Absolution

A Palestinian Israeli Love Story

By: R.F. Georgy

a novel

R.F.Georgy

Published by Parthenon Books, New York

Paperback ISBN-13: 978-0692216088

Paperback ISBN-10: 0692216081

LCCN: 2014940578

Library of Congress Catalog Number: 2014940578

1. The Grand Hotel. 2. The Grand Café. 3. The University of Oslo.

4. Demons. 5. Absolution.

Printed in the United States of America

Absolution

For: Alexandra, Antoinette, Athanasius,

&

Rosalie Albair Georgy

"Whoever saves one life saves the world entire."

-Talmud

"Whoever saves the life of another, surely he saves the lives of all of humanity."

-Holy Quran

"Blessed are the peacemakers: for they shall be called the children of God."

-The Bible

Absolution

"And in this respect, the Israeli-Palestinian conflict has been a tragedy, a clash between one very powerful, very convincing, painful claim over this land and another no less powerful, no less convincing claim."

-Amos Oz

"I am an American Jew and aware of the sensitivities involved in the Israeli-Palestinian conflict."

-Steven Spielberg

"I take criticism so seriously as to believe that, even in the midst of a battle in which one is unmistakably on one side against another, there should be criticism, because there must be critical consciousness if there are to be issues, problems, values, even lives to be fought for…Criticism must think of itself as life-enhancing and constitutively opposed to every form of tyranny, domination, and abuse; its social goals are noncoercive knowledge produced in the interests of human freedom."

-Edward Said

"Two households, both alike in dignity, In fair Verona, where we lay our scene, From ancient grudge break to new mutiny, Where civil blood makes civil hands unclean. From forth the fatal loins of these two foes A pair of star-cross'd lovers take their life; Whose misadventured piteous overthrows Do with their death bury their parents' strife."

-Shakespeare, Romeo and Juliet

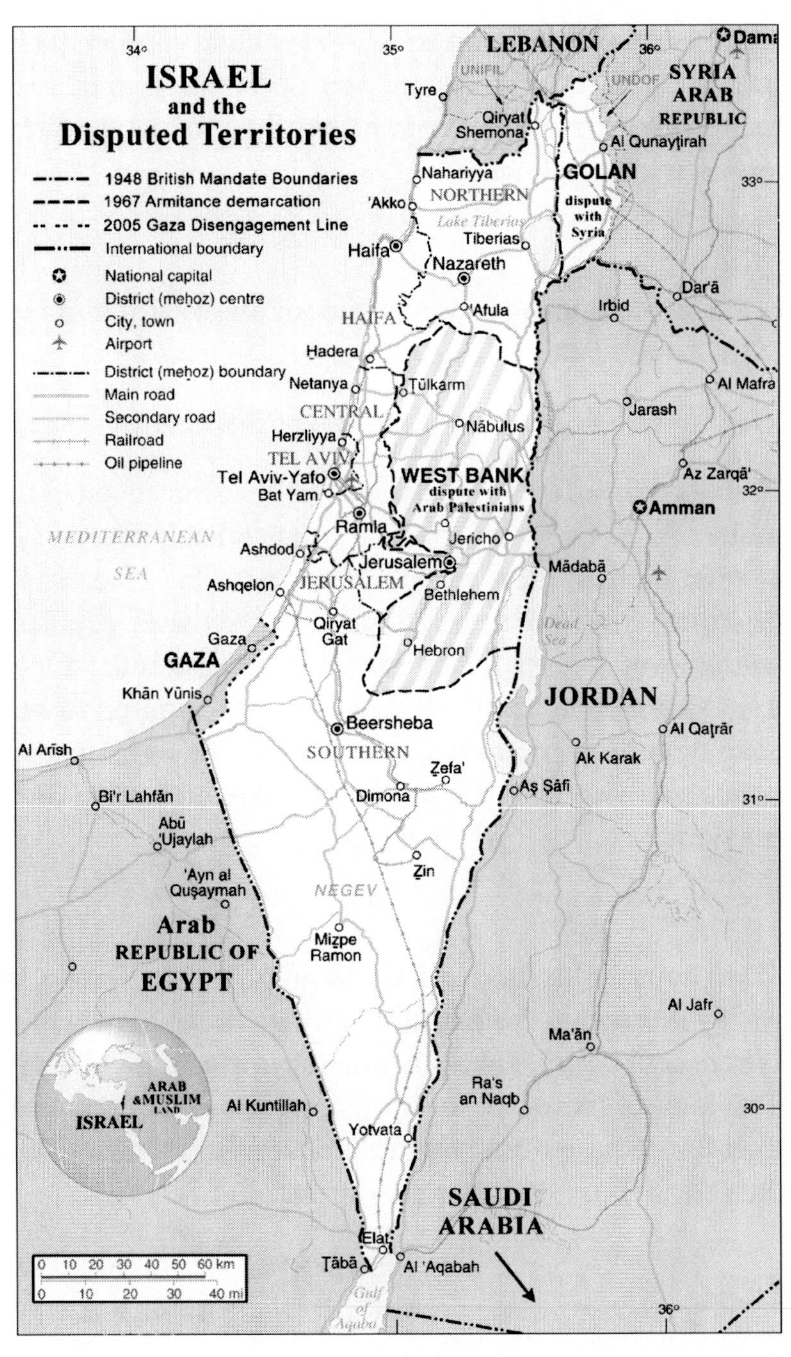
ISRAEL
and the
Disputed Territories
1948 British Mandate Boundaries
1967 Armitance demarcation
2005 Gaza Disengagement Line
International boundary
National capital
District (meḥoz) centre
City, town
Airport
District (meḥoz) boundary
Main road
Secondary road
Railroad
Oil pipeline
34°
35°
36°
33°
32°
31°
30°
LEBANON
UNIFIL
UNDOF
SYRIA
ARAB
REPUBLIC
Dama
Tyre
Qiryat
Shemona
Al Qunayṭirah
Nahariyya
GOLAN
dispute
with
Syria
'Akko
NORTHERN
Lake Tiberias
Tiberias
Haifa
Nazareth
Dar'ā
Irbid
'Afula
HAIFA
Hadera
Netanya
Ṭūlkarm
Al Mafra
Jarash
CENTRAL
Nābulus
Herzliyya
TEL AVIV
Az Zarqā'
Tel Aviv-Yafo
WEST BANK
dispute with
Arab Palestinians
Bat Yam
Amman
Ramla
MEDITERRANEAN
SEA
Jericho
Ashdod
Jerusalem
Mādabā
Ashqelon
JERUSALEM
Bethlehem
Dead
Sea
Qiryat
Gat
Gaza
Hebron
GAZA
Khān Yūnis
JORDAN
Beersheba
Al Qaṭrār
Al Arīsh
SOUTHERN
Ak Karak
Ẓefa'
Aş Şāfī
Dimona
Bi'r Lahfān
Abū
'Ujaylah
Ẓin
'Ayn al
Quşaymah
NEGEV
Arab
REPUBLIC OF
EGYPT
Miẓpe
Ramon
Al Jafr
Ma'ān
ARAB
&MUSLIM
LAND
ISRAEL
Ra's
an Naqb
Al Kuntillah
Yotvata
SAUDI
ARABIA
Elat
Ṭābā
Al 'Aqabah
Gulf
of
Aqaba
0 10 20 30 40 50 60 km
0 10 20 30 40 mi

"History teaches us that men and nations behave wisely only after they have exhausted all other alternatives."

-Abba Eban

"I can certainly put myself in Israel's shoes. They are humans just like we are. They want peace and security inside their borders."

-Mahmoud Abbas

"A diplomatic peace is not yet the real peace. It is an essential step in the peace process leading towards a real peace."

-Yitzhak Rabin

"Fear is, I believe, a most effective tool in destroying the soul of an individual- and the soul of a people."

-Anwar Sadat

"The metaphor for Palestine is stronger than the Palestine of reality."

-Mahmoud Darwish

"I would like to see real peace and a state of Israel living peacefully alongside a state of Palestine."

-Elie Wiesel

"As a Zionist youth leader in the 1940s, I was among those who called for a binational state in Mandatory Palestine."

-Noam Chomsky

Prologue

It used to be a universally accepted axiom that the Palestinian Israeli conflict is an intractable and immovable impasse of epic proportion. Its Sisyphean nature cemented its reputation as an insoluble focal point of hatred and endless violence. Such universal truths, of course, derive their power and resonance from within the constraints of geography, ideology, and the construction of the imagination that is always trapped under the feeble nature of temporal movement. One can certainly say that Jewish history is filled with the grotesquery of blind hatred; that Jews were singularly reduced to an alienated other. Their disjointed and fractured identity was preserved only by the portability of a religion that would help them survive the darkest hours.

But fate is not without irony, as the Palestinians were forced to accept the collective guilt of all those who committed unspeakable acts against the Jews. The Palestinians had to endure the systematic dispossession of their land and loss of identity. They were forced to accept defeat as a bitter reminder of their subaltern status in a world of proud nation states. Palestinians and Israelis were connected by a fatalistic dialectic, whose movement was punctuated by violence and directed towards an apocalyptic conclusion. One might argue that this dialectic enveloped a land, mythical and actual, spiritual yet earth-bound, ancient yet very much poised towards unfolding actualities.

This land conjures images of return and redemptive possibilities. Palestine and Israel are two strands intertwined in our collective imagination. They are linguistically exclusive and yet reference a singular place. We are embarking on a peaceful resolution to a conflict that has left deep psychological scars. Of course, peace is not determined by the signage of treaties or the wishes of leaders. Peace is not a discrete event; rather it is a renewable proposition, filled with affirmations designed to mitigate against the collective distrust of two people who knew little beyond hatred, suspicion, blame and counter blame, intellectual gamesmanship, fear, paranoia, historical necessity, retribution, and a host of other deeply engrained emotional projections that are constantly lurking beneath the surface.

Part I

I

The Grand Hotel

Oslo, Norway

2018

No one understood the dangers of peace better than Avi Eban. He came to Oslo to accept the Nobel Peace Prize. The city was abuzz with journalists and foreign dignitaries from around the world. The security detail was particularly heavy given the nature of the event. It was only last year that the historic signing of a peace treaty between Israel and Palestine became a reality. Palestine became the 194th country to be recognized by the United Nations, and Palestinians danced with tearful jubilation. From the streets of Gaza to al-Manara Square in Ramallah, from the Church of the Nativity in Bethlehem to the Al-Aqsa mosque in the old city of Jerusalem, Palestinians everywhere celebrated a reality that only existed in the hopes and dreams of a people who suffered extraordinary loss. Israelis in Tel Aviv celebrated by the thousands as a new chapter of hope and optimism was greeted with eager anticipation. However, Avi knew that not everyone embraced peace. History was filled with those who paid the price for their courage.

The memories of what happened to Gandhi, Martin Luther King, Jr., Anwar Sadat, and Yitzhak Rabin served as constant reminders that peace had a price. Extremists were united by the necessity of conflict. Avi arrived in Oslo on Saturday, December 8th; a full two days prior to the awarding of the prize. It was unusual for a head of state to arrive this early for the ceremony. As prime minister of Israel, Avi was aware of the dangers. In fact, his security detail tried in vain to persuade him to arrive Monday morning for the ceremony, but Avi insisted on arriving early. His itinerary was meticulously planned: the Nobel Peace Centre, the University of Oslo, Oslo City Hall, the Grand Hotel, and the Oslo Spektrum. If it was up to the Shin Bet (Israel's internal security service), Prime Minister Eban would only attend the ceremony at Oslo City Hall and the banquet that followed at the Grand Hotel.

However, Avi had other plans. He wanted to tour the Nobel Peace Centre and attend the concert at the Spektrum. The Nobel Peace Centre was established in 2005 to honor past Nobel Laureates. He was also asked by Palestinian and Israeli students to give a lecture at the University of Oslo. It was an honor he could not refuse. As he sat in his hotel room at the Grand Hotel, he felt a tingling sensation, as if a wave of nostalgia was gradually enveloping him. He was in this very same hotel almost ten years ago, long before he was prime minister. As a Nobel Laureate, he was put up in the Nobel suite, the same suite that Barack Obama occupied when he won the prize in 2009. It was an opulent suite, with a marble entryway, an elegant sitting room with a table that sat up to six, a bedroom with its own bath, and two balconies. The entryway was adorned with pictures of past Nobel laureates. As Avi paced back and forth in the sitting room, he noticed the pictures of several Nobel winners. The four portraits that provoked an emotional reaction were those of Anwar Sadat, Menachem Begin, Yasser Arafat, and Yitzhak Rabin. He walked around the room, oblivious to the clamor around him. There were two security agents inside the suite, four stationed outside the room, and an additional six outside the hotel. He also had several aids with him to coordinate the details of his visit, such as who would meet with the Prime Minister, his Nobel lecture, the speech at the Spektrum, and various interviews. As Avi stood by the window lost in thought, he was suddenly interrupted.

"Mr. Prime Minister, it would not be wise to stand by the window," said Yoram, the head of his security detail.

"I thought you said that a three-mile perimeter is secure," said Avi with some frustration.

"It is, sir, but–"

"Yes, I know. I know. Protocol," said Avi with disquiet. "Why do I feel like a prisoner?"

"Mr. Prime Minister, could I have a word?" It was David Barkovic. Avi's senior aide and close friend. David knew Avi when they were undergraduate students at Columbia back in the '80s. Avi was a double major in philosophy and comparative literature. David was unsure of what to study, but settled on political science. When Avi became prime minister in 2015, he asked David, who was teaching at Tel Aviv University, to be part of his government. David was one of the people close enough to Avi to know when something was wrong.

"What is it David?" Avi asked.

"Nothing."

"Avi, what is going on?" David was one of a select few who privately addressed the prime minister by his first name.

"I don't know what you're talking about."

"Don't give me that. I've known you for over thirty years and I know when you're spacing out. What's going on? You have a lecture to give at the university tomorrow, your acceptance lecture, the lecture at the Spektrum, and countless interviews. Tell me, what's troubling you?"

Someone knocked on the door.

"Give us a few minutes!" David yelled in frustration. He turned back to the prime minister. "Is there anything you want to talk about?"

"I'm fine, just a little tired. Why don't you find out what's going on outside?"

"I will, Avi. But I know something is bothering you." David looked at Avi, who stared into a kind of disturbing void as though nothing mattered; not the Nobel Prize, peace with the Palestinians, or the popularity he enjoyed, the most of any world leader since Barack Obama in 2009. David was beginning to worry. After all, it was his job to know everything about the prime minister. He was there to anticipate problems so they would be solved before the media grew wary, and certainly before anything became viral. David left the room to check on things. He returned to inform Avi that his first interview had arrived.

"It's Anderson Cooper. Do you want me to reschedule?"

"No!" Avi said emphatically, willing himself back to reality.

"I just need a few minutes. Did you bring the Carl Orff CD?" Avi asked with a sense of preparation, as an actor would while getting ready to go on stage.

David left the room for a minute to retrieve the CD. He found several versions, including the London Philharmonic Orchestra, Chicago Symphony Orchestra, Boston Symphony Orchestra, New York Philharmonic, and Israeli Philharmonic. He knew which one to pick out. Avi always preferred the New York Philharmonic version, which reminded him of his nostalgic days as a student at Columbia.

"I brought you the New York Philharmonic version."

"Which conductor?"

"You are unbelievable!" After all these years, David never felt that he really knew the prime minister. Avi kept people at a distance. It was both his strength and weakness. David considered Avi to be freakishly brilliant, an anomalous accident that baffled all who met him. In addition to holding a Ph.D. in philosophy, Avi spoke six languages fluently: English, French, Hebrew, Arabic, Italian, and German. He wrote a dozen books on subjects that ranged from Nietzsche's "*God is Dead*" declaration to a response to Edward Said's *Orientalism*. He was also a brilliant orator in the tradition of his great uncle, Abba Eban. Despite his extraordinary intellectual gifts, Avi suffered from periodic depression. He was prone to drinking and preferred solitude to the company of others. Avi was also the first Israeli prime minister to not marry. What David came to realize over the years was that Avi had a mystery quality. It was as if he was hiding something of epic proportion, and could not trust anyone to confide in. Of course, David could never prove this. But it was a belief he held privately for years.

"It says here, Alan Gilbert is the conductor."

"I have the one with Zubin Mehta as conductor. It's in my briefcase. Can you please get it for me?" Avi asked absent-mindedly.

"Here it is. I remember in college, when you would always listen to it. But I never understood the power it had over you."

David could not have realized that *Carmina Burana,* or more specifically, *O Fortuna,* the opening and closing movement of the CD, penetrated Avi's soul in such a way that he became transfixed when he heard it. The piece did something to him; something that he could not understand. He felt a visceral reaction that caused his hands to twitch and his face to become contorted. He would often tilt his face sideways in a 45-degree angle and look at people in such a way that made them feel uncomfortable. He did not listen to the music. Rather, the music enveloped his soul in an unsettling way. People close to Avi often told him that he changed when he heard *O Fortuna*. He became so intense that it frightened those around him. Avi always believed that people listened to the piece without understanding what the lyrics meant. *Carmina Burana* is considered by many to be one of the greatest cantatas ever written. It was composed between 1935 and 1936 by Carl Orff, a German composer and music instructor.

Orff languished in anonymity as an instructor of music at the Günther School for Gymnastics, Music, and Dance. *Carmina Burana,* or to be more precisely, *Carmina Burana: Cantiones profanae cantoribus et choris cantandae comitantibus instrumentis atque imaginibus magicis,* is part of a *Trionfi,* which is the musical triptych that also includes *Catulli Carmina* and *Trionfo di Afrodite*. Orff based his work on a collection of medieval poems, also called *Carmina Burana,* or Songs of Beuem. Beuem refers to the Benediktbeuern Abbey, a monastery in Bavaria, where the original poems were found. However, there was speculation that the poems originated in Sekau Abbey, in Austria. The poems were written in Latin by students and clergy around 1230 A.D.

Although there were 254 poems in all, Orff organized 24 of these poems into a libretto. The lyrics had haunted Avi for over thirty years. *Fortuna Imperatrix Mundi,* better known as *O Fortuna,* is a poetic meditation on the cruel irony of fate. After all, it was fate that forged realities both transcendent and utterly devastating. Fate defined Avi's existential condition in such a way that his teleological direction was destined to be tragic. After listening to *O Fortuna* countless times, Avi memorized the text in several languages. His favorite was Latin. David inserted the CD and sat down to observe anything unusual in Avi's behavior.

"It's too low. Please increase the volume," Avi said, with agitation in his voice.

"I don't want them to hear us in the other room," David said. Of course, he knew that when Avi heard *O Fortuna* in a loud volume, his behavior grew unholy.

"Make it louder, damn it!" Avi snapped. He listened to each word in Latin:

> *O Fortuna velut luna statu variabilis, semper crescis aut decrescis; vita detestabilis nunc obdurate et tunc curat ludo mentis aciem, egestatem, potestatem dissolvit ut glaciem. Sors immanis et inanis, rota tu volubilis, status malus, vana salus semper dissolubilis, obumbrata et velata michi quoque niteris; nunc per ludum dorsum nudum fero tui sceleris. Sors salutis et virtutis michi nunc contraria, est affectus et defectus semper in angaria. Hac in hora sine mora corde pulsum tangite; quod per sortem sternit fortem, mecum omnes plangite!*

Though Avi understood Latin, his private inner experience – his *qualia,* as he described it in philosophical terms – was mediated through English. Those 82 Latin words served as bitter reminders of what he couldn't have; of his longing for a woman he lost twice to fate. The English version of *O Fortuna* tore at the interstitial space of his soul:

> *O Fortune, like the moon you are changeable, ever waxing and waning; hateful life first oppresses and then soothes as fancy takes it; poverty and power it melts them like ice. Fate – monstrous and empty, you whirling wheel, you are malevolent, well-being is vain and always fades to nothing, shadowed and veiled you plague me too; now through the game I bring my bare back to your villainy. Fate is against me in health and virtue, driven on and weighted down, always enslaved. So at this hour without delay pluck the vibrating strings; since Fate strikes down the strong man, everyone weep with me!*

Of course, it was fate that Avi found to be monstrous and empty. For all his considerable accomplishments, he always believed his life to be a complete failure. He often compared himself to Dostoevsky's underground man. His interior monologues were schizophrenic, and he would constantly dwell on circumstances that tormented him. He often suffered from psychotic episodes brought on by trauma that occurred thirty years ago. Although there was some correlation between trauma and psychosis, it was not clear if the trauma caused the psychosis or if the trauma triggered a pre-existing condition. David witnessed Avi's psychotic episodes over the years and tried repeatedly to convince him to get help. Avi always maintained that he had his condition under control. Only a handful of people were aware of Avi's psychosis. The Israeli people were not aware that their prime minister suffered from self-inflicted demons that haunted him with disturbing regularity.

As David increased the volume, he witnessed Avi physically react to the music, as he had many times. He noticed Avi's hands twitch and curl into some kind of unnatural claw, his head tilting sideways and his eyes taking on the look of something unholy. As the first movement crescendoed, David noticed Avi cracking his jaw as he tilted his head sideways. Avi reacted to the music with greater intensity, as if trying to fight the demons inside. As the explosive part of *O Fortuna* burst in his ears, Avi was disturbed by a knock at the door.

II

nderson Cooper is ready for the prime minister," a voice said calmly.

"Ask him to wait," David said.

"Are you ready to do this interview?" David asked, turning to Avi.

"Yes, let's get this over with."

It was at that moment that David realized Avi was ready to be engaged. Avi relied on a remarkable ability to focus on the task at hand. When the moment dictated it, he always rose to the challenge.

"Anderson," Avi said as the familiar face entered the room. He stood erectly and polished his words. "It's so good to see you again. I'm sorry to have kept you waiting."

"Mr. Prime Minister, it's always a pleasure to talk to you. Thank you for granting us this exclusive." Anderson spoke with modesty. He was an international star, whose reporting style departed from the traditional role of an anchor as an omniscient narrator of current events. Cooper developed a style that was known as emo-journalism. He was known for emotionally connecting to the stories he covered. Anderson had interviewed Avi many times, and had come to consider the prime minister a friend.

"Can we have you seated here for the camera, Mr. Prime Minister?"

Avi nodded and smiled. He was suddenly composed and amiable as a production assistant attached the lavaliere mic beneath his second shirt button. He paused a moment, letting his eyes adjust to the lighting.

"Whenever you're ready, Mr. Prime Minister."

"I'm ready when you are, Anderson."

"Mr. Prime Minister, let me congratulate you on sharing the Nobel Peace Prize with President Hanan Ashrawi of Palestine."

"Thank you, Anderson. It is indeed an honor and an affirmation of what is possible when people of good will are committed to peace."

"Have you talked with President Ashrawi since your arrival here in Oslo?"

"I will meet with her tomorrow, but I know she is very pleased."

"As you know, your popularity on the international stage is something we haven't seen since President Obama. But inside Israel, you continue to be a controversial figure. How do you balance the two?"

Avi paused with a well-rehearsed demeanor, despite the fact that he was prepared for the question.

"First, let me remind you that it was President Obama who paved the way for the eventual peace between Israel and Palestine. He made it his number one foreign policy priority during his second term. In fact, I will be meeting with him tomorrow to personally thank him for his enduring contribution to peace. I know he won the Nobel Peace Prize back in 2009, but that award was for, and I'm paraphrasing, his extraordinary efforts to strengthen international diplomacy. There were voices of disagreement suggesting that President Obama did not actually accomplish anything to merit such a prestigious award. I, of course, have disagreed in the past over such objections. According to Nobel's will, the peace prize shall be awarded to those who have done the most or the best work for fraternity between nations."

"But, if you recall, the Israelis were quite apprehensive about the sweeping change in the Arab World, especially in Egypt."

"Of course, we were apprehensive. When you are living through the unfolding of history, filled with temporal uncertainties, you do not always have the luxury of determining your own fate. At the time, I embraced the sweeping democratic change in Tunisia, Egypt, Syria, Libya, Yemen, and other countries in the region. I wrote numerous articles urging Israelis to embrace the change. I also argued that it would only be a matter of time before the Palestinians realized their own destiny in the form of a Palestinian state."

"Are you worried about your safety, Mr. Prime Minister? I'm sure you're aware of what happened to President Sadat and Prime Minister Yitzhak Rabin."

"I do not worry about my safety," Avi said, smiling and looking around the room. It was filled with several members of his security detail.

"But as a student of history, I'm sure it's something you think about, right?" Anderson knew the prime minister was not comfortable discussing personal issues, and was uncertain if Avi was going to elaborate.

"If fate decides to take me, then there isn't much I can do about it. I've always believed that enlightened leaders should be active participants in writing history. If I allow myself to be influenced by the irrational behavior of those whose aim is to exact vengeance under some misguided religious or ideological view, then, I'm afraid, the Palestinian-Israeli conflict would have remained intractable and insoluble. Change, as President Obama eloquently framed it, is the realization that we are the agents to bring it about. If we wait for others or place the burden of change on future generations, then we would be guilty of moral cowardice."

Anderson interrupted, sensing that Avi was about to go into lecture mode. He had seen interviews with the prime minister go down this path before.

"On that subject of change, you have been called a traitor by many Israelis, especially the settlers. Some have compared you to Noam Chomsky, who was one of the harshest critics of Israel."

"First of all, to be compared to Noam Chomsky is an honor. I have had numerous discussions with Professor Chomsky on subjects that ranged from Foucault to Zionism. Our disagreements, which were many, have been chronicled in various academic journals as well as the *New York Times*. As far as our views on Israel, we had fundamental disagreements. He did not agree with the idea of having a uniquely Jewish state. I remember one night back in the 1990's when we debated this point until four in the morning. He believed that Israel's existential justification, grounded in religious affirmations, would eventually contribute to the moral degeneration of a people whose history is filled with noble aspirations. The problem with his logic is that he equated the idea of being Jewish with other religions. His syllogism, of course, works if we accept the premise that being Jewish is *ipso facto* being religious. Are you following me on this, Anderson?"

"Sure." Anderson nodded.

"If it is objectionable to establish a state along religious lines and being Jewish is exclusively a religious affiliation, then it is objectionable to have a Jewish state. The Jews, however, unlike any other people, have, by historical necessity, become something that transcends the narrow confines of religion. There is no one-to-one correspondence between Jewish identity and Judaism. Jewish identity is shaped and defined by a complex set of forces; historical, political, linguistic, diasporic, psychological. I could go on.

What binds these forces is the asymmetrical suffering and treatment of Jews as a subaltern other who were blamed for all the sociological ills by cultures who found it convenient to transfer blame onto those who were stripped of power centuries ago."

Avi's passion lit up the room. While the camera focused on Avi, Anderson glanced sidelong at David and others, as if to point out his brilliance. He didn't want to interrupt the prime minister, but he knew the viewers at home needed a pause.

"But you have gone on record as saying, and I quote, 'we are guilty of committing a monstrous crime; we are individually and collectively responsible for dispossessing a people of not only their land, but their identity.' How do you reconcile that statement with Israel's desire to live peacefully and with a sense of security with its neighbors?"

"Of course, I acknowledge the remarkable nature of my statement. But what I find more remarkable is the startling reaction around the world. In Israel, people said it was a matter of time before my coalition government dissolved. In the States, American Jews were divided, with many denouncing me as a self-hating Jew. In the Arab world people were struck by its honesty, but were skeptical."

"Are you saying you anticipated this reaction?"

"Yes, I did expect it. But what I do find remarkable is that we Israelis are still ignoring our past. We wanted for so long to maintain moral legitimacy while simultaneously denying the role we played in stripping the Palestinian people of their fundamental right to self-determination. We fought for this right, only to deny it to those who had a greater claim to Palestine."

"Are you aware that you have gone farther than any Israeli Prime Minister in acknowledging Israel's role in Palestinian dispossession?" Anderson crossed his legs and interlocked his fingers. It was clear he was thoroughly enjoying this exchange. It was always refreshing to speak with the prime minister, who was always honest and forthcoming. Many of the world leaders he interviewed couched their responses in diplomatic speak. Avi was never afraid to speak his mind.

"I will defend Israel's existence with my dying breath, but I do question the process by which we delegitimized Palestinian aspirations. That is to say, we fought so hard for our right to exist in Palestine while dismissing the national aspirations of a people who found themselves absolutely humiliated. We were on the wrong side of history. Part of the peace treaty with the Palestinians, as well as the broader Arab world, was to correct the mistakes made. You cannot have peace as long as you deny your responsibility in what has happened."

"But the Palestinians have also had their shortcomings, right? Poor leadership, terrorism, their inability to make peace, infighting, Hamas, corruption, and so on. It was your great-uncle, Abba Eban, who is known for the famous quote, 'the Arabs never miss an opportunity to miss an opportunity.'"

"Absolutely, and President Ashrawi will agree with much of that. Both sides have engaged in what I call 'bad faith'. Both Israelis and Palestinians used sweeping, and even dehumanizing language to discredit each other. Golda Meir considered the Palestinians to be a manufactured people. They did not exist as far as she was concerned. Yasser Arafat, who shared the Nobel Peace Prize with Yitzhak Rabin, has often stated the Palestinian desire to eliminate the state of Israel and establish a purely Palestinian state. As far as what my great-uncle said about the Arabs never missing an opportunity to miss an opportunity, I simply don't agree. The Palestinians have for too long suffered representations that reduced them to a paradigmatic other. They–'

Anderson had to stop Avi once more to interject a question. Avi, who taught philosophy for many years, was a lecturer by nature and Anderson didn't want to lose the viewers at home.

"You're talking about Edward Said, right? His groundbreaking work, *Orientalism,* is in essence about how the West reduced the orient to representations. You actually wrote a book in response to Said.

"Yes, and Edward Said and I had numerous discussions about the meaning and implications of cultural representations. My book, *Cultural Illusions,* argued that Jews have historically suffered the same bifurcated reality that the Arabs were forced to endure. You know, Said's book was nothing short of brilliant. It was essentially an intellectually penetrating analysis of the general idea of 'othering', which was developed by Foucault and other postmodernists. Said focused this idea and directed it towards the Orient. He was correct that the Orient has been reduced to illusory representations and imaginative constructs that are divorced from reality. Nietzsche often said that truths are illusions about which one has forgotten that this is what they are. Let me put it another way, representations are illusions that are apprehended as *ipso facto* real. Both Jews and Arabs have suffered from sweeping representations that are divorced from the historical and cultural actualities which define who they are." Avi stopped when Anderson leaned forward.

"Prime minister, I feel as if I'm interviewing a philosopher. But, of course, you are a philosopher, which makes this interview all the more interesting. If I recall, you spoke at Edward Said's funeral. Were you close to the family? I know you attended Columbia with his niece, Alena Said, back in the 1980s."

Avi froze at the sound of the name Alena Said. He didn't know how to react. He turned his head sideways and looked as if he was in pain. He wanted to end the interview immediately. His thoughts were in disarray. He was asked about Alena Said before, but only in a professional capacity. No one had asked him about the fact they studied at Columbia at the same time. He always supposed it was public knowledge, but he simply was not prepared for this question. David immediately noticed Avi's reaction.

"Anderson, would it be possible to take a break?" David asked. "There are some documents the prime minister needs to sign."

"Of course." Anderson smiled at David. "I could use a break as well. The prime minister has given me plenty to think about."

§§§

Anderson understood that something was wrong. He wanted to pursue this line of questioning, but was unsure of how to proceed. He knew Avi vigorously guarded his privacy and didn't want to affect the rest of the interview. He also read unconfirmed reports, mostly blogs and tabloids, that Avi may have been romantically linked to Alena Said. Avi's reaction at the mere mention of her name sparked Anderson's curiosity. Could the gossip columns be correct? What made this a sensitive issue was not so much the possibility that Avi and Alena may have been romantically linked in college. It was the possibility that these two political and intellectual heavyweights may have had an affair. One tabloid suggested that they were seen together in Oslo back in 2009. Other reports placed them together in Cairo, Paris, London, and several other locations. At the time, Alena was a professor of Linguistics at Columbia and Avi taught philosophy at Harvard. Though both published several books and occasionally appeared on television interviews, they were hardly public figures.

Such stories and rumors never interested Anderson. He was considered the pre-eminent journalist of his generation. His work was respected throughout the world and he would never allow himself to entertain such silly gossip. Still, Avi's reaction to Alena's name provoked him to consider the possibility. He considered posing a veiled question to Alena, who was in Oslo as part of the Palestinian delegation. He was scheduled to interview President Ashrawi after he was finished with Avi. David went into the bedroom with Avi and wasted no time.

"I think I understand what's going on here, Avi." He stood rigidly while Avi slumped onto the bed.

"You don't understand anything, so stop trying to figure things out." Avi stood with his hands on his hips, glaring at David.

"Something did happen between you and Alena back in '85. This is extraordinary. After all these years, I never connected the dots."

"There are no dots to connect. Just drop the subject. I don't want to talk about her."

"What do you mean, drop the subject? You're going to see her tomorrow, remember? She is travelling with President Ashrawi and will sit in on the meeting. You worked with her several times in the past few years. Both of you helped iron out the peace treaty, do you remember that?"

"That should tell you there is nothing between us, but tell me how did Anderson Cooper know I was invited by Edward's family to speak at the funeral? Who told him?"

"Avi, you're reading too much into the question. My God, he asked an innocent question. Now you have aroused his suspicion. You know about the tabloids and the things they say about you. He must have picked it up somewhere, but I want to know what happened between you and Alena back at Columbia." David was not about to give up. He was now convinced something happened and felt he deserved to hear the truth.

"Why are you so interested in such matters?"

"How long have we been friends?"

"You are a close and dear friend, so I'm telling you nothing happened between us."

"Then tell me this. Why did you attend so many of the Palestinian events at Columbia? You always told us it was to better understand their arguments, but that's not the whole story, is it? Remember Shimon Berman? He saw you once staring at Alena and suggested to me that something was going on, but I told him he was imagining things. Do you remember the time the Arab organization was putting on a falafel fundraiser?"

"I don't remember a falafel fundraiser."

"Sure you do. Remember, we were going to the Low Memorial Library when you noticed the falafel stand. I told you the Arab Student Organization planned this event for weeks and posted it on campus. There was an Egyptian, I don't remember his name now, who was working the stand. You didn't care and we went to the library to study. A couple of hours later, we left and wouldn't you know it, Alena was behind the stand selling falafel. Do you remember what happened next? Of course you do, but let me refresh your memory. You suddenly became hungry and told me you would like to try a falafel sandwich. I stood at a distance, wondering why you would want to contribute money to the Arab Organization. It took you several minutes to get the sandwich. I thought at the time you got into an argument with Alena. I never thought there was something going on between you too."

"We did get into an argument."

"Ah, so you do remember." David smiled.

"Why are you convinced something happened? I told you we got into an argument over Zionism. Do you remember her article in the *Daily Spectator*? She argued that Israel is an illegitimate entity."

"Yes, I remember that and you responded with your own article a few days later, defending Israel's right to exist."

"That's what we argued over. I bought a sandwich and she proceeded to tell me that Israel is illegitimate. You know me. I couldn't let it go. We got into a heated discussion. That's all that happened." Avi could see that David wasn't convinced.

"Even if there was something between you too, that was a long time ago. I mean, I don't understand why the secrecy. I'm your friend, and if anyone can understand the need to keep this away from the media, it would be me. It's my job to keep the media at bay. Why can't you tell me what happened. Are you protecting her? Is that it? She's married now and holds a distinguished place in Palestinian politics. Could this be why?"

"I'm not protecting anyone. Nothing happened. End of story." Avi stood up and walked towards the window. He heard noises on the street, but didn't know what they were. David must have heard the noises too, because he walked to the window and stared onto the street below. He was clearly distracted, but turned to face Avi anyway, an accusatory look plastered across his face.

"Ok, do you remember the night before you were leaving to go to Harvard? Edward Said threw a going away party for you at his home. You and Alena were inseparable that night. You stepped out on the balcony with her, remember?"

"She wanted to apologize for her article."

"You have an answer for everything, but I'm not buying it."

"I don't care if you are buying it or not. Nothing happened between us."

"Then why did you react the way you did when Anderson mentioned her name?"

"I was bothered that he suggested Alena asked me to speak at the funeral."

"You see, that makes no sense. Why would you be troubled by that? It was an innocent question. Look, we're not getting anywhere. We need to get back out there and finish the interview."

"Can I have a few minutes alone to collect myself?"

"Don't be long. I'll tell Anderson that you're on the phone."

Avi paced back and forth as soon as David left the room. His thoughts were moving too fast to focus on any single idea. Of course, he knew David didn't buy his explanation. He simply didn't want anyone to know. He thought of the falafel stand and what happened that day. As he looked around the room, his mind wandered from 2009 to 1985. The memories were overpowering, and he tried to ignore them. But he was unable to fight the past. He felt himself growing angry and bitter again. He was angry at God, at fate, and at the forces that conspired to keep him and Alena apart. He made mistakes and suffered a lifetime for them. He went into the bathroom and stared at the bathtub. A flash from the past slapped him with such ferocity that he felt light-headed. It was in this very same bathtub that he stood where he was standing now, admiring Alena's transcendent beauty as she relaxed in the tub, drinking wine and enjoying chocolate-covered strawberries. The memory was overpowering. He decided to splash his face with cold water. As he looked into the mirror, the image reflected back was unsettling if only Avi was able to perceive the distortion

What stared back from the mirror was a wide-eyed 21-year-old; tall and slender, with long, curly brown hair parted to the back, blue-eyes, and an intense look crafted to intimidate opponents. The mirror revealed a young man wearing blue jeans and a white T-shirt. His face wore a youthful, rugged expression. His rimless glasses gave him an intellectual air, as if he belonged in rarefied intellectual circles. One might think him vain to embrace such a self-portrait, but this phenomenological bracketing of his own physical form was the result of trauma.

The idea of bracketing was developed by the German philosopher, Edmund Husserl. Husserl argued that bracketing is the process of setting aside, or bracketing off, the question of the objective nature of reality; what Kant called the *noumena*. The phenomenologist considered only the experience of the phenomena in question, rather than the ultimate nature of reality. It is our experience of phenomena that should be examined.

Phenomenology, as developed by Husserl, was the systematic process of analyzing and reflecting upon the structures of consciousness, and how consciousness itself apprehends phenomena. Avi's distorted self-perception was the result of psychological injury and not phenomenological bracketing. As he stood in front of the mirror, Avi's mind wandered to the summer of 1985.

III

It was August and Avi had just arrived in New York for the first time. He transferred to Columbia after completing the mandatory three years of military service demanded of all Israeli citizens. Born in 1964 in Kfar Shmaryahu just north of Tel Aviv, Avi came from a long line of distinguished Israeli diplomats, politicians, writers, musicians, and notable cultural figures. His great-uncle, Abba Eban, was universally esteemed within Israel and beyond as a towering intellectual figure who defended Zionism as the moral necessity in response to the Holocaust. At the age of 31, Abba Eban became the youngest permanent ambassador to the United Nations. David Ben-Gurion, Israel's first prime minister, called him the voice of the Hebrew nation.

He was born in Cape Town, South Africa and moved to England when he was a child. He studied classics and oriental languages at Cambridge. He spoke ten languages, including Arabic, Hebrew, Farsi, German, and French. It was Abba Eban who successfully obtained approval for United Nations Resolution 181, which called for the partition of Palestine into two states, one Jewish and the other Arab. The influence that Abba Eban had on Avi was most evidenced in Avi's voracious learning style and intellectual stamina.

Avi was also related to Chaim Herzog, who became the sixth president of Israel. Herzog was born in Belfast. His father, Rabbi Yitzhak HaLevi Herzog, was the chief rabbi of Ireland from 1919 to 1937. Chaim joined the British army during World War II and helped liberate several concentration camps. It was Chaim Herzog who identified a captured German prisoner as Heinrich Himmler, the man responsible for coordinating the extermination of six million Jews.

Avi's uncle, Eli Eban, who is not much older than Avi, is a world renowned clarinetist, who was invited by Zubin Mehta to join the Israeli Philharmonic Orchestra. This was the reason that Avi preferred Mehta's version of *Carmina Burana*. Eli Eban divided his time teaching at Indiana University and touring as a soloist. He spent his summers playing principle clarinetist at the Chautauqua Symphony Orchestra in New York. Avi's father, Levi Eban, was minister of education and a member of the Knesset. Avi had what most would call a privileged childhood. He attended the famous Herzliya Hebrew Gymnasium and graduated at the top of his class. After completing his mandatory military service, Avi applied for, and was accepted, at Columbia University. His parents – especially his mother – did not want him to travel to America. As a child, he was constantly reminded of his special place in Israeli society. The Eban name always loomed large for Avi, both as inspiration and as a stifling reminder of all that awaited him. The pressure on the young man was overpowering, and he often felt powerless in choosing his own path. He was expected to enter public service, marry a girl from a respected Israeli family, and honor the Eban name with contributions that would eclipse all who came before him. Avi was a child prodigy from a very young age. He mastered English, Arabic, and French before the age of ten. Abba Eban took an early interest in Avi and tried to duplicate what James Mill did for his son, John Stuart Mill. James Mill, along with Jeremy Bentham, wanted to create an intellect powerful enough to carry out the implementation of Utilitarianism. John Stuart Mill was raised with none of the socialization that children his age normally had. His precocity was such that he learned Greek at the age of three, and by the age of eight, he had read Aesop's Fables, Herodotus, Plato, Diogenes, Isocrates, and several other ancient texts. He also mastered Latin, Algebra, and Euclid's Geometry. By twelve, Mill began studying scholastic logic, Aristotle, political economy, and the sciences. It was said that by the age of eighteen, Mill had an intellect that was equivalent to three Ph.D.'s.

Early on, Avi demonstrated a kind of freakish precocity that even Abba Eban was impressed with. Abba Eban routinely showered Avi with special attention. He encouraged him to read Plato and Aristotle, master algebra, geometry, trigonometry, and calculus. Avi went on to read Shakespeare, Milton, Newton, Dostoevsky, Tolstoy, and other classic works before he was twelve. Abba Eban also recognized Avi's talent for music and sent him to learn the piano at the age of three. In every respect, Avi was not a normal child. He did not socialize with other children and never participated in social activities. Though he was not brought up in a religious household and embraced agnosticism at an early age, he would later develop the kind of spiritual sensibility that leaves one in a perpetual state of contemplating insoluble questions. He was considered a freak of nature; a genius child who combined the penetrating intellect of Einstein with the literary and psychological insights of Freud. What Abba Eban failed to realize was that John Stuart Mill would suffer dearly as a result of being a guinea pig for his father's grand ideas. Avi would suffer not only the loss of his childhood, but the torment of feeling alone in a world that couldn't fully understand him. This was partly why he wanted to study abroad.

When he first arrived in New York, he was struck by the massive scale of the city. Although he read quite a bit about the history of New York and grew up listening to stories from Abba Eban, he was stunned by the magnitude of a city that moved faster than the time it took to hail a taxi. During orientation week, Avi followed tradition by exiting Lerner Hall through the back doors, turning right, and entering the campus through the main gates. Avi quickly embraced being a Columbia student. He knew all about the long, rich history of Columbia. He marveled at the names that preceded him: Alexander Hamilton, Theodore Roosevelt, Franklin Roosevelt, Warren Buffet, and a host of luminaries. Another graduate, Barack Obama, finished up at Columbia two years prior to his arrival.

Avi was alone as he strolled along the College Walk from the Butler Library to Low Memorial Library on September 9, 1985. It was twelve noon when he started heading to his next lecture, backpack slung over his shoulder. It was Activities Day, where all the clubs and organizations on campus set up tables to attract new members. Avi wore blue jeans, a white T-shirt, and an ugly gray jacket with a white fur collar. His hair was parted in a haphazard manner to the side and he was unshaven, as usual. As he walked through the Quad, he saw banners for a host of organizations festooned over plastic banquet tables: the International Socialist Organization, the Columbia Anti-War Coalition, Students against Imperialism, Students for an Orwellian Society, Columbia University College Republicans, the Hamilton Society, Pro-Israel Progressives, and dozens of others, each manned by eager undergrads armed with piles of flyers and pamphlets.

Up ahead and off to the right was a young woman standing handing out flyers to students as they walked by. She looked European, perhaps Swedish or from some other Nordic country. Avi could not take his eyes off of her flowing red hair. He was immediately attracted to her; though he couldn't understand why. He was mesmerized by her beauty, which accounted for his disinterest in the banner in front of her table. Soft freckles peppered her creamy white skin. He approached the table without thinking. Only when he was a few feet away did he notice several people talking to her. He stood awkwardly clutching his backpack. As he waited, he realized he was running late for his Philosophy class. At the same time, the table cleared. He smiled awkwardly.

"Hello."

"Hi," the girl smiled back. "We're having our first meeting this Thursday in Philosophy Hall. It would be great if you can come."

Avi was stunned by her beauty. He watched her alabaster skin, high cheek bones, and perfect button nose. She had teeth that glistened like pearls and impossible dimples when she smiled. She also had a body that rivaled anything Leonardo painted. She wore jeans and a white blouse poking from beneath a blue sweater.

He was anxious and nauseated in a way he never before felt. He only knew he didn't want to leave. He was suddenly speechless. He wanted to talk to her, but the words escaped him.

"So, do you think you can make it?" she asked.

"I'm sorry, what?" he stammered.

"Our meeting." Her smile evaporated and Avi realized he had no idea what she was saying. "It's our first one and it'd be great if you could make it."

"Oh, yes, of course. I'd love to come. Where is it?"

She smiled again. "Philosophy Hall, Thursday at 6 pm in room 106," He watched her talking again. There was something about her smile; something that seared his core and would never let go. He knew he was gawking at her but couldn't stop.

"Here, take this flyer." She handed him the flyer. Just as Avi was about to take the flyer, she pulled it back.

"Wait, let me write my phone number on the back in case you have any questions." She leaned over and scribbled on the back of the flyer.

"Thank you," Avi smiled. "I'll be sure to attend."

"That's what I like to see," she said.

"What?"

"You smiled." He stared at her a moment longer, at the dimples perched at the corners of her mouth. Her red hair tumbled over one shoulder and she tucked it behind her ears. He stared until it would have been strange to stare any longer, until other people were staring at him for staring.

He backpedaled and turned around, catching a glimpse of the banner draped over the table. It read *Turath: The Arab Student Organization.* Avi walked away and turned the flyer over, catching sight of her name. Alena Said. He froze and stared at the name to make sure he read it correctly. Avi knew Said was an Arabic name. He knew prior to attending Columbia that Edward Said taught English and Comparative Literature there. He read Said's groundbreaking work, *Orientalism,* back in Israel and was hoping to meet him. He turned the paper over to see the flyer.

> *Turath: The Arab Student Organization of Columbia University cordially invites you to our first meeting of the fall term.*

The flyer listed the details of the meeting in small print beneath the banner. Of course, Avi knew the word *al-turath* meant "heritage" in Arabic. He was stunned and stumbled to his lecture in a fog. He couldn't focus or concentrate at all.

"How could she be an Arab?" he thought. After all, he had seen many Arabs and none of them had naturally red hair or freckles. He figured she had to be an American with pro-Arab sympathies. It was the only way.

§§§

David returned to the room to see if Avi was ready to finish the interview. He noticed the bathroom door closed, so he knocked on the door. There was no response. As David knocked again, Avi felt himself being pulled back from a place he didn't want to leave. Water still dripped from his face.

"Give me a minute, David. I'm just washing up."

"It's been twenty minutes and we need to finish the interview. You have other interviews, you know? The BBC, Egypt's Nile Television, Israel's Channel 1, an online forum, and a few others are waiting to talk to you."

His tension reverberated against the bathroom wall. Avi opened the door and David noticed his wet hair.

"You need to dry your hair and comb it. When you go out there, don't give any indication that the question concerning Alena bothered you. We don't need anyone asking questions about your private life."

"Let's get this over with. I'm not feeling well." Avi walked out of the room in a hurry.

"I'm sorry to keep you waiting, Anderson." Avi picked up his lavaliere from the chair and sat down. He reattached it and smiled, seeming as composed and amiable as before he left. "I had some business to attend to."

"Of course, Mr. Prime Minister. I understand how busy you must be. Are you ready to continue?"

"Yes, please let's go on."

"Mr. Prime Minister, did Edward Said's family ask you to speak at the funeral?"

"Actually, I was the one who asked the family if I might say a few words. They were kind enough to allow me the opportunity."

"What did you say?"

"It was actually a very emotional speech for me. Here was a man that I had numerous battles with, and fate would have it that I would offer some final words. It was during the speech that the full force of his influence on my thinking came gushing forth. I had to stop for a moment in the middle, to collect myself. Edward Said and Abba Eban represented two opposing natures of the intellectual war that raged within me for many years. They died a year apart and

I spoke at both funerals. One of the things I said at Said's funeral was how generous he was to me. I remember the grief I used to give him as an undergrad. I said things that I would later regret. He always–'

Avi began to tear up. It was rare for anyone to see him emotional. He did not shed a tear at his uncle's funeral, though he was distraught. Pain was always a private affair, and no one was allowed to see his human side. Everyone marveled at his detached nature. For most of his life, Avi identified with Nietzsche's Übermensch, or the *overman*. He believed in his capacity to transcend the constraints of human emotions, or to impose his will on the world. This was another reason he loved *O Fortuna*. Listening to it always strengthened his highly controlled, Nietzschean self-image. For some reason, he was unable to control his emotions when remembering Edward Said.

"Do you need a minute, Mr. Prime Minister?" Anderson was also taken aback by the genuine show of emotion.

"No, I'm fine. It's just that Edward Said meant so much to my own understanding of Palestinian aspirations. You know, for a long time I insisted that genuine and lasting peace could not happen unless the Palestinians truly understood Jewish suffering. What Edward Said made me realize was that we Israelis had to also psychologically navigate our way to acknowledging Palestinian suffering, and our own contribution to such suffering. At the funeral, I simply spoke of the extraordinary influence he had on my life. He did not live to see the birth of Palestine, but so much is owed to him. Many people remember him as a brilliant defender of the Palestinian people and an eloquent writer, but he was also an accomplished pianist and an authority on music. He was the music critic for *The Nation* and wrote three books on music. He collaborated on one of his books; I believe it was *Musical Elaborations: Parallels and Paradoxes,* with his good friend, Daniel Barenboim, the Israeli conductor. In fact, Said and Barenboim founded the West-Eastern Divan Youth Orchestra in Spain. This youth orchestra was made up of musicians from Israel and Palestine."

"I'm curious. Did you have a chance to thank Edward Said?"

"Fortunately, I did. I was teaching at Harvard and he came to give a lecture. The year must have been 2000 or 2001. I asked him if he had time for a cup of coffee. He looked frail as a result of his battle with leukemia. I simply told him how much he meant to me and the impact he had on my intellectual development."

"What did he tell you?"

"Well, as I was in the middle of apologizing, he interrupted me and said that I had nothing to apologize for. He was one of the most decent people I've ever met."

"Did you talk about anything else?" It was clear Anderson was referring to Alena.

"We didn't actually talk about politics. We just reminisced about the old days. We also talked about my book, *Cultural Illusions*. Edward wrote a review for the *New York Times* back in 1998. His review was mostly positive in spite of our differences."

Avi knew he was treading on thin ice. He knew Anderson was trying to get him to open up about Alena, but he was not about to reveal anything. When he met Said at Harvard, they did indeed discuss Alena. Said wanted to know what happened in 1986 when he suddenly transferred to Harvard. Avi and Alena were supposed to meet in Cairo in 1986, but Avi never made it. Avi was not ready to answer any questions about her, but he did ask Said about her. Said told him Alena was now married with two children. He also told him she was teaching at Columbia. What Edward Said didn't know, and what no one else knew for that matter, was that Avi never stopped thinking about Alena. In fact, she was the guiding spirit of his life.

"Was that the last time you talked to him?"

"Yes, I'm afraid it was the last time I saw him."

The ice was growing thinner. This was another lie. Avi talked to Edward Said just weeks before he died. He called him in August of 2003 to tell him what exactly happened between him and Alena. He explained why he didn't go to Cairo to meet Alena and why he decided to leave Columbia. He gave Said a tearful apology and told him he would go to New York to visit him soon. Avi never had that opportunity, as Edward Said died on September 25th of that year.

"There was a recent article in the *Jerusalem Post* that suggested it was your friendship with Edward Said and Noam Chomsky that gradually changed your perspective. You also knew Alena Said while you were a student at Columbia. To what extent did they shape your understanding of the conflict?"

"It would be too simplistic to reduce how I arrived at certain conclusions to the influence of a few people. I was influenced, to a great extent, by my great-uncle, who defended Israel with passion and eloquence. I was also influenced by the three people you mentioned. I also read a great deal about the conflict from both Arab and Israeli sources–"

"To what degree did Alena Said influence your thinking?" Avi was not surprised this time. He knew Anderson was headed in this direction.

"I remember we argued quite a bit in college, but I always respected her passion and tireless effort on behalf of the Palestinian cause. It helped that she was on the negotiating team which resulted in the creation of Palestine."

David suddenly rose from his chair. At the same time, Avi was oblivious to the shouting that was taking place outside the hotel. Yoram stood and walked to the window and peered through the curtains. He looked back at David, grim-faced and anxious. David knew what had to be done.

"Anderson, the prime minister has several other interviews today. Could we possibly continue tomorrow?"

"Of course. I understand. Thank you, Mr. Prime Minister for giving us this interview." Anderson turned to David. "We can deal with the details of tomorrow a little later?"

"Of course."

"Thank you, gentlemen, for your time today." Anderson removed his lavaliere and stood up. His crew quickly turned off their lights and disassembled their equipment.

"Thank you, Anderson, for your understanding," Avi said. "I look forward to finishing our interview tomorrow." Avi rose and left the room.

Part II

The Grand Cafe

IV

Avi went back to the bedroom. He was tired and wanted to be alone for a while. David walked in behind him and closed the door. They had both heard it. There were demonstrators outside the building and their numbers were growing. David walked over to look out the window. He saw a few hundred people gathered below. He could barely make out their chanted calls – something about the fallacy of peace.

David ran his fingers through his thinning hair. This had a chance to turn bad in a hurry. He scanned the street for a police presence but saw nothing. Just some metal barricades lining the street that the protestors walked around. David knew their numbers were growing and things could soon get worse for all of them.

David turned to face Avi. He didn't want the prime minister to be burdened anymore. He was clearly distracted during the interview with Anderson Cooper. He was afraid Avi's disposition could turn sour for the entire weekend if he knew about the demonstrations below.

"The BBC should be here shortly," he said.

"I don't want to do anymore interviews today."

"Avi, your schedule is already booked for tomorrow. We need to finish these interviews."

"I don't care. Move them back to tonight. I just need some time alone. What time is it?"

"It's 3:30. Do you want to rest for a while? You hardly slept on the plane."

"I want to go down to the Grand Cafe."

"Whatever you need from the cafe, we can have it brought up." David couldn't have known that Avi wanted to sit inside the Grand Cafe and be left alone to reminisce.

When Avi looked back at his life, he divided it into two categories; magical moments and everything else. Everything else meant work; writing, teaching, politics, deep sorrow, suffering, and psychotic breakdowns. The magical moments, though fleeting and rare, were powerful enough to sustain him. What kept him going was the possibility of being alone with Alena. That's all he ever wanted. He loved the Palestinian people simply as a result of his deep, enduring love for her. He masked his love for Palestinians with sophisticated arguments designed to keep everyone from realizing the truth. Of course, he felt the arguments were morally valid. But what drove him to make deep concessions in the negotiations was the love he had for a woman he could never be with. His love for Alena both transcended and embraced every category of human understanding.

Avi couldn't understand Alena's control over him. He often thought of Kierkegaard's observation that passion is primary and intellect is only used to justify our pathos. He never agreed with Kierkegaard when he first read *Either/Or* in college, but the fullness of time and the scars of experience had taught him the painful lesson that our emotional disposition can mask truths beyond our immediate capacity to comprehend them. But at that moment, all Avi was able to think about was sitting at the Grand Cafe.

"Look, David. I simply want to be able to sit there like a normal person."

"Avi, you know security has not cleared the cafe for you. It was not on our itinerary. Why didn't you mention that you wanted to visit the café before?" David's agitation was obvious.

"I don't care. I'm going down to have some coffee." Avi was acting irrationally. All he knew was that he wanted to have the experience of being at the Grand Cafe. After all, he had one of the most magical moments of his life there.

"At least let our people make sure it is secure."

"I was told we had a three-mile perimeter secure. Listen, the Grand Cafe is just downstairs. I'm just going to slip in, sit down, and have a cup of coffee. You can station two security guys outside."

"Are you kidding me? Don't you know that you will be immediately recognized?" David felt his blood boiling.

He paced toward the door and back. "Journalists are waiting outside the hotel and paparazzi are everywhere. We can't prevent people from going places." He exhaled deeply and stared into the ground. "Look, let me send our guys to make sure there will be no one to bother you and alert the staff. Is that okay?"

"How long will it take?"

"About an hour, alright?"

"Thank you."

David left the room, the door slamming behind him. Avi didn't care what it took. He sat down at a chair adjacent to the bed and let the memories of Columbia flood back to him. He closed his eyes for a moment and found himself back at his Philosophy lecture thinking of Alena Said.

§§§

His upper division Political Philosophy course was taught by an aging gaunt man with a goatee named Professor Sidorsky. There were only eighteen students in the class. The lecture topic was Marxism, but Avi was too busy thinking of the girl he met minutes earlier. He stared at the flyer and wondered who she was. His blood raced and he tried to relax.

He knew he was the enemy to much of the Arab world. He spent six months in the West Bank during mandatory military service and dealt with Palestinians all the time. He couldn't understand why the Arabs hated Israel so venomously. It was the Arabs who rejected the partition plan of 1947. It was the Arabs who vowed to destroy Israel. It was the Arabs who caused the refugee problem in 1948 by attacking the fledgling Jewish state. That's what Avi was raised to believe. He believed that Arabs were generally a violent people incapable of rational discourse. He believed that Zionism was the only nationalism capable of protecting the Jews. If history taught him anything, it was that the Jews would always be considered outsiders wherever they went. The Holocaust magnified this stubborn reality in front of the whole world. The only time Avi dealt with Palestinians was as a soldier or engaging in shouting matches in Tel Aviv. Deep down, Avi never trusted Arabs and wanted to avoid them as much as possible.

"Excuse me, but I noticed you're not paying attention," said Professor Sidorsky. "Do you want to share with us what you were thinking about?"

Avi scanned the room and saw the eyes of the entire class on him. He recoiled in his chair. "I'm sorry, Professor."

"I remember you came to see me last week to ask if you can add this class. You realize this is an upper division course and I typically don't allow freshmen. What is your name, young man?"

"Avi."

"Avi what?"

"Avi Eban."

"You wouldn't be related to Abba Eban?"

"He is my great-uncle."

"Well, I hope you can live up to your great-uncle's reputation as a brilliant thinker."

"I'm terribly sorry for not paying attention, Professor. I was just distracted."

"My class is not compulsory, but I do expect my students to be engaged."

"Of course, Professor."

Avi felt terrible that he made a bad first impression. He approached Professor Sidorsky when class ended. The man was bent over his desk, sliding notes into a briefcase.

"I'm very sorry for not paying attention, Professor. I actually finished the paper you assigned on Feuerbach. I'm eager to get your reaction. I know you asked for ten pages, but I wrote fifteen. I hope you don't mind."

"You already finished the paper? It's not due until next week. I'm impressed, young man. I look forward to reading it."

Avi walked to Butler Library to study after class. He had an English paper to write on Chaucer and another Philosophy paper on Kant. His thoughts gravitated to Alena as he read in a tiny cubicle. He wondered why she couldn't have been Jewish. He decided to go home at 8 pm. He didn't live on campus and he had no interest in social life. In fact, he always felt awkward in social situations and he had made no friends so far at school. He could engage in conversation, but never learned how to socialize. He could speak in front of a large crowd with ease, but could never mingle in social groups.

He bought a motorcycle to get around New York. He didn't really need one, but he had a motorcycle in Israel and felt it would be easier to get around town. As he was riding along 116th Street, he stopped at a traffic signal on Broadway. In one fateful moment, Avi found himself on the ground, lying prone next to his bike. It happened suddenly. He got up slowly and brushed himself off. He picked up the bike and pushed it to the sidewalk. Apparently, a car hit him from behind. The force of the impact threw him several feet in the air before he landed awkwardly on his head and shoulders. He was unaware that any of this had happened. He was fortunate to have been wearing a helmet, as the impact of him falling on his head would surely have killed him. The girl driving the car ran up to him to apologize. She was a student at Columbia and had a little too much to drink at a sorority party.

The next thing Avi remembered was lying prone in the Emergency Room. He broke his clavicle, three fingers on his right hand, and the radius bone on his right arm. The doctor said he was lucky to be alive. After getting a cast and sling, the nurse asked him if he had someone to pick him up. That was the moment Avi realized he was alone in New York. His mother gave him the names and phone numbers of several Jewish families in New York in case of an emergency. But Avi didn't want to call any of them, as he knew the news would quickly reach his mother. He figured he could take the subway home, but he was too dizzy to walk to the station. He asked the nurse if he could use the phone to call a cab. The nurse told him to use the payphone in the waiting room. He didn't have any change on him, so he pretended to search for money in his pockets. That's when he realized that he was still carrying the flyer that Alena gave him. He took it out and remembered she wrote her phone number on the back. It was at that fateful moment that he decided to call her. He asked the nurse if he could use the hospital phone. He didn't have any change and he didn't know what to say. He was alone in New York City and calling someone he just met seemed impulsive. He wanted to hang up immediately when he heard the phone ringing, but a soothing voice answered and he gasped.

"Hello."

"Hi, is this Alena?"

"Yes it is."

"Hi, you probably don't remember me, but I met you earlier today. You gave me a flyer and wrote your name on the back."

"Yes, I remember you. You were wearing that gray jacket with a white fur collar."

"I'm so sorry to call you in the middle of the night, but I just…I was in a motorcycle accident and I don't have a way of getting home. I don't know anyone and I was wondering–"

"Oh my God! Are you okay?"

"I broke my collarbone.."

"Where are you? I can come pick you up."

"I'm in the Emergency Room at the Columbia Medical Center."

"I'll be right over."

He couldn't believe what he just did. It was completely unlike him. He instantly regretted it. She was Arab, after all. He didn't want to trouble her in the middle of the night. However, his attraction for her was undeniable. He hadn't stopped thinking of her since that afternoon. He sat in the waiting room and thought about her. A young woman approached him as he stared absently in the distance.

"There you are. Oh my gosh, I'm so sorry about what happened. Are you okay?"

Avi was confused and light-headed. He did not recognize the girl that hit him and scanned the waiting room.

"I'm sorry, but do I know you?"

"I'm the one who hit you from behind. I'm so sorry. I wasn't paying attention. I wanted to give you my insurance information and phone number. Please, if there is anything you need just call me. Of course, I'll pay for the hospital bills. Are you a student here?'

"Yes, I just started this term."

"I'm a junior here as well."

"Do you need a ride anywhere? I'd be happy to take you wherever you need to go,"

"I have someone coming to pick me up, but thank you for the offer. What happened to my motorcycle?"

"I'm not sure, but I can find out for you. Can you give me your phone number?"

Avi gave her his number and continued to wait. He shook his head, thinking about his misfortune. He wouldn't have called Alena if he had known the woman who hit him was going to follow him to the hospital. Of course, Avi desperately wanted to talk to Alena, just under different circumstances. He lowered his head for a few minutes when he heard her soothing voice call out to him.

"Hi, are you alight?" Alena looked down at him with pity. Avi wore a cast and a sling, and looked tired and disheveled.

"I'm so sorry to have bothered you like this. I do apologize. It's just that–"

"It's fine, really. I just hope you are okay. What happened?"

"Someone hit me from behind. Apparently, she had too much to drink and was coming from a party. She's a student here at Columbia.'

"Can you walk? My car is right outside."

Avi got up slowly. Alena held him by the elbow and guided him outside into her sedan. She got in and closed the driver's side door, locking them inside from the rest of the world. Her bucket seat was close to the steering wheel, as though someone much shorter than her taught her how to drive. Avi saw the lights of the city reflected in her eyes when she turned to him.

"So, do you live on campus?" she asked, pulling into traffic.

"No, I live in a loft on 72nd and Columbus. I'm so sorry to drag you out in the middle of the night like this. I just…I don't know anyone in New York and I couldn't walk to the subway." Avi was nervous talking to her. He tried to look at her again without her noticing. She didn't speak with an Arabic accent.

"So, what's your name?"

Avi froze in place. He thought about not telling her his name. She obviously would recognize that he was Jewish. If he lied about his name, she would eventually find out, and Avi didn't want to risk that.

"Avi," he said in a low voice, as though trying to change the subject.

"Oh, are you Jewish?"

Alena was curious. She remembered him immediately when he called because of the absent-minded way he approached and his ridiculous fur jacket.

"I'm Israeli. I just transferred to Columbia." An awkward silence hung over them as she turned onto Broadway.

"Why did you take the flyer from me then? I mean, I don't mind, but if you knew I was part of the Arab organization, why did you bother stopping at the table?"

Avi didn't know how to respond. He couldn't tell her the truth; that he didn't realize it was the Arab organization because he was too busy gawking.

"I was just curious."

"I take it you won't be coming to our meeting then."

"I noticed your name is Said. Where are you from?"

"I'm Palestinian," she said, smiling. Avi found himself gawking again when a calm quiet surrounded them. She stopped at a traffic light that filled the compact car with red, lighting up her face. She caught his stare, darkness pooling at her dimples. He didn't look away.

"I know you're surprised that I'm Palestinian. Everyone's surprised at first. I think my red hair throws people off."

They drove silently, Avi occasionally looking out the window. He felt a tinge of sadness when he realized they were close to his loft. Suddenly, a car cut them off rounding a turn and Alena honked her horn, shouting profanity in Arabic. Avi smiled.

"Why are you smiling?" Alena said, turning to him with a smile. Her eyes held his. "Do you know what I said?"

"Actually I do."

"You're kidding!"

"No, I speak Arabic."

"Really? Okay, what did I say?"

"It's difficult to translate, but you literally said 'get off my ass.'"

"Oh boy," she said, laughing. "I have to be careful what I say around you." The tension in the air melted and he laughed with her.

"Where is your apartment?" Alena asked, scanning the address numbers on the buildings as they approached his.

"I'm on the 7th floor. Apartment 714."

"Do you want me to help you up?"

"I've troubled you enough. Thank you for doing this. I'm terribly sorry for the burden."

Of course, he desperately wanted her to come up. He tried to be modest but found himself unable to take his eyes off of her.

"It's no bother. I'm just glad you're okay." He opened the door and gingerly pulled himself out of the car. "Take care of yourself," she said. For some reason, she didn't want to leave. She sat on the curb as he turned and faced her through the open window.

"Thank you so much for your help. Good night." Avi trudged to his building's doorway. Suddenly, he heard her call out.

"Wait, what's your phone number?" Avi turned and smiled. He gave her his number and she wrote it down on a scrap of paper. He thanked her again and waved as she drove off.

§§§

Although he was in tremendous pain, he couldn't get any sleep that night. He couldn't stop thinking about Alena. His thoughts meandered between her impossible beauty and his horrible luck. Of all the people in the world, the most beautiful one he had ever seen was Palestinian. As he lay down on the bed thinking of her, the phone suddenly rang. It had to have been past midnight. He answered it, certain that it was his mother calling to check up on him.

"Hello." Avi didn't want to sound as if he was in pain. He didn't want his mother to know that he had been in a motorcycle accident. In fact, he never told her he bought a motorcycle.

"Hi, Avi." Alena's soothing voice made Avi instantly melt. She prolonged the word *hi,* emphasizing the 'i'. He didn't expect a phone call and didn't know what to say. His heart raced and his breathing accelerated.

"Hi, Alena."

"I just wanted to make sure you're okay."

It was Alena's turn to feel nervous. Her attraction was not as clearly defined as Avi's. She thought he was handsome, but there was more. She couldn't put her finger on it. She was bothered by the fact he was Israeli, but that didn't stop her from thinking about him since she dropped him off. She had met Israelis before. Her uncle, Edward Said, had Israeli friends and she interacted with them regularly. She met Noam Chomsky through her uncle and knew he was a brilliant man. Though Chomsky was Jewish, he was the harshest critic of Israel. She never looked at him through an Arab-Israeli prism. There was something different about Avi. He was polite to a fault and respectful, which was not at all like the other college boys she knew.

"I'm trying to sleep but the pain is getting worse," Avi said.

"Didn't they give you something for the pain at the Emergency Room?"

"Yes, I took a couple of pills just now. I want to thank you again for the ride home and for the phone call. I was thinking about you before you called."

He admitted to it before he could consider what he was saying. He was nervous despite the aching pain in his ribs. He never had feelings like this before, but they were unmistakable. He was attracted to a few Israeli girls back home, but the feelings were never this intense. There was Arielle, whom he met during his military service, but it was purely a physical attraction. This time, he knew there was something different about the feelings stirring inside of him. It wasn't just her beauty. He felt a profound emotional connection already.

"Good thoughts, I hope," Alena said.

"Yes, of course."

"So what were you thinking?"

"I was thinking of how kind you were to come out in the middle of the night and help out a stranger. Thank you for doing that."

"I hope we're not strangers anymore."

"I wanted to ask you if you are related to Edward Said."

"I'm his niece."

"I was hoping you would say that."

"Really. Why?"

"I read *Orientalism*. Your uncle's a brilliant writer."

"Thanks, I know." Nobody could understand how proud Alena's family was of her uncle; how his success raised the fortunes of her family. To the rest of the world, he was the greatest Arab thinker of his generation. But to Alena, he was a hero.

"I mean, I don't agree with everything he wrote, but it was an amazing book." Avi heard silence on the other end of the phone and immediately regretted his words. He didn't want her impression of him to be shaped by intellectual disagreement.

"So what didn't you agree with?"

Avi paused. He wanted to backpedal, anything to get out of this conversation. In fact, he was a huge admirer of Edward Said.

"I'm sorry. I didn't mean to–"

"It's ok; I didn't mean to put you on the spot."

"So what's he like? I mean, he's one of the smartest people in the world. People must come up to you all the time, asking about him. I don't mean to belabor the point, but you must be proud."

"Yeah, we all are. He's a great man." She told him the story of her uncle's life – of his love for music and passion for peace. She told him about the many nights at his beautiful home, talking with Chomsky and the countless intellectuals she met. She told him about her uncle's love for art, books, culture, and politics. It always came back to politics, and she grew up with the sense that the world was in constant flux, and she was at the nexus of it. Her uncle told her from her youth that she would grow up to provoke change; that she was destined for something that will transcend the hatred and animosity. This was her childhood.

"Wow," said Avi, pausing after she finished. Her world was foreign and yet identical to his. He too grew up next to a great thinker, surrounded by philosophers, musicians, and politicians. He realized as she spoke that he admired Edward Said more than he knew, and that he intimately knew her already. This one conversation changed his life and he would never be the same again.

"So, tomorrow? What time should I pick you up?" she asked, breaking him from his spell.

"I can't keep imposing like this. I can take the subway. It's not a big deal–"

"No, don't be silly. You shouldn't take the subway in your condition. I'll pick you up around eight. Is that okay?"

"I'm really embarrassed, but that sounds fine. I'll be waiting outside. Thank you."

"It's no problem. I look forward to it. I'll see you in the morning." He heard the smile in her voice. The sound stayed with him as he fell asleep.

V

Avi sat in his chair, gripped by memory and staring into the dark hotel curtains. He sat in this way for more than an hour before being startled by David.

"Avi, we've cleared the café for you. You'll enter through a side door and someone from the café will escort you to your table. The staff knows not to approach you. One of our people will act as the waiter to take your order."

"Thank you, David."

"I told Anderson he could finish the interview tonight. Tomorrow is difficult as you have your lecture at the University of Oslo, meetings with heads of state, and I'm sure you are going to want some time to yourself."

As Avi entered the café, he noticed how little it had changed in the last ten years. He noticed the cherry wood-paneled walls and the large, crystal chandelier. He remembered the large mural on the wall that featured famous diners, including Henrik Ibsen and the symbolist painter who inspired expressionist art, Edvard Munch. He spent some of the happiest times of his life here. As Avi sat down, one of his security men, acting as a waiter, gave him a menu. Avi didn't need it. He simply asked for coffee. As much as he consciously wanted to return to 2009 – when he had lunch here with Alena as their romance suddenly reignited – he found himself thinking back to their time at Columbia. It was remarkable that his memories thirty years removed were as fresh as yesterday. The reason for his extraordinary memory had little to do with cognitive ability, rather it was trauma that trapped him in a perpetual loop that haunted him. Avi was running late and he knew Alena would be waiting for him any minute. He rushed downstairs to find her waiting in the car.

"Good morning," Alena said with a smile.

"Hi. I hope I didn't keep you waiting." Avi's anxiety and joy filled him with energy as he plopped down in the passenger seat.

"I just got here. How are you feeling? Are you still in pain?"

"I feel better. Thank you."

"Wait. Do I detect a British accent?" Alena narrowed her eyes on him.

"My great-uncle was raised in Britain and I learned English from him."

"Who is your great-uncle?"

Avi was shocked. He hadn't thought of her reaction to his family. He realized he should have made up a name, but he was not quick on his feet. He knew the sound of his uncle's name would probably create friction. His attraction to her prevented him from being forthcoming.

"Do I have to tell you?"

"Of course you do when you put it that way." Alena was quiet and gawked at him playfully.

"Come on. I told you who my uncle is,"

"My uncle is–"

"What's the big secret? Is he is an axe murderer or something?"

"Could I just tell you my last name? Would that be alright?"

"I love the way you say 'alright,'" she said, laughing. "It sounds so British." She mocked him playfully, repeating the word with his accent. Avi didn't laugh. "Okay, what's your last name?"

"My name is Avi Eban."

"So you are Abba Eban's nephew?"

"I'm his great-nephew." Avi watched Alena's expression grow blank. The car was again filled with awkward silence. A few blocks passed on the way to campus with neither of them speaking. She finally spoke again with a pensive look on her face.

"I don't care for his views." A few moments passed and they stopped at a red light. She turned to him. "So, why did you stop by my table? Were you spying on the Arab Organization? Why did you call me after your motorcycle accident? Of all the people to call, why did you call me?"

"I didn't mean–"

"Why do I always help people who have an alterior motive ?" She said in angry French. She was upset with herself for helping people, only to be taken advantage of.

"I'm sorry to have upset you."

"What else should I know about you?"

"I'm really sorry to have upset you. I would never spy on you. I'm very grateful for your help." Avi stared out the passenger window. It was a cold day and the street looked like it could be picked up and broken in a thousand pieces. He absently shook his head and leaned it against the window.

"Look, I'm sorry," Alena said. "But while your great-uncle was defending Zionism, my people were systematically being dispossessed of their land. Are you aware of that?"

Alena could tell Avi wasn't going to say anything. He was too worried about upsetting her.

"I guess you're not going to say anything." He was silent until they reached campus. She wound slowly through a parking garage and pulled into a tight spot. He was going to have to hike downstairs and across the Quad, but he didn't care. All he can think about was the possibility he would never see her again.

"Well, we're here."

"Thank you so much for the ride. Once again, I'm so sorry for upsetting you."

"Don't worry about it. Take care of yourself,"

She pulled her bag from the backseat and slammed the door. He slung his backpack over his stiff neck, wincing as he did. He watched as she walked toward the elevator, heels clacking on the asphalt. He strode slowly and turned around.

"Look, I'm sorry–"

She stopped and turned.

"It's just that I've never met anyone like you. You're–"

"I'm what?"

"Nothing…I have to go."

He watched her walk to the elevator and turned to walk before she turned around. He walked briskly, certain he would never see her again. He had no idea why, but he missed her terribly already. He shook his head quietly in his Philosophy lecture while pretending to listen to Professor Sidorsky again. The more he tried to think about her perspective, the more he grew confused. After all, Abba Eban was an intellectual giant. He was revered in Israel for his contribution to the establishment of the state of Israel. He could understand her reaction if it was directed at Ariel Sharon or some other dyed-in-the-wool right wing stalwart, but Abba Eban was in favor of a two-state solution.

When Avi was stationed in the West Bank during his military stint, he sympathized with Palestinian suffering, but blamed the Arabs for the stubborn reality that Israel inherited as a result of the Six-Day War of 1967. *They were the belligerent ones,* he thought. He believed that Israel had powerful historical and moral claims to Palestine. He knew the people of Israel had suffered enough. The world stood by while the Jews were slaughtered for no other reason than being Jewish.

Avi rode the subway home immediately after class. He held onto the vacuous hope that she would call. But he knew it was remote. She was fiery, and he attached this quality to her red hair, as though one led to the other. He knew people of Arab descent could be fiery, but had never seen a beautiful woman seem so cold and distant. His mind wandered and he settled on the idea that he was destined to feel empty, that this was part of his life. It was okay in its own way. He just never knew emptiness until now.

He tried to read until midnight, when he threw his book across the living room and gave up. He understood that she wasn't going to call and thought about calling her instead. He could apologize and that would be it. But he thought of her ignoring his calls – or worse –listening silently and answering him coldly. He got up and paced across the room, running his fingers through his hair.

Suddenly, the phone rang. Avi ran across the room, hitting his knee on the edge of the coffee table and stumbling. He stood in front of the phone for a second, frozen in place. Finally he picked up.

"Hello?" Avi tried his best to be calm.

"Avi, why didn't you call home yesterday?" He heard his mother's voice, sounding worried.

"Hello, mama," he said with resignation. "How is papa and everyone else?"

"Everyone's fine. We're worried about you. Did you contact the Greenbergs?"

"I'm fine, mama. I'll call the Greenbergs if I need anything. I promise."

"Are you eating? I know how absent-minded you are. I know studying is important, but you can't concentrate on an empty stomach."

"Yes, I'm–"

"Wait, your uncle wants to say hello."

"Hello, Avi." He heard Abba Eban's familiar gravelly voice. "How do you like Columbia?"

"Hello, Uncle. It's fine."

"Did you contact some of the people I told you about? They can be very helpful to you in New York,"

"No, I haven't had an opportunity yet, but I will." Avi was hesitant to call any of his uncle's contacts. He wanted to earn his own reputation rather than be given special consideration just for being related to Abba Eban.

"How do you like your classes?"

"They're easy so far. I'm thinking of adding another class. Maybe Said." Avi wanted to get his uncle's reaction to taking a course from Said.

"How many units would you have if you add Said's course?"

"I'd have 24. I know what you're going to say, but I'm not being challenged. Much of what I'm studying, I've already read."

"Why Said?"

"You encouraged me to read Orientalism and I decided to major in Philosophy and Comparative Lit."

"When did you add Comparative Literature? I thought you might do Mathematics along with Philosophy."

"I can do Math on my own. I prefer literature, since it complements my philosophical studies."

"Be careful with Said. His conclusions suggest that anyone who attempts to study the Orient will be governed by a prism that distorts reality."

"I'm not sure about that. We Jews were also objects of illusory constructions, what Said calls imaginative geography." Avi felt recharged. He missed having philosophical discussions with his uncle.

"Let's not forget that Said takes the idea of imaginative geography from Foucault and directs it towards the Orient. Remember, for Foucault, space and subjectivity are mutually constitutive. That is to say, we all have a historically specific way of not only apprehending but imagining geography." Abba Eban was going into lecture mode, something Avi learned at an early age.

"I think that Said might be correct that the Orient, in general, and the Arab world in particular, have been largely reduced to representations by imperial powers whose only connection to that part of the world was textually referenced."

"Did you read Merleau-Ponty or Husserl yet?" Avi was using his great-uncle's apartment rather than staying in the dorms, and the living room held an extensive library. The apartment was adorned with books and paintings that gave it the feel of an English library. It had mahogany panels, with books stacked to the ceiling. The New York collection alone housed over a thousand books. It helped Avi to feel at home.

"I haven't read them yet, but I'll start soon. There's a graduate seminar on Phenomenology offered next semester. I'll talk to the professor about adding the course."

"Is there anything you want to talk about?"

"I'm fine. New York is an amazing place. Oh, I went to Carnegie Deli. It was loud and expensive, but the Reuben was delicious. People in New York are loud and short-tempered. How did you live in this city? You're always calm and rational."

Avi heard numerous stories from his uncle about New York, but the reality of the city was different from his stories. He realized now that New York had to be experienced to be understood.

"You'll adjust soon enough. I might come visit you in the summer."

"That would be great. Say hello to everyone for me."

"I will. Take care of yourself and tell me how Said's course turns out. Good night, Avi."

"Good night, uncle." Avi hung up the phone and felt calmer. He looked around for Merleau-Ponty's book, *Phénoménologie de la Perception*. He sat down on his uncle's giant leather chair and started reading. It must have been half past midnight when the phone rang again. Avi's heart raced again.

"Hello." Avi's voice quavered.

"Hi, Avi." He heard Alena's soothing voice.

"Alena, I want to apologize for upsetting you this morning," Avi said. "I also want to thank you for–"

"No, I'm the one who should apologize to you, Avi. I overreacted and I'm so sorry for losing my temper."

"There's nothing to apologize for. I understand how you could have thought I would be spying on you."

"Listen, do you want to get some coffee?"

"Now?"

"Yes. If that's alright."

"Yes. I mean, I would love to."

"Great. I will pick you up in fifteen minutes."

"Okay, I'll wait outside."

Avi couldn't believe it. He was desperately hoping to hear from her and now he was going to have coffee with the most beautiful girl he had ever met. It was at that moment he knew he was falling in love. Electricity ran through his veins. He quickly washed his face and looked in the mirror. He wore jeans and a white T-shirt. He thought of shaving but knew he didn't have time. He grabbed a sweater and ran to the elevator. He opted to run downstairs so as not to keep her waiting. He noticed her car approaching as he stepped outside.

"Hi, Avi." Alena waved through the open passenger window, smiling. The gesture and sight of her sent his heart racing.

"Hi, Alena."

"Let's go to Tom's on Broadway. They're open 24 hours."

Avi slid into her passenger seat and slammed her door. She drove slowly, stopping for endless red lights even though there was little traffic this late.

"So tell me. How many languages do you speak?" Avi could tell Alena was staying clear of any talk about politics.

"Six."

"You're kidding me, right?"

"Well, I know you speak at least three languages."

"How do you know that?"

"Well, I know you speak English, Arabic, and you said something to yourself in French this morning. Do you speak any other languages?"

"I also speak Spanish. Okay, I know you speak English, Hebrew, Arabic, and French. What else?"

"I also speak Italian and German." While they were cataloguing how many languages each spoke, Avi noticed a song playing on the radio. He didn't recognize the song, but the melody was beautiful. He sat and listened for a minute and turned to see her staring at him and smiling.

"What's the name of this song?" he asked.

"I'm not sure, but I think its *Cherish* by Kool and the Gang. Why?"

"It's beautiful." They listened quietly as they pulled up before the restaurant.

Cherish the love we have / We should cherish the life we live.

Alena smiled and stared at him. They were quiet until they sat down at a booth.

"What are you going to have?" Alena asked. "I'm hungry."

"I'm not hungry. I'll just have some tea."

"Oh, come on. My treat." Avi felt as if his heart was about to stop. He was experiencing love for the first time. It was a magical feeling.

"I'm truly not hungry, but thank you."

"Well, I don't like to eat alone, and if you don't have something with me, I'll just have coffee."

"What if I share whatever you're having."

"Great. Let's see now, what should we have? How about a turkey sandwich?"

"That would be fine." Alena placed her order and turned around. She felt eager to get to know Avi. She was finding it difficult to hide her attraction for him, even as she wasn't sure where it came from. She cursed her fate at feeling attracted to an Israeli, but she couldn't help it. Her mind was struggling to make sense of an attraction that seemed impossible to reconcile.

"So what's your major?"

"I'm a double major in Philosophy and Comparative Lit."

"Wow! I guess you're going to be pulling some all-nighters. And you'll have to take courses from my uncle."

"Actually, I'm going to see Professor Said tomorrow to try and add his class on Foucault."

"Don't worry. He'll let you add his class."

"I hope so. It's an upper division course. What are you studying?"

"I'm a linguistics major. In fact, I have to finish a paper on Chomsky that I keep putting off."

"What's the topic?"

"Why? Are you familiar with Chomsky?"

The waitress placed their food on the table. Alena thanked her and ignored her sandwich.

"I've read some of his work."

"It's on Chomsky's disagreement with Piaget's cognitive development."

"I'm familiar with that. Chomsky actually debated Piaget in 1975."

"How do you know this? Oh my God! I mean, I met Chomsky several times and I didn't know that he debated Piaget."

"There's an interesting book on the debate that outlines the fundamental disagreement between the two. It's really interesting."

"Wait, let me get out a pen so I can–"

"Oh, no need. I actually have the book if you want it. It's called *Language and Learning: The Debate between Jean Piaget and Noam Chomsky*."

"You just happen to have the book."

"Yes, I read it last year. Like I said, it's fascinating."

"Do you think you can help me with the paper?"

"Of course, I'd be happy to help. It's the least I can do. You've been so kind to me."

"Our food is getting cold. Here is your half of the sandwich."

"I'm not really–"

"You said you would eat half, remember?"

"Okay, thank you." Avi smiled and took half of the turkey sandwich. He took a bite and set the sandwich down. He watched quietly as she ate. After two bites, she looked at him with her mouth full and smiled.

"Can I make a confession, Alena?"

"Sure, what is it?"

"I want to tell you why I approached your table yesterday. This is difficult for me to say, so I hope it comes out alright. You see, I was walking along the College Walk and I noticed you from a distance. I–" Avi paused, unsure of what to say.

"Avi, what is it?"

"The truth is that I was stunned by your beauty. I didn't notice the banner in front of your table simply because I was mesmerized by how beautiful you looked. Forgive me, but I didn't really care what organization you represented. I simply wanted to meet you. You're…you're the most beautiful girl I've ever met." Avi was trembling when he finished. He couldn't believe he confessed such a thing to her. He was dying to tell her but fearful of her response.

"What?" Alena dropped her sandwich on the plate. She felt there was an attraction between them, but didn't expect such a romantic confession.

"I'm so sorry if I upset you. I just don't want you to think I was spying on you. I noticed your red hair from a distance and, you'll probably find this funny, I had this weird feeling that you were Swedish. I walked a little closer and noticed how beautiful you were. I hope you're not upset."

"Heavens no! I just didn't expect this. I'm flattered. My God! Look at me, I must be blushing. But after I gave you the flyer, didn't you notice my name was Alena Said?"

"Yes, after I walked away. I couldn't focus all day."

"No, I mean you must have realized I was Arab. Didn't that change your opinion of me?"

"Well, I must admit that I was disappointed at first. We come from different worlds and have antithetical perspectives on the conflict. The truth is that I couldn't stop thinking of you. When you were upset with me this morning, I was afraid I would never see you again."

"So you don't mind that I'm Palestinian?"

"All I know is that I love talking to you."

Alena looked at her watch and gaped at Avi.

"Oh my goodness. It's almost two. I've got a lecture in the morning."

"Me too." She drove him home and told him she would pick him up in the morning.

VI

Avi was nervous about meeting the Palestinian scholar. Though he never told this to anyone, he considered Edward Said to be the Palestinian equivalent of his great-uncle. Both were intellectuals who passionately defended their people. Both men were steeped in the Western intellectual tradition and used their position to construct arguments to defend their respective national pride.

Edward Said was born in Jerusalem in 1935 to Protestant parents. His father, who was a United States citizen, served under General Pershing during World War I. Said's childhood was marked by a disconnected sense of identity that shaped his intellectual development. During Israel's war of independence in 1948 – what the Arab world called *al-Nakba,* or catastrophe – Said's family moved to Cairo. Young Edward felt out of place while studying at Victoria College. He was a Palestinian, with a British first name (his mother named him after the Prince of Wales), and an American passport, studying in Egypt. By the age of fifteen, Edward was on the verge of being expelled from Victoria College for mischief, which prompted his father to send him to study at the Mount Vernon School in Boston. Although he excelled academically, first at Princeton and then at Harvard where he earned his Ph.D. in English Literature, Said would always feel an uprooted sense of dislocation, isolation, and fragmentation.

His groundbreaking book, *Orientalism*, fundamentally changed the nature of postcolonial studies. It impacted fields as diverse as history, philosophy, literature, anthropology, and the arts. Though *Orientalism* was largely praised as an intellectual exploration of how the West constructed the Orient as an ontological and epistemological paradigm that reduces a vast geography of otherness to essentialist realities, critics argued that Said's view of the West is itself a distorted representation.

As Avi approached Professor Said's office at Philosophy Hall, he noticed several students waiting in the hallway to talk to him. He decided to wait, but realized that Said's Foucault lecture would begin in twenty minutes. He had no choice but to sit in on the lecture and hope to talk to him about the possibility of adding the course later. Upon taking a seat in the back of the lecture hall, he was immediately struck by the number of students waiting for him to speak. He guessed there were at least two hundred students. Edward Said entered from a side door up front and immediately began his lecture on the discursive nature of representations. As Avi listened, he was awestruck by Said's rhetorical power. He was impressed by Said's ability to convey complex ideas. Avi was transfixed. Whenever Avi was enchanted by a powerful speaker, he would cross his legs, rest his elbow on the arm of the chair, and bury his face in his hand. He was frozen in this posture for the entirety of the lecture.

"So, for Foucault, knowledge as a whole – truths, morality, and meaning – are created through discourse. In his book, *History of Sexuality*, Foucault tells us that it is in discourse that knowledge and power are joined together, connected in a multiplicity of discursive elements. Discourse both transmits and produces power. It is – and we talked about this last time – similar to the Hegelian spirit that dialectically moves through history."

Avi was inspired by Foucault's insight into power relations as outlined in *History of Sexuality*. He wanted to ask Said about the topic, but was unsure of the etiquette in this particular course. Some professors would allow students to interrupt at any time and others demanded that questions and comments be addressed at the end of a lecture. Twenty minutes into the lecture, a student sitting up front raised her hand. Much to Avi's delight, Professor Said acknowledged her. This first question opened the door to several more questions and Avi raised his hand, Said acknowledged a student sitting in front of Avi, who asked Said about his view of imaginative geography.

"I addressed imaginative geography last time," Said responded. "So I don't want to repeat everything I've said. Let me explain it this way. Our ideas about the paradigmatic other are shaped by the production of images and rational discourse about those we are representing. It is these representations that are divorced from reality. When it comes to the East, you have a repertoire of images that become part of the fabric of accepted representations. You know, the sensual woman, the exotic east or what is often referred to as the marvels of the East. These images become self-referential. That is to say, writers and poets relied upon them, almost subconsciously, to articulate a body of knowledge about a geographic location that was divorced from the actuality of that place. So the Orient, unlike the West, becomes an amorphous sea of exotic and uncivilized culture that is timeless and immutable."

Avi was listening and waiting for the opportunity to jump in. He had to raise his hand up high since he was in the back. He was nervous and anxious as Said pointed to him. Avi froze for a moment but proceeded.

"I have a question, Professor, but I would like to offer a framework if I may. The idea of constructing or representing a paradigmatic other, the discursive elements that Foucault discusses, is predicated upon certain epistemic assumptions that are somehow treated as axiomatic givens. In *Orientalism,* you argued that when Napoleon invaded Egypt, he arrived with an enormous army of not only soldiers, but scientists who studied and catalogued Egypt for the benefit of France. You go on to say that what allowed this to happen was the sheer power of a European country to be able to represent the Egyptians. The converse of that process would not be possible. That is to say, the Egyptians lacked the necessary power to be able to represent Europe. My question is simply this: Is the act of representation inherently governed by an overarching epistemology that, as Foucault would say, transmits and produces power?"

Before Avi could complete his thought, he noticed the creeping glares of other students. The entire lecture hall lay in front of him, and he noticed other students looking at each other. He felt gratified and terrified all at once, but he continued.

"What I'm asking is if, hypothetically, the Egyptians, or any other subaltern group, had the power to represent the West, would the representation not also suffer from the burden of imaginative geography? And if that is the case, can representations, as produced by hegemonic or subaltern powers, ever get at some kind of Kantian reality?'

He was surprised that he got through the question. He was emboldened by the moment and the chance to address Said in person. It was something like an out-of-body experience. It seemed as though all those years of reading and studying were converging toward this moment. Professor Said was taken aback by the question and paused for a moment.

"That's an extraordinarily insightful question. What's your name young man?"

"Avi."

"So you are Avi Eban? I heard about you. I'm impressed." Professor Said proceeded to answer the question while other students strained to look toward the back of the lecture hall. Avi grew uncomfortable at the attention. He also knew people might approach him after class.

He rose quickly once the lecture ended. As he got up, he was surprised to see Alena standing up front and waving for him to come down. He walked slowly down the steps. A crowd of students stood around Said as he held court.

"Well, you know how to make an impression," Alena said. "I want to talk to you about the question you posed, but I want you to meet my uncle first."

Alena felt proud. There were several students surrounding him, but Alena tapped her uncle on the shoulder. He turned on his heels and smiled.

"So, you are Avi Eban. Well, it's very nice to meet you. Alena mentioned you. Where in Israel are you from?"

"It's truly a pleasure to meet you, Professor Said." Avi's nerves shot through his body. He spoke quickly and stood stiff. "I read *Orientalism* and *The Question of Palestine*. I was born in Kfar Shmaryahu, just north of Tel Aviv.'

"How are you feeling? Alena told me about the motorcycle accident."

"I'm feeling much better. Thank you, Professor. Would it be possible to add this course?"

"I don't usually allow freshmen in this course, but judging from your question, I think you can handle some of my graduate seminars. Where is your add card?"

Avi pulled his schedule card from his backpack and handed it to Professor Said, who signed it.

"Come see me this afternoon so I can give you the syllabus. I'll be in my office around four."

"Of course. Thank you, Professor." Avi and Alena left the lecture hall together, walking shoulder-to-shoulder down the hallway.

"Do you want to have lunch?" Alena asked.

"Actually, I have a lecture to get to. How about if we have lunch at 2:30 or so?"

"That would be great. Do you know where Amir's is?"

"I'm not sure actually."

"Don't worry about it. Meet me in front of Philosophy Hall and we can walk together."

"Sure, thank you."

Avi waved goodbye and walked to his political philosophy class. He couldn't believe his good fortune, to be having lunch with Alena and to have met one of his childhood heroes in one afternoon was a dream come true. It was the first moment that he truly felt like a Columbia student, like he really belonged.

His thoughts rested with Alena and Professor Said as he sat down in his usual seat, dropping his backpack onto the floor with a thud. His thoughts raced with images of Alena, and so he didn't see Professor Sidorsky approach him.

"I read your paper, Mr. Eban. Please see me after class."

Avi looked at Professor Sidorsky with confusion. His stern tone and focused eyes suggested there was a problem. Avi wondered what was wrong with his paper. It was on Marx's view of religion as outlined in his 1843 essay, *A Contribution to the Critique of Hegel's Philosophy of Right*.

What Avi could not have known was that Sidorsky was skeptical that a freshman could have written such an eloquent paper. It may have been the most insightful and scholarly work he received from any undergrad or grad student at Columbia. He was unwilling to accept that Avi actually wrote it.

He continued his lecture on Marx's view of religion from the previous class.

"Let's continue with Feuerbach's views on religion, which had an enormous influence on Marx's own thinking. For Feuerbach, religion is the process of objectifying man. God, under this view, becomes the alienated, objectified, personality of man."

As the professor continued, Avi realized what a pleasure it was to listen to Said's lecture. By contrast, Sidorsky's style was dry and uninspired. Nevertheless, Avi waited patiently for an opportunity to jump in. Underneath his polite exterior lied a killer instinct. He sat among upper division students – juniors and seniors. Avi scanned the room and saw most students taking copious notes. He failed to understand this ritual in a humanities course. If it was mathematics or science, perhaps notes would help. But he was never able to understand why students took notes in a philosophy course. He always found it more beneficial to listen to lectures and think actively. He found his opportunity halfway through the lecture. Sidorsky was discussing Marx's constructionist view of religion.

"For both Marx and Feuerbach," he said with his monotone delivery. "Religion is a creation; a construction of the mind. As Feuerbach puts it, thought arises from being, but the converse is not true, being does not arise from thought. So religion is a construction; though Feuerbach and Marx would not use that term, a projection of the imagination. Marx wrote in his essay on Hegel's *Philosophy of Right*, that man makes religion, religion does not make man. Again we see an inversion of Hegel. It is the materiality of this world that maintains the belief structures regarding the next world. Now–"

The Professor paused, distracted by Avi's hand.

"Yes?" he asked, as though burdened by the interruption.

"I'm curious about the term *construction*," said Avi. "While, as you pointed out, Feuerbach and Marx never used the term, they certainly implied a process of projecting man's attributes. My question has to do with the nature of this construction. In his Essay on Hegel's *Philosophy of Right*, Marx does not address the construction itself, but accepts it as something coterminal with an illusion of happiness. I'd like to know if the act of constructing a reality that is beyond this world is necessarily an act of producing illusions?" The classroom fell silent. Avi again felt the eyes of the students upon him.

"I don't think Marx's aim was to explore the sociological nature of constructions in general," Professor Sidorsky said. "Marx would respond by arguing that religion is a human enterprise and, as such, it diverts attention from the political reality that conspires to keep people in a perpetual state of denial. I don't think you're correct in saying that Feuerbach and Marx accept the illusory projection of religion as a given. They spend a great deal of time in describing the process of how religion is created."

Avi held back his rebuttal. Professor Sidorsky continued for a few more minutes before time ran out. Avi waited for the students to leave in order to talk to him. As he was waiting, a student came over to introduce himself.

"Hi, I didn't understand half of what you said, but, man, I was impressed."

"Oh, thanks."

"I'm David, by the way. What's your name? Oh wait, I forgot, you are Avi Eban, right?"

"Yes, how did you know?"

"Sidorsky asked for your name last time, remember?"

"Oh, yes. I'm sorry I forgot."

"So were you born in Israel?"

"Yes, and I take it you're Jewish."

"Yes, my name is David Barkovic. I was born here in New York. I visited Israel two years ago. I loved it there. I went to Jerusalem and Tel Aviv. We have a ten-page paper on Feuerbach due next Wednesday and I haven't even started it yet. I'm so lost. Did you start the paper yet?"

Avi didn't know how to respond. He didn't want to project conceit.

"I actually finished it and turned it in."

"Damn, you finished it already? Listen, do you suppose you can help me with it?"

"Sure." Avi saw Professor Sidorsky packing up his briefcase. "Excuse me, but the professor is waiting to see me."

"Sure, I'll talk to you later."

Avi turned and walked to Professor Sidorsky.

"Professor, you wanted to see me?"

"Yes, it's about your paper. I read it last night." Sidorsky took the paper out of his briefcase. It had comments throughout made in looping red cursive, but no grade.

"I thought it was brilliant, but until today, I didn't believe you wrote it. After the way you discussed Marx just now, I'm going to give you an A for the paper."

Sidorsky took out his pen and wrote an A on the cover sheet. "I'm impressed, young man. Your great-uncle must be proud. Listen, I'm wondering if you would like to join my graduate seminar on Marx. We meet twice a week, Tuesdays and Thursdays from 4:00 to 5:30."

"I'd be honored, Professor. Thank you.' Avi was overjoyed with the attention. He also realized his workload would leave him little time for anything else. Avi realized it was 2:40 and Alena was waiting for him.

'I'll see you tomorrow at the seminar, Professor. Thanks again." As Avi was leaving the room, the professor called him.

"Don't you want to know where the seminar is?"

"Yes, of course. I'm terribly sorry."

"Don't worry. We meet in room 206, Philosophy Hall."

"Thanks again. I'll see you tomorrow."

§§§

Avi ran to meet Alena and found her standing in the Quad, waiting for him. She hugged her books and smiled as he approached her. He was out of breath and smiling back at her. They immediately started walking to her car.

"I'm so sorry. I was detained by my Philosophy professor."

"It's okay. I understand. So did you wow your philosophy class too? People are talking about you."

"My professor thought I didn't write a paper I did for him. He changed his mind and gave me a grade."

"Don't tell me. You got an A, right?'

"Yes, I'm happy to say I did."

"How did you like my uncle's lecture?"

"He's extraordinary. He certainly knows how to command an audience. Oh, who am I kidding? I was mesmerized. There's something about his lecture style that is inviting. He is stunningly brilliant, yet down to earth."

They got in her car and drove to Amir's. It was just a couple of blocks away. It was a warm day and Avi rolled down the window to take in the air. He felt liberated in her car, completely separated from the world beyond. He privately wished they were going somewhere much further.

"I hope you like falafel."

"Of course. I had falafel all the time back in Israel."

"Well, I hope you don't tell me that the Israelis came up with falafel?"

"No, I don't think so." Avi read something arcane on the history of falafel from his great-uncle's library. He also wanted to offer a concession, or so it seemed in his mind, so as not to spoil the moment.

"Well, I'm glad to hear you say that. Of course it was the Arabs who introduced falafel."

"Actually, I read somewhere it was the Coptic Christians of Egypt who introduced falafel."

"I have a friend who is Coptic. They seem to fast year round. I don't blame them for coming up with it."

They parked and walked inside the tiny falafel store. It was a cultural hotspot for Columbia students and out-of-towners – a place where people worked, talked and met. Avi had been here once before but hadn't tried the falafel. He was beginning to think that Alena had been here many times.

"I hope they're not too crowded," Alena said. "They're usually packed."

They walked in and saw that the line was short. Avi walked with Alena to get in line, but she asked him to grab one of the two remaining tables while she ordered.

"Remember," Avi said. "You promised I could treat this time."

"Well, I'm the one who suggested Amir's so it's my treat."

"Please, let me treat you this one time. I feel like I'm a burden to you. You drive me everywhere and–"

"Didn't you say you would help me with my Chomsky paper?"

"Yes, of course I will, but what does that have to do with me treating you?"

"Avi, we can stand here arguing over who's going to pay or you could grab that table before someone takes it."

Avi went to claim the table while Alena ordered falafel. As Avi waited, he experienced an overwhelming sense of bliss. His private world was suddenly bifurcating between schoolwork and obligation, punctuated by fleeting moments like these that were magical and dreamlike. Alena ordered the food and sat down with Avi.

"My uncle was really impressed with you," she said.

"How do you know? I mean, we left together."

"When you went to your lecture, I went to see him. He told me that you remind him of someone he knew in college."

"I wanted to thank you for introducing me. Is it okay if I tell you that I missed you?"

"Avi, you just saw me." Alena wanted to be cautious with her feelings, though she was clearly attracted to him.

"I know, but I–" Avi was interrupted as their order was called out from the counter. He went to pick it up. He returned with their order, sat down, and stared at Alena.

"Can we talk about Foucault?" she asked. She was not as interested in Foucault as she was in Avi. His intelligence was unusual and freakish. She was anxious to know everything he knew. She was a voracious reader and somewhat of a loner until her final year of high school. The truth was that she often preferred being alone to spending time with her friends. She was a precocious child who lived in her own private world of ideas. Edward Said's influence on her was unmistakable and she wanted to know the extent of Avi's extraordinary precocity.

Avi's intellect startled and amazed her. He was a new benchmark for brilliance. She wasn't sure that it was healthy to be as bookish and awkward as he seemed to be. But his intelligence was a source of attraction to her. It was the reason she wanted his help with her paper on Foucault. She knew enough to write knowledgeably about Chomsky. In fact, she could call the man if she had any questions, but she wanted to test Avi's intellect; his cognitive insights for arriving at a completely new idea, carved out of the same textual foundation she already knew.

"Sure, of course. But I thought we could start on your Chomsky paper."

"We can work on that later. So tell me what have you read by Foucault?"

"Let's see, I read the *Archeology of Knowledge* and *The Discourse on Language, The History of Sexuality, Order of Things,* and *History of Madness.*"

"What did you mean when you asked if representations can ever get at some kind of Kantian reality? I'm sorry, but I never understood Kant."

"Oh, you see Kant distinguishes between two realms, right? The *phenomena* and *noumena*. The phenomenal world is that which we can apprehend through sensory experience and the *noumena,* or the thing-in-itself, is beyond our capacity to understand. So in a way, Kant is saying that we can never know the true nature of reality independent of how we perceive the world. The point I was trying to make about representations is that the very act of describing a culture is inherently limited by the constraints of the observer."

"So are you saying that the idea of imaginative geography is false?"

"No, I actually agree with Professor Said that Western images of the Orient are made possible by positional authority and legitimized by a kind of self-referencing and self-fulfilling framework that continues to maintain a hold on our collective imagination."

"Do you always talk like this?"

"I don't understand."

"I mean, we're not in lecture anymore. You can relax now and talk normally."

"It's difficult to talk informally when you ask me about Kant and Said."

"So the images we have of Arabs as terrorists, irrational, barbaric, and so on. Are they grounded in reality or are they manufactured?"

"I believe they are manufactured, but let me ask you this question. Do you think the image of Jews as conniving, blood-sucking people grounded in reality or a manufactured image?"

"Could we talk about something else?" Alena didn't want the conversation to end in acrimony.

"Of course, but I just want to make my point that imaginative geography is not exclusively spatial in the sense that it positionally moves from Western dominance to the Orient. We Jews suffered grotesquely distorted representations while supposedly being assimilated into

Western culture. We were always the convenient scapegoat for all the ills of Europe."

"I understand that, but why did the Palestinians become the scapegoat for what Europe did to the Jews? I mean, Zionism was a national movement whose aim was to remove us from our homes."

"Maybe you're correct. We should talk about something else. I don't think we're going to persuade each other over lunch."

"Well, you hardly touched your sandwich. Don't you like it?"

"It's quite good, actually. Please don't be upset with me."

"I'm not upset. Look, you are brilliant. Why can't you see that my people are suffering as a result of Israel?"

"I would concede that point if you would acknowledge the role of the Arabs in Palestinian suffering. Don't forget that when we declared statehood in 1948, five Arab armies attacked us."

"You were attacked because you were an illegitimate entity in the region. You can't just go to a land that does not belong to you and derive legitimacy from brute force."

"I'm sorry, but I simply don't agree with that. You must understand that a great deal of the land was purchased from absentee land owners who lived in Lebanon and elsewhere. As far as moral legitimacy, we were slaughtered by the millions. Look, you never asked me about my views for a solution. I believe in a two state solution."

"Well, that's encouraging."

"Speaking of your uncle, I have to go see him."

"Do you know how to get back?"

"Yes, thank you for lunch, but you must let me treat next time."

Avi sensed that Alena was irritated. In fact, he was irritated too. He didn't know how she could call Israel an illegitimate entity. He wondered how many Jews had to die before Israel could be considered legitimate. He couldn't understand why the vastness of the Arab world was unable to accommodate a Jewish state. The Arabs had their chance in '48 to accept partition, but instead they attacked. This is what Avi believed, and he would use his considerable intellect to defend Israel's right to exist. He hadn't reached the point where he could entertain the notion that Israel's *raison d'etre* came at a price. Israel's moral legitimacy was intimately bound to Palestinian dispossession.

Avi thought Alena was simply incapable of understanding the magnitude of Jewish suffering that culminated in the senseless murder of millions. After numerous debates with Palestinians, Avi seemed to have memorized the basic format of the argument-counterargument chess game. It was getting old for him. It lost its luster. If a Palestinian questioned Israel's moral legitimacy, he would invoke the Holocaust or the United Nations. Palestinians, in turn, would counter with something to the effect of 'why should the Palestinians suffer for the misdeeds of Germany?' What he didn't care for was how easy it was for people to dismiss the Holocaust. This was the one thing that hurt him the most in these debates.

For Avi, the Holocaust represented the savagery of a so-called civilized society; an unprecedented brutality directed at a defenseless people. It was the Jews who became the imagined other. It was the Jews, who were supposedly assimilated in imperial Europe, that were slaughtered on an unimaginable scale. Avi felt that the entire world was morally responsible by its glaring inaction. This was the psychological barrier that Avi had to confront. He had to navigate his way beyond this universal blame and acknowledge how Israel's existence came at a heavy price.

VII

Avi sat quietly, reliving his days with Alena at the Grand Café. He was suddenly interrupted by David, standing in front of him with hands on his hips.

"We have to leave immediately."

"Why? What's wrong?"

"There's been an attack. Three Israeli protestors were injured. A right-wing Israeli man was taken into custody at the scene and the protestors are growing anxious. I'm afraid tempers are escalating. We have to go upstairs and speak with Yoram. I'm afraid the rest of the weekend's events are uncertain."

Avi looked around the café. The people he saw around him were suddenly gone. The room was empty and even many of the servers seem to have vanished. In the distance beyond the café's lobby, he could see an empty hallway. Beyond a man sitting alone in the corner, there appeared to be no one else in the café except for he and David.

"What? How can this be? Yoram said this was a secure perimeter."

"What you don't seem to understand is how volatile this situation is. Look, Avi. This isn't the place. We have to get upstairs."

Avi shook his head and stared into the wall behind David. His country needed their leader. This moment was a watershed in Israel's history, and he needed to see it to its conclusion. He knew this and David knew it too. He looked at David and felt the fiber of their friendship collapsing. He didn't need David to say anything else. The remainder of the weekend's events might be in doubt if they didn't act soon. But he couldn't get up from his chair. He told David he needed a few more minutes. David was frustrated and left for a few minutes to get Yoram. Avi returned to that magical year he couldn't seem to escape from.

This time it was November 2nd, 1985. It was Saturday and Avi was home working on a paper for Said's class. He was expecting Alena a little later and he was nervous, as this would be the first time she visited his apartment. Avi knew he was in love with a fiery redhead, but at the same time, their arguments were growing more feverish. Neither could abandon their love for their people. At the same time, they were growing more connected to each other. It was a colossal paradox that neither could escape. For Avi, she was becoming his addiction, and he knew he was powerless against her.

There was no way he could tell his mother about her, as he knew she would not approve. He did not even confide in his great-uncle, whom he trusted and was accustomed to sharing everything with. He tried to ignore his feelings by reminding himself that Alena was Palestinian; that she believed the Jews didn't belong in their ancestral homeland. None of it worked, however, and he found himself thinking of her all the time. There was something about her; something deeply genuine and honest. Despite her hostility toward Israel, she was remarkably kind toward him. They talked daily and he would often help her with her papers. People started seeing them as a couple, though they tried to avoid that perception. This is why Alena wanted to come to his apartment to study. She was uncomfortable having her Arab friends see her with an Israeli. She was, after all, the president of the Arab Organization on campus.

Avi was the topic of conversation among Jewish and pro-Israel students, though he didn't belong to any of the pro-Israel organizations. He was asked to speak at various events. Several Jewish groups repeatedly asked him if he would persuade his great-uncle to speak at Columbia. Avi and Alena were aware of their on-campus reputations and tried to avoid the inevitable gossip swirling around them. As Avi was busy writing his paper, the phone rang.

"Hello."

"Hi, Avi." His heart raced at the sound of Alena's voice.

"Hi."

"Am I still invited to come over?"

"Of course. It would be an honor to have you."

"Aren't you sweet. Are you sure I won't be bothering you?"

"Heavens no. What if I tell you that I miss you terribly?"

"I miss you too, Avi. I'll see you in a few minutes."

Avi was nervous. He spent all morning cleaning the apartment and organizing the books strewn all over the floor. He tried to study, but his mind was just as scattered as his books. Though he spent every day with Alena since his motorcycle accident, he wasn't sure if she shared his romantic feelings. There were times when he could see it in her eyes. She had a way of slumping forward as though she was surrendering to the feeling of being with him. But there were other times when she sat erectly and probed him with questions. He could see the frustration boiling in her, especially when they discussed their perspectives on the conflict. It was these times when he was most confused.

The fact that she had a temper only increased his attraction to her. Avi always admired strong women. He was relieved when their dialogue sidestepped their political and cultural backgrounds. She never gave an inch, and always reminded him of the suffering of her people, and the lack of attention from the rest of the world. The phone rang again a few minutes later and he heard his doorman's voice. It sounded strange because he had never had a visitor before, and didn't know the protocol. The man's voice was familiar, but he didn't know who it was immediately.

"Sorry to bother you, sir. There is an Alena here to see you."

"Oh. Yes, of course." Avi said. "Please send her up." He shot up and ran to the bathroom to check his appearance. He was wearing jeans and a white T-shirt. As usual, he didn't shave and his hair was haphazardly parted to the side. It was at this moment that he panicked as he realized he had nothing to eat or drink to offer. He ran to the refrigerator to see if he had anything, but it was empty. The doorbell rang.

"Hi, Avi." Alena smiled when he opened the door.

"Hi. Please come in," Avi said breathlessly.

"My God, Avi." He felt uncomfortable at Alena scanning his sparse apartment. "You have your own private library in here. Wow! How many books do you have?"

"Well, this is my great-uncle's apartment and these are his books. I never really counted them, but I would estimate there are about a thousand books here."

"I love the dark wood and the matching furniture. Here, I got you a present." She handed him a gift-wrapped box.

"Oh, thank you. You didn't have to."

"Why don't you open it?"

"Okay." He struggled to open the gift wrapping before finally pulling out a cassette tape. "Wow, it's Kool and the Gang. Thank you."

"Do you have a cassette player?"

"Yes, it's here on the kitchen table. I study here and I tend to play music as I'm studying."

"What do you listen to?"

"I listen to mostly classical. Beethoven, Mozart, Tchaikovsky, Vivaldi, Carl Orff... "

"Avi, I didn't mean for you to give me a full list."
"Oh, I'm sorry. It's just that I'm a little nervous."

"Why?"

"I have the most beautiful girl in the world in my apartment and you are asking me why?"

"Aren't you sweet!" Alena was blushing and didn't know what else to say. She wanted to change the subject before her feelings for him become obvious.

"I see you like Dostoevsky. He's one of my favorite authors. What have you read by him?"

"Let's see, I read... wait a minute, I'm not going to list them." Avi and Alena laughed a bit over this awkward moment.

"You know, I read *Crime and Punishment* while listening to Vivaldi's *Four Seasons*. My favorite, however, is Orff's *Carmina Burana*.

"I never heard of Orff."

"Well, it's very intense. I can play it for you if you like."

"Sure, but put in Kool and the Gang first. I know how much you enjoy the song, *Cherish.*" Avi put in the cassette and fast-forwarded to the third track. As the song played, Avi felt as if he was transported to heaven. He savored every moment. She was his first love and he was feeling an otherworldly sense of happiness.

"Come and sit down, Avi." Avi sat down on a brown leather chair that was facing her. He was trying to maintain his composure, but he couldn't believe she was actually in his apartment, staring at him. He was starting to believe that she mirrored his feelings.

"So have you read many of these books?"

"Well, I haven't been here long enough to read them. My great-uncle has a similar set of books in Tel Aviv and I read most of them there."

"You're kidding."

"I'm so glad you're here. I'm so sorry that I don't have anything to offer. I'm afraid I'm not very good with cooking. I could have a pizza delivered or maybe some Chinese food."

"It's fine. I'm not hungry."

"Please let me order something. You've been

wonderfully kind to me these past couple of months. Actually the Chinese restaurant down the street is quite good. I've had them deliver before. Their pepper shrimp is quite delicious."

"That sounds good."

"Great, let me call them." Avi was ecstatic that he could finally pay for a meal. He placed the order and went to sit down.

"Oh, I forgot to tell you. I got an A on my Chomsky paper. Thank you for all your help. I still need to give you the book back. Now I have a paper to write for my Sociology class and it is due in a few days."

"What's the topic? Perhaps I can help. I love helping you, you know." Avi smiled.

"Well, remember the class I'm taking on sociological theory? We're discussing Berger's book, *The Social Construction of Reality*, and I'm so lost. I mean, I understand the process of social construction, but this paper is on another book Berger wrote called *A Rumor of Angels*. I'm so lost with it."

"Oh, I've read it. I believe it is here somewhere. Let me look for it." He went to look for the book.

"Here it is."

"Who are you? I mean how is it that you read all these books? My God, you can talk politics, literature, philosophy, history, sociology. Wow."

"I just happened to read it, that's all."

"What was your childhood like?"

"I didn't have friends so all I did was study. My great-uncle encouraged me to read at a young age."

"So you read *A Rumor of Angels*?"

"Yes."

"What's it about?"

"Well, it's unusual. You see, if you read Berger's other books like *The Social Construction of Reality* and *The Sacred Canopy*, you get the distinct impression that he's an atheist. So you can imagine how surprised I was when I read *A Rumor of Angels*. He says in the preface that his other works represented his professional, sociological view of religion, namely that it is a constructed reality. He goes on to talk about his Protestant faith, and rather than attempt to prove the existence of God, it might be better to find, what he calls, signals of transcendence."

"That's what I'm confused about. I don't know what that means"

"Well, rather than attempt an all-encompassing proof for the existence of God, which Berger believes is doomed to failure, he settles for clues – what he calls signals that point to the divine. He gives several examples of these signals, like the way time appears to stop when a mother comforts her child in the middle of the night or when children are at play and completely immersed in the joy of playful activity. It's this sense of the eternal that serves as a signal of transcendence."

He noticed Alena staring at him without speaking.

"What?"

"I'm just blown away. My God, Avi. I've never met anyone like you."

"Well, this is one of those moments, isn't it?"

"What?"

"A signal of transcendence. I actually can't believe you are sitting here with me."

'What's wrong?'

"Oh God, I'm just going to say it before I burst. Alena, I'm so…I'm so attracted to you that I can't seem to think straight anymore."

"I'm attracted to you too." She smiled and leaned forward.

"I don't think you understand. I'm in love with you, deeply in love with you. You're all I think about. When I'm with you, it feels like I'm in heaven."

"I know." She smiled and looked into the hardwood floor. She didn't say anything and he grew alarmed. Could he have just confessed his love, with her saying nothing in return? He waited for her to say something for endless moments when she finally looked up at him.

"I'm there."

"What?"

"I'm there."

"Where?

She laughed and looked up at him. "This isn't what I planned, you know? I wasn't supposed to fall in love with an Israeli boy." She shook her head. He could see tears pooling in the corner of her puffy eyes. She sniffled without looking away from him. "But I'm there. I'm wherever you want me to be. It's been that way ever since I met you the night of the motorcycle accident. I haven't stopped thinking about you. I didn't want this, but I can't help it. I'm in love with you."

"Dear God," Avi exhaled. "I thought my feelings for you were unrequited."

"The fact that I spent every day with you for the past month should have given you a clue." She sniffled again and laughed. He was nervous and fidgety with possibilities, and she rose from her chair and sat on his lap, straddling him. She ran her fingers through his hair and he tucked his index fingers into the belt loops of her jeans. "Are you nervous?" she asked.

"Yes. I can't help it. I adore you."

"I love you too," Alena whispered in his ear. He felt a rush of euphoria. It was a feeling he never felt before.

"I love you, Alena Said." Alena caressed his hair and embraced him. She kissed him, first on the cheek. The kisses gradually moved toward the edge of his mouth. The phone suddenly rang, startling Avi.

"Avi, we're not doing anything wrong. It's probably the delivery guy." Avi answered the phone and heard the doorman's voice again, announcing the arrival of their Chinese food.

"Send him up, please," he said to the doorman. He turned to Alena smiling sheepishly. "Sorry, it's just that I'm nervous."

"What are you nervous about?"

"It's not every day that I have the most beautiful girl in the world in my apartment."

"Are you always this romantic?"

"I've never been romantic in my life."

He had been breathing fast and turning pale rapidly. Alena walked to him and wrapped her arms around him. It was the first romantic kiss of Avi's life. She kissed him on the lips, and Avi was moved beyond anything he had ever experienced before. Alena's lips were soft and warm. She wrapped her fingers around the back of his neck and Avi closed his eyes, ready to die. She let go of him for a moment and started to caress his hair.

"Where is the bathroom?" she asked. Avi pointed and she got up, returning with a comb.

"You should comb your hair to the back, rather than part it to the side." Alena combed Avi's hair to the back. The door knocked when she finished and she rose to answer it. The delivery man looked at her and then at him. Avi gave him some money, took their food, and closed the door.

"Where would you prefer to sit?" he asked.

"Why don't we sit at the kitchen table? Let me find some plates and silverware."

"Oh, please let me do that, you're my guest."

"This is my first time in your apartment, but I probably know my way around the kitchen better than you. You have to let me cook some Palestinian food for you. When was the last time you had a home-cooked meal?"

"Not since I got here. I miss my mother's cooking."

"Have you told her about me?"

Avi froze. He couldn't imagine telling his mother about Alena.

"It's okay," she continued. "I'm having a hard time telling anyone about us. I told my mother that I have an Israeli friend just to see her reaction. You know, my mother was kicked out of her home in 1948, so I knew the fact I have an Israeli friend might not go over very well. You'd be surprised what she told me."

"I'm truly sorry to hear that. What did she say?"

"She told me I should try to prove to you that not all Palestinians are terrorists."

"You know I don't think that."

"I know you don't." Alena pulled out some plates and forks while she spoke. She moved around the kitchen as though she had been here many times. She opened the Styrofoam boxes and looked at their dinner.

"Everything looks so good. We should share." She began to spoon a little from each box onto both plates. Avi laughed when she was finished.

"What's so funny?"

"I don't know. Do you think Palestinians and Israeli's can share?"

"I don't think in our lifetime, but who knows." Alena took a forkful of his pepper shrimp and laughed. She chewed slowly and her eyes lit up. Avi watched her eat, following his pattern of not touching his food.

"Let's talk about something else," Alena said. "I don't feel like a debate tonight."

"I think we can agree that I like watching you eat."

They ate quietly, Avi pausing to watch her take tiny bites. Finally Alena dropped her fork on the plate with a loud clink.

"Tell me more about Berger's book."

"Okay, what do you want to know?"

"Well, is he saying that there are signals that point to God? If that's the case, how does he reconcile the social construction argument?"

Avi smiled. He was realizing that she was exceptionally bright. She merely lacked confidence in her abilities.

"What?" she asked after he smiled for too long.

"You're very smart."

"Thank you, but I know my limits. I don't have your brain so don't try to make me feel good."

"Alena, why do you do this to yourself? My God, you are both stunningly beautiful and brilliant."

"Aren't you the charmer? Okay back to Berger."

"Oh, right. Well, Berger separates his professional activity as a sociologist from his own private feelings about religion."

"I'm not sure one can separate the two. I mean you can't arbitrarily use the convenient cover of professional sociology to argue that religion is a construction, which debunks the idea of God, and then turn around and say that you personally believe in God."

"Actually, he addresses your point, which I think is a fair criticism. He argues that constructions are not, in and of themselves, debunking agents. Let me ask you a question, do you suppose that all construction is false?"

"I believe that if an idea is constructed by us, then it ends with us. An idea cannot transcend itself."

"Wow, the way you put that is brilliant. I'm not sure that it is true, however. I mean mathematics is a construction, but we don't ignore it."

"True, but we are not about to worship pi. We don't elevate mathematical construction as a transcendent reality."

"The Greeks, especially Plato, felt that mathematics exists as a separate reality. My point is that if we allow for the possibility of one construction as being valid, then perhaps there are other constructions that are equally valid."

"Are you religious?" Alena asked, with her elbows on the table. She hung on his answer.

"No, I'm not."

"Are you spiritual?"

"I don't believe I am. I'm simply making the argument that constructions are not inherently illusions. For Berger, signals of transcendence offer us a sense of the divine without the logical problems of proof."

"Do you believe in God? I'm an agnostic so you can tell me."

"I have a problem with agnosticism. I know it's fashionable for intellectuals to apply such a seemingly benign label, but I find it empty."

"So you do believe in God."

"I don't think God is knowable."

"But isn't that what agnosticism says?"

"Well, agnosticism, as developed by Thomas Huxley, simply states that we do not have sufficient proof to either affirm or deny the existence of God."

"Exactly, that's why I have a difficult time with religion. I need proof before I can surrender my identity to something that might be an illusion."

"But the problem with that formulation is the idea of sufficiency. I mean, what constitutes sufficient proof, right? How will we know the proof is sufficient? What are the epistemic criteria necessary to judge a proof as satisfying sufficiency?"

"Avi, you're confusing me."

"Alright, alright, let me illustrate with an example." Avi was animated and absorbed in the discussion. Alena was seeing the full force of his intellect for the first time.

"Let's suppose that I parade a thousand proofs in front of you. How will you know which proof is the one that you've been looking for? Think about it, Alena, it's fashionable to say that–"

"What if I know what is sufficient? I mean what if I demand empirical proof?"

"You can certainly demand empirical proof, but you will do so at the expense of all other knowledge domains."

"Why does it have to be at the expense of other forms of knowledge?"

"Well, if you are limiting yourself to empirical proof, then what about literary, mathematical, textual, and other forms of knowledge? Would you entertain them? You see, what you seem to be saying is that if the proof is not scientific, that is to say, demonstrable and repeatable, then it will not satisfy the sufficiency criteria."

"Avi, you're a freak of nature. I mean that as a compliment."

"Alena, forgive me for saying this, but you are the one who is a freak of nature. You are by far the most beautiful girl I've ever encountered. On top of that, you are brilliant. Can I tell you how I know that you are brilliant?"

"Oh, do please enlighten me."

"By the type of questions you ask. Haven't you noticed that students often ask secretarial questions?"

'Secretarial? What does that mean?"

"I mean they simply ask for clarification of a term or concept. They're not engaged in the topic at hand. You, on the other hand, ask penetrating questions."

"Well, that's very kind of you to say, but I ask secretarial questions all the time. You can't expect everyone to be like you."

"It's amazing to me that you don't recognize your intellect."

She smiled and looked away. It was clear that Alena didn't know how to take his compliments. She looked for a diversion to avoid further compliments.

"You hardly touched your food," she said. "The pepper shrimp is amazing."

"Not hungry, I guess."

"Oh, I forgot to ask," Alena said. "Thanksgiving's coming up. Are you going anywhere?"

"No, I'm just going to stay home and catch up on work."

"This will be your first Thanksgiving here. You do know that everything will be closed, right? Why don't you come over to my house? My mom always prepares an amazing meal. She'll have the usual turkey dinner, but she also prepares Palestinian food. Have you tried *mansaf*?"

"I've heard of it. Isn't it a Jordanian dish?"

"It's also a popular Palestinian dish. So will you come? My uncle will probably stop by."

"I'd love to, but I'm not sure I would fit in."

"Don't be silly. Of course, you'll fit in. We Palestinians are a very warm people. You'd be surprised. Besides, I want you to come and visit my parents before Thanksgiving."

Alena had been thinking about this off and on for days. She wasn't sure if Avi would be accepted, but she didn't want him to be alone on Thanksgiving. That would be too much to bear. She thought of asking her uncle to talk to her mother, but decided to do so herself. Her mother would have trouble accepting the fact of their relationship the first time, so it was important that Avi meet her in advance to get any awkwardness out of the way before he met the rest of her family. One big meeting in front of her family was too much to ask of anyone.

"Can you imagine it, Alena? An Israeli and a Palestinian having Thanksgiving dinner together. Wouldn't that be something?"

"Who knows? Maybe we'll solve the conflict. What do you think? I mean, Abba Eban and Edward Said will probably be arguing to the bitter end. Maybe it's up to our generation to solve the conflict, right?."

Alena got up to take their dishes to the kitchen. Avi watched her take two trips to the kitchen and return to the table. She was right, of course. It was up to future generations to solve the conflict. But it didn't matter right now. None of it did. He knew this as he watched Alena clean the table around him.

"Oh my gosh. What time is it?" she asked. "I better get going."

"Do you have to? Can't you stay for a little while longer?"

"I promised my mother I would go shopping with her today."

Avi stared sadly into the table. He didn't look at her as she walked around the table towards him. She stood next to him, rubbing her fingers softly through his hair.

"Why don't you play some of the music you like? What was that one you mentioned?"

"Oh, Carl Orff. I don't know. It's kind of intense."

"What do you mean intense? Like Beethoven's 9th?"

"I think it's more intense than the 9th. Actually, I'm not sure it's a good idea if I play it. It does something to me."

"What do you mean?"

"It's difficult to explain. It just affects me in a physical way."

"Oh, now I have to hear it." She smiled.

"I'm sure you'll recognize it when you hear it. It's been played countless times. My uncle, Eli, introduced me to it while I was in high school. I'm sure Edward Said is well aware of it. He is an accomplished pianist and a music critic."

"You should hear him play. He is quite good. He plays Beethoven better than anyone I know. Now, can you please play Orff for me?'

Avi stood up from the table and picked up the *Carmina Burana* cassette from the top of the player. He dropped it in and pressed play. The orchestra rose and Alena watched as Avi was slowly transformed. It was the same disturbing transformation he always experienced when listening to *O Fortuna*. She watched as Avi tilted his head sideways while staring at her. He cracked his jaw and an intense look overtook his eyes. His fingers curled sharply and he stood ramrod straight. The transformation frightened Alena. She stopped the tape player before it crescendoed.

"Okay, what's going on Avi? My God, you scared me."

Avi decompressed slowly and shook his head, as though returning from another place. He blinked and stepped toward Alena, putting his hand on her shoulder.

"It's okay. It's just part of me. I can't explain it. There's something about it."

"I don't understand. I know it's intense, but I've never seen anyone react this way to a piece of music. I have heard it before, by the way. At my uncle's house. So tell me what do you feel when you hear it?"

"I'm not sure I can explain it. I feel as if an electrical current is surging through me; as if the electricity is moving up through my body toward my head. I tilt my head and crack my jaw instinctively. I do this every time. It's like demons are trying to invade me."

Alena looked shocked. She walked around him and picked up the tape. She held it before him and shook it.

"You shouldn't be listening to this."

"I wouldn't be the same person if I stop listening to it. Did I tell you that I play the piano?"

"Why am I not surprised? What do you play?"

"I play mostly classical pieces."

"Can you play Beethoven's Moonlight Sonata?"

"Yes, of course. It's one of my favorites."

"You must promise to play it for me. You have your Carmina Burana and I have the Moonlight Sonata."

"I love you Alena!" Avi whispered in her ears.

They kissed breathlessly until she had to leave, standing by the doorway until it was getting late, until Alena thought of her mother, wondering where she was. The moment sealed Alena's fate, for it was at that moment she knew there was something mysterious about Avi; something she could never control or even fully know. She needed to understand him better, but knew she never could. The challenge filled her with something unknowable, and rendered his Jewish-ness obsolete. She didn't care anymore, and she wouldn't care if her mother or anyone in her family cared. She felt all of this in the tinge of sadness as she left his apartment. She needed to see him again and she needed to know more about him.

VIII

Alena couldn't stop thinking about Avi. She couldn't focus on the drive home and she was in no position to write her paper on Berger's signals of transcendence. She got up and turned on the radio, then picked up a magazine. She ate an apple and sat on the couch. Finally, she turned off the radio and sat in silence, her class notebook open to her notes on Berger staring back at her. Nothing worked. She couldn't stop thinking of him.

There were two questions that stood out. She had to know what he had done to her, and she had to know how she could ever tell someone about them. She was ruined. She had dated boys before, but never felt anything like the obsession she felt now. It transformed her into a completely different person and she didn't know how to navigate her turbulent emotions.

Alena was always passionate about her studies. She attended the prestigious American Community School in Beirut, where she graduated at the top of her class. She was driven to attend Columbia to be close to her uncle and to live in the beautiful city she heard so much about. She idolized Edward Said and felt that the national identity of the Palestinian people was largely due to his intellectual efforts. She harbored dreams of shaping Palestinian identity since she was a teenager; since she was old enough to consider her role in the future of her people.

Those dreams felt oddly absent, covered with a fresh

coat of paint. She struggled to think about Berger, but she also struggled to think about her former self and her personal aspirations. All of it was gone suddenly, replaced by uncontrollable thoughts of what Avi was doing at that precise moment. There was no blueprint for how to proceed. She needed to talk about it before it drowned her in grief.

It was 2:30 in the morning when she thought of calling her aunt in London. Her Aunt Rosemarie Said Zahlan was one of the foremost academic historians of the Gulf States. In addition to writing books on Qatar, Dubai, and the United Arab Emirates, Rosemarie, like her older brother, Edward Said, made great contributions to the Palestinian struggle for self-determination.

The phone rang several times before Alena realized it was 7:30 in the morning in London. She was about to hang up before she heard her aunt's voice.

"Hello?"

"I'm so sorry to call you so early, but I just need to talk to you."

"Alena?"

"Yes."

"What's wrong? What time is it in New York? Are you alright?"

Alena listened as Rosemarie's voice grew alarmed.

"It's 7:30 in the morning. Did I wake you?"

"No, but is everything alright?"

"Yes, everything's fine. I just have a problem and I need someone to talk to." Alena felt herself getting emotional at the sound of her aunt's voice.

"What's wrong?"

"I think I'm in love with someone."

"Oh, Alena. You scared me. I thought something might have happened. Well, I was around your age when I first fell in love. It's not that Egyptian you dated for a while, is it?"

"No, it's someone else. I met him two months ago and I've been seeing him every day since then."

"Sounds serious. Have you told your mother yet?

"I mentioned him, but I didn't tell her yet. There's something you need to know and it may shock you."

"Sweetie, nothing shocks me anymore. What do you want to tell me?"

"He's Israeli."

Alena heard the kind of silence that she dreaded. She began to regret calling her aunt.

"I see. Well…so tell me–"

"I'm so sorry to upset you like this. It's just that I'm feeling so confused."

"Alena, you didn't upset me. I was just surprised, that's all. Tell me about him."

"It's really quite romantic actually. He noticed me from a distance, but he thought I was Swedish."

"Well, that's not the first time someone thought you were European."

"I was handing out flyers at the Turath table and he came up. I thought he knew the name of the organization, which was clearly placed in front of the table. I gave him a flyer and wrote my number on the back."

"Sounds like you were attracted to him right away?"

"I'm not sure. He seemed so absent-minded that I felt sorry for him. Anyway, that same day, he got into a motorcycle accident and he called me to ask if I can pick him up. We've seen each other every day since."

"How did he react when he found out you are Palestinian? I'm sure he knows that Edward is your uncle."

"He is taking his course on Foucault. Oh, he is utterly brilliant. I mean he is a freak of nature. He's also related to Abba Eban. It bothered him at first that I'm Palestinian, but I don't think he cares."

Rosemarie paused. The silence on the phone was a concern. Alena fidgeted nervously while she waited for her aunt to say something.

"Do people know? You know, Columbia is a hotbed of Arab-Israeli animosity."

"I know. Rumors have started, but Avi and I agreed to not be seen in public. Why couldn't he be Palestinian? I'm just so confused and I don't know what to do."

"Alena, listen to me. Your identity is not exclusively Palestinian and his is not exclusively Israeli. This does not mean the relationship will work out, but don't let your identity and ideology interfere with your happiness."

"I don't know how to tell Mama. How do you think she'll take it?"

"Well, maybe not well at first. But Grace is open-minded, and if she gives you any grief, I'll talk to her."

"Oh, I love you. Thanks so much. You've always been so helpful. When are you coming to visit? I want you to meet him."

"I've been asked to speak at Harvard in February, so I will stop in New York to see all of you then."

"I have another question. I submitted an article to the campus paper a few weeks ago where I say that Israel is an illegitimate entity in the region. I know it's going to create a problem between me and Avi, so should I ask the paper not to publish it?"

"Why should you? You can't suddenly change your political views simply because you're in love with an Israeli. If you start changing who you are simply because of who you love, you won't be able to live with yourself. It's good if he challenges you to develop your ideas. But you can't start changing how you think because of a man. You have to be strong."

Alena was surprised to hear Rosemarie speaking this way. Silence returned to their phone call, and Alena wasn't sure what to say.

"Do you still feel Israel is an illegitimate country?" Rosemarie asked.

"I don't know anymore. I can't think straight now. He believes in a two-state solution and so do I. I suppose you can make the case for Israel's illegitimacy, but I'm not comfortable saying that anymore."

"If you're uncomfortable with your article, you should ask the paper not to publish it. The question of legitimacy is a difficult one. There are legal, political, ideological, and moral considerations. There is one undeniable truth, and that is the fact that Israel exists regardless of whether it has a right to exist or not. You also know that your uncle believes in a two-state solution. I agree with Edward on this point. There are radicalized elements within our people who feed us this garbage about reclaiming all of Palestine. The days of depending on the Arab world to liberate Palestine are long gone. We have become a political convenience, a nationalist banner, but in the end we have to deal with the Israelis."

"I know that I don't care for Zionism. I never have and never will. Their nationalist aspirations occurred at our expense."

"Did you talk to Edward about the article?"

"I talked to him briefly, but I didn't tell him that I described Israel as illegitimate."

"Are you aware that he argued that the Zionist claim to Palestine as well as Palestinian self-determination have legitimacy and authenticity? Both nationalisms converged toward the same land, with each side dismissing the claims of the other. Both present themselves as mutually exclusive. Alena, you must go beyond this binary prism that distorts understanding. If you're falling in love with this young man, then have an open and honest conversation about the conflict with him."

"Whenever Palestine comes up, we just end up arguing. It's a problem. Actually, he has been very polite and I just get nervous and agitated."

"You need to confront this issue, both of you. You need to listen to what he has to say and he needs to listen to you."

"I'll try. Why couldn't he be Palestinian, Aunt Rosemarie?"

"We never know what fate has in store for us. You know, if more Palestinians and Israelis interacted and listened to each other, there might be hope for peace."

"I thought you didn't believe in fate."

"I use the term in the sense of what the future holds."

When Alena realized she was sleepy, the feeling hit her hard. It was after 3 am and she had no choice but to get off the phone.

"I'm so sorry to call you so early. Thank you so much for talking to me. I can't wait to see you in February."

"Call me whenever you want to talk, Alena. Remember, talk to him."

"Good bye."

§§§

Alena decided to ask the *Daily Spectator* to change the wording of her article. Later that day, Alena realized she was falling behind on her studies. She isolated herself in the library and concentrated on her work. She and Avi settled into a comfortable routine by then. She always went over to his apartment in the evening. He would help her with her papers and they would talk about anything from philosophy to literary theory. She loved their conversations. He managed to have informed opinions on everything she brought up, and this challenged her to examine his thoughts and develop opinions of her own. She found herself reading more outside of her studies, and scrambling to challenge his air of certainty.

But the one topic they couldn't discuss was the Middle East. They could never agree on the terms of the conversation, let alone their opinions. It always ended in silence, so what was the point of starting?

For Jews around the world, Israel was an existential necessity, a geographical reality that would protect them from the whims of political instability. Israel represented a convergence, where identity, history, religion, culture, and political freedom found tangible expression in a land that always informed Jewish hopes and aspirations. For Palestinians, the land of Palestine was a construct of images and realities, whose resonant power shaped and directed a people who felt disconnected from their home. Palestinians endured humiliating representations in the West that dismissed them as a paradigmatic other, bent on the destruction of Israel. Each side accused the other of falsifying history, engaging in indiscriminate violence, and perpetuating propaganda. Each side claimed moral superiority.

For all his intellectual sophistication, Avi was incapable of grasping the human dimension of Palestinian suffering. Though he was stationed in the West Bank and witnessed the dehumanizing effect of the occupation, he never allowed it to penetrate his well-defined sense of self.

The occupation was the result of the 1967 war, in which Israel launched pre-emptive air strikes against Egypt, Jordan, and Syria. Within a few days, Israel more than tripled in size, a result of an overwhelming victory against the Arabs. Israeli forces captured the Sinai and the Gaza Strip from Egypt, the West Bank and East Jerusalem from Jordan, and the Golan Heights from Syria. Avi knew this history intimately. But history had a habit of being non-history, of being remembered in ways that affirmed a comfortable narrative. For Avi, the Israelis engaged in a pre-emptive strike against the Arabs, but it was Egypt's Gamal Abdel Nasser who engaged in fiery rhetoric aimed at the destruction of Israel. Several years before the 1967 war, Nasser, who was the de facto leader of the Arab world, vowed to liberate Palestine by violent means if necessary. His vitriolic speeches – heard on the radio across the Arab world and in Israel – forced Israel to defend its existence. Avi believed that the Israeli occupation of Arab land came as a result of a war that Israel was forced to wage in self-defense.

To Alena, the Israelis clearly seemed to be the aggressors. She believed the war was part of a Zionist master plan to take more Arab land under the pretext of self-defense. Though Alena was born in Beirut, she considered herself part of the Palestinian Diaspora. Palestine was a construct of existential urgency. She was young and filled with idealistic dreams. The conflict for her was an intellectual exercise in persuading anyone who would listen of the righteousness of the Palestinian cause. Though she acknowledged Jewish suffering, she was quick to dismiss the relevance it had on a conflict that stripped a people of their land. She never allowed the Holocaust to influence her understanding of the conflict.

Alena tried in vain to avoid Avi on campus, but always melted when she saw him approaching. Avi lacked the same fear of reproach from their classmates. He was too proud to be concerned about what anyone thought of them being together. It seemed to Alena that his freakish intelligence made him immune from the glare of others. In fact, she began to believe that he was this way because he was introverted; that the two facets of him were somehow related. In his many years alone, cloistered safely from social surroundings, he managed to never understand that a social environment could make one more self-aware . It was a facet of being around people that he never adopted.

Slowly, her fear of their relationship being detected dissipated, especially in light of his lack of concern. This made it only a matter of time before her Palestinian friends saw them together. They were walking to get coffee. They developed the habit of going out for coffee in the evening. As soon as they entered, Alena noticed her friends, Eileen and Elizabeth, sitting in the corner of the coffee shop, her face peering above the spine of a book she held. Alena instinctively looked away, but it was too late.

"Damn!" she said to Avi. "Don't look, but two of my friends are sitting over there. They have a big mouth, too."

Avi instinctively turned around to see a woman smiling and waving. He waved back. Alena pushed his forearm down but it was too late.

"Oh no. They saw us." The women got up from their table and walked over to see them, standing in line.

"Hi, Eileen. How are you? Hi Elizabeth."

"Hi, Alena. What are you doing here? I mean, I usually see you at the library." Elizabeth said with a smile.

"This is Avi." Avi shook their hands and smiled.

"So you're Avi Eban. I heard quite a bit about you. Your Israeli, right?" Eileen exclaimed with a smile.

"Yes, I am."

"Alena, can I talk to you for a minute?" Alena excused herself and walked with Eileen to her table. Eileen smiled at Avi and turned around, the two of them walking shoulder-to-shoulder. Elizabeth stayed in line with Avi in an effort to get to know him.

"What's going on here, Alena? Why are you standing with him?"

"What are you talking about Eileen? We just came from my uncle's lecture."

"Alena, I saw you looking at him. I know that look. You are attracted to him, aren't you?"

"Eileen, you don't know what you're talking about. I don't appreciate being accused of –"

"Wait a minute. I'm not accusing you of anything. I'm simply pointing out that you are attracted to him. Calm down. You don't have to get defensive."

"Well, I'm not. Of all people, you actually think I'm going to be attracted to an Israeli? That's ridiculous."

"Why is it ridiculous? Your uncle has many Jewish friends. My father has Jewish friends. Alena, it's not about being Jewish or Israeli. It's about their capacity to understand our cause."

"Well, that may be the case, but I'm simply not attracted to him." Alena saw through Eileen's noble gesture. She knew that Eileen wanted her to confess the truth about her and Avi. Eileen was a caring person, but Alena knew that she was the type who couldn't hold her tongue.

"So tell me. What's he like? I heard that he's brilliant."

"Well, that's true. He's very intellectual. Listen, I better get back. I just want to finish discussing Foucault with him and go home." Alena smiled and walked back to Avi, who was still waiting in line with Elizabeth. She thought about leaving but knew that would look suspicious. She looked at Elizabeth as if to tell her to leave.

"Of all the people that we had to bump into, it had to be Eileen and Elizabeth. She has a seriously big mouth. Do you know what we call her? Reuters."

"Reuters? Why do you–? Oh I get it, she's always reporting the latest news. That's clever."

They reached the front of the line and Alena placed their order. They got their food and sat down quietly. Alena felt too self-conscious to talk seriously about anything with him. She didn't know what to say.

"How about if I just stare into your beautiful eyes?"

"Avi, be serious. God I hope they leave."

"I'm curious. Why all the secrecy? I mean who gives a damn about what people say."

"Avi, if this gets out, we won't hear the end of it. All my Arab friends and all your Jewish friends will say we sold out. Believe me, they won't understand."

"Alena, I don't have many friends here."

"Well, what about David? And what will your parents think? Have you told them about me?"

"No, I haven't. Your point is well taken." Four more of Alena's friends walked in. She cursed herself for getting a bite to eat near campus. She looked to see them approaching and she ducked.

"Wow, this is not happening. There's no time to explain, just act natural."

"Hi, Alena," said one of her friends. He was a bright looking, impeccably dressed young man with a backpack around his shoulder and a smirk on his face. “What are you doing here?”

"Hi, Nabil. This is Avi."

"Hello, it's very nice too meet you." Avi stood up to shake Nabil's hand.

"Avi, this is Nabil, Rashad, Khaled, and Luai. They are all engineering majors and members of Turath." The men smiled at each other and Alena clenched her jaw. Avi shook each of their hands. There were six of them now and not enough room to accommodate them. Rashad and Khaled decided to go sit with Eileen and Elizabeth.

"So, you are Avi Eban? Alena mentioned you," Nabil said. He was a graduate student and an elder statesman of the Arab Organization. Although he was an engineering major, he was an intellectual who spoke calmly and with confidence. Nabil was a Jordanian-born Palestinian. He heard about Avi's brilliance and was eager to have a conversation with him.

Alena had no choice but to invite them to sit down. To not do so would be obvious. It would also be rude. But she could see the writing on the wall. Nabil was a notorious anti-Zionist and passionate speaker. She was afraid he would be tempted to provoke Avi, which would surely end their afternoon together. It would also leave her between a rock and a hard place, unwilling to repeat her passionate defense of Palestinian statehood in front of Avi, but unwilling to deny it at the same time. She stared into her coffee with disgust.

"Have a seat," she said to Nabil and Luai, motioning for them to take the open chairs. "Rashad, why don't you grab a couple of extra chairs?"

"It's ok, me and Khaled are going to join Eileen and Elizabeth."

"Are you sure? You are welcome to join us." Alena tried to act naturally. She invited Nabil and Luai to sit down once more.

"Thanks," Nabil said.

"So are you from Tel Aviv?" Luai asked. Avi's elbows were on the table, as though he had rehearsed for this conversation.

"Yes, I was born there."

"I heard that you are Abba Eban's nephew." Nabil said.

"Actually I'm his great-nephew. Are you all Palestinian?" he asked.

"We're all Palestinian, Avi," said Alena. She looked disapprovingly at him, but he didn't notice.

"You know, Abba Eban has often said that anyone who criticizes Israel is anti-Semitic," Nabil said. "Do you share his views?"

"No, I don't agree with him on this point. I believe that is an *ad hominem* fallacy. I think what he was saying, though, is that some of the criticism is existentially negating.

That is to say, it is directed at Israel's destruction. In this case, I do believe it is anti-Semitic.

"Actually, he said any criticism of Israel is anti-Semitic" Nabil countered.

"Well, let me ask you a question. Let's imagine that you believe Israel is an illegitimate entity. Do you then subscribe to its destruction?"

Avi felt he could take all of them on in a debate. He looked Nabil in the eyes. What he couldn't have known was that Nabil was an intellectual powerhouse. He was thoughtful, brilliant, and offered reasoned arguments. He smiled at Alena before he spoke.

"All this talk about the destruction of Israel is nonsense," said Nabil. "Israel is a *fait accompli,* and however we feel about it won't change this stubborn fact. I would argue it is a remnant of the colonial period that is supported by the United States. Let me ask you this question. Are you saying that Jewish life, with its rich history and contribution to every conceivable field, is exclusively connected to Zionism and Israel? Do you consider Jews who criticize Israel to be self-hating, as your uncle said in 1973?"

"Well, I'm flattered that you're familiar with my great-uncle's work. When he made those comments, he was thinking of Noam Chomksy and I.F Stone. I have to tell you that I don't agree with my great uncle on this point. You certainly don't expect me to mirror his views. Jews should have the right to criticize Israel or Zionism without being labeled as self-hating. Back to your question about equating

Jewish life with Israel. Jewish history is a broad canopy of human experience and Zionism is a modern expression of an aspect of this experience. Zionism cannot be equated with the overarching Jewish narrative. But at the same time, it cannot be denied as a central current of 20th century Jewish thought."

"But that narrative of 20th century thought came at the expense of the Palestinians," said Nabil. He was leaning forward now with his elbows on the table. "Do you deny that?'

"I'm sorry," said Avi. "But I don't believe that. The Holocaust was perhaps the most horrific event in the modern era. Our people were slaughtered by the millions."

'You know what I'm tired of?" Nabil interrupted. "I'm tired of the Holocaust being used to justify the taking of our land."

Alena felt her blood boiling. She saw her friends growing more animated and worried that Avi was going to feel cornered. She knew his temperament, and saw him growing more animated in turn.

"Let me tell you what I'm tired of," Avi said. "I'm tired of hearing the Holocaust being glossed over as if it was a walk in the park. It was one of the seminal events of human history, not just Jewish history. The Nazis systematically slaughtered millions, and you contemptuously respond by dismissing it as a premise in a twisted syllogism?"

"Hey, look, nobody's going to solve the conflict tonight," said Luai. "There's no need to get defensive." Luai was usually reticent to speak. He was also a Jordanian-born Palestinian who studied engineering. He was not as political as the others and rarely got involved in heated debates.

"You're right, of course," said Avi. "I'm sorry. It's just that the Holocaust is a sensitive issue."

"Did you lose family members in the Holocaust?" Nabil asked.

"Yes, I lost several relatives."

"I agree the Holocaust was a horrific event," said Nabil. "And no people deserve such degradation, but the Jews were not the only ones who suffered from genocide. The Armenians, Cambodians, Russians, Chinese, Ethiopians, and numerous others suffered catastrophic loss. You don't see the Cambodians or the Armenians migrating to a distant land, taking it by force, and justifying it by referencing the mass killings of their people."

Alena slunk into her seat. She knew Nabil wasn't the sort of person who would back down, and Avi was impossible to defeat in a debate. They were both intransigent, and she didn't see how this could end well.

"The only problem with your argument is that each of these people you've correctly identified suffered extraordinary loss on their own soil. They were not dispersed throughout the world. The Jewish people lived in the Diaspora for two thousand years."

"Do you see the irony here?" asked Alena. Avi turned to face her. "The Palestinians are now living in the Diaspora. Many of us are refugees. We were forced out of our land, humiliated, and on top of that, we are conveniently labeled as terrorists." She spoke with a kind of tenderness, as if to make Avi understand the plight of the Palestinians.

"Look, let me say that I strongly believe in a Palestinian state. I also believe that both Israel and the Palestinians have their own radicalized elements."

"I'm glad to hear you say that," Nabil said. "But do you acknowledge what Zionism did to the Palestinian people?" Nabil was not interested in empty platitudes. He heard them before – probably his whole life – without any substantive movement toward a Palestinian state.

"I'm not sure what you want me to acknowledge. There was violence on both sides. There was the civil war in 1947 and 1948, the war of independence, what you call *al-Naqba*. We were attacked by five Arab countries."

"Actually, I was not referring to the establishment of Israel just yet. I'm asking you a philosophical question about Zionism. It is inherently flawed in its racial attitude toward the Arabs. Herzl himself has often pushed the ridiculous idea of transporting a people without a country to a country without a people. Think about that statement for a moment. The Arabs in Palestine were not simply irrelevant. They were non-existent. Do you see the imperialist mindset of Herzl? The fact there were nearly a million people living in Palestine was simply a footnote to his imperialist aims."

Nabil felt that he made a lucid point and paused, ready to hear Avi's response.

"First, I'm not sure you've made the case that Herzl's nationalism was exclusively imperialistic. He lived, as with most Zionists, during the Imperial Age. He was a child of his time. He witnessed anti-Semitic marches in the streets of Paris in response to the Dreyfus affair. He was a secular Jew, fully integrated into the European intellectual tradition. His experiences made him realize that Jewish assimilation was impossible. There were many Jews who disagreed with him, who felt his dream of creating a national home for the Jews was a pipe dream. The religious Jews argued that only a messiah would lead them back to the Promised Land. You must realize the world back then was not constituted as today. It was a world of empires and Herzl used whatever leverage he had in securing a home for the Jews."

"So, are you saying–'

"Let me finish my thought, please," Avi interrupted. "You made some excellent points and I want to respond. The Arabs in Palestine at the time were not formally constituted as a nation state. They lived on a land controlled by the Ottoman Empire. Herzl met with Sultan Abdulhamid II in order to secure Palestine, but he was rebuffed. Now, were the Palestinians absolutely ignored in this international chess game? Yes, of course they were. Was it morally justified? Absolutely not, but before you condemn Zionism as some kind of colonial extension, you must understand the political, social, and cultural reality of that period. Your uncle, Alena, wrote a groundbreaking book on how the

Western intellectual tradition reduced the Orient to convenient images and representations wholly divorced from reality.

My point is that the Jews, in the very heart of Western culture, were also stigmatized by that very same culture. We may have been well educated, accomplished, and for some very few, wealthy, but none of that secured our equality. We were living in post-Enlightenment Europe, with science and technology flourishing and reason becoming the celebrated force of human potential. The Holocaust showed that none of that mattered. When it came down to it, we were still Jews. We were reduced to the same essentialist realities that Said so eloquently described. So did the Zionists deal with colonial Europe to help them secure a Jewish home? Yes, of course they did. Who else should they have dealt with? Did the Zionists share the same Oriental prism under which they perceived the Arab world? Perhaps they did. That's the tragic irony of it. Here you have Jews, discriminated against, persecuted, vilified, and whose fragile inclusion into the enlightenment experiment was punctuated by dehumanizing exclusion, observing and reducing the Arab world in the same minimal categories as the West."

Avi saw Alena's friends glancing sidelong at each other He waited for Nabil or someone else to rebuff his argument, but nobody spoke.

"You know something," Nabil finally said. "I think you're a true intellectual. You listen and you are honest and measured in your critiques. We may not agree on a lot, but at least we can have a conversation." Nabil extended his hand and Avi shook it.

"I agree," Luai said with a smile. "Why can't other Israelis be open-minded like you?"

"Thank you, and I'm sure if we have more of these discussions, maybe we can reach a level of understanding that transcends the hatred."

"You know what I never cared for?" Luai asked. "The scripted arguments. It's as if someone read a manual on how to respond to every conceivable criticism."

"Me too," said Alena. She felt relieved that things hadn't escalated. Luai got up suddenly, saying he had to get to the library. Nabil rose as well. Eileen, Elizabeth, Rashad, and Khaled noticed their friends leaving and decided to return back to campus with them.

"Hey Alena," said Eileen. "Can you give me a ride back?'

"I would love to, Eileen, but I have to get home." Alena fibbed in the hope that Avi would get the hint and stick around.

"I better get home too," said Avi, looking at his watch. "I have to prepare for midterms as well. It was a pleasure to meet all of you. I hope we can do this again." Avi was the first to leave. He decided to wait across the street, thinking that the rest of the group would follow his lead. But no one else left.

"He's different than what I expected." Eileen said to Alena.

"I heard he's brilliant. What did you think of him, Nabil?" Rashad interjected.

"I was impressed." That was saying something coming from Nabil.

"What did you think of him, Luai?" Khaled chimed in with a question.

"I was impressed with him as well," said Luai. "At least he is open to ideas and he listens. I think we should invite him to give a talk at our next meeting. Wouldn't that be a good idea?" Luai felt that understanding came from listening, rather than engaging in endless back-and-forth arguments.

"Actually, you know what I would love to see?" said Nabil. "You'll probably think I'm crazy, but I would love to see Edward Said debate Abba Eban. Alena, I'm sure you can persuade your uncle to do a debate and maybe Avi can get Eban. That would be the event of the year, wouldn't it?" He turned to Alena. "What do you think?"

"That's an interesting idea, Nabil. I'll talk to my uncle. Maybe he would do it for the organization."

"He seems to be very polite." Elizabeth added. She was neither Palestinian nor Arab, but she attended all the Turath meetings and her sympathies to the Palestinian cause was clear.

"Well, we better go," Nabil said. "Do you want a ride, Eileen?"

"It's ok. Thanks, Nabil. I came with Elizabeth. Are you going back to the library, Alena?"

"I'm too tired. I think I will just go home. I'll see all of you tomorrow."

"We'll walk you to your car." Alena was furious. She didn't know how to excuse herself without drawing suspicion. She wanted to try one last maneuver before surrendering to fate.

"I have to go the restroom. Do you want to wait for me?"

"We'll just see you tomorrow. Call me Alena."

"Ok, I will. See you tomorrow."

Alena went to the restroom hoping her friends would leave quickly. After a few minutes she ran out the front door and across the street, and leaped with a spasm of joy when she saw that Avi had waited for her. Part of her knew he would, and her hopes were confirmed. She hugged him with such tenderness that Avi recoiled at the thought that her friends might be nearby.

"What is it?" Avi asked.

"Nothing. You were great. They really liked you."

"Yes, it was quite enjoyable. Nabil is very smart. I thought it was a great dialogue."

She rambled. It was all she could do. She told him about Nabil's idea to have Abba Eban debate her uncle, and reminded him about Thanksgiving at her parents' house. He agreed and said he would be there, and kissed her once more to silence her. She said her uncle was having Noam Chomsky over next Saturday, and that he had asked if Avi would like to attend. It was an informal dinner, just a few faculty members and friends.

"It starts at 5," she said. "But feel free to get there early. I'm sure there will be plenty to talk about."

She looked at him with plaintive eyes, lips pursed and dark pools forming in the dimples that bracketed them.

"Yes, of course."

That was it. She exhaled and melted in his arms, the two of them embracing on a New York sidewalk, pedestrians swerving to miss them.

§§§

It was four days later that Avi was walking across the quad to his English lecture when he noticed David Barkovic approaching him quickly. David was already one of Avi's few friends on campus. It was at least partly a friendship based on Avi's willingness to help him with his papers. But Avi had never seen David in a hurry for anything, and he knew before he heard David's voice that something was wrong.

"Avi, did you read the *Spectator* today?" He clutched it in his hand with his textbooks.

"No, why do you ask?"

"You know Alena Said, right?"

"Yes, we've talked a few times. Why?"

"Well, you should read her article. You're not going to believe what she said about Israel."

Avi grabbed the newspaper from David and began reading.

"Hey, I got to go to class. Do you want to go to the library later? I have to work on a Psych paper due tomorrow."

"Sure." Avi stared at the article. He was not sure what upset him more; the reference to Israel as illegitimate or the fact that Alena didn't tell him she had written such an article.. "I'll meet you back here around 1:30." Avi continued to read as David walked away. He felt himself growing more furious with each paragraph. He couldn't understand why she would deceive him. In the article, Alena described Zionism as an imperialist plot to take over Arab land. She argued that the Balfour Declaration offered the Zionists an imperial cover to build a Jewish state in Palestine. The Balfour Declaration became one of the most controversial documents of the conflict. It was a letter written by the British Secretary of State for Foreign Affairs, Arthur Balfour, to one of the leaders of the Zionist movement, Lord

Rothschild. In the letter, dated November 2nd, 1917, Britain viewed with favor the establishment of a Jewish national home in Palestine. The letter was a mere sixty-seven words, but the textual power of these words would serve as a divisive force in a bitter conflict that spanned a century. Alena's final paragraph summed it up:

> *The foundation of Israel was based on colonial ideas whose sole purpose was to divide the Middle East into spheres of influence. The Balfour Declaration epitomized this Western attitude towards the Orient. Here we have a foreign power (Britain) helping another foreign group (the Zionists) occupy a land that never belonged to them. Israel is an illegitimate entity in the Arab world and the international community must recognize this fact.*

Avi read the article twice and was stunned each time. He sat outside Philosophy Hall, confused and disoriented. She was duplicitous. He couldn't have seen that coming. He didn't know how she could claim to love him and write so scathingly about his people. He felt so injured that he began to question everything: his feelings for her, his trust, all of it. He tried to reconcile his feelings but couldn't. On the one hand, she was the most wonderful person he had ever met. On the other hand, she was capable of such hateful language. He skipped his lecture and wandered the hallways until he bumped into David again.

"Hey, Avi. Ready to go to the library?"

"Yes, let's go."

"So what did you think of the article? You know you need to write a rebuttal."

"I thought it was a typical Arab attack against Israel. I've heard these arguments so many times. It's nothing new."

"Yeah." They walked quietly through campus. David made small talk occasionally but Avi was clearly lost in thought. He stared into the ground and lost track of where they were headed. They walked slowly across the quad and past a row of tables. It was only as they approached that David saw the sign.

"Look, the Arab organization is having a falafel sale," David said.

"Oh, really?"

"Yeah, I told you about it last week, remember? They've been planning it for several weeks now. Look, it's that Egyptian that you once had an argument with."

"Who cares? Let's just go to the library."

"Alright,"

Avi was quiet again. David observed as Avi tilted his head and cracked his jaw, but this time there was no Carmina Burana. They both walked quietly the entire way and David respected his silence, though something was clearly wrong. They walked through the library lobby and up the giant stairway, negotiating the oncoming crush of traffic.

"Hey, do you think you can help me with a paper on William James?" David asked.

"What makes you think I know anything about James?"

"I don't know. I mean, I just thought you may have read his book, *The Varieties of Religious Experience*."

"Actually, I did read it. But I have to work on a paper of my own. Can I help you tomorrow?"

"Yeah, sure."

"Are you okay? You don't seem like yourself. I mean, did something happen?"

"I'm fine. It's just that I'm falling behind on my work."

"Don't worry about it. I have to study for midterms anyway. We can work on it tomorrow."

David found a cubicle and Avi went to sit alone at a table. Avi opened his textbook and tried to study, but he couldn't avoid thinking about the article. He decided to leave after an hour, during which he accomplished nothing. David noticed he was leaving and grabbed his books to walk out with him.

"You seem out of it," David said, catching up to Avi.

"I'm just tired. I think I'm just going home and rest for a while. Do you want to study tonight?"

"Sure, how about I meet you here around nine?"

"That's fine."

They walked quietly back through the quad. Avi didn't know why they walked this way. He clenched his jaw again. There was nothing he could say to her. A thousand questions raced through his head, but he knew she couldn't possibly have any answers. He considered an attack on his people to be an attack on himself, and so he felt injured by the person he loved the most. It was too confusing to wrap his head around. He was considering the possibility of ending the relationship when he saw her behind the falafel stand.

"Hey, there's Alena." David pointed and Avi looked away from the table, toward David. He squinted as the sun fell behind Philosophy Hall. It was getting cold and he was irritable.

"You know what? I just realized I'm hungry. Maybe I will try a falafel sandwich."

"Are you kidding me? Why would you want to support their organization?"

"I just want to tell her what I thought of her article. And I want some falafel. You want me to get you a sandwich?"

"No thanks. I don't feel like talking to her right now. I'll wait here."

"Okay, I'll only be a minute."

Avi approached her table, where a throng of students stood in line. It was exactly like the first time he saw her, except this time it engendered the antithesis of the sublime feelings he felt the first time. He approached from the library end of the quad and dreaded the thought of locking eyes with her. Avi lowered his head and hid behind other students, not wanting to be seen. He brainstormed for something to say, but could think of nothing. He fished for money in his pocket and realized he only had a couple of dollars on him. The line parted suddenly and he stood in front of the line, staring at her.

"Oh my gosh, Avi. I didn't see you." She looked away and looked back, wearing an empty expression.

"Just tell me why you deceived me. That's all I want to know."

"Avi, I didn't–"

"I mean, I don't mind so much that you called Israel an illegitimate entity. That's…whatever. But why didn't you even tell me you had an article coming out today? I had to hear about it from David."

"Avi, I didn't know it was coming out today, Honestly, I submitted the article weeks ago and I was meaning to go and change the reference to Israel being illegitimate."

"Reference? That was the whole article."

"I know." She dropped her head.

"You didn't even tell me you submitted an article. I thought we were closer than that. I thought I mattered to you, but I guess I was wrong."

Alena looked over Avi's shoulder to the line of students waiting for falafel. She exchanged glances with a few people.

"Avi, you're making a scene."

"You're damn right I'm making a scene. I always treated you with respect. Why is it that all I get in return is deception? You couldn't trust me to tell me that you submitted an article to the *Spectator*? That's fine, but when you need help with papers, I know all about that."

"Is all this because I dared say that Israel is illegitimate?"

"You don't get it, do you? It's not about the content of your article, though it is ridiculous. It's about not trusting me enough to tell me."

"Look, can we talk about this later?"

"Well, I'm here to buy a falafel sandwich."

"Fine, let me make one for you. Do you want tahini on it?"

"Yes, thank you."

Alena turned around and spread tahini onto the sandwich. She handed it to him in a perfunctory manner.

"Here you go."

"How much?"

"It's okay. It's on me."

"No, I would like to pay for this sandwich."

"In that case, it's $2."

He threw the two crumpled bills on the table. They were the last dollars he had. A man stood shoulder-to-shoulder with him, waiting to get Alena's attention. The line was clearly growing, but Avi felt rage building inside of him.

"You know, I thought you were different from the others."

"What does that mean, *different*? So are the others now a bunch of terrorists or something? My God, are you listening to yourself? Have you not learned anything about representations?"

"You're unbelievable." He shook his head.

"Could you please step aside? There are others who want to order."

"Gladly. Goodbye." Avi walked away with his sandwich before turning back around. His patience eroded into nothing and he only saw anger. He brushed the student aside who had stepped to the front of the line.

"You know, maybe this was a mistake," he said. "Maybe we shouldn't see each other anymore."

She looked startled at him and turned to the other student. She shook her head and he walked away. He found David where he left him, standing impatiently.

"What took you so long?"

"We got into an argument. Let's go."

"If I knew you were going to take that long, I would have had you get me a sandwich."

They resumed walking. Avi stuffed his sandwich in his backpack and continued staring angrily into the ground.

"What did you do, Avi? Go up to her and start arguing over Zionism? You know her uncle is Edward Said, right?" David continued when Avi didn't respond. "I don't see what's so special about Said. I mean people treat him as if he is a God on campus. I don't see why he gets so much attention."

"David, just shut up."

"What's wrong with you today?"

"Look, I'm going home to rest for a while."

"Fine, are we meeting later?"

"I don't know. I'll try. I'll see you later."

IX

Avi had no choice but to walk home. He was angry and confused. He was angry with himself for trusting her. He couldn't understand why Alena turned on him so quickly. He decided to write an article of his own in defense of Zionism. Two hours later, he had six scratchy pages on a notepad, but something was not quite right. As Avi read over his article, he realized his language was too harsh and too dismissive of Palestinian aspirations. He didn't want to be guilty of the same sweeping language that Alena used. Though his great-uncle equated Zionism with anti-Semitism, Avi was never comfortable making this claim. His need for intellectual honesty made him feel that such a blanket accusation was nothing but a sophisticated *ad hominem* attack against anyone who criticized Zionism or Israel. He rejected labeling any Jew who criticized Israel as self-hating.

Perhaps it was confidence, but Avi believed that arguments should stand or fall on their own merit. It was this openness to ideas – the willingness to move beyond the rigid confines of ideology – that would help him understand the conflict from multiple perspectives. Avi also rejected all theological arguments that would attempt to offer biblical justification for Israel. As a secular Jew, Avi's moral defense of Zionism was based on Theodore Herzl's argument that the assimilation of Jews in Europe was impossible. Though the term Zionism was coined by Nathan Birnbaum, it was Herzl who was responsible for a Jewish national movement that began in the late 19th century and culminated in the creation of Israel in 1948. Herzl, after studying law and working as a journalist in France, gradually came to the realization that the Jewish question could only be solved by the creation of a national home. Although Herzl has often been connected to the Dreyfus Affair, it was perhaps the Austrian politician, Karl Lueger, who preceded and inspired Adolf Hitler in his virulent anti-Semitism, that animated and informed his belief that Jewish assimilation could never work. In his controversial book, *Der Judenstaat* (published in 1896), or The Jewish State, Herzl argued that the only way to avoid anti-Semitism in Europe was the creation of an independent Jewish state. In anticipation of fate's grand design; Herzl, while writing the outline for his book, planned to give it the title, *An Address to the Rothschilds*. Twenty-one years later, the Balfour Declaration was sent, in the form of a letter, to Baron Rothschild.

Avi read Herzl's book with great interest and was influenced by his argument. Herzl appealed to Avi in that he was a secular, Jewish intellectual who himself was well assimilated into European culture. Despite his own assimilation, Herzl was prophetic in the sense that he understood, better than most Jewish intellectuals of his time, that the Jews would never be fully accepted by Europe. Avi would see Zionism as a moral necessity. The Holocaust, which for Avi was a seminal event in Jewish history and identity, proved once and for all that the Jews need a national home. The reason Avi was receptive to Said's arguments in *Orientalism* was the fact that Jews suffered representations that reduced them to, and targeted them, as a dehumanized other. Although he did not discuss this with Abba Eban, Foucault and Said gave him the intellectual underpinning to use the idea of representation as a moral grounding for Zionism.

Avi came to realize that representations, if unchecked, could have historic consequences. The problem, however, was how to justify the Zionist takeover of Palestine at the expense of the Palestinians who were already there. He has used the Balfour Declaration, the partition plan, the systematic attacks by the Arabs, terrorism, and other readymade arguments. But deep down, he was not convinced of the merits of such arguments. For Avi, Zionism was not a clearly defined, historically demarcated struggle of a subaltern people who fought for their rights. Zionism was messy and filled with contradictions that needed to be resolved. It would be this unsettling sense of injustice towards the Palestinians that would serve as the spark for his transformation.

He was deeply hurt by Alena's article because of his inability to convey his deepest feelings about the conflict to her. He was injured by the sense that she was personally attacking him. But he was also deeply hurt by her inability to trust him enough to talk about the article before it was published. By the time Avi finished polishing his article, it was 11 pm. He decided to call his great-uncle.

"Hello?" His great-aunt, Susie Eban, answered. She sounded groggy and only then did he realize how early it was there.

"I'm so sorry to wake you, but I wanted to catch Uncle Eban before he left."

"Avi, you didn't wake me. It's so good to hear from you. How are your studies going?"

"Fine. How is everyone back home?"

"We are all fine here." They chatted a few minutes before she handed the phone off to his uncle.

"Hello, Avi. How are your studies going?"

"Fine, do you have a minute?"

"Of course, is there a problem?"

"Oh, no. It's just that I wrote an article for the campus paper on Zionism and had a couple of questions."

"Yes, of course."

"Why did Herzl propose Uganda? Was the goal of the early Zionists simply to find a national homeland for the Jews, regardless of location?"

"This is a common misconception, Avi. Herzl wanted Palestine all along, but you must remember that our people were suffering terrible persecution around the turn of the century. There was rampant anti-Semitism and pogroms in Eastern Europe and Russia. I'm always fascinated when Arabs suggest a kind of conspiracy between the Zionists and Britain in the form of the Balfour Declaration. In fact, around

1900 there were talks between Herzl and the Ottomans for the express purpose of securing Palestine. However, the talks failed to produce a result. You will remember from our conversations that on May 17th, 1901, Herzl met with Sultan Abdulhamid II in the hopes of securing Palestine. Although the Sultan refused, he later offered land that is today part of Iraq, Syria, and Turkey for the price of 2.6 million pounds."

"But what about Uganda?"

Avi knew that when his great-uncle got into lecture mode he could talk for hours. He wanted to hurry the conversation in case Alena called.

"As I said, our people were suffering terrible atrocities and there was an urgent need to alleviate the suffering by finding a national home for the Jews. By 1902, Joseph Chamberlain, who was at the time the Secretary of State for the British colonies, offered part of what is today Kenya."

"I thought it was Uganda."

"History books often refer to it as the *Uganda Plan*, but the land was in Kenya. On August 23, 1903, Herzl brought the proposal to the sixth Zionist Congress. It was a limited proposal to settle Jews in East Africa. It was this proposal that nearly destroyed Zionism. There were heated debates and acrimony, with some Zionists accepting the so-called *Uganda Plan*. The majority, however, insisted upon Palestine as the ultimate goal of Zionism."

"I think I have a better idea. Thank you for your help."

"Wait one moment. Tell me more about this article. Why are you writing it? Is it in response to something that happened on campus?"

"Yes, someone published an article against Zionism so I thought that I should respond."

"I'm glad that you are responding. You should mention that any criticism of Zionism is anti-Semitism."

"I wanted to talk to you about that. I know that has a powerful emotional impact, but I don't feel comfortable equating the two. It smacks of an *ad hominem* attack. I think we have the intellectual capacity to debunk an argument based on its merit."

This was unfamiliar territory. Avi was developing his own ideas for the first time. He was challenging the authority of his great-uncle, and they both knew it.

"Avi, those who criticize Zionism or Israel do so from the perspective of bringing about its destruction. It is not as clean as simply making arguments. We are fighting for the survival of our national identity. If the Arabs lose a war or two, there will continue to be Arab nations. If Israel loses a war, we lose our existential identity."

"I understand that, but you must realize that not all criticism of Israel is intended to destroy it. The *ad hominem* attack of equating criticism with anti-Semitism eliminates the possibility of any meaningful discourse."

"Avi, you sound like Noam Chomksy. Remember that Chomsky's criticism of Israel is intended to undermine the Jewish state. Don't go down the path of I.F Stone, who was in favor of Zionism and then became an Arab sympathizer."

"I read his book, *Holy War,* and I agree with him that the Arab problem is also the number one Jewish problem."

"Avi, we need to talk about this more in depth, but I'm afraid I have to leave for a meeting."

"I wanted to ask when you might come to New York. I have several Jewish friends here who would love to see you debate Edward Said."

"Does he want to debate me?"

"I think so. Would you be interested? I know that both the Arabs and the Jews here would love to see both of you in a debate."

"Well, if he agrees to meet for an intellectual discussion, I would be happy to debate him."

"That's great. I'll try to arrange it. I will be so happy to see you here at Columbia. Thank you for taking the time to talk to me."

"Of course. Call me again soon."

"I will. Bye."

He got off the phone and stared at it. It was the first time in weeks that Alena wasn't at his house. He wondered if she would call. His anger evanesced into hope and worry, and he eventually sat down on the leather couch next to the phone, curling into the fetal position and feeling lost.

Part III

The University of Oslo

X

No one knew the historical significance of Zionism and Palestinian nationalism better than Avi. The two converged toward seemingly irreconcilable historical moments that defied and resisted universal clarity. The Arabs claimed that Zionism was an extension of colonial Europe; that the Jews, wealthy and educated, used their considerable influence to secure Palestine from Britain. What the Arabs failed to appreciate was that the Jews of Europe – also known as Ashkenazi Jews – regardless of their status, were subject to the whims of a Christian culture that opened and closed the doors of freedom and opportunity on a whim. Despite their multi-layered integration into European culture, Jews have often been discriminated against, persecuted, and forced to live in ghettos. Regardless of their level of success – be it academic, professional, political, or economic – Jews were never fully embraced as Germans, French, English, Austrian, or as anything other than Jewish.

Throughout their two thousand-year Diaspora, it was the portability of their religion that sustained and animated their cultural orientation. In post-Enlightenment Europe, the majority of Jews were integrated into European society. It would be this people; this culture that produced some of the greatest minds, both in Europe and America, to usher in the modern world. The list is extensive, with names such as Baruch Spinoza, Moses Mendelssohn, Karl Marx, Sigmund Freud, Theodore Herzl, Edmund Husserl, Albert Einstein, Hannah Arendt, Theodor Adorno, Henri Bergson, Ludwig Wittgenstein, Marcel Proust, Jacques Derrida, Emile Durkheim, Claude Levi-Strauss, Gabriel Marcel, Maxime Rodinson, Simone Weil, Mortimer Adler, Ronald Dworkin, Walter Kaufman, Thomas Kuhn, Karl Popper, Thomas Nagel, Ayn Rand, Leo Strauss, Isaac Asimov, Saul Bellow, E.L. Doctorow, and Noam Chomksy. Of the more than 800 Nobel Prize recipients since 1901, a full 20% were Jewish. Jews were not monolithic in terms of belief structures, religion, ideology, politics, philosophical production, art, literature, and a host of other categories that naturally distinguish a people.

Some were atheists or agnostics, others converted to Christianity. Some were Zionists, who strongly believed in a Jewish national home, others believed in assimilation. Regardless of their differences, the Jewish people were bound by a singular identity, historical and locatable, filled with spectacular achievements as well as unspeakable degradation. Jewish identity is unique in its dispersive capacity to establish and maintain a cultural hold on a people for millennia.

For the Palestinians, both the accomplishments and the devastation of the Jews imposed a reality that denied them the very freedom and self-determination that the Zionists struggled to achieve. Fate, it seemed, had singled out the Palestinians to bear the cruelties of historical events that converged toward a land that had religious, cultural, historical, and psychological significance. The Palestinians, who are the most educated group in the Arab world, suffered cruel representations in the West. They were the indigenous Arab population, then they were simply referred to as refugees, and once they became a conscious political force, they were contemptuously labeled and identified as terrorists. During their brief Diaspora, the Palestinians produced their own set of gifted intellectuals, professionals, politicians, artists, writers, and poets. Though these figures are not well known in the West, their achievements are extraordinary. The list includes: Ibrahim Abu Lughod, Edward Said, Rashid Khalidi, Walid Khalidi, Sari Nusseibeh, Rosemarie Said Zahlan, Anis Sayigh, Khalil Suleiman, Hanan Ashrawi, May Ziade, John H. Sununu, John E. Sununu, Nasser Khader, Pierre de Bané, Said Musa, Carlos Flores Facusse, Shafik Handal, Antonio Saca, Tala Abu-Ghazaleh, Naim Attallah, Elia Suleiman, Naji Salim al-Ali, Khalil al-Sakakini, Mahmoud Darwish, Mourid Barghouti, Joseph Massad, Nur-eldeen Masalha, Laila Al-Marayati, Naseer Aruri, Nabil Abu-Ghazaleh, and numerous others.

As with the Jews, Palestinians were a multi-dimensional people with different perspectives about the conflict. Politically, they disagreed about how to go about realizing their own state. Some were radical in their views in demanding a return to all of Palestine, and others were accommodating to the idea of a two state solution. Some prescribed to violent struggle as a means of achieving their goal, while others preferred diplomacy and peaceful resistance. Some Palestinians resorted to suicide bombings and other violent attacks that defied any moral justification.

Others, such as Edward Said, moved away from a two-state settlement and opted for a one state, non-Zionist solution.

§§§

Avi's thoughts were removed from the urgency of the situation as he sat at the Grand Café, oblivious to the world around him. He was snapped back to reality by Yoram, his Head of Security. Yoram was closely followed by David.

"Mr. Prime Minister, it is urgent that you return to your room. It is no longer safe for you to stay here." Yoram looked apprehensive, as if the Prime Minister was in imminent danger. Yoram was nervous, given Avi's propensity for spontaneity and irrational behavior. Yoram Rubin had served as Head of Security for two years. Back in 1995, he was the only security guard to be injured in the assassination of Prime Minister Yitzhak Rabin. That fateful day haunted him ever since.

It was the evening of November 4th, 1995, and a large peace rally was under way in Tel Aviv's Kikar Malchei Ysrael square. More than 100,000 people attended the rally in support of the Oslo Peace Accords, which were officially signed in 1993 in a public ceremony at the White House. It was 9:30 pm when Rabin walked off the stage and toward his official car with the door already open. As he approached the car, three shots were fired. The first two shots hit Rabin and the third shot slightly injured Yoram. He was immediately rushed to Ichilov Hospital. Though the hospital was 600 meters from the square, Rabin did not survive the shooting. Yoram, who was treated for a gunshot wound to the forearm, was devastated by the news that the man he was assigned to protect was assassinated. Though his career flourished as a result of taking a bullet, he constantly regretted not doing more. He wallowed in failure for not doing enough to save the man who courageously pursued peace. This episode served as a constant reminder of the dangers lurking beneath the threshold of anticipation.

Yoram went on to become the personal body guard of Shimon Peres and Ariel Sharon. It was only after Avi negotiated the peace treaty with the Palestinians that Yoram was asked to become the head of his security team. Given his tenuous past, Yoram fixated on every detail and left nothing to chance. Overseeing Avi's security, however, proved to be the most challenging job of his career. Of course, Avi made matters worse with his erratic behavior. There was the time in 2016 when Avi was in New York addressing the United Nations, when he suddenly decided he wanted to visit Columbia. He was adamant about going despite Yoram's insistence that his security team did not have the opportunity to secure the area. There was also the time in Cairo when Avi was on an official state visit when he, without warning, wanted to visit the Nile Hilton. Of course, Yoram could not make sense of his Prime Minister's erratic and unpredictable behavior.

"What's so urgent that you want me to leave now?" Avi asked. "I haven't been here that long."

"Mr. Prime Minister, the protests outside are growing more violent. Already there have been five people taken to the hospital. The police are doing what they can, but there are no guarantees."

Avi shot up from his chair. He looked at David and back at Yoram.

"Can you follow me, Mr. Prime Minister?" What Yoram was about to do was unorthodox, but he wanted Avi to realize the gravity of the situation. It was dangerous to take the prime minister to the window, but he needed a way to convince Avi of the danger lurking outside. Avi followed Yoram to the window. Hundreds of people were gathered there, most of them demonstrating peacefully. Yoram pointed to a throng of people in the middle, shoving and shouting like a moshpit. Most of the protestors looked to the window, as though they expected Avi to address them at that moment.

"Damn it."

"Avi, you need to go up to the room immediately."

Avi turned to Yoram and David. He could see the dark circles under David's cheerless eyes, and he knew it was an uncertain time.

"Yes, let's go."

They walked briskly to the café's back door and up the service stairs. It was a long climb and Avi was winded when they reached his floor. He resented the interruption but understood the gravity of the situation. Once back in his hotel room, Avi informed David he wanted to rest for a while. David waved to Yoram to wait outside. They walked into the bedroom.

"Yoram believes we should cancel the remainder of the weekend's events immediately; the speech, everything. He believes the situation is growing too tenuous to control and there are no guarantees for your safety. This is a serious issue. I told Yoram I would tell you this myself. I think we need to get you out of here."

Avi slumped forward. He looked sad and defeated. David had never seen him this way. He took great pride in his appearance and demeanor, but that had changed. His thinning hair was rumpled and his suit jacket was wrinkled and uneven. David wasn't sure he would be ready for any interviews later that day.

"No," Avi said.

"What?"

"I said no."

Avi ran his fingers through his hair. The fact was that he only cared about seeing Alena. She was going to be there for his acceptance speech. He knew how important this moment was for his country's history – a Nobel Peace Prize to cap off the monumental resurgence of his people on a global scale. But, in the end it was about her. It always was.

"No, David. We're not leaving. We're staying and delivering this speech. Look, we can cancel the Anderson Cooper interview and the remainder of my meetings. But we're not leaving Oslo without that award. We can't do that to Israel."

Avi waved dismissively, and David shook his head. He walked for the door and turned around.

"You're making a huge mistake, Avi."

"We're going to be fine, David." He looked at David closely and smiled. "Trust me. We'll be fine."

David shook his head and closed the door behind him. Avi lay on the bed contemplating a past that shaped the very meaning of the peace between two sworn enemies.

§§§

It was Saturday morning and Avi was thinking of Chomsky. He might never have the chance to meet the man again. It wasn't right to go. Although he had a bitter argument with Alena, he couldn't pass up the chance to see Chomsky and Said in the same room, and maybe even engage them in dialogue. There was no way he could pass it up, even if Alena was going to be there. It was completely out of character for him. He was painfully awkward and incredibly nervous, of course, and didn't know what kind of impression he would make. He contemplated calling his great-uncle, but he already knew what Abba Eban would say. He was also worried about seeing Said in an informal setting. It is not common for undergraduates, especially freshmen, to have dinner with their professors. He paced back and forth in his room, unable to focus. He decided to call David to get his mind off the thought of that evening. David answered on the first ring.

"Hello?"

"David, are you busy?"

"Hey, Avi. Not really. I might go to the library later but that's it."

"Listen, there's something I have to ask you. Did you know Chomsky is in town?"

"What, are you serious? There was no mention of him coming. Is he giving a lecture at school?"

"I don't think so. He is going to Said's for dinner tonight and I've been invited."

"What the hell? Who invited you?"

Avi froze for a second. He hadn't thought of David asking this question. He didn't want to let David know about Alena. Alena was the first friend he ever confided in, and that had gone poorly. He knew he couldn't confide in David now.

"Said invited me. He wanted me to meet Chomsky."

"You've got to be kidding. That's incredible. You're going, right?"

"I'm not sure." Avi tried to feign indifference. He didn't want to appear too eager. Do you think I should go?'

"Wow, Said and Chomsky together. Do you think you can take them?"

"Take them? What does that mean, David? You're talking about two of the greatest intellectuals of our time. I'm just a naïve undergraduate who's lucky to have been invited." In fact, Avi couldn't wait to take on the two intellectual giants. This hubris was one of the side effects of his precocity, and he knew it came off as conceit at times. He knew there was a chance they would ignore him, but the thought of debating them made his heart race.

"Avi, what the hell are you talking about? Man, you're a freak of nature. If I had your brain, I would take them on myself. Said, I can understand. I mean he is Palestinian and is defending his people, but Chomsky hates his own kind. He discredits Israel everywhere he goes. He deserves a good debate from the next generation."

"What do you care, David? You're an American."

"Do you have any idea what Israel means to Jews all over the world? After I finish Columbia, I'm going to visit and possibly stay.

"Really?"

"Yeah. So are you going to do it? Are you going to take on Chomsky?"

"I haven't decided if I'm going, but if I do go, it's a dinner, not a lecture. I never cared for social settings. I never know what to say in polite company."

"Hey, what are you doing now?"

"Not much. Why?"

"I was thinking of stopping by to borrow that book on Locke. I have a paper due next week on the natural rights of man and I thought you could–"

"You need help with it, don't you? Sure come on over."

"Where is your place again?"

"72nd and Columbus. Apartment 714."

"Okay, I'll see you in a few minutes." As soon as Avi hung up the phone, he regretted inviting David over. He knew Alena wouldn't call. He decided to brush up on Chomsky as he waited for David. Fifteen minutes later his phone rang.

"Sir, there is a Mr. Barkovic to see you."

"Send him up please." David knocked on his door a moment later. Avi looked around and realized his apartment was very messy. He hadn't cleaned since Alena last came over, and his books and dishes were scattered everywhere. It was only at this moment that he realized that he didn't know what to wear, or even how he was getting to Said's building. He thought of Alena, who could answer all of these questions for him.

"Hey, Avi," David said after Avi answered the door. "Wow, this is a nice place."

"Come in. Please."

David marveled at the massive library and mahogany furnishings. He stared back at Avi. "Man, is this why you don't spend much time in the library?"

"I study better here. These aren't my books. They belong to my great uncle."

"These are Abba Eban's books?"

"Yes, I'm using his apartment while I'm studying here."

David sat down and continued gawking at the vaulted ceilings and recessed skylight. Avi could tell he was imagining Abba Eban in this room.

"You know, he's going down in history as one of Israel's greatest diplomats. I know he was foreign minister, but what's he doing now?"

"He is the Chair of the Knesset's Foreign Affairs and Defense Committee."

"So, did you get him to accept a debate with Said? That would be something to see."

"Wait. How did you know about that?"

"Everyone's talking about it at school. It would be amazing for Columbia. Eban and Said in the same room? Incredible!"

"Yeah, well. He told me he's willing to do it. We have to see if Said would accept. Maybe I'll ask him tonight."

Avi got up to make some tea, while David stared at the bookcases. He got up and thumbed through a few volumes, and sidestepped toward the vinyl collection lining the shelf of the far wall. He thumbed through the albums and set them back to lean against the wall. He stared at a pile of tapes before pulling out the top one.

"What's this?" David turned toward Avi in the kitchen as he returned with two cups of tea. He set the cups down on coasters.

"You never heard of *Carmina Burana*? Where have you been? This is one of the most powerful pieces of music ever written. It's more powerful than Beethoven's 9th."

"Are you serious? Classical music?"

"It was written in the classical style in 1936 by Carl Orff. He died just three years ago."

"Okay, now I'm curious. Can I play it?"

"Sure, but I guarantee you've heard it before."

"You have many versions of it here. Which one do you recommend?"

"Oh, the New York Philharmonic is the best." He walked over and put the tape in. He pressed play and the orchestral power filled the room.

"So this is *Carmina Burana*? Wow, you're right. I've heard it many times before, but I didn't know what it was."

"Most people have. They just can't connect the music with the composer."

As the music played, Avi tried his best to control his reaction to it, but within seconds he was in his own world. David stared at Avi, slowly growing concerned. Avi's fingers twisted and the tissue of his neck tensed. His jaw was clenching as David stopped the cassette, just as the music began to overpower him.

"Wait, what just happened? Why did you react like that? You looked like you wanted to kill someone."

"It's nothing. The music just makes me feel intense, that's all. Now where's the book?"

Avi walked over to grab the book on Locke from the bookshelf and was struck with horror. It was already 4:15 and he wasn't ready to go. Alena had told him that dinner was at 5:00. He had nothing to wear and no way to get to Said's house. Worse yet, he didn't know where Said lived. He looked at David, who gawked at him.

"What is it?"

"I…I need your help."

"Sure, you're helping me write my paper on Locke. What do you need?"

"I need a ride to Said's apartment."

"No problem. Maybe he'll invite me in too."

"The thing is, I don't know where he lives. And I have no idea what to wear."

Avi walked to his bathroom mirror and stared at his reflection. He was wearing blue jeans and a white T-shirt, as always, and his hair was matted on one side. He scooped handfuls of water on the side of his head and turned around when he saw David standing behind him.

"What am I going to do? I have to get to Said's."

"Relax. Just grab a button-down shirt and a blazer. You have those, right?"

Avi nodded and glanced back at his reflection. He needed a shave, and he needed to wear a tie.

"Start getting dressed and I'll take care of the rest."

Avi knew he was lucky that David was there. He was also lucky it was a different time, when a professor's phone number and address would be in the white pages, and they could call a building and get directions quickly. Avi rushed to shave and throw on some clothes. He was standing in his living room ten minutes later and staring at David, who held the Locke book at his side.

"Um, you have an iron, right?"

XI

Edward Said lived at 448 Riverside Dr. near the corner of 116th Street. David and Avi were struck by the beauty of the building, known as the Colosseum Apartments. The building was constructed by Paterno Brothers in 1910 and later acquired by Columbia University. It had a distinctive, curved façade and an imposing marble lobby. They were luxury, four-bedroom apartments with a sweeping view of the Hudson River, and they housed some of the most notable faculty members of Columbia. Harlan Fiske Stone, the 12th Chief Justice of the United States Supreme Court, took up residence here during the early part of the 20th century. The Colosseum was also home to David Weiss Halivni, who was an American-Israeli scholar and served as Classical Rabbinics scholar in the Department of Religion at Columbia.

Avi thanked David and crossed his fingers as he got out of his car. David smiled and nodded. Avi turned and walked nervously to the doorman.

"Your name, sir?"

"Um…I'm sorry?"

"Your name?" The doorman wore white gloves and a shiny hat, and Avi momentarily stared at him.

"Oh, Avi Eban."

"Very good, sir." The doorman called upstairs and Avi thought of Alena's shock if she heard his name. It was at this moment that he was consumed with fear over Alena's reaction at seeing him.

"Please go on up, sir," said the doorman. He skulked into the elevator and cringed as the doors closed. *Maybe Alena wouldn't be there,* he thought. He shook his head. *Of course, she would be there*. He had to apologize to her. He overreacted. She was entitled to her opinion. In fact, it was brave of her to publicize it, especially when there were so many Israelis on campus. He was lost in his thoughts when he knocked on the door.

Alena gasped when she saw him. "It is you," she smiled. She stepped into the hallway and threw her wrists around his neck. "Oh, Avi. I'm so glad you came. I was hoping you would come, but I figured–."

Avi recoiled and Alena stared at him. The world seemed to disappear for both of them at that moment. Alena wanted to explain why she didn't inform Avi of the article.

"Avi, I'm so sorry for hurting you,"

"It's perfectly fine, Alena. I'm sorry for reacting the way I did."

"No, Avi. Please let me explain. You see, the Arab organization wanted someone to write an article on Zionism. I volunteered and wrote my opinion on the subject. I sent it off to the *Daily Spectator* without knowing if they would publish it or not. You must know this, Avi, during the last few weeks; I began to doubt my own conviction about Israel being illegitimate. I planned on asking the paper to delete the illegitimate reference, but I simply got busy with work. They didn't give me a warning that they were about to publish it. I'm so sorry for hurting you. I should have told you I was writing it. Listen, would it be okay if we started discussing the conflict openly and honestly?"

Avi glanced up and down the hallway for fear that someone would see them. He relaxed when Alena didn't seem concerned. He heard distant voices behind the front door and wondered if someone would come outside to check on them.

"I tried repeatedly to discuss the conflict, but you always got nervous and agitated."

"Yes, I know and I was wrong to do so. I was scared it would be the end of us. I was scared you might persuade me with your considerable intellect. Can I confess something to you?"

"Yes."

"I avoided discussing the conflict because somehow I've convinced myself, almost subconsciously, that you are not Israeli. You are Avi, the nicest and most brilliant person I've ever met. I love discussing philosophy and literature with you. Whenever Palestine comes up, it reminds me that you are Israeli. I know that sounds cruel, but that's the real reason I avoid the topic."

"It's not cruel at all, Alena. I actually understand what you are saying. There is a part of me that wants to transcend our identity. We must be able to engage the topic without ending in a heated argument."

"Oh, Avi. You have to forgive me. I've been so miserable." Tears formed in her eyes and he knew she was telling the truth.

"It's okay. I'm sorry. I've been miserable too. I haven't been able to eat or sleep or focus on anything else but you."

"Avi, promise me this won't happen again. The last few days–" She turned and stared into the ground, biting her bottom lip. Avi felt horrible, but at the same time thought that she had never looked more beautiful. Just then the door opened behind them and Avi saw a woman who could only be Professor Said's wife, Mariam.

"Hi," she said to Avi. "Alena, I wondered where you went."

"Aunt Mariam, this is Avi." Alena introduced Avi with a proud smile. Mariam shook his hand and looked at Alena, smiling widely. What Avi couldn't have realized was Mariam Said suspected that he and Alena were becoming an item. She was alerted by Alena's mother, who had yet to meet Avi.

"So nice to meet you, Avi. I've heard so much about you."

"It's great to be here, Mrs. Said," Avi smiled.

"Thank you for inviting me."

Mariam Said turned to usher them in, but Alena stopped Avi and straightened his tie. She tugged the hem of his jacket and dusted his shoulders. She smiled and took his hand. She led him to the kitchen, where her mother was helping to prepare hors d'oeuvres.

"Mama, this is Avi.' Alena introduced Avi with a proud smile.

"So, you are Avi. It's very nice to meet you. Alena talks about you all the time."

"Mama, I don't talk about him all the time."

"It's a pleasure to meet you, Mrs. Said," Avi said. He didn't know what else to say and stared around the apartment. He was immediately struck by its spacious elegance. He noticed the Chippendale furniture, the layers of Persian carpets, and the imposing grand piano. He was struck by Said's aristocratic domestic life. It was not at all what he imagined. Avi was brought up reading Dostoevsky, Tolstoy, Sartre and Camus, and he romanticized their ascetic lives as something noble. While reading *Orientalism,* he conjured images of Said as a professor with little care for the material world. In his discussions with Abba Eban about Said, there was no mention of his personal life.

He couldn't believe he was here now, standing in his home. Avi felt like a fish out of water as an Israeli in a Palestinian household. And it wasn't just any household. He was attending a dinner at the home of perhaps the greatest Palestinian intellectual the world has ever seen.

"So, have you recovered from your motorcycle accident?" Alena's mother asked. She had a direct tone and stared at him with unwavering eyes.

"I'm much better, thank you."

"Alena tells me you are the great nephew of Abba Eban."

"Yes, I am."

"How do you like New York?"

"I think it's a magical city." Avi looked at Alena with a smile.

"I'm glad you like it here. I prefer Washington, D.C. We are staying in New York so we can be closer to Alena." Mariam Said walked into the kitchen to check on dinner and turned to the three of them.

"I hope you like Palestinian food, Avi."

"Yes, I'm sure I will. Thank you so much for inviting me."

"Oh, I almost forgot. Do you keep kosher, Avi?" Avi turned to Alena, who appeared surprised. She and Avi never talked about his diet.

"Avi, my uncle is asking for you," Alena interrupted. She noticed his tense posture and wanted to get him out of the kitchen, and away from the interrogation from his mother and aunt. She decided to take him to meet Chomsky. As she walked Avi over to the living room, Edward Said waived to Avi. He stood in a circle of people, several of whom Avi recognized. There were a few graduate students and several professors, including Rashid Khalidi who would eventually become the Edward Said Professor of Modern Arab Studies at Columbia. He noticed the graduate students and the other professors huddled around Said and Chomsky. Said wore a tweed jacket and a white collar over tan slacks. He commanded the full attention of the room. Avi was not new to this. He remembered the times when he accompanied his great-uncle to the Knesset and the parade of people jostling to talk to one of Israel's founding members. In contrast to Said, Chomsky wore brown pants, a striped white shirt, and a dull brown sweater. Avi never met Chomsky, but had seen him many times on television. He remembered watching him in a 1969 debate with William F. Buckley. He was only five years old at the time, but remembered his great-uncle saying something to the effect that Chomsky was a brilliant man who turned against his people.

They approached Said and Alena tugged on his elbow when he was finished speaking.

"Avi, it's great to see you." Said smiled warmly and shook his hand. "I want you to meet some people. Noam, do you know who this is?"

"No, I don't think we've met before," said Chomsky. He was sitting in a chair with his legs crossed and foot dangling.

"This is Avi Eban, Abba Eban's great-nephew." Said presented Avi with pride, which warmed Avi's heart.

"Hello, young man. So you are Abba Eban's great-nephew." Chomsky stood up from the chair to shake Avi's hand. He offered a perfunctory smile and sat back down.

"It's a pleasure to meet you, Professor." Avi sensed cold indifference from Chomsky. He wondered if it was because of Abba Eban's comment that Chomsky was a self-hating Jew. Avi grew more nervous than before. He scanned the room awkwardly.

"Avi, I also want you to meet Rashid Khalidi. He teaches Middle East studies here."

"It's a pleasure to meet you, Professor."

"Edward speaks highly of you, young man."

"Well, I hope to be worthy of his kind opinion."

"And this is Professor Gayatri Spivak. She pioneered the study in literary theory of non-Western women." Gayatri Spivak, who was born in India in 1942, would go on to become University professor at Columbia, making her the only woman of color to achieve this prestigious post.

"It is a pleasure to meet you, Professor. I've read your translation of Derrida's Grammatology."

"It's very nice to meet you, Avi. Edward has told us that you are one of his most promising students. It's great of you to come here tonight. How old are you?"

"I'm twenty one."

"And you read Derrida? I'm impressed. Edward, where have you been hiding him?" She looked toward Said and smiled. Avi shrank at their praise. It was too much at once and gave him a prickly sensation, as though he wanted to leave. He looked again at Chomsky, who stared toward the kitchen.

"Come and sit next to me, Avi." Said motioned for Avi to follow him.

"Avi, I don't think you know these grad students."

"No, I don't think I've had the pleasure."

"This is Moustafa Bayoumi, Joseph Massad, Nabil Abu Jildeh, and this over here is Shelley Wanger, my editor." Said pointed around the room and several people smiled and waved at Avi. "Standing over there with Alena is my nephew, Saree Makdisi and my two children, Wadie and Najla." As Said was making the introductions, Avi nodded his head awkwardly. He smiled at Alena, who smiled proudly and waved back.

"So what were we talking about?" Said asked the group of grad students.

"We were talking about the language of postcolonialism," Moustafa answered.

"Yes, as I was saying, Europe constructed an Orient that is a paradigmatic other as a means of defining a more cohesive European identity. In this sense both the Occident and the Orient are mutually constitutive." Said had the rapt attention of the group.

"So are you saying that the Orient constructs the Occident as much as the Occident constructs the Orient?' Nabil asked.

"Yes, but the way the Occident constructed the Orient, the discursive process, has enabled a kind of control over subaltern cultures."

"Would Zionism be a part of this Western construction of the Orient?" Nabil seemed more interested in Avi's reaction than Said's.

"Are you asking this because Avi is here?" asked Said.

"I'm just curious about his reaction. We've actually met before." Nabil looked at Avi as he spoke. Said seemed hesitant to put Avi on the spot so he continued.

"I will get to Zionism in a minute, but I want to emphasize a point I made earlier and that is neither the term Orient nor the concept of the West has any ontological stability. Each is made up of human effort, partly affirmation, partly identification of the other."

"Excuse me, Professor Said," Avi interrupted. "But I'm not entirely clear what you mean by ontological stability."

"I'm glad you asked. That's a good question. You see, the Orient is a Western construction whose aim has been to articulate in discursive fashion something that is authoritative and credible. The only problem is that such a construction lacks stability. Its very essence is fractured and disjointed."

"Forgive me, Professor Said. But are you using the term as self-evident knowledge? I mean, I'm sure both the Orient and the Occident are ontologically fractured, but–" Avi paused for a moment. He wasn't sure if he should continue.

"What are you trying to say, Avi?"

"It's just that when you say that construction x, y, or z lacks ontological stability you presuppose that such stability is possible. I'm not sure if ontological stability is possible. The process of constituting a reality is complex and messy. The construction itself is temporally unstable, always shifting, always moving forward in a dialectic effort to get at some level of cultural truth." Alena and Saree joined the group while Avi spoke.

"I don't think Edward meant it's unstable in that sense." It was Chomsky. Avi didn't notice that he had approached the group until he spoke. "I think he meant that the West has described the Orient in sweeping generalizations. In this sense, Zionism has accepted such generalizations about the Orient. The Arabs and Muslims are looked upon as backward, barbaric, uncivilized, and so on. Zionism was part of Europe's colonizing project."

§§§

This was the first time Avi had the opportunity to listen to Chomsky in person. He was neither eloquent nor forceful in his speech. Chomsky spoke in a calm monotone, and one had to listen carefully in order to fully understand his arguments. Said jumped in before Chomsky could continue.

"Hold on, Noam. Avi what are you trying to say?"

"I'm simply trying to say that the Western construction of the Orient, as you have so eloquently argued in your book, as an amorphous mass of undifferentiated other, is a compelling indictment against the Western intellectual tradition, but I find it difficult to accept that Zionism was a significant contributor to that discursive process. Gramsci himself tells us that cultural hegemony is neither monolithic nor a unified value system. We Jews, regardless of our dispersive integration into European culture, have had to endure the persistent image of the other. We–"

Before Avi could continue he was interrupted by Professor Spivak.

"Just a minute, young man. Are you saying you've read Gramsci?"

"Yes, I read his prison notebooks." As soon as Avi said this, he noticed more sidelong glances from the group of grad students. Antonio Gramsci was an Italian philosopher, linguist, and a founding member of the Communist Party of

Italy. He was imprisoned by Benito Mussolini's regime and died of poor health at the age of forty six. Edward Said was influenced by Gramsci's ideas and was surprised to hear that Avi read his prison notebooks.

"If you read Gramsci," Said interjected, "then you should be aware of his ideas on cultural hegemony."

"Yes, and it is cultural hegemony that brings me to the point that we Jews have always suffered under the enlightened culture of Europe. Regardless of whether we were part of the proletariat or the bourgeoisie, we were relegated as outsiders. Our history is punctuated by disturbances that served as reminders of our subaltern status. These disturbances would converge toward the systematic slaughter of millions."

Avi grew aware that everyone was fixed on him and held back. Avi saw Alena's wide-eyed look of concern and thought for a moment that he had gone too far.

"Don't forget that I'm Jewish as well," Chomsky said. "What you don't seem to understand is that the Palestinians have become the victims of the victims. Did you know I lived in a kibbutz in Israel back in 1953? I was a Zionist, but not in the sense you understand the term. I was a cultural Zionist, which meant that I believed in a bi-national state where Jews and Arabs could coexist. The Zionism your great-uncle supports, and apparently you as well, is quite different. The Zionism you believe in came at the expense of the Palestinian people. That's racism, when you exclude those who are different from you."

"Forgive me, Professor Chomsky. But I simply don't agree that Israel is a racist state. Let me quote Gramsci. In one of his famous passages, he said, and I quote, 'the starting-point of critical elaboration is the consciousness of what one really is, and is knowing thyself as a product of the historical process to date which has deposited in you an infinity of traces, without leaving an inventory.' It is this inventory that allows me to justify Zionism. Jewish history has left an infinity of traces upon my consciousness, and without a critical inventory of these traces, we cannot possibly understand the meaning and implication of a Jewish home.

"Do you know what your great-uncle called me?" Chomsky asked. He appeared agitated and Avi looked back to Alena for help.

"Yes I do, Professor. I'm sorry that he chose such harsh language. I certainly don't agree. I believe that Israel should be criticized for its actions, just as any state should be. Jews should be allowed to criticize Zionism and Israel without being labeled as self-hating Jews. I never cared for ad-hominem attacks."

"I noticed you used the term *Jewish home* and not Jewish state," Rashid Khalidi said. This was not the first time Avi used the term to describe Israel. Alena corrected him in the past.

"I realize that, but I meant to say Jewish state."

"Are you sure? Noam would agree with you about the need for a Jewish home. You do realize there is an oceanic separation between the meaning of home and a state? The problem with Zionism is that it came at the expense of a people who were systematically dispossessed of their land."

Suddenly, Said spoke up. "You told me that you read my book, *The Question of Palestine*. Did you read the section entitled 'Zionism from the Standpoint of its Victims?' If you did, you would know that I articulated what Zionism means to Jews. Though not many Arab intellectuals would be sensitive to the suffering of Jews, I understand that suffering. I even went so far as to appreciate the meaning of Israel for Jews. You see, Zionism is a great narrative filled with idealistic hopes, historical identification, and redemptive possibilities. It is a story of spectacular achievement, of bringing Western sensibility and enlightenment to a degraded and unworthy part of the East. The only problem with this narrative, the one you defend, is that it is based on illusions. You see, there were inhabitants living in Palestine. These inhabitants lived and died in Palestine. They tilled the soil, built villages, and looked upon themselves as organically connected to that land. The Arabs who lived on that land for centuries were irrelevant to the more important goal of establishing a Western leaning civilization in the Orient. The indigenous population was a nuisance; a troublesome detail to be dealt with.

"You mentioned Gramsci, one of my favorite writers, and his ideas on history as depositing an infinity of traces upon our consciousness is relevant to this discussion. We are all a product of historical moments that find expression in each of us. You cannot ignore the history of Zionism from the history of colonial expansion. You argued that Jews suffered degradation throughout their Diaspora in Europe. This suffering converged towards one of the most horrific events in human history. Fair enough, but the question that confronts you now as an Israeli is this: does suffering, regardless of the magnitude, justify the oppression of others? If the Jews suffered catastrophic loss, does this entitle them to oppress those who had nothing to do with that suffering? This is a moral question and a question that Israelis as a whole must come to terms with."

Said spoke with soothing compassion. Avi was taken aback by his thoughts. He never met a Palestinian who went this far in acknowledging Jewish suffering.

"Avi, I must admit that I'm impressed by your precocity," Professor Spivak said. "I want to ask you a basic question. Why are you here attending this dinner?"

Avi was caught off guard. Only he knew the real answer was watching him from the kitchen, smiling widely.

"I'm not sure what you mean, Professor. I was invited."

"Yes, of course, and I'm glad you accepted. But I want to know why you accepted? You were aware the dinner would be with Palestinians and possibly other Arabs, right?"

"Yes."

"Nevertheless, you chose to attend. What I'm getting at is that it took courage for you to come. Most Israelis would have stayed away, but you chose to come. I admire that sense of openness. You spoke so eloquently just now about Jewish suffering; of how Jews were reduced to a paradigmatic other. You see, Avi, the concept of the other is something that has always interested me and Edward as well. *Orientalism* is essentially about the idea of the other. Edward, what was that quote from Nietzsche you often use?"

"It's of one my favorite quotes. I believe it goes something like this. 'What is the truth of a language but a mobile army of metaphors, metonyms, and anthropomorphisms—in short, a sum of human relations, which have been enhanced, transposed, and embellished poetically and rhetorically, and which after long use seem firm, canonical, and obligatory to a people: truths are illusions about which one has forgotten that this is what they are.'"

"So you see," continued Professor Spivak. "Truths are illusions, constructions, if you will, about which we forget they are constructions."

"Are you saying that what we know about the Other is an illusion?" Avi asked. He was finding himself mesmerized by Spivak's logic and demeanor. She spoke with disarming warmth, as though she didn't want to make Avi feel defensive. Avi thought that was the problem all long with this conflict. Part of Avi's intellectual development was to use knowledge as a weapon to defeat those who would undermine the legitimacy of Israel.

"Yes, that's exactly what I'm saying. The idea of the Other helps to define or constitute our sense of identity. What are you studying here at Columbia?"

"I'm a double major in philosophy and comparative literature."

"Impressive. Tell me, have you read Hegel?"

"Yes, I read *Phenomenology of Spirit*."

"Excellent. Do you recall the passage called the Master-Slave dialectic?"

"Forgive me, Professor, but I found Hegel rather dense."

"Yeah, where are you going with this?" Moustafa interrupted.

"You will see." Said remarked with a smile.

Spivak continued. "It is in Hegel that we first encounter the idea of the other. In the Master-Slave dialectic, the idea of the other becomes a constituent in self-consciousness. Absolute knowledge, or spirit, cannot come unto existence without first having the self-conscious awareness of another self-consciousness."

"Forgive me, but I don't understand what this has to do with Zionism?" Avi was confused and a little out of his element. He was accustomed to dominating intellectual discussions. He was, however, not the only one to be confused by what Spivak was getting at. The graduate students were also uncertain as to where she was going.

"I mean, every culture in history has demonized the enemy by creating an 'us versus them' paradigm," Avi added.

"Yes, that is certainly true," Professor Spivak said. "But the systematic study of the other would begin with Hegel. This is why Edward's work is so critical to the study of subaltern people. *Orientalism* traces the discursive process by which Europe reduced the Orient to something wholly imagined and constituted, something to be articulated, shaped, and controlled by the enlightened West. You see, to me the term *subaltern* should have a more precise meaning than simply those who are oppressed. Some believe that Gramsci used the term in reference to the proletariat, but I think he was also looking for a more precise meaning. I think it should include all those who have limited or no access to the cultural imperium, which brings me to Zionism. You see, Jews in Europe have become both part of the cultural imperialism and victims of it as well."

"This is the point you seem to be overlooking," Joseph Massad interrupted. "European Jews used the positional authority of the West to articulate a nationalist agenda that came at the expense of the Palestinian people."

"Look, everyone. I don't want this evening to be about the Palestinian-Israeli conflict," Said interjected. "Alena, why don't you show Avi the view of the Hudson."

Alena took Avi to one of the bedrooms so he could see the sweeping view. Avi stared at the tiny faraway buildings and the haze over the city. It looked like he could see for a hundred miles. He looked back at Alena, who was staring at him. He figured she had seen this view too many times to be impressed.

"How are you holding up? You seemed uncomfortable."

"I'm just not very good in social settings. Professor Spivak is brilliant though. I should read her work on Derrida again."

"She is very funny once you get to know her." Alena wrapped her arms around Avi and leaned her head against his shoulder. Avi felt her warmth on his back and her hands around his waist. He turned reflexively to see if anyone was coming.

"What if someone walks in?" he asked.

Alena kissed his neck and Avi turned around to embrace her.

"Avi, please let's never argue again. I had no idea how deeply in love I was until you were gone. It was like I couldn't breathe."

"I know. I tried to avoid thinking about you but I couldn't. It's like you were everywhere."

"What are we going to do?"

"What do you mean?"

"I mean, look at all the people here tonight. What if they knew we were together? It's like being between a rock and a hard place."

Avi shook his head. Alena buried her head in his chest and inhaled, breathing him in. His collar was crooked again and somehow his hair had gotten tousled, but it didn't matter. A tear streamed from her eye and stained his shirt. She sniffled deeply and wiped it away. She smiled, forcing him to smile with her.

"We better get back," she said.

"Yeah."

"Hey, you should talk to Chomsky."

"I don't think he likes me."

"Avi, you just met him. Give the man a chance. I'm sure you want to ask him questions. Come on let's go." Alena walked back to the living room where the large group broke up into smaller groups. Chomsky was talking to Edward Said and Avi stopped to stare at the two intellectual heavyweights.

XII

Avi and Alena walked back to the living room and approached Chomsky. As they approached, Avi's eyes were on Chomsky. He was unpretentious and modest. It was at that very moment that Avi realized he was standing in the presence of a historical figure.

"Professor Chomsky?" Alena interrupted. "Avi wanted to ask you a few questions." Chomsky stared at Alena and Avi, who smiled awkwardly.

"Of course, Alena."

"Come sit here, Avi." Said rose from her chair. "I need to check on dinner."

"I'm impressed with your learning, young man," Chomsky said. "Did you know that my daughter's name is Aviva? Most people call her Avi for short."

"No I didn't, Professor. Is she studying at MIT?"

"No, she's doing graduate work in history at Berkeley."

"That's great."

"Yes, we're really proud."

"I just wanted you to know that my great-uncle is a kind person. He taught me much of what I know and has always encouraged me to read as much as I could. Though he has shaped my understanding of the conflict, I still have much to learn, especially the Palestinian perspective. I think you know that Abba Eban is for a two-state solution."

"I'm sure your great-uncle is sincere in his views, but you must realize that you simply cannot equate anti-Zionism with anti-Semitism. If you do, you cover all possible cases of criticism against Israel. This process of equating the two exploits racist sentiments for political ends. Israel is no different from any other state and is subject to criticism."

"Fair enough, but what if the criticism is existentially threatening? I mean, Israel has a right to exist as any nation does."

"The term, 'right to exist', is unique to the Israeli-Palestinian conflict. No state has a right to exist and no one demands such a right. It's interesting that Israel demands that Palestinians accept their right to exist. Think about it. The Israelis are asking the Palestinians to accept the legitimacy of their own dispossession."

"I'm not sure about that." Avi looked up to see Moustafa Bayoumi and Joseph Massad with awestruck expressions. He guessed they were surprised that an undergraduate student would dare challenge Chomsky. He didn't care and continued his thought.

"Modern nation states have an inherent right to exist. In his 1882 essay, *What is a Nation,* Ernest Renan, argued that a state has a right to exist when members of a defined community are willing to sacrifice their own self-interest. In

1823, Sir Walter Scott, argued that Greece has a right to exist as a nation state. I'm sure you're aware of the Greek revolution to separate from the Ottoman Empire. Jews are members of a defined community. Many of us sacrificed our own interests for the sake of establishing our own independent state. What I'm trying to say is that there is historical precedent for a nationalism based on ethnic identity."

Avi looked away from Chomsky to see that several people had stopped what they were doing and gravitated closer to them.

"I'm glad you brought up Renan," Chomsky said. "In that very same essay you reference, Renan argued that nationalism cannot be based on religion. He goes on to say within modern nationalism one can be French, English, German, Protestant, Jewish, or atheist. You cannot base your nationalism on religious affiliation. As far as Scott defending the nationalism of Greece, you fail to mention that the Greeks have continuously lived on their land for millennia. They did not dispossess another people in order to realize nationhood."

"Okay, if you equate Jewish identity with religion, then, of course, Renan is correct when he argues that religion cannot be a component of nationalism. The problem is that being Jewish is far more nuanced than what a religious label would allow. I'm sure you know far more Jewish history than I do, so you must acknowledge that our Diaspora is something quite unique in terms of how long we suffered systematic degradation. Are the Jews a race, religion, ethnicity, community? Our identity has always been fractured, disconnected and, as the Holocaust has shown, precariously on the verge of collapse. Do you recall the concluding words to Renan's essay? He said, and I quote, 'a soul, a spiritual principle. Two things, which are really one, constitute this soul and spiritual principle. One is in the past, the other, the present. One is the possession in common of a rich trove of memories; the other is actual consent, the desire to live together, the will to continue to value the undivided, shared heritage.' This is our history: A rich trove of disjointed memories, discrimination, pogroms, endless hostility, and a deeply held desire to live together. Do you want to leave our fate in the hands of those who would use us as a convenient scapegoat? We tried assimilation. From the French Revolution to the Weimar Republic, and it was a spectacular failure."

Avi lost track of where he was and who he was talking to. He exhaled and looked at Chomsky, who looked back at him with a perplexed expression. Just then, Mariam Said approached them

"Noam, I don't think you are going to solve the conflict tonight. Dinner is ready."

They got up and went into the living room. Avi's heart was racing, but he stayed calm. Chomsky began walking and Avi touched his elbow, forcing him to turn around.

"So which is it?"

"Excuse me?" Chomsky asked, and Avi knew he had gone too far. Alena stood at the edge of the dining room, her mouth open.

"Which is it? A two-state solution or no solution? You can't have it both ways."

Chomsky glared at Avi with a mixture of objection and respect. "There are too many diplomatic factors involved now. You have two superpowers with overarching political and economic concerns. It's an impractical question, but I favor a one state, binational solution."

Mariam Said returned and waved for Chomsky to come in. He looked back at Avi and walked toward dinner. A throng of people stood around the table, and it was clear there was no seating arrangement. There was obviously not enough room to seat everyone at the main dining table. Avi noticed that the professors were going to the main dining table and the grad students were going to the breakfast table. As he walked toward the breakfast table, he heard Said call out to him.

"Avi, come sit next to me."

Avi was not sure why Said was showering him with special treatment. He also felt uncomfortable that he was taking attention away from the others. What Avi was unable to understand was that Edward Said was vastly impressed with his precocity. Said felt there was something unique about Avi. Though he defended Zionism and Israel with passion, Said sensed conflict in him.

Avi looked at the breakfast table where Alena sat. She watched him as he walked toward the dining room table and sat down. He sat next to Said and directly in front of Chomsky. Seated at the table were Spivak, Khalidi, Shelly Wanger, Mariam Said, and Grace Said. As Avi sat down, he was mesmerized by the array of food on the table. The aroma alone was heavenly. He noticed a large dish filled with rice, pine nuts, lamb, and a yogurt-like mixture sitting atop flat bread. He also noticed a dish with stuffed grape leaves and another dish with stuffed bell peppers. There was another dish that he thought he recognized as *kibbeh*, but he wasn't sure. There were also several small dishes that he couldn't identify.

Avi quickly realized this was no ordinary dinner. It was a gastronomic journey that would define the Palestinian experience for him in ways that went beyond intellectual arguments. Said served as his culinary guide.

"Do you know what this is, Avi?" Said pointed to the *mansaf*.

"I'm not sure, but it looks quite appetizing."

"Well, you are in for a treat. This is *mansaf*. It is a popular dish in Jordan and Palestine. What I love about this dish, aside from being delicious, is the communal way it is eaten. It is often served on special occasions, you know, weddings, graduations, and it is eaten by hand. I'm sure you are familiar with the stuffed grape leaves and vegetables, but do you know what this is?"

"I believe it is *kibbeh*." Kibbeh is a popular Levantine dish made of ground beef or lamb, bulghur (cracked wheat), and minced onions.

"Yes, it is. Have you had it before?"

"Yes. It was quite tasty."

"Well, wait until you try Mariam's recipe. My wife is Labanese and prepares excellent dishes."

"Thank you, Mrs. Said. It all looks amazing."

"You are quite welcome, Avi. I hope you like it."

"Do you know what these smaller dishes are?"

"Edward, let the young man eat." Mariam Said interrupted. Avi waited for the others to start eating before he picked up a plate. As the guests were eating and engaging in light conversation, Avi felt this would be a good time to ask Chomsky some personal questions.

"Professor Chomsky, I know you debated Foucault in 1971 and I'm curious as to what your impression was of him."

"I liked him better than his public persona, which was off-putting to me. He seemed to be pretentious, in the Paris style, though not as extreme as most. He seemed to be an interesting and decent person. I think Edward had a different impression than me though."

"I didn't know you met Foucault, Professor Said."

"Yes, but it was a brief encounter. It was January of 1979, I believe, and I was home preparing for a lecture when I got a telegram. As I tore the telegram, I noticed it was from Paris. I will never forget what the telegram said as I was shocked by who sent it. It said, 'you are invited by *Les Temps Modernes* to attend a seminar on peace in the Middle East on 13 and 14 March. Please respond, Simone de Beauvoir and Jean Paul Sartre.'"

"You met Sartre? This is unbelievable. I read most of his work."

Avi was fascinated by the biographical intersection of people he read about. The Palestinian-Israeli conflict faded and he was speaking to Chomsky and Said as literary figures.

"Avi, you've hardly touched your food," Grace interjected. "Don't you like it?"

"It's delicious. Thank you."

"Well, then. Eat. Don't be shy."

"I will. Thank you, Mrs. Said. Please continue, Professor Said."

"Well, at first I thought it was a joke. It took me two days to ascertain from friends in New York and Paris that the invitation was indeed genuine. I quickly responded with my unconditional acceptance. I was quite surprised at the time to get an invitation from Sartre and de Beauvoir. I mean it might as well have been an invitation from Cosima and Richard Wagner to come to Bayreuth. When I arrived in

Paris, there was a message waiting for me at the hotel I booked in the Latin Quarter. The message basically said that for security reasons, the meeting would be held at the home of Michel Foucault. The next morning, I arrived at Foucault's apartment. There were several people there, including de Beauvoir with her famous turban. As soon as we were introduced, Foucault made it clear to me that he had nothing to contribute to the seminar and would be leaving shortly. I was surprised and pleased to notice my book, *Beginnings*, on his bookshelves."

"Did you have an opportunity to talk?"

"Yes, we talked briefly. I found him to be amiable, but mysterious and aloof." What Said did not realize in 1979 was that Foucault was firmly in support of Israel. Said would learn of this in the early '90s from the French philosopher, Giles Deleuze, who was one of Foucault's closest friends. Deleuze and Foucault had a falling out over the question of Palestine, with Foucault expressing support for Israel, Deleuze for the Palestinians.

"My great-uncle told me a great deal about Foucault."

"Did Abba Eban meet him?" Said asked.

"Yes, they met in Paris, I believe in 1978. He was impressed with him, but I would have loved to meet him. It's too late now. He passed away last year, but tell me, Professor Said, what was your impression of Sartre?" Mariam Said jumped in before Said could answer.

"Avi, you are not eating. Don't you like it?"

"The food is absolutely delicious, Mrs. Said. I love the *mansaf* and the stuffed vegetables." Avi found the food to be intoxicating. He was just too excited to eat.

"Please have some more." Mariam picked up his plate and filled it with *mansaf* and stuffed vegetables.

"That's too much. Thank you."

"Meeting Sartre was quite a disappointment. Here I was waiting for one of the great intellectuals of the 20th century. I'm not sure what I imagined, but what transpired during the meeting was something altogether different. Sartre showed up well past the appointed time. You know what's interesting, Noam, I don't think I ever told you this. I actually introduced Sartre to Foucault." Before Said could continue, the table erupted in laughter, except Avi.

"What is so funny?" Avi looked at Mariam in confusion.

"Avi, Sartre and Foucault were old friends," she said. "So Edward must have been nervous."

"Yes, of course." Avi smiled and clinked his fork against his plate.

"The first thing that struck me when Sartre came in was how old and frail he looked. He was also surrounded by a retinue of people on whom he was totally dependent. As the meeting proceeded, I noticed that Sartre hardly uttered a word. When it was time to break for lunch, I was rather surprised by the elaborate and methodical affair. I mean, what would ordinarily take an hour, took us three and a half hours. It had been raining non-stop and we were transported by cabs. It was a four-course meal, so by the time we got back much of the day was wasted. I remember sitting in front of Sartre and trying repeatedly to engage him, but it was an exercise in futility. He looked disconsolate and was totally uncommunicative. It was quite a site to see. Sitting in front of me was the shadow of a man who was one of Europe's greatest intellectuals."

"When you say you tried to communicate with him, did he…I mean did he ignore you?" Avi hung on Said's story. He certainly knew how to tell a story, and Avi thoroughly enjoyed the biographical details of writers he admired. Avi was not aware that Alena was looking at him from a distance. Alena noticed that Avi was fully immersed in the conversation and was happy to see him growing more comfortable.

"It was not that he ignored me," Said continued. "But I think he might have been deaf at that point. It was quite a site to see him sitting there with egg and mayonnaise streaming haplessly down his face. By that evening, I grew tired of his silence and brazenly interrupted the meeting, insisting to hear from Sartre forthwith. What happened next was quite comical, really. Looking quite perturbed by my request that Sartre address the meeting, his handlers adjourned the meeting in order to have a consultation about letting the old man speak. It was quite a spectacle."

"Wait, I don't understand," Rashid Khalidi said. "Sartre's handlers asked to adjourn the meeting simply to have a conference to determine if he would speak or not?"

"Yes, and what made things more bizarre was the fact they informed us that Sartre would have a statement in the morning. Eagerly anticipating what he had to say, I was quite disappointed that he read a prepared statement. I mean, it was obvious that someone wrote the statement for him. I was completely disillusioned by the whole thing."

"Well, Edward, don't leave us hanging." Spivak said. "What did he have to say?"

"He spoke in platitudes. It might as well have been a Reuters dispatch. He praised Anwar Sadat for his courage. I found it remarkable that this intellectual that I admired for so many years had nothing of substance to say about the Palestinians. Let's not forget that Sartre was always a champion of the oppressed. He wrote the preface to Fanon's groundbreaking book, *The Wretched of the Earth,* but had nothing to contribute to the suffering of the Palestinian people."

"Did you respond to what he said?" Khalidi asked.

"Respond to what, Rashid? I mean this was the theater of the absurd. It was truly sad to watch this bigger than life philosopher, my hero you understand, being reduced to this. I recall an apocryphal story where Sartre traveled to Rome in the late '50's to meet Frantz Fanon, who was then dying of leukemia, and harangued him for 16 non-stop hours, until Simone made him desist. Gone forever was that Sartre who championed the oppressed."

Avi was engrossed in Said's story. He had so many questions to ask and didn't know where to begin. He decided to ask a question that had little direct reference to the conflict.

"Professor Said, I would like to ask if you or anyone else here met Heidegger."

"Why do you ask?" Said responded.

"I'm reading *Being and Time* and I'm just curious."

"How is it coming along?" Spivak asked.

"He is very difficult to read. It's as if he is reinventing a language to communicate a concept so primordial that it defies language altogether."

"I didn't meet the man," Chomsky said. "But I met someone who was close to him."

"Who would that be?" Avi asked.

"Hannah Arendt."

"This is incredible. I just finished reading her book, *Eichmann in Jerusalem*. What was she like?"

"Didn't you have a debate with her in the late sixties?" Said asked.

"Yes, I never liked her," Chomsky said. "She was arrogant and too absolutist in her views."

Avi was beginning to realize that Chomsky was not as good a storyteller as Said. Chomsky was brilliant at dissecting arguments and referencing arcane details, but was less fluid when it came to telling a story. His answers were often curt and kept the listener in suspense.

"I did not know that she knew Heidegger?"

"Wasn't it rumored that she had an affair with Heidegger?" Spivak jumped in.

"I think it was more than an affair." Chomsky responded.

"What? This is unbelievable! Arendt was Jewish and Heidegger collaborated with the Nazis." Avi was shocked at hearing this.

"Wait, what do you mean it was more than an affair, Noam?" Said asked. "From what I know and heard, she had an affair with him in the 1920's, but it ended before he joined the Nazis."

"There is evidence emerging that she corresponded with him and may have seen him long after the war." Chomsky spoke with calmness, but seemed surprised by the reaction of everyone at the table.

"What evidence?" Rashid Khalidi asked.

"Elzbieta Ettinger, who teaches literature at MIT, informed me that she came across some of the correspondence between them. I believe she might be planning a book on their relationship."

"Did they correspond after the war?" Avi asked. He found this revelation difficult to comprehend.

"I believe they corresponded until his death in 1976." The details of the Arendt-Heidegger relationship would fill several books in the years to come. In 1924, a young and impressionable Hannah Arendt was taking a course on Plato at the University of Marburg. Heidegger at the time was 35, married with two children, and working on his book, *Being and Time,* which would elevate him into the rarefied circle of philosophical immortality. It was Heidegger who initiated the affair, which would last a couple of years. In 1933, in what would be her last letter until after the war, Arendt wrote to Heidegger complaining that she heard he was barring Jews from his seminars and refusing to speak to other Jewish professors. Although he would deny these allegations, the truth was far more disturbing. It was during 1933, when Hitler seized power, that Heidegger joined the Nazi party. He banned all Jewish professors, including his mentor, Edmund Husserl, whom he replaced as rector of the University of Freiburg, from setting foot on the university campus.

The evidence that would later emerge painted a portrait of someone with strong anti-Semitic leanings, coupled with the personal ambition of becoming the leading philosopher of the Nazi regime. After the war, Heidegger tried to paint an exculpatory picture of his time as rector, but the evidence was simply overwhelming. Shortly after the war, Arendt wrote a letter to her good friend and mentor, Karl Jaspers, referring to Heidegger as a potential murderer in the death of Husserl. This, of course, would all change in 1950, when Arendt reunited with Heidegger and forgave him everything. The love between Hannah Arendt and Martin Heidegger can be described as poetic tragedy.

This sounded familiar to Avi. What he couldn't have realized was that his love for Alena would be tragic in ways he could not yet comprehend. For now, Avi was blissfully enjoying his time at Said's apartment. The dinner and rich conversation would continue late into the night. These and countless other memories would be burned into Avi's consciousness. His perspective on the conflict would slowly begin to change. Although he would forever embrace Israel as a moral necessity, Avi would begin to experience critical epiphanies that would shape and inform his understanding of Palestinian aspirations. He would begin to realize that Arabs, Palestinians in particular, are not a monolithic group that can be reduced to generic representations. Avi would begin to doubt what he was raised to believe. The conflict was no longer a Manichean battle between the noble and virtuous Zionist cause and the backward, uncivilized Arabs whose singular aim is to drive the Jews into the sea. Such beliefs, densely layered and engrained in the imagination, would gradually bend and become malleable enough to entertain ideas that were once anathema.

His experience in New York opened him up to ideas and perspectives that were far more nuanced than the sophisticated arguments he proudly offered in defense of Israel. His love for Alena, a love that had epic overtones, would forever change his understanding of a people that had largely been maligned in the West. The conflict was no longer a struggle for moral superiority. His binary understanding of the Palestinian Israeli conflict, clearly defined and meticulously demarcated in existential terms, was about to undergo a dramatic and epiphany filled transformation. Doubt replaced his once serene and comfortable certainty. His love for Alena would be magnified and projected as love for a people who have been used as a political football by all the actors involved in the conflict, including the Arab world. The Palestinians, he would come to realize, have suffered as a result of Zionism. It would be this one singular realization, profound and yet unsettling, that fundamentally reshaped his understanding of a conflict that he once apprehended in moral absolutes. In the coming months, Avi would be fully immersed in a reality that he would look back upon as the most intense and magical moments of his life.

XIII

It was early evening and Avi was lying on his bed completely oblivious to the world around him. His dress shirt was disheveled and partly untucked, and his hair was matted to his head on one side again. His arms had lost feeling from resting over his head, but he didn't care to move them. He flinched at the sound of a knock at the door and rose up on his haunches. He knew it was David before he said anything.

"Come in."

David was composed and grim-faced as always.

"Avi, are you awake?"

"Yes, I'm just resting."

"Good. You have a phone call. I think you'll want to take this one."

"Who is it David, and why can't it wait?"

"It's Alena."

"Alena? Why is she calling?"

"She didn't say. Do you want to take the call or not?"

"Yes, I'll take it in here. Please don't have anyone enter without knocking."

Avi got up and walked to the video monitor on his desk, where he took all of his calls. He straightened his shirt and tried running his fingers through his hair before picking up. He immediately smiled when he saw Alena smiling back at him.

"Foreign Minister Said. It's good of you to call."

"Prime Minister Eban, I want to offer you my personal congratulations on winning the Nobel Prize." Alena spoke with the reserved dignity appropriate to her position. Though Alena was married, she chose to follow her mother's example and keep her maiden name. Avi, of course, was thrilled to see her. He had not seen or spoken to her in several months. He always watched her on television whenever she gave interviews, and was awestruck by her composure and command of the issues. He knew that she was destined for greatness in the new Palestine.

"Thank you, and please allow me to extend warm congratulations to President Ashrawi." Avi acted cautious and official. He hoped for a signal from her to let him know she was alone.

"She wants to congratulate you in person. Would a brief meeting tomorrow be acceptable? She is currently swamped with interviews and wanted me to tell you how proud she is of what we have been able to accomplish. Together I believe we can–"

"Could I have you hold for one second?" Avi interrupted. He could tell she was alone by the lack of voices in the room. He rose from his chair and acted as though he was ushering people out of the room.

"Of course." Alena heard the door close, which was his signal to her that he was alone.

"I'm terribly sorry, but there was too much commotion in here."

"Avi, are you trying to tell me you are alone?"

"Alena, why didn't you tell me you were alone?"

"I was not certain you were alone, Avi."

"It is so good to hear your voice. Do you have any idea which suite I'm in?"

"Avi, I need to talk to you now that you're alone.

"I'm in the Nobel suite. Doesn't that remind you of anything?"

"Yes, Avi. But I need to talk to you."

"I miss you, Alena."

"Avi, please don't do this."

"I'm sorry, but I'm still deeply in love with you. Why did you leave me? You never gave me an answer. Can you just tell me what I did wrong? Just that. That's all I want to know."

"Avi, stop."

"But I can't. I've told you. I'll never be able to–"

"No, I mean, listen. You have to get out of Oslo."

"What?"

"You have to leave. I've gotten some dangerous reports of growing unrest in the neighborhood outside your hotel. The demonstrations are growing. It's all over the news now. There's a chance the Oslo police won't be able to contain the demonstrators. They're not used to handling angry mobs."

Avi sat and stared at Alena and shook his head.

"Did David call you?"

"What? No. Look, you have to leave Oslo, right away."

"Alena, I'm not leaving without speaking at the award ceremony. You know that. I have to deliver this speech. It's for the future of our peace. It's for the future of our two-state union."

"Avi, please do this for me."

They paused and the silence overwhelmed them, haunting and fuzzy as it was amplified by the satellite connection between them. Avi watched as a tear appeared beneath her eye.

"I just…I have a horrible feeling about tomorrow. I don't want anything to happen."

"Then you should return home. I'll be fine."

Avi was quiet and heard noise from the hallway. He wondered if he was about to be interrupted.

"David knows about us."

"What? Are you serious? How?"

"He noticed how I reacted to a question about you in an interview with Anderson Cooper. He confronted me about it."

"What did you tell him?"

"I told him it was an absurd notion. I told him to drop the subject, but he would not let it go."

"Why is he so curious? I mean, it's none of his business."

"He feels hurt that I never told him."

"Are you going to tell him the truth? Avi, if this ever gets out it will create problems not only for us, but for the peace between us."

"Alena, I trust David completely. Don't worry I will not reveal anything."

"You can't give this lecture tomorrow. You just can't."

"I have to, Alena. I haven't actually prepared for it, but in a way I've been preparing for it my whole life. You know that."

"If you're going to give it, I'm going to be there."

"That's fine. I was hoping you'd be there."

"There's something I need to tell you in case I don't get a chance to talk to you again."

"What do you mean? I will see you tomorrow and we have negotiations coming up on several joint projects."

"You know what I mean, Alena. In case I don't see you alone."

"What is it?"

"I finally solved the mystery about you."

"What mystery?"

"Come on, Alena, don't you remember? For years, I've asked you *ad nauseum* why you always had a powerful psychological hold on me."

"Avi, why do you do this to yourself? This is something that happened over thirty years ago. Why can't you let it go?'

"I don't know why." Avi was tearing up.

"I'm sorry, Avi. It's just that I don't think you solved it. You were the one who told me back in 2009 that I will forever be a mystery to you. Do you remember? I told you back then to let it go. Now, tell me what you have figured out since then."

"That's just it, Alena. I have always tried to deduce an answer; to analyze the past for clues as to why I'm so deeply in love with you. For over thirty years, I've been unable to breathe. I've been intoxicated by your beauty for so long that

I don't remember what life was like before I met you. I never understood this power you have over me."

"Do you have any idea how honored I feel? I never did anything to deserve this lofty construction you have of me. I mean, you are the most brilliant man I've ever met, including my uncle."

"I'm so deeply in love with you, Alena. I just can't breathe. The answer came to me almost in a dream-like state. I've been looking for the answer in all the wrong places. I've been looking for an intellectual explanation that would make sense to me, but what I realized recently slapped me with such ferocity that everything suddenly made sense to me."

"My God, Avi. You truly have me curious now."

"Do you remember the motorcycle accident back in college?"

"Of course. How can I forget?"

"Something happened that night which sealed my fate

forever. When I–"

"Avi, we discussed the accident countless times before."

"But I did not have this memory at the time. You see, the memories I had of that night were always memories of events. What I experienced recently was an emotional memory. I was riding my motorcycle home, remember? A drunk driver hit me from behind. When I called you from the emergency room, I was frightened. Remember when I told you I had no one to call? That was not entirely true. My great-uncle gave me the phone numbers of several Jewish families to call in case of emergency. The problem, of course, was that I didn't want to call people that my mother knew. They would surely have told her, so that was out of the question. It was at that moment I realized I was alone with no one to call. I was frightened and didn't know what to do. When I found the flyer you gave me in my back pocket, I desperately wanted to call you, but didn't know how to justify it. I mean, I just met you a few hours earlier so what was I supposed to say?"

"Avi, we've gone over this before."

"I know, but the emotional memory that jolted me a few weeks ago is different from what I told you before. When you came to pick me up from the Emergency Room, something happened when I saw you. Something so profound it has haunted me ever since. Do you remember when I compared you to a Pre-Raphaelite painting?"

"When was that?"

"It was November of 1985.It was at the dinner I attended at your uncle's home. Remember, it was the first time I met Chomsky."

"I remember. You impressed the hell out of everyone, but I don't remember you mentioning Pre-Raphaelite paintings."

"On our way home together. Remember, we got into an argument earlier that day and David gave me a ride to Said's apartment. When you took me home, I told you that you remind me of Milais' The Martyr of the Solway. In fact, if my memory is correct, you told me that you've always admired that painting. I was taken aback by your knowledge of art and you said something to the effect that there is a lot I don't know about you."

"My God, how do you have such a detailed memory? I remember now. You were so disheveled that night, like you couldn't dress yourself."

"I was nervous. But that painting was burned in my subconscious long before I met you. When I was around eleven or twelve, I read Plato's *Republic* for the first time. I was also studying Pre-Raphaelite paintings. That's when I came across the Milais. I was struck by her red hair and perfect features. Her beauty seemed utterly transcendent and, as a prepubescent boy, I was smitten. She represented archetypal beauty, eternal and immutable. When I was in the Emergency Room, something happened to me. Something so profound that I have not been able to breathe for over thirty years. When you walked in, you appeared as an angel before me. You appeared as otherworldly. Maybe it was the trauma of the accident, I'm not sure. I was dizzy and disoriented when you walked in with your flowing red hair. It was at that moment that my fate was sealed. That's what I'm trying to tell you, Alena. You have always been the angel who saved me. You are the angel who descended upon me to guide me. You are the angel who taught me the value of humility. You are the angel who possessed beauty beyond this world."

Avi glanced at the screen and noticed Alena in tears. He was engrossed in his thought, and had no idea how long she had been crying.

"I have to go."

"Wait. Don't go."

"I have to go. Just... remember that your people need you. I need you. Be safe, please."

She hung up and he sat back down on the bed, falling backward completely dejected and exhausted. He fell asleep without trying.

§§§

David knocked on the door and awoke him two hours later. Avi rubbed his eyes and walked to the window. The nighttime sky around the buildings was lit by city lights. He saw hundreds of people below, shouting and carrying signs. The demonstration looked peaceful enough, but it was hard to tell from his room. He could see police lights flashing and barricades had been set up. He couldn't understand why the police hadn't moved the protesters further away from the hotel, but maybe the demonstrations weren't threatening to get out of control. Alena had grown more worrisome as she got older. Perhaps it was her maternal instinct, but she felt that Avi was in danger.

David knocked again and entered. He looked at Avi and grimaced.

"What's wrong?"

"Nothing, What do you need?"

"Clearly, you're not considering giving the lecture."

"David, I don't see the–"

Avi paused when David walked over to turn on the international news feed. Cameras showed a much different scene on the ground outside the hotel, and Avi had difficulty believing the scene on the news feed was the same one he saw from his window. Police separated the protestors, but the crowd had grown to several thousand. Some of them carried signs demanding that Avi step down immediately, claiming that the Nobel Prize was a sham. It was clear that many of them were not Norwegian, and that they must have flown thousands of miles to make a statement against Avi and the bipartisan peace process. This small, yet vocal minority, clinged to views that were no longer embraced by the vast majority of Arabs or Israelis. Avi was stunned by the sight. He hadn't even thought to turn on the news feed.

"This is happening a few hundred meters away, Avi. This is why the time is now. We can get you out the back door and no one will–" Avi shook his head and David stopped.

"David, I'm not talking about this any longer. I am delivering this speech, and that is final. How will it look if I leave now? I'm the Israeli Prime Minister, damn it! I'm not about to acquiesce to the demands of a vocal minority. They do not represent the wishes of millions of people who crave peace. We are staying here, and delivering this lecture in the name of freedom for both parties. Everything will be made clear once the lecture has been given. David, look we've been through a lot together. We've faced tougher situations before, right? This is something that I need to do, ok?"

"I understand. In that case, we should prepare for tomorrow's speech now and go over your appointments. President Obama called while you were asleep. I'm certain he wanted to congratulate you and warn you about the protests. I told him you'd call back as soon as possible."

"Thank you, David. But I don't need to prepare. I just want to be left alone."

"Avi, you've wanted to be left alone since we arrived. What the hell is wrong with you? Pull yourself together." David turned to leave before Avi called after him.

"David, wait."

"Yes?"

"Come and sit down. I have a few things to tell you."

David sat down on the corner of the bed and interlocked his fingers. He could see the strain in Avi's eyes and sensed something grave. Avi got up and turned his desk chair toward the bed, sitting down on it.

"What I'm about to tell you is between us, and between us only. It never leaves this room. First, you need to know that your suspicions about me and Alena are true. She is the love of my life and has been since our time at Columbia."

Avi told David the entire story. He explained their separation and how it consumed his life, even after all these years. Avi was exhausted after David left, and barely slept. He awoke before sunrise and began preparing for his lecture. He felt exhausted and relieved. What really mattered was that Alena would be there. Perhaps he would consider cancelling it if she said she wasn't going to make it. He smiled in spite of his fatigue as David knocked on his door early the next morning.

"How are you feeling this morning?" David asked. He had left the night before, saying that they needed to iron out a few details for the day's lecture and agenda.

"I'm much better, thanks." David sat on the corner of the unmade bed, hands on his crisp pants. He took off his glasses and rubbed his eyes.

"I just want to thank you for trusting me, Avi. I'm sure it wasn't easy." David knew the answer was to let go of her, but wasn't sure how to say so. Avi was such a prideful man. It was difficult to give him advice, even after all these years. Avi sat with a slumped posture.

"Something has to change, Avi."

"You're right. I know. This isn't fair to anyone."

"Let me ask you a question. Do you feel that she is in love with you?"

"No. I mean I did once, but I don't know about now. She is so damn mysterious and complicated."

"Avi, all women are mysterious and complicated. I mean, I don't understand my wife half the time.

Avi nodded and looked toward the window.

"There is a lot more at stake here than chasing the past." David pointed out the obvious in the hope of redirecting Avi's attention.

"Yes, you're right, of course. I need to focus here and get ready for the lecture. Fate has always worked against me and I'm tired of fighting it."

David rose from the bed and paced toward the door. He checked his phone and looked at Avi

"You have several interviews after the lecture, a meeting with President Obama, another meeting with President Ashrawi, and several phone calls to make. We also need to prepare for your acceptance speech tomorrow."

"Well, I should get ready for the lecture today. Can you send some breakfast up? I'm starving."

David left feeling relieved. He knew Avi's hunger was a sign that he was back on track. It was just in time. He left and closed the door carefully behind him. Avi thought about his lecture. He wanted to emphasize the narrative of redemptive possibilities. He was an off-the-cuff speaker. His preparation included a few note cards to avoid tangents. His impromptu style frustrated his staff, since none of them were sure what he was going to say.

XIV

At 10:15 am, it was time for Avi to make his way to the university. Yoram, David, and the rest of his security detail escorted him downstairs to his awaiting convoy. The lecture would be held in the Atrium. The Nobel Peace Prize was awarded in this very same Atrium from 1947 to 1989. The compactness of the Atrium, combined with the density of the crowd, created a security nightmare. The overflow forced university officials to project the lecture on giant monitors outside. Television cameras were everywhere filming this historic event.

Avi entered through a side door for security reasons. Israeli and Arab students chanted together and waved flags. Dignitaries from all over the world were in attendance, including former President Barack Obama, President Hillary Clinton, Hanan Ashrawi, and representatives from dozens of countries. Before the lecture, the West-Eastern Divan Youth Orchestra performed to a roaring applause. The ensemble served as a reminder of the once oceanic divide between two people who accepted their reality as inextricably linked by conflict. Their performance left Avi certain that delivering this lecture was the right thing to do. He smiled at David, who smiled back to him.

With the crowd growing restless, it was time for Avi to be introduced. Thorbjørn Jagland, the chair of the Nobel Committee, was scheduled to introduce him, but at the last minute, the king of Norway, Haakon VIII, wanted the honor.

The King lavished Avi with praise for his tireless contribution to peace. Avi took the podium to a thunderous ovation. He motioned to the crowd to take their seats, but the ovation continued. He thanked the students for coming as well as the general public. He thanked His Majesty, King Haakon VIII, for his kind and gracious introduction. He thanked the heads of state and other dignitaries. He also thanked both Israeli and Palestinian students for coming.

"Please allow me some prefatory remarks. The kind ovation you have given me should be directed toward President Hanan Ashrawi of Palestine for her courage, wisdom, and implacable determination to achieve peace."

The audience stood up and applauded at once before Avi could continue. President Ashrawi rose to acknowledge the crowd and bowed toward Avi in appreciation.

"I also want to thank the foreign minister of Palestine for her tireless work toward peace. It was her uncle's dream to realize a just and enduring peace for the Palestinian people. We all, both Palestinians and Israelis, owe Edward Said a ton of gratitude. Ladies and gentlemen, Alena Said." The crowd once again erupted in thunderous applause. Alena did not stand up to acknowledge them, partly due to her desire to avoid the limelight.

"This peace that we are celebrating today was a century in the making. It is clear even today that not everyone is engaged in this process. The ongoing demonstrations outside this building are a reminder that not everyone is committed to a prosperous peace between Israel and Palestine. Unfortunately, the road to peace is an arduous one, full of acts of tragedy. But those devoted to peace will be rewarded with prosperity. This prosperity has been built on the backs of brave people who labored on both sides of this conflict. It is as a result of the tireless efforts of those brave souls that millions will live in peaceful harmony in the years to come."

The assembled crowd cheered at his words, and Avi realized for the first time that the room was charged with hopes for the future and concerns about the present. The true gravity of the moment energized him, and he allowed himself to scan the room before settling on Alena's proud eyes.

"I have lectured a great deal throughout my academic career," he continued. "On a conflict that seemed to many of us to be insoluble, intractable, and insurmountable. The topic for my talk today is redemptive possibilities. I want to take this opportunity to tell the Palestinian people in unmistakable language that we Israelis acknowledge the role we played in your dispossession. As Prime Minister of Israel, I also want to offer my deepest apology for our contribution to Palestinian suffering."

The audience erupted in applause again, which turned into another standing ovation. Many of the Palestinians and Arabs in attendance were visibly moved. The Israeli students seemed equally moved.

"Let me talk briefly about the Holocaust. It was this singular outburst of madness, an aberration beyond human comprehension, that contributed to the collective trauma of Jews everywhere. Throughout our Diaspora, our fate remained in the hands of others. Our scattering left us vulnerable and fractured.

"For centuries our existential direction was a schizophrenic trajectory of trying to assimilate into a culture that simply did not want us while simultaneously dreaming of a redemptive return to Jerusalem. We lived as a marginalized people looking for absolution that would not come. We lived a history punctuated by extraordinary intellectual production as well as the grotesquery of savage treatment. Wherever we ended up in Europe, we were treated as the paradigmatic other. We were convenient targets, focal points, if you will, of ignorance and hatred. Our education and passion for knowledge allowed some of us to reach exalted states of learning, only to be brought down to size for our accomplishments. Our psyche was fractured and we banded together as a people defined by our otherness. When the nihilistic nature of German madness was projected onto a defenseless people, the collective trauma would create in us a blind and absolute affirmation of never again. Never again would we leave our fate in the hands of others. Never again would we accept a subaltern status. Never again would we experience the concentrated brutality of so called enlightened cultures."

Avi spoke in short bursts of declarative sentences. His voice rising and the audience was mesmerized by the force of his lecture style. As Alena heard him speak, an avalanche of memories crashed down upon her. Tears trickled down her cheeks as the memories overwhelmed her. Avi would always tell her that her voice sounded like a symphony in his mind, but he couldn't have realized the power his voice had over her.

"You see, ladies and gentlemen. It was this trauma, singular in its sustained capacity to scar us for generations, that clouded our ethical judgment. For many Jews, Israel became our existential salvation, our redemption from the cold wilderness of naked terror, our ancestral protection from the whims of those who tolerated us when it was convenient, and raped our collective psyche when it suited their warped nature. We felt that we had the moral high ground when it came to Israel. We defended Israel with every fiber of our being. We used sophisticated arguments to legitimize the sanctity of Israel. We told the world that we were going to transform a barren desert into a land of milk and honey. We told the world the refugees that resulted in our war for independence should be absorbed by the Arab nations that attacked us. There is only one problem with this narrative: it was a mythology.

"Just as individuals must undergo a coming-of-age experience, so too must cultures. I, myself had to undergo a profound transformation of thought and perspective. I had to come to terms with the damage inflicted on an innocent people by the ideas and actions of Zionism. When Zionism was formed in the late 19th century, though noble in its intentions, the existing population in Palestine was seen as a burdensome detail that had to be dealt with. Herzl and other Zionist leaders were Western in cultural orientation, and perceived the Arab world through the Orientalist lens that Edward Said so eloquently described. Here is the profound and disturbing irony, ladies and gentlemen. We Jews, who were reduced to a subaltern other and wholly removed from the universe of cultural acceptance, turned around and stripped the Palestinian people of their humanity.

"People often ask me how I, as the Prime Minister of Israel, could speak such words. It's simple. I tell them it is the truth. It is this psychological transformation that we Israelis had to navigate both collectively and individually in order to realize an enduring peace. This lecture that I've been asked to give is not so much an academic exercise, but a confessional. It is a confessional that accepts responsibility for our own moral shortcomings. As difficult as it was to confront this ethical dilemma, it had to be done in an honest and methodical manner. I've been asked in countless interviews about my own transformative experience. I would often say it was a natural evolution of a man plagued with doubt about the moral absoluteness of the Zionist position. Some have suggested that Edward Said and Noam Chomsky had a powerful influence on my thinking. While there is no doubt that both impacted my thinking, the transformation came from someone else."

Alena froze at the thought that he might mention her again. She tried to motion to him with her hand to let him know that she didn't want to be mentioned in this way. Once was more than enough. She didn't want the attention and the fallout. She remembered Avi telling her back in 2009 that one day the whole world would know how special she was, that she and she alone changed his perspective on the conflict. It was too late. Avi was determined to tell the world what she meant to his own evolution of thought.

"This person is not only an intellectual whom I deeply respect and admire. This person has been a tireless advocate of peace between our people. Without this person, I would probably still be spewing sophisticated arguments and the creation of Palestine would still be a distant dream. This person taught me the value of humility, the–"

Avi paused for a moment, leading to encouraging applause. It was clear to all that he was growing emotional, and had to work to maintain his composure.

"She taught me the meaning and value of acknowledging mistakes to your enemy. She showed me the human dimension of a conflict that I largely ignored as a young man. Today, I not only respect the Palestinian people as a result of this person, but I have grown to love and admire the Palestinian people."

The audience once again rose in thunderous applause. Though Alena didn't want him to mention her, she was in tears listening to him.

"Ladies and gentlemen, I want to reveal to you who this person is. I'm deeply proud and honored to acknowledge Foreign Minister, Alena Said, for her–"

The crowd exploded in thunderous applause before he could finish. Alena was in tears and President Ashrawi, who sat next to her, told her to stand up and acknowledge the standing ovation. Cameras focused on Alena as she wiped away her tears.

"Thank you, Foreign Minister Said, for your compassion. Thank you for your wisdom and guidance during the lengthy negotiations. Thank you for your patience in allowing me to evolve and appreciate the Palestinian struggle for statehood. Thank you for not only acknowledging Israel, but also for accepting us as friends. Both Israelis and Palestinians owe you a debt of gratitude. I want to now tell you why this talk was billed as a lecture. You see, I wanted to open for a Q &A session. I have been known to lecture for hours and in the process put people to sleep."

Laughter cascaded from the back of the room.

"The media has always dominated this area of asking questions, and perhaps rightly so, but I want to give the students here an opportunity to ask questions."

This spontaneous gesture infuriated Yoram, as it compromised security. Yoram walked quickly to the podium, but Avi shooed him away. David was also unsettled, but he was accustomed to Avi acting on a whim. Dozens of students raised their hands at once.

"Yes, over there in the back."

"Mr. Prime Minister, I'm Palestinian and I never thought I would ever say this, but it is an honor to be able to ask you a question. I want to know when your transformation occurred concerning the Palestinian people."

"First of all, I want you to know it is an honor for me to be here and I thank you for your kind sentiment. My transformation was a gradual evolution of thought and emotions. Let me quote Kierkegaard. 'Life can only be understood backwards; but it can only be lived forwards.' I've always liked that quote. At one time, I was an arrogant and narcissistic young man. I believed in my intellectual capacity to penetrate any topic, to engage in philosophical conversation. To all you young people in the audience, I want you to listen carefully. Intellect alone will not solve the problems of the world. It was when I first tasted Palestinian food that I started to develop an emotional reaction to the conflict."

The audience erupted in applause.

"It's true, thanks to Foreign Minister Said, I was fortunate to have a gastronomic experience, which I remember to this day as a turning point. What I'm trying to say is that my transformation occurred over time. What saved me was–"

Avi caught himself before he went too far. He took several more questions before concluding his talk. He was surprised at the insight of many of them, and spoke much longer than anyone expected. After the lecture was over, his security took him to a private room where he would greet the many dignitaries who attended. He was exhausted by the time his security team was ready to escort Avi to the car.

Yoram was uncomfortable with the crowd waiting for the prime minister to depart. There were thousands of people celebrating and chanting his name. Many waited to get a glimpse of the Prime Minister. Some hoped to get close enough to get an autograph. Avi's car was waiting just a few meters from the side door. The crowd erupted when Avi emerged. Several members of his security detail surrounded him as he walked to the car. Avi waived to the crowd to acknowledge them. Yoram yelled for Avi to move faster. David was waiting in the car with the doors open. Avi was a couple of meters from the car and Yoram was beginning to breathe a sigh of relief.

Suddenly, several shots were heard. Pandemonium broke out and everyone scattered. Screams fell upon them. Yoram instinctively hugged the prime minister and ducked, pushing him toward the car. He yelled for his men to clear a path. It was not clear where the shots came from, and the security team scrambled to locate the shooter. Cameras were rolling and the incident was being televised live. Once Yoram shoved Avi inside the car, he yelled at the driver to move. Oslo University Hospital was only a few minutes away.

"Sir, are you alright?"

"What happened?" Avi asked weakly. David was sitting on the other side of the prime minister and saw blood on Avi's cheek and inside his jacket.

"He's shot! Oh God!" David screamed. Yoram spoke calmly into his radio, directing his crew to establish a security perimeter around the hospital. He asked David to help take Avi's jacket off.

"We need to stop the bleeding," he said. Avi slumped against David. A bright red circle was growing on his chest, darkening his light blue shirt. David balled his jacket and pressed it against his chest.

"Hang on, Avi," David said. "We're almost at the hospital, Stay with me!"

"Step on it!" Yoram yelled at the driver.

§§§

The story broke on every major news outlet within seconds. Alena was on her way to an interview when she was alerted. Her initial reaction was shock. Her mind could not grasp the thought. A few seconds later, she yelled at her driver to stop the car. She uttered a sound that was inaudible to the others in the car. She started crying and asking why. She sat in the car repeating the question. She quickly grew hysterical. Her security insisted that the car move to a safe location. Alena asked to be taken to the hospital. She wanted to run to Avi, to be with him during this darkest of hours. In the midst of her panic, her phone rang. It was President Ashrawi.

"Alena, where are you?"

"I don't know! I don't know! I asked them to stop the car. Why? Why did this have to happen?"

"Alena, listen to me. We don't even know if he was hit. All we know is that shots were fired. You need to compose yourself and act like a leader. This is no time for you to fall apart. I know about you and Avi, but you must be strong."

Hanan Ashrawi knew for some time about Alena and Avi. She saw them in Paris back in 2009, but never said a word. She saw them stare at each other during the negotiations. She knew through Edward Said that both were deeply in love while at Columbia. What Hanan did not realize was the emotional depth of Alena's feelings for Avi. Her love for him was so powerful that it threatened to tear her world apart.

"I don't care that you know. I don't care if the whole world knows." Alena was yelling on the phone. She was incoherent. It's as if she snapped and there was no way to contain her.

"Alena, I'm begging you to calm down. The whole world is watching and we can't add fire to the situation. You are a married woman and the foreign minister of Palestine. You are going to give the tabloids everything they want and more. As we speak, Twitter has exploded with conspiracy theories and accusations, and you know that Palestinians will be the prime suspects. I'm in contact with Israeli officials and they promised me frequent updates. I have to return to Ramallah for security reasons. Alena, are you listening to me?"

"Yes, I hear you, but I…I need to see him."

"Alena, you will not be able to see him. Please return to the hotel and wait for further instructions." Her driver accelerated when she got off the phone.

"Take me to the hospital! I'm ordering you to take me to the hospital!"

"I'm sorry, foreign minister. But I have orders." Alena frantically redialed Hanan, and screamed into the phone.

"Hanan, please let me go see him. I need to be with him. Please! I'm begging you."

"I can't let you do that, Alena. You are not thinking straight." President Ashrawi was quite shocked by Alena's reaction. Alena opened the car door while it was moving. She wanted to jump out and run to him. One of the security men immediately pulled her in and hugged her.

"Alena, what the hell are you doing? Have you lost your mind? This is not love. This is madness, my dear. Look, please go to the hotel and stay there until you hear from me."

Alena fell into a deep silence. She felt like a prisoner of culture and an unwitting participant in fate's cruel design.

Avi's car pulled up to the hospital with medical personnel waiting with a gurney. He was quickly rushed inside to a secure location. The doctors found a gunshot wound to the side of his head, another entry wound under his clavicle, and a third one through his abdomen. Avi was losing consciousness, and the doctors had to immediately rush him to surgery. The doctors were in surgery for several hours. David sat quietly alone, perfectly still the entire time. Yoram came and went occasionally. No one else could enter the room for security reasons. No one else in Oslo had clearance, and so David waited quietly. Finally, Dr. Anders Bjornsen emerged through the swinging door with a look of resignation.

"He had a bullet lodged in the temporal lobe and we took it out. He also had a bullet that was several millimeters from his heart, and another one in his liver. We removed them as well."

"Will he make it?"

"He is in a coma."

"What does that mean? Will he recover?"

"It is difficult to tell with a coma. He may recover in a few hours, days, or…I'm sorry, I will have an update for you in a few hours. The media is waiting for a word. I think you need to address them. My team of surgeons will be with you to answer any medical questions."

David accepted the challenge with stubborn resolve. There were dozens of things to take care of. He had to update his government on the situation, update heads of state, many of whom were in Oslo, and inform the media. The future of Israel was suddenly in flux. After informing his government of Avi's condition, an emergency cabinet meeting selected Foreign Minister Dalia Rabin-Pelossof, the late Yitzhak Rabin's daughter, as acting Prime Minister.

Meanwhile, the search for the gunman continued and speculation ran rampant. Many were already pointing a finger at Palestinian groups vocally objecting to the peace treaty. Others felt it might be a radical right-wing Orthodox

Jew opposed to the creation of Palestine. The Nobel Committee met in an emergency session to discuss the ceremony scheduled for tomorrow.

The good news was that Avi exhibited measurable brain activity. His private inner experience was intact. The boundary between dreams and reality was indistinguishable and he wanted to return to Columbia. As his consciousness temporally shifted back in time, he was unsure if he was actually visiting the past or his memory was guiding him. Avi felt a sense of serenity and an inner calm. There was no pain and reality appeared for the first time to be welcoming and seductive. He felt himself being pushed back to a different time, a time of innocence and magical moments. His flashbacks were racing with movie trailer speed. He did not feel he was in control. Finally, the cinema reel slowed down and he found himself back in 1986. He couldn't focus on an image just yet, but the sounds and smells flooded back to him. He was in Alena's car going to school.

Part IV

Demons

XV

It was January, 1986 and Avi was fully immersed in his studies. He established a comfortable routine with Alena. She would pick him up each morning to go to school and take him home in the evenings. These were the magical moments that would haunt him throughout his life. Alena would often invite Avi home to have lunch or dinner with her family. Alena's mother embraced him with love and compassion. The debate between Avi's great-uncle and Edward Said was fast-approaching by then. Remarkably, the Saids seemed to embrace Avi more in anticipation of the intellectual exchange, as though Avi was becoming part of their family. This made Avi grow more excited about his great-uncle's arrival, and the prospects for a groundbreaking debate between the two great men.

Avi grew to feel at home eating Arabic food. Grace often prepared Lebanese and Egyptian food, which Avi enjoyed. He particularly enjoyed *molokheya,* an Arabic dish quite popular in Egypt, but enjoyed by many other Arab countries. *Molokheya* was a green leaf vegetable of the *chorcorus* species. It was prepared by removing the central spine from the leaves and chopping the leaves into a fine paste. The paste was added to chicken or beef broth with sautéed garlic and coriander. The resulting dish was a viscous soup that could be poured over rice and eaten with chicken or lamb.

As Avi immersed himself in Alena's life and, by extension, Palestinian life, his ideas about the conflict slowly evolved. He began to view the conflict not as a struggle between the righteous longing of the Jews to have a uniquely Jewish state, but more as a struggle between two people desperately fighting for a land they perceived as their legitimate home. Avi began to question the historical truths he lived by. He questioned his political and moral convictions. It was something as simple and yet infinitely complex as love that forced him to reexamine the Israeli perspective.

It was Monday, January 13th, and Avi was busy writing two major papers. Alena needed his help with a paper on Plato's *Theory of Knowledge*. She told her mother she would be up all night studying at the library. It was 10 pm, and she decided to drive to Avi's apartment to study.

She knocked and he smiled gratefully when he saw her. She came in and dropped her books on his kitchen table. Avi could tell she was overwhelmed by her classes.

"I better make us some coffee," Avi said.

"Avi, you put on some music and I'll make us the coffee. Where did you put the Turkish coffee I got you last time?"

"It's in the cupboard above the stove." Avi put on *Cherish* by Kool and the Gang and sat down on the couch.

Avi quickly felt himself intoxicated by the aroma of coffee and seeing her in his apartment. It felt as if he was in a dream, unable or unwilling to wake up.

"Avi, if you keep playing *Cherish* over and over you'll wear the cassette out."

"We should order something. What are you in the mood for?"

"We're not ordering anything. I will prepare us something to eat, but first we must study."

"Why does it feel like we're married?"

"Avi, are you proposing to me?"

"Oh dear God. It would be a dream come true to marry you."

"Avi, I thought you didn't believe in God."

"With you, I can believe in God, heaven, and unicorns."

"Aren't you the romantic one tonight?"

Avi approached her as Kool and the Gang played in the background. He wrapped his arm around her and kissed her neck. Alena moved her head back and breathed deeply.

"Avi, what are you doing to me?"

"I am so deeply in love with you that I can't think straight. All my learning, all my studies did not prepare me for this."

Alena turned around and they embraced for an eternity. It felt to Avi as if they both exited space and time altogether.

"Can we go into your bedroom?" Alena whispered.

"You have no idea how I've longed to hear you say that."

He had never kissed a woman the way he kissed Alena, and she had never been kissed so slowly and with such care. He carefully undressed her and kissed her an inch at a time, until he unbuttoned her pants and pulled them down. He had been naked with a woman before, but he never felt as intimate with anyone as he did at this moment. She clearly felt the same way, and he knew somehow that nothing that happened between them could be wrong. She matched his intensity and they held each other with intense passion.

The experience of making love to the woman of his dreams was far more intense than he envisioned. Making love to Alena for the first time produced a physical reaction that would never leave him. The experience was so intense that he became dizzy. Her natural scent was intoxicating, and her taste was sweeter than anything he could have imagined. When they were done, Alena wrapped herself in Avi's arms. Suddenly, she jumped out of bed and ran toward the kitchen. She was still naked as he watched her scamper out of his room.

"The coffee! Oh God, I bet it's burned." She had forgotten to turn the stove off and the coffee spilled all over the stove top. "I'm so sorry, Avi, I forgot to turn the stove off. I'll clean it up."

"Alena, you will do no such thing. Please sit down and relax."

"You're so sweet. Let me get dressed and I'll make us coffee without burning it."

"It's entirely my fault, Alena. I was the one who interrupted you."

"Hey, that's right. It is your fault." Alena laughed. She never felt more comfortable with anyone. She was deeply in love with an Israeli and didn't care about the consequences.

After Avi cleaned the stove, Alena made coffee and they sat down to get some work done. Avi marveled at how she cared for him. She loved taking care of him, and doing so made her think about marriage.

"Avi, I want to ask you a question."

"Sure, what is it?"

"Do you think you and I could possibly get married one day?"

"I don't know. Are you proposing?"

"Avi, I'm being serious."

"Alena, I'm deeply in love with you. To live one lifetime with you is not enough. I love every second I spend with you. It's difficult to explain, but there's something about you I don't want to ever be without. Sometimes I feel the fate of the Palestinian-Israeli conflict will somehow involve us. Perhaps a marriage between Abba Eban's great-nephew and Edwards Said's niece would move us closer to a Palestinian state.

Alena nodded. A contented glow consumed her.

"You want to hear something bizarre, Alena? I'm not just falling in love with you. I'm also beginning to care about the Palestinian people."

Avi sat next to Alena on the couch, caressing her hair. Alena nestled her head into Avi's shoulder.

"You know that people are openly talking about us now," she said.

"Yes, I know. Some of the Jewish groups on campus are calling me a traitor."

"What do you think? Does that bother you?"

"They can go to hell. I don't care what they say."

"Don't worry. I'm getting similar reactions from the Arabs on campus. It's probably going to get harder this week, with the debate upcoming. Have you told your mother about us yet?

"Yes, of course, I did." Avi lied to Alena. He had not mentioned her and was unsure how to tell his mother. He lied to avoid making her feel more nervous than she already was. He knew this was going to be a major problem this week when Abba Eban arrives. He had no idea how to tell his family, and knew his mother would take it the worst.

"My Uncle Eli is excited to meet you. He gets here tomorrow."

"Avi, I'm nervous about the debate this Saturday. I mean are we going to sit next to each other?"

"Of course, we'll sit next to each other. We can show everyone that peace is possible. I know it sounds naïve, but you have taught me it takes more than fancy arguments to understand the conflict. I'm truly indebted to you for opening my eyes."

"I heard the debate will be held at Havemeyer Hall, Room 309."

"I know, but I don't think it will accommodate everyone. The buildup to the debate is unlike anything I've ever seen. It seems everyone is talking about it. The news media will cover it and I hear people from as far away as Boston will be coming."

"Okay, Avi. Let's not kid ourselves. Who will you be supporting in the debate."

"I honestly don't know, Alena. I love my great-uncle and I think he is an eloquent speaker, but I'm not sure how he will do against Said. I'm sure he will put the same arguments I've put forth in the past. He is a man set in his ways and I'm not sure he will be persuaded. I've had disagreements with him on the phone and he tells me that I'm young and don't fully understand what is at stake. The only problem is that I'm beginning to understand what is at stake. Our survival is inextricably linked to Palestinian statehood. The longer we wait, the more settlements the Israelis build, the harder it is to forge a lasting peace."

"My God, Avi. Do you remember just three months ago you were passionately defending Israel. How did that change so fast?"

"I fell in love." Avi smiled and caressed Alena's face.

"I'm serious, Avi. What made you change your perspective?"

"I'm serious, Alena. It was you. It was entirely as a result of your love that I started to see the conflict from a different perspective. Look, you know that I will defend Israel until my dying breath, but I also want to see a Palestinian state. We Israelis are so damn busy defending our right to exist that we fail to notice the suffering of the Palestinian people."

"You're a special person, Avi. I'm deeply in love with you. Look at me. You're all that I think about now." Alena held his face and kissed Avi with such tenderness that it brought tears to his eyes.

"You cannot possibly know how I feel about you, Alena. I don't even understand it. There is something about you."

"Avi you keep saying that. What is it about me?' Alena wiped away his tears.

"I'm so attracted to you on so many levels. I'm attracted to your intellect. I'm attracted to your stunning beauty. I'm attracted to your body. I'm deeply in love with you, but there is something else and I don't know what it is. One day I'll figure it out."

"Avi, it's getting late and we should study. Are you going to help me with my paper on Plato?"

"I will if I get a kiss."

"Avi, please be serious. I need to finish this paper by tomorrow."

"Alena, I can finish it for you in an hour. Don't worry."

"Avi, I don't want you to do it for me. I want you to help me understand Plato so I can write it myself."

"Very well, Plato's Allegory of the Cave is found in Book VII of the Republic. Plato uses the Allegory to elaborate on his Divided Line Theory."

Alena sat erectly next to him, smiling widely. "Avi, you are too much. Who are you? My God. Please keep going. I love listening to you."

They adjourned to the kitchen table. They spent the night together. It was a night Alena would never forget. He helped her finish her Plato paper and they slept for a few hours before the sun rose and classes started. Avi was curious to see how Alena would look when she woke up. He knew people looked very different first thing in the morning. He divided people according to this morning ritual: those who look radiant and adorable and those who are not to be seen. Avi knew he was in the latter group. He hated allowing people to see him this way. Alena awoke next to him, looking like a red-haired angel. She smiled and curled into him, and he dreaded the idea of getting out of bed.

"Avi, what time is it?" she asked. She turned to him and gasped. "Oh God, please don't look at me. Why are you staring at me? I must look atrocious." She turned away from him, so that the sun pouring through his open curtains shone on her back. He playfully fingered the notches of her spine.

"You look beautiful."

"Avi, what do you mean? I must look horrid."

"You look like an angel to me." Avi caressed Alena's hair and smiled. It was at that moment that Avi knew he could never fall out of love with her.

"Avi, I assure you I do not. We better get ready for class."

§§§

Eli Eban arrived that afternoon and met Avi at his apartment. Avi was very happy to see him and excited to break the news about Alena. He felt it would be easier to talk to Eli before his mother arrived. Eli was only nine years older than Avi, making him feel more like an older brother than uncle.

"I'm very happy to see you, Avi." Eli set his suitcase down and hugged his nephew. He smiled widely and pulled off a scarf. "I've been hearing great things about you."

"I'm taking 24 units, which keeps me busy. How is the Israel Philharmonic going?"

"I'm truly enjoying it. I'm playing and recording the entire major orchestral repertoire. Our conductor, Daniel Barenboim, is traveling with me. He wanted to see the debate. So tell me how is your piano playing coming along?"

"I hardly play anymore. I've been so busy with my studies. Where are my manners? Let me prepare some tea. I'm afraid I don't have any crumpets to offer."

"Hmm, tea and crumpets. You do have your great-uncle's British manners. Avi, you don't have to be formal with me. Tea is fine."

"Why are you staying in a hotel? I mean, you can certainly stay here."

"I would love to, but I don't think there is enough space with my father and your mother staying here."

"Yes, but…I suppose you're right." Avi walked to the kitchen and put a teapot on the stove.

"So tell me. How do you like New York? It's your first time here and the city can be overwhelming."

"It was at first, but I got used to it quickly."

"How do you like Columbia? Are you fitting in? You know it is a hotbed of Arab-Israeli animosity."

"Actually, the Arabs I met here are not what I thought. I have conversations with them and they are quite civil. We may not agree on everything, but we are not shouting at each other."

"I hear you're taking a course with Said. What do you think of him?"

"I know you like milk with your tea, Eli, but I'm out."

"It's perfectly fine, Avi. Come sit down so we can catch up." Eli sat down on the couch in the very spot where Alena sat on so many occasions. Avi walked over and sat down on the chair. The curtains were closed and the room was darkened. It was strange seeing someone so familiar in a different place, and it seemed to transform his apartment into a foreign land.

"I actually like Said. He's not what I expected at all."

"I'm sure he is aware of your brilliance by now."

"I don't know about that, but I feel he likes me. I actually had dinner at his house a couple of months ago."

"How did you manage that?"

"Eli, I have to talk to you about something. I'm not sure how to say it."

"Well, just come out with it."

"You see, it's just that. I–"

"Avi, what is it? You're making me nervous."

"I fell in love with a girl here at Columbia."

"Is that all? My God, you had me worried for a minute. So who is she? I bet she comes from a nice family."

"Eli, you don't understand. It's far more complicated than that."

"I think I understand. She's not Jewish, is she? I don't think your mother will be happy."

"I wish it was that simple."

"Avi, I don't understand. Who is she?"

"She is Edward Said's niece."

"What? You're kidding, right? Avi, this is insane. Your mother will never agree to it. You know that. How did this happen? Why didn't you say anything?"

"I didn't know how. What did you want me to tell her? 'Hello, mother. I fell in love with a Palestinian girl.'"

"How did this happen?"

"It's a long story."

"We have plenty of time."

"Shortly after I arrived, I bought a motorcycle."

"What? Did you tell your mother about the motorcycle?"

"Heavens no, she would have been frantic. Eli, do you forget that I had a motorcycle in Israel."

"Riding a motorcycle in Israel is different than in New York. Go on. What happened next?"

"Well, I got into an accident. Some drunk driver hit me from behind. I was taken to the Emergency Room and–" Avi proceeded to tell Eli about that fateful night. He told him about Alena's kindness and the help she offered him. Eli sat erectly on the edge of the couch.

"Avi, listen to me. You don't have to persuade me. I'm sure she's a wonderful girl, though I think you are exaggerating a bit about her beauty. Look, she is your first love, right?"

"Yes, and I'm not exaggerating about her beauty. You'll meet her soon and you decide. I'm so in love with her I can't think straight."

"You do realize this will crush your mother. Avi, you are brilliant. Your mother, uncle, and the whole family have such hopes for you."

"I'm sick to death of being labeled as brilliant. Do you realize the pressure I have? I don't want it anymore. I never wanted it. I just want to be normal, like everyone else."

"You've never been just like everyone else. I remember when you were eleven or twelve reading Plato and Aristotle. I think you're intelligent enough to know that the extraordinary gift you have comes with responsibility. Look, I know you are in love, but what you have is an idealistic kind of love."

Avi got up and poured Eli a cup of tea. It was clear it was going to take a while to understand how to tell his mother. He was grateful Eli had arrived a couple of days early. They talked throughout the night. The romantic idealism that he was experiencing was going to be tested. His mother and great uncle arrive Thursday. Avi did not want to break the news to them just yet. He also asked Eli not to mention it. Avi only hoped that once he introduced them to Alena, they would see for themselves how beautiful she is and accept her.

XVI

It was Saturday morning, and Avi was working on the debate with his uncle at the kitchen table. The topic for the debate was Zionism: Nationalism or Colonialism. Abba Eban was upset by the title, but agreed to go ahead with the debate, partly to satisfy Avi. His mother was in the kitchen preparing breakfast. Avi was anxious to help his great-uncle refine his debate topic, but his thoughts gravitated to Alena.

"Are you going to mention that the Arabs should absorb the refugees?" Avi asked with some concern. His great-uncle was not yet aware that Avi's views were gradually changing.

"Well, the Arabs did attack us in 1948 and again in 1967. They created the refugee problem. The Arabs have a vast amount of land that could comfortably absorb the refugees."

"They are known as Palestinians. Why can't you refer to them as Palestinians?"

"You seem upset. What's wrong, Avi?"

"Nothing, it's just that I'm hoping you emphasize the need for a Palestinian state."

"There is something different about you, Avi. Is there something you want to tell us?"

"Uncle Solomon," his mother said. "Let the boy be." Avi's mother was accustomed to calling Abba Eban, by his middle name. Abba Eban was born Aubrey Solomon Meir Eban. In 1947, while serving as a liaison officer to the United Nations Special Committee on Palestine, where he succeeded in the effort to approve partition for Palestine, he decided to change his name to the Hebrew word, *Abba,* meaning father. While one might think this title to be self-centered, it was an apt description of a man who played a pivotal role in the founding of Israel.

"Breakfast is ready. Avi, I made your favorite omelet."

Avi's mother, Ayala Eban, was born and raised in England. While studying literature in England, Ayala fell in love with a dashing young man by the name of Meir Eban, Abba Eban's nephew. They married before Ayala could finish her studies. Ayala invested all her hopes and dreams in Avi, her only son. Avi's love for his mother was otherworldly, and he would do anything to make her happy. He knew this love was going to be put to the test.

"Avi, are you alright? You've been rather distant since we've arrived. How are your studies?"

"I'm fine, mama. I've just had a lot on my mind. I'm taking on too many units."

"Avi, I've never heard you complain about your academic load before. Something is amiss. Is it the big city? I never cared for New York." His mother walked over and kissed him on the forehead. "Come along, you two. You need to eat something. Avi, go call the security men outside to come in and eat something."

In 1985, at the age of 70, Abba Eban served as Chair of the Knesset's Foreign Affairs and Defense Committee. As a member of the Knesset and former Foreign Minister, he was given a small security detail whenever he travelled.

"Ayala, leave the men alone. They're doing their job."

"They must be hungry. Very well. You and Avi must come and eat. Avi what time is the debate?"

"It's at 1 pm. We must hurry up and eat if we are to make it on time."

"We have plenty of time, Avi. Why are you in such a hurry?"

"I suppose you're right, mama. I'm just a bit anxious."

"There is nothing to be anxious about, Avi. We have the moral high ground in this debate."

"What if the Palestinians have the moral high ground? We are the ones in power. We are the ones who.... Oh never mind."

"What's gotten into you, Avi? Is this what happens when you take one course from Said?"

"You always taught me to be open-minded and to listen, remember? Of course we have a moral claim, but the Palestinians also have a moral claim."

"Avi, many of these so-called Palestinians would have us thrown into the sea if they could." His mother was growing agitated by Avi's sympathy toward the Arabs.

"This is simply not true, mama. The Palestinians simply want to be treated with respect and dignity. Have we not learned anything from our own victimization? We took their land, mother. We, the sophisticated and enlightened Zionists, took the land of the Palestinian people and then turned around in a self-righteous tone and labeled them as terrorists."

"Avi, what's gotten into you? What has this university done to you?" His mother stood over him with her hands on her hips. Her posture and tone reminded him of his childhood. It was a feeling he hadn't had in many years. She was clearly dismayed by her son's transformation. She looked to Abba Eban.

"This is why I didn't want to send him off to New York."

"Ayala, this is just a phase." Abba Ebban looked at Avi with displeasure.

"Look, I'm sorry to upset both of you like this. Let's talk about something else. Tell me how is everyone back home, mama."

"Everyone is fine, Avi. They are all asking about you. Do you remember Hadasah?"

"Hadasah Goldberg?"

"She's a good girl, Avi, and comes from a good family. Her father is the deputy foreign minister now."

"Mother, I haven't even finished my undergraduate studies and you want me to get married?"

"I'm not suggesting you get married right away. Can you blame a mother for wanting the best for her son? I just want you to be happy, Avi. She gave him a kiss on the top of his head.

"We should get ready if we are to make the debate on time."

"It's only 11:30," said Abba Eban.

"There is a small reception for uncle to attend. The president of Columbia wants to greet him. Professor Said also wants to meet both of you prior to the debate."

"Did you arrange all this, Avi?" his mother asked with pride.

"Actually, a couple of the Jewish organizations on campus planned this and the Arab groups also contributed as well. It was professor Said who asked to meet both of you."

"There is no need for all this fuss, Avi," said Abba Eban, who never cared for social attention.

"Nonsense. You are the elder statesman of Israel and you shall be accorded the respect of your position. You see, uncle, you completely misunderstood what I was trying to say. I'm simply hoping that you stress the need to have a Palestinian state. That's all."

"Avi, I've always advocated a two-state solution. You know that. As I've said many times, the Arabs never miss an opportunity to miss an opportunity."

§§§

It was 12:30 by the time Avi and his family arrived on campus. Avi took his great-uncle and mother to a reception room in Havemeyer Hall, where President Michael Sovern and dozens of professors and graduate students waited to greet him. Avi noticed Alena from a distance and excused himself to go talk to her.

"Hi, Avi. God I missed you." She pulled her hair behind her ears and smiled. She was hugging a binder full of flyers for the debate.

"I missed you, too, Alena."

"I didn't know Abba Eban was so tall." As Avi was talking to Alena, Eli showed up and approached them. He smiled and nudged Avi, who turned to him.

"Eli, it's so good of you to make it. This is Alena Said. Alena, this is my Uncle Eli."

"When Avi told me about you, he didn't do your beauty justice."

"Thank you. That's very nice of you to say."

"Is Edward Said coming to this reception? I would love to meet him."

"He should be here shortly. Is Abba Eban your uncle?"

"Actually, he is my father."

"I see. Are you in politics as well?"

"Eli is a musician," Avi said. "He's with the Israeli Philharmonic."

"Really? What instrument do you play?"

"I play the clarinet. The conductor for the Israeli Philharmonic is here and he would love to meet Edward Said."

"I will make sure that he gets to meet him." Alena turned to Avi and smiled.

"Great. Thanks. I will be over there with Daniel Barenboim." Eli pointed to a corner in the reception room, where the conductor stood talking to someone. Alena watched him walk away and turned to Avi.

"So, Avi, when do I get to meet your mother?" Avi could tell that Alena was nervous. She looked around the room as though trying to pick her out from the crowd.

"Let me introduce you right now. Come on."

"Avi, wait. I'm really nervous."

"There's nothing to be nervous about. I'm sure you will make a great impression."

"Could we take a walk outside for a bit?"

"Of course. Is everything alright?"

"Oh, yes. It's just that I'm a bit anxious about meeting your mother." Avi held out his elbow and Alena hugged it. They walked outside arm in arm, where they found themselves alone.

"Nothing to be anxious about, Alena. I assure you. Did you see how Eli reacted to you? He was shocked by your beauty."

"He seemed very down to earth."

"He's my favorite uncle."

"Avi, I want you to know something. I'm deeply in love with you. I'm afraid that meeting your family will change things."

"Oh, Alena. Don't worry. It won't change anything. Look at me! I adore you, Alena Said. I love you in such a way that I cannot easily explain. There is something about you, something otherworldly and transcendent. I'm not sure what it is, but you haunt my every waking thought." Avi wanted to hug her and closed his eyes for a moment.

"Avi, there are people all around us."

He smiled and held her eyes with his. She turned just then and Avi saw Edward Said approach them. A retinue of professors and graduate students walked with him.

"Should we say hello or go back in?" Avi asked.

"Too late. He saw us. Let's say hello and go inside."

"Hi, Uncle Edward. This is going to be a memorable debate."

"Alena, how are you?" Edward Said hugged his niece and turned to Avi. "And it's good to see you, Avi. Are you going to introduce me to Abba Eban?"

"Of course, Professor Said. It would be my pleasure." They began walking inside but Alena didn't budge.

"Alena, aren't you coming?" Said asked.

"You go on ahead. I have to take care of some last minute details." She held up her binder, as though showing him evidence. "I will see you inside in a few minutes."

Avi walked back to the reception room with Said and the others. He found Abba Eban and his mother talking with President Sovern and several faculty members. There were also several members of the media present and cameras were rolling everywhere.

"Uncle, please allow me to introduce Professor Edward Said." The two great men shook hands firmly. They stood in a tight circle.

"Ah, Professor Said. It is a pleasure to meet you," Abba Eban said. "How is Avi doing in your class?"

"The pleasure is mine. Your great-nephew is a brilliant student, as I'm sure you know. You must be proud."

"Professor Said, this is my mother." Avi interjected.

"It is very nice to meet you, Professor Said. Avi speaks very highly of you."

"Thank you. He's one of my brightest students."

"I hope our discussion will contribute to a better understanding between our people," said Abba Eban. "I've always maintained that Israel needs to establish a context in the Middle East."

"I do hope the context you speak of will result in the acknowledgment of Palestinian aspirations," Said countered. Avi noticed Alena watching from a distance. She wanted to approach them and introduce herself, but she stood there frozen in place, unable to move. As she stood there, Eli noticed her and decided to bring Daniel Barenboim in the hopes of meeting Said.

"Hello, Alena. Please allow me to introduce Daniel Barenboim."

"It's very nice to meet you, Mr. Barenboim."

"The pleasure is mine. You are Edward Said's niece?"

"Yes, I am. Oh right, you would like to meet him, of course."

"If it is not too much trouble."

"Oh, God. No trouble at all." Alena approached Edward Said and waved to him to let him know she needed a minute.

"Uncle Edward, I would like to introduce you to Abba Eban's son, Eli."

"It is a pleasure to meet you, Professor Said. I found *Orientalism* to be quite fascinating."

"It's very nice to meet you. I'm glad Israelis are reading my book."

"Professor Said, please allow me to introduce the conductor of the Israeli Philharmonic Orchestra, Daniel Barenboim."

"It's a pleasure to meet you, Professor Said. I've wanted to meet you for some time."

"The pleasure is mine. Perhaps it will be music that will bring us together."

Little did Edward Said or Barenboim know at the time that they would become the best of friends. Said and Barenboim would form the West-Eastern Divan Orchestra in 1999 and would go on to coauthor the book, *Parallels and Paradoxes,* which explored certain political and social parallels to music. In 2005, Barenboim would give the Edward Said Memorial Lecture at Columbia University. These and other cultural exchanges would serve as necessary building blocks for the eventual peace to come, but for now, both sides were cautiously talking to each other.

"I've heard a great deal about your musical abilities. Do you agree that music transcends politics, ideology, and other barriers that keep people apart?" Barenboim asked.

President Sovern interrupted as Said and Barenboim became lost in conversation.

"Edward, I believe we should enter the lecture hall."

"Yes, of course. Michael this is Daniel Barenboim. He is the conductor for the Israeli Philharmonic Orchestra. We've been having the most interesting conversation about music."

"It's a pleasure to meet you, Mr. Barenboim. We should really get to the lecture hall." The lecture hall was full beyond capacity, with tiered seating and mahogany chairs. A balcony overlooked the proceedings, and hundreds of students clamored in the aisles to find room. Several thousand watched the debate outside Havemeyer Hall. The president took to the podium to introduce the speakers. He asked the students sitting in the aisles to watch the debate outside. Avi gave his mother and Eli third row seats and he sat in the first row with Alena.

XVII

"Thank you, President Sovern, for the kind introduction," began Professor Said. "I also want to thank my distinguished colleague, Abba Eban, for agreeing to participate in this discussion. While it is tempting to label this event as a debate, I want to think of this conversation as an honest exchange of ideas between two people who find themselves on opposite sides of a conflict that has left bitter memories, violent confrontation, deeply engrained hatred that is imprinted on our collective consciousness, as well as a host of exigent demands and counter-demands that never seem to amount to much.

The topic for today's discussion is Zionism: Nationalism or Colonialism. Before I deal with this topic, I must tell you that I've never been entirely comfortable with topics that are framed in terms of their binary outcome. That is to say, I don't care for questions that require mutually exclusive answers. In my book, *The Question of Palestine,* I've discussed Zionism at length. In one section of the book, Zionism from the Standpoint of its Victims, a section that somehow gets lost in the conversation, I discuss Zionism from a Jewish perspective. One simply cannot dismiss the power of Zionism as an idea for Jews. We cannot minimize the complex set of forces that characterize and animate Zionism, its true meaning, and messianic message."

You must realize that, for an Arab, any attempt at an honest discussion of Zionism is rather a difficult matter.

Much of my education and intellectual orientation is Western. In what I've read, in what I have written about, in my politics, I have been profoundly influenced by Western attitudes toward Jewish history, anti-Semitism, as well as the destruction of European Jewry. Unlike most Arab intellectuals, most of whom obviously have not had my background, I have been immersed in those aspects of Jewish history and experience that have mattered singularly for Jews and Western non-Jews. Let me also say that I know as well as any educated non-Jew can know what anti-Semitism has meant for Jews, especially as it culminated in the horror of the Holocaust. This understanding allows me to appreciate the intertwined terror and exultation out of which Zionism has been nourished. What I'm trying to say is that I think I could grasp the meaning of Israel for Jews as well as any enlightened Western liberal.

All that I've said thus far is valid and genuinely felt, but, alas, I'm not exclusively a product of the Western intellectual tradition. I'm also a Palestinian Arab who sees and feels other things that complicate matters considerably. It is my Palestinian identity that compels me to focus on Zionism's other aspects. It is this other reality; a reality that I think is worth describing, not because what I think is crucial, but because it is useful to see the same phenomenon in two complimentary ways that are not normally associated with each other. It is these complimentary ways that are critical here. One is either a Zionist and views Zionism from a Jewish lens or appreciates Zionism from a Western perspective, or one is anti-Zionist and looks upon it as the victim of its accomplishments.

Let me discuss Zionism as an idea. Ideas in general, or if you like, system of ideas are shaped by circumstances and are apprehended as reality. An idealist would tell us that ideas exist in the realm of ideas, as abstractions that are essentially perfect, good, and uncontaminated by human desire or will. This view also applies when ideas are considered to be evil, absolutely perfect in their evil. Those ideas that have gained widespread acceptance begin to take on some of the characteristics of brute reality. Zionism, for all its political tribulations and struggles, is an immutable idea that expresses the yearning for Jewish political and religious self-determination, for Jewish national statehood, to be exercised on the Promised Land. The fact that Zionism as an idea culminated in the creation of the state of Israel would have many argue, and quite effectively I might add, that the historical realization of the idea confirms its unchanging essence.

Israel, of course, is a story of remarkable political and cultural achievements. Quite apart from its spectacular military successes, Israel is a subject, at least in the West, where one can feel positive. Israel is looked upon as a triumphant story of overcoming extraordinary odds. Together, Zionism and Israel produced a prevailing view of the question of Palestine that almost totally favors the victor. The only problem with this narrative is that it leaves out the victims. To the Palestinian, for whom Zionism was somebody else's idea imported into Palestine and for which in a very concrete way he or she was made to pay and suffer, these forgotten things about Zionism are the very things that are centrally important.

Let me pose some fundamental questions from the standpoint of the victims of Zionism. What did the victim, in this case the Palestinian, feel as he watched the Zionists arriving in Palestine? What does he think as he watches Zionism described today? Where does he look in Zionism's history to locate its roots? These are the questions that are never asked. I will attempt to answer these questions and many more by examining the links between Zionism and imperialism. What I want to explore this afternoon is the far reaching impact Zionism had on Palestinians. Antonio Gramsci's observations are relevant here; that the consciousness of what one really is…is knowing thyself as a product of the historical process to date which has deposited an infinity of traces, without leaving an inventory. The process of producing an inventory is a first necessity, Gramsci reminds us, and it is this inventory of what Zionism's victims endured that is rarely exposed to public view.

Imperialism was and continues to be a political philosophy whose purpose is territorial expansion and its legitimization is imaginative geography. Gaining and holding *an imperium* means gaining and holding a domain, which includes a variety of operations, among them constituting an area, accumulating its inhabitants, having power over its ideas, people, and of course, its land. Laying claim to an idea and laying claim to a territory-given the extraordinarily current idea that the non-European world was there to be claimed, occupied, and ruled by Europe-were considered to be different sides of the same, essentially constitutive activity, which has the force, the prestige, and the authority of science. In multiple knowledge domains such as biology, philology, and geology, the scientific consciousness was principally a reconstituting, restoring, and transforming activity turning old friends into new ones, the link between an outright imperialist attitude towards distant lands in the Orient and a scientific attitude to the inequalities of race was that both attitudes depended on the European will, on the determining force necessary to change confusing or useless realities into an orderly, disciplined set of new classifications useful to Europe.

The imperialist found it useful to incorporate the credible and seemingly unimpeachable wisdom of science to create a racial classification to be used in the appropriation and organization of lesser cultures. The works of Carolus Linnaeus, Georges Buffon, and Georges Cuvier, organized races in terms of a civilized us and a paradigmatic other. The other was uncivilized, barbaric, and wholly lower than the advanced races of Europe. This paradigm of imaginatively constructing a world predicated upon race was grounded in science, and expressed as philosophical axioms by John Locke and David Hume, offered compelling justification that Europe always ought to rule non-Europeans. This doctrine of cultural superiority had a direct bearing on Zionist practice and vision in Palestine.

A civilized man, it was believed, could cultivate the land because it meant something to him; on it, accordingly, he produced useful arts and crafts, he created, he accomplished, he built. For uncivilized people, land was either farmed badly or it was left to rot. This was imperialism as theory and colonialism was the practice of changing the uselessly unoccupied territories of the world into useful new versions of Europe. It was this epistemic framework that shaped and informed Zionist attitudes towards the Arab Palestinian natives. This is the intellectual background that Zionism emerged from. Zionism saw Palestine through the same prism as the European did, as an empty territory paradoxically filled with ignoble or, better yet, dispensable natives. It allied itself, as Chaim Weizmann said, with the imperial powers in carrying out its plans for establishing a Jewish state in Palestine.

The so-called natives did not take well to the idea of Jewish colonizers in Palestine. As the Zionist historians, Yehoshua Porath and Neville Mandel, have empirically shown, the ideas of Jewish colonizers in Palestine, this was well before World War I, were always met with resistance, not because the natives thought Jews were evil, but because most natives do not take kindly to having their territory settled by foreigners. Zionism not only accepted the unflattering and generic concepts of European culture, it also banked on the fact that Palestine was actually populated not by an advanced civilization, but by a backward people, over which it ought to be dominated. Zionism, therefore, developed with a unique consciousness of itself, but with little or nothing left over for the unfortunate natives. In fact, I would go so far as to say that if Palestine had been occupied by one of the well-established industrialized nations that ruled the world, then the problem of displacing German, French, or English inhabitants and introducing a new, nationally coherent element into the middle of their homeland would have been in the forefront of the consciousness of even the most ignorant and destitute Zionists.

In short, all the constitutive energies of Zionism were premised on the excluded presence, that is, the functional absence of native people in Palestine; institutions were built deliberately shutting out the natives, laws were drafted when Israel came into being that made sure the natives would remain in their non-place, Jews in theirs, and so on. It is no wonder that today the one issue that electrifies Israel as a society is the problem of the Palestinians, whose negation is the consistent thread running through Zionism. And it is this perhaps unfortunate aspect of Zionism that ties it ineluctably to imperialism- at least so far as the Palestinian is concerned. In conclusion, I cannot affirm that Zionism is colonialism, but I can tell you the process by which Zionism flourished; the dialectic under which it became a reality was heavily influenced by the imperialist mindset of Europe. Thank you."

Edward Said ended his lecture to thunderous applause. Discernible boos also cascaded from the back of the audience. Avi's mother turned to Eli.

"Eli, who is that girl sitting with Avi?"

"I'm not sure. I think she's Edward Said's niece."

"She can't be Palestinian, can she? Are you sure, Eli? She has red hair. She's beautiful."

"Why isn't Avi sitting with us or with the Jewish groups on campus?"

"I don't know. Maybe you should ask Avi."

"What do you mean?"

"I don't know. Ask him."

"I'm asking you, Eli. You've been spending time with him. What do you know?'

"I think he has feelings for her. That's all I know."

"That's all I needed to know." His mother's face was stricken as Abba Eban approached the podium. The lecture hall reverberated with applause, but she stared into the back of a stranger in front of her.

"Thank you, President Sovern for your kind introduction. I also want to thank the faculty and students of Columbia for making this event possible. I wish to thank my distinguished colleague, Professor Edward Said, for agreeing to this lively exchange. I agree with Professor Said in that I don't think of this discussion as a debate. I would much rather think of it as an exchange of ideas between two people who perceive two seemingly contradictory realities. I must also tell you that I appreciate Professor Said's open and honest portrayal of Zionism in terms of its meaning to Jews. In this spirit of esprit de corps, I would like to say that I'm in favor of a two state solution: A Palestinian state and a Jewish state living side-by-side in peace and harmony. The topic, however, is a more abstract one – namely is Zionism nationalism or colonialism?

Here I must disagree with my distinguished colleague and affirm that Zionism is a Jewish national movement whose aim has always been to provide a Jewish national home. Professor Said has graciously stated that Zionism has experienced spectacular success, but whatever success Zionism achieved pales in comparison to the unimaginable horror of the Holocaust. Six million of our people were senselessly slaughtered as the world stood by. Perhaps the number, six million, is so large that it becomes an abstraction and, therefore, difficult to comprehend. How does one confront the magnitude and horror of this aberration? How does one deal with the fact that nearly all of European Jewry was wiped out? How do you process such evil? How do you make sense of the unimaginable nightmare that scarred and injured a people for centuries to come?

Professor Said informed you that he is a product of Western culture. He also stated that not many Arab intellectuals can appreciate what Zionism means to Jews. Let me also say that I, too, am a product of the Western intellectual tradition. Not to put too fine a point on it, my way of thinking about the world, the analytical structure of my mind, as well as my emotional sensibility is Western in nature. However, as Professor Said pointed out, I as a Jew am not exclusively Western in terms of how I see the world. I see other things, to borrow my distinguished colleague's phraseology, and I feel other things. I filter the world through a rich prism filled with thousands of years of Jewish history. Allow me to say a few words about what it means to be Jewish.

My identity as Jewish cannot be reduced to a religious affiliation. Professor Said quoted Gramsci, an author that I'm familiar with, that, and I quote, 'to know thyself is to understand that we are a product of the historical process to date which has deposited an infinity of traces, without leaving an inventory'. Let's apply this pithy observation to Jewish identity. While it is tempting to equate Judaism with Jewishness, I submit to you that my identity as someone who is Jewish is far more complex than my religious affiliation. The collective inventory of the Jewish people rests on my shoulders. This inventory shapes and defines my understanding of what it means to be Jewish. The narrative of my people is a story of extraordinary achievement as well as unimaginable horror.

For millennia, the Jewish people have left their fate in the hands of others. Our history is filled with extraordinary achievements as well as unimaginable violence. Our centuries-long Diaspora defined our existential identity in ways that cannot be reduced to simple labels. It was the portability of our religion that bound us together as a people, but it was our struggle to fit in; to be accepted that identified us as unique. Despite the fact that we excelled academically, professionally, industrially, we were never looked upon as anything other than Jewish. Professor Said in his book, Orientalism, examined how Europe looked upon the Orient as a dehumanized sea of amorphous otherness. If we accept this point of view, then my question is: How do you explain Western attitudes towards the Jews? We have always been a convenient object of hatred and violent retribution whenever it became convenient.

If Europe reduced the Orient to an essentialist other, to borrow Professor Said's eloquent language, then how do we explain the dehumanizing treatment of Jews who lived in the heart of Europe? We did not live in a distant, exotic land where the West had discursive power over us. We thought of ourselves as assimilated. We studied Western philosophy, literature, music, and internalized the same culture as our dominant Christian brethren. Despite our contribution to every conceivable field of human endeavor, we were never fully accepted as equals. On the contrary, we were always the first to be blamed for the ills of Western Europe. Two hundred thousand Jews were forcibly removed from Spain in 1492 and thousands more were forcibly converted to Christianity in Portugal four years later.

By the time we get to the Holocaust, our worst fears were realized. Jewish history and consciousness will be dominated by the traumatic memories of this unspeakable event. No people in history have undergone an experience of such violence and depth. Israel's obsession with physical security; the sharp Jewish reaction to movements of discrimination and prejudice; an intoxicated awareness of life, not as something to be taken for granted but as a treasure to be fostered and nourished with eager vitality, a residual distrust of what lies beyond the Jewish wall, a mystical belief in the undying forces of Jewish history, which ensure survival when all appears lost; all these, together with the intimacy of more personal pains and agonies, are the legacy which the Holocaust transmits to the generation of Jews who have grown up under its shadow.

Our situation at the end of World War II was as follows: we were wallowing in the fearful anguish of the Holocaust; the visual effects of the Holocaust had an effect that went far beyond the mere statistical enumeration of the victims. Our promised homeland was being assailed by regional violence and by international alienation. The victorious powers, the three of the them – the United States, Britain, and the Soviet Union – showed no intention whatever, at first, of recognizing the Jews of Palestine as a political reality. There wasn't a single ray of light on the horizon. The Jewish representatives at the United Nations conference in San Francisco were humiliatingly seated in some distant balcony, looking down at the fifty member nations, none of which had made anything like the sacrifices demanded of the Jewish people by its own martyrdom. That was the situation. Two years later – *just two years* – the gates were opened; masses of our kinsmen were coming back to their national home. The war of survival had been won, and our flag was aloft in its own name and pride. And there has never been, I believe, in the history of any nation, a transformation of fortune as abrupt and as speedy and as providential as that which the Jewish people had in that period, during the first two years of its existence.

Let me say a few words about the Arab-Israeli hostility. It is too easy, too simplistic to reduce the hostility to the colonial-settler argument. We are not a colonial-settler people. We did not have a power center in Europe from which to exploit other land and other people. Let me go so far as to say that I regard the hostility of the Arabs to Israel as deterministic inevitability. In a way, because there was no way in which the Jews, after their trials and ordeals, could renounce the idea of Jewish statehood, and there was no way in which the Arabs could possibly accept the Israeli demand for statehood. In other words, this was not a tragedy of choice; it was a tragedy of compulsion. It was really a Greek tragedy in that sense that what the Jews had to insist upon was something which the Arabs could not possibly accept.

Let me turn my attention to the idea that Zionists forcibly took land away from the Palestinian people. When the early Zionists found their way to Palestine prior to World War I, there was no such thing as a Palestinian identity. The entire region from Damascus to Lebanon, Palestine to Iraq, was controlled by the Ottoman Empire. Now I am not saying that the Palestinians are a manufactured people. I'm simply saying there was no nationalistic consciousness for the Zionists to engage. Early Zionists dealt with the reality of empires. It did not matter which empire would help us secure Palestine as a Jewish national home. Theodore Herzl, who was indeed Western in his orientation, negotiated with anyone who would help the Jews settle in Palestine.

In 1898, Herzl traveled to Palestine and Istanbul to meet with Kaiser Wilhelm II of Germany and the Sultan of the Ottoman Empire. Kaiser Wilhelm refused to commit to backing a Jewish national home and the Sultan, who offered Jews other areas in the empire on the condition that we become Ottoman subjects, was unwilling to give up Palestine. It was a result of these failures that Herzl turned his attention towards securing a temporary home for the Jews in Uganda and Argentina. This move proved to be controversial within the Zionist movement and eventually abandoned. In 1904, Chaim Weizmann, my mentor, settled in England and quickly worked towards securing a Jewish national home. Lord Arthur Balfour, who was at the time the Prime Minister of the United Kingdom, informed Dr. Weizmann to accept the Uganda plan. It was only as a result of our concentrated lobbying efforts that we were able to secure the Balfour Declaration."

Abba Eban proceeded to give a detailed history of Zionism and the establishment of Israel. He spoke eloquently and forcibly. When he was done, the audience gave him a thunderous ovation. Though he argued for a two-state solution, Avi was hoping for him to acknowledge some of the transgressions of Zionism. What Avi was not aware of at the time was that Abba Eban went out of his way to strike a conciliatory tone.

The exchange between Said and Eban continued for another hour. Following the event, a reception was held for the speakers and invited guests. Avi noticed his mother sitting with Eli. He suggested to Alena that it was time to meet his mother Avi was nervous as they walked over. He could not have known that Alena was terrified. She followed him stiffly before stopping altogether.

"Avi, can we do this another time? This isn't right."

"Don't be silly, Alena, you'll be fine. She's really a kind person." Avi grabbed her hand and squeezed it. He dragged her, almost forcibly, toward his family. His mother and uncle turned and smiled when they saw him approach.

Avi was relieved to see his mother smiling.

"Mother, I would like you to meet, Alena Said. She is Edward Said's niece."

"Hello, Alena. It is very nice to meet you. My, but you are beautiful! I've never met a Palestinian with such beautiful red hair."

"It's very nice to meet you, Mrs. Eban." Alena extended her hand and Avi's mother grasped it. "I hope this exchange can bring our people together."

Alena could see that Avi's mother was examining her thoroughly. Although she clearly saw Alena's beauty, she dismissed her outright as unsuitable for Avi.

"I'm an eternal optimist, so I hold the same hopes. Your uncle is quite an eloquent speaker. I was impressed."

"Thank you, and Abba Eban is equally impressive. Now I see where Avi gets his accent." Avi's mother glared at Alena, who felt herself moldering under her gaze.

"So, mother, did you enjoy the debate?" Avi asked, interrupting the silence between them.

"Oh yes, I did, Avi." She caressed Avi's face with the back of her hand, smiling proudly.

"Avi, when will you be visiting? We all miss you back home. Hadasah has been asking about you."

"Who is Hadasah?" Alena looked at Avi curiously. It

was at that moment that Alena knew his mother didn't approve. She soldiered on, even though she wanted no part of the remainder of this conversation.

"Hadasah is a good friend of the family," Avi's mother interjected. "Avi and Hadasah practically grew up together. Isn't that right, Avi?"

"I think my uncle is calling me," Alena said, looking over Avi's shoulder. "Would you excuse me? It was very nice to meet you, Mrs. Eban."

Alena walked away stiffly. She felt rejected and insulted by Avi's mother. She disappeared into the crowd. Avi turned to his mother, who glared at him with a self-satisfied smile.

"Mother, why did you insult her like that? She is a sweet girl and she's been so kind to me. Did you know I was in a motorcycle accident when I arrived here?"

"What? Why didn't you call us? Since when do you keep secrets from your mother?"

"I didn't want you to worry. Mother, you're missing the point. Do you know who came to pick me up from the Emergency Room? She did. She didn't even know who I was, but she came to help out a complete stranger."

"Why didn't you call the Greenbergs?"

"Mother, I don't appreciate what you did to her. It's not fair to her or me. I'm in love with Alena. Can you understand that?"

"Avi, she is simply not the one for you. I'm your mother, Avi, and you are my one and only precious child." Avi's mother started tearing up.

"I know that, mother. But why did you have to treat her this way?"

"I don't know why. I wanted her to know that you can't possibly be serious about her." She stared into the ground for a moment in thought. She looked up at Avi, trying to compose herself. "Well, I'm feeling a bit tired. Can we go home now?"

"I need to talk to Alena," Avi said, turning to his uncle who just walked up. "Eli, can you take mother home? I'll return with uncle a little later."

"Sure, Avi. Don't worry, I will talk to your mother. I think Alena is a lovely girl."

Avi knew that this was the pivotal moment of his relationship with Alena. It was clear that his mother would never accept her. He was confused, hurt, and saddened. He turned away from his family to look for Alena. He did not know what he was going to say to her. He felt embarrassed and ashamed. Though he adored his mother, Avi had never seen this possessive side of her. Avi noticed Alena with some of her friends and decided he didn't care anymore. He approached her without thinking about them, or his family, or anyone in the world but her.

"Hello, Alena. May I talk to you for a second?"

Alena smiled at Avi. "Sure." They walked to a corner of the lecture hall's vestibule, surrounded by strangers.

"I'm so sorry, Alena. I didn't expect this from her at all. Please forgive me."

"My God, Avi. You didn't do anything wrong. Why are you apologizing? It's perfectly fine. She's protective of you. You can't blame a mother for that."

"No, Alena. She was rude and insensitive. I am…I'm so sorry." Avi felt tears surging within. He didn't know how to react, or what to say. He feared that Alena would never look at him the same way.

"Let's not talk about it anymore," Alena said. Her eyes lit up at thinking about her uncle and Abba Eban, of watching the two great men sitting shoulder to shoulder with Avi. "What did you think of the debate? I was surprised by Abba Eban. He is very eloquent."

"Alena, you're changing the subject. I know you pretty well, you know. You're upset and hurt by what my mother said."

"Avi there's nothing I can do about it. Your mother will never accept a Palestinian as a daughter-in-law. She would not even accept me as your girlfriend."

"Alena, you are not my girlfriend."

"Oh, really. So what am I to you?"

"You are the love of my life. I'm so in love with you, it's crazy."

"Avi, you better go." She looked over Avi's shoulder. "Your uncle is looking for you."

"Would you like to meet him?"

"'Maybe another time."

"Can I call you tomorrow?"

"Of course. Take care of yourself." Alena spoke as if she was saying a final farewell. It was at that moment that Alena realized there could be no future with Avi. Her love for him was deeper than anything she had felt before, but she also knew nothing would come of it. Her future seemed uncertain. The love between them was too idealistic and Alena knew she would never be accepted. It was a matter of time before things changed.

XVIII

Avi floated in that interstitial space between life and death, his mind wandering rapidly between eras of his life. He found himself in January, 1987. He resisted the haunting memories awaiting him there, but he was a mere passenger on this mental train. He felt as if his life was on trial and couldn't stop the prosecutorial elements of his guilt. The images from that dark period of his life were growing further into focus now. He was suddenly at a gathering held for him at Edward Said's home. Avi was transferring to Harvard, and Alena decided to throw him a farewell party.

As far as everyone was concerned, Avi had an opportunity to attend one of the premier colleges in the world. What no one knew, of course, was that Avi engineered his exit so as to avoid an awkward separation. He knew his family, especially his mother, would never accept Alena. He was simply afraid to confide to Alena about his fears and doubts. He was not strong enough to fight for the love of his life. Alena, of course, was not surprised that Avi was leaving. She was deeply hurt that Avi did not fight for her. She often felt that perhaps there was something wrong with her; that she wasn't good enough for his family. When Avi submitted his transfer application, he told Alena that he simply wanted to see if Harvard would accept him. Throughout its long and distinguished history, Harvard rarely accepted transfer students and mid-year transfers were unheard of.

When Avi was accepted into Harvard, he knew he found his ticket out of New York. Though he was deeply in love with Alena, he didn't want to disappoint his family. He lacked the maturity that would allow him to confront others about his love for a Palestinian girl. He was confident that if he left New York, he would eventually forget about Alena. He tried to rationalize his cowardly actions by convincing himself that the memory of his first love would naturally recede and that time would heal his guilt. His master plan was to convince Alena that a long-distance relationship was possible. After all, Boston was only a four hour drive from New York. Avi promised Alena they would see each other on weekends and holidays.

For her part, Alena sensed that Avi was hiding something. She sensed that Avi had changed. He always seemed preoccupied. Whenever talk of marriage came up, Avi would try to avoid the subject. Though Avi would profess his love for Alena, something was different about the way he said it. He avoided conversations about the future and had stopped telling her he loved her. Alena always enjoyed those quiet moments with Avi where they dreamed of a utopian world, where Palestinians and Israelis would find an enduring peace and lasting friendship. The realization of such dreams was decades away, but for now Avi was distant and removed from his immediate reality. It was at his farewell party that Avi began to feel the full weight of his actions. As Avi stood next to Alena, Edward Said approached.

"Avi, can I talk to you for a minute?"

"Of course, Professor." They walked over to two chairs in the living room, the same two chairs where Avi once saw Said and Chomsky debating the validity of a two-state union.

"Why are you leaving, Avi? I know you told me that Harvard is a chance of a lifetime. Ordinarily, I would agree with you. I did my graduate work there and it was the most intellectual stimulation I had as a student. I want to know if there is another reason."

Avi could tell that Said was suspicions. He noticed Alena was not the same since the debate with Abba Eban. Said suspected that something happened between them, and Avi's sudden departure was proof.

"I'm not sure what you're talking about. I simply wanted to try and see if I could get into Harvard."

"But is everything alright between you and Alena. Whenever I talk to her lately, she seems distant, not at all like herself."

"May I tell you something, Professor? I think you've known this for some time. I'm deeply in love with her. She is the kindest person I've ever met. It was entirely because of her that my views on the conflict have changed. Intellectually, I owe you a ton of gratitude, but in terms of the human dimension of the conflict, I owe it all to Alena."

"Tell me something, Avi. If that is the case, and I do believe you, why are you leaving? What are you running from? Could it be that your mother does not approve of Alena, and you found a way to escape the situation?"

Avi felt his heart racing. He didn't understand how Said could know so much about them.

"Good heavens! No… It's just that this is a once in a lifetime opportunity."

"I see. Well, I wish you all the best. Please write me and tell me how you are getting on."

"I can't thank you enough for all your help, Professor Said. You've influenced my intellectual direction so much."

Avi was drowning in guilt. He looked as if he was in a daze as he rose from the chair. Alena walked in the living room at that moment to check on him.

"What are you two talking about?"

"I'm just giving Avi some advice about Harvard. I think he's trying to follow in my footsteps."

"Well, can I steal him away for a few minutes?' Alena smiled calmly. She projected serenity throughout the previous months, but deep down she feared she would never see Avi again. She didn't want anyone to see her broken heart. Though she went along with Avi's charade about calling each other and weekend visits, she knew it was over. She had too much pride to confront him. What hurt most was the fact that Avi wouldn't confide in her.

Avi got up and approached Alena, who snaked her arm around his elbow and leaned into him.

"What did my uncle want to talk to you about?"

"He just offered some advice about Harvard."

"Well, there are people who want to say goodbye to you."

"Is it possible to have a few minutes alone?"

"Sure, give me a minute to let the others know. Wait on the balcony for me."

"Yes, of course, don't be long."

Part of him wanted to cancel the transfer to Harvard. He felt lost and confused. He loved his mother and could not bring himself to disappoint her. He was afraid his cowardly response to love would haunt him for the rest of his life. Fear was at the heart of this betrayal. It was the kind of fear that could trap someone into an unalterable course of action. He didn't know how to confront his mother in an honest and mature manner. He didn't know how to talk to Alena about his fears and doubts. He stood on the balcony thinking of the two women in his life and his inability to be honest with either of them.

Avi couldn't have known his choice to leave New York would define his life forever. He thought Alena would simply recede into distant memory. Only his arrogance would have him believe that he could overcome this unpleasant experience. He used his intellect to mask his fear.

However, he knew intellect could be a convenient tool to wield in order to avoid the emotional reality that lurked within the depths of our soul. Despite his meticulous planning and sophisticated rationalization, Avi was weighed down by uncertainty. Deception had a certain density that could weigh the best of men down.

As Avi stood on the balcony, he thought of Milan Kundera's *The Unbearable Lightness of Being*. It was Kundera's curious title that struck most people. Of course, he knew what Kundera was saying. The fact he read Nietzsche at the age of fifteen helped him understand, but the title made more sense than ever right now, standing on the balcony overlooking the city at night. The title referred to Nietzsche's idea of eternal return. Nietzsche argued that our existence is an infinite manifestation in a temporal loop that is cyclical. The idea that our existence has an infinity of antecedent expressions and an infinity of future recurrences is not new. But it was Nietzsche who gave it serious philosophical consideration. For Nietzsche, the idea of eternal recurrence is a haunting concept, but through philosophy, one can learn to embrace the unbearable heaviness of an existence that becomes ontologically dense. It is only by embracing our fate, what Nietzsche called *amor fati*, or the love of fate, that we are able to give our lives meaning. Kundera rejected Nietzsche's premise of circular time and embraced time as a linear path. If eternal recurrence results in a weighty existence, then linear time can only produce an existence that is as light as a feather. For Kundera, what happened but once might well not have happened at all. If we have only one life to live, we might as well not have lived it at all. This is the theme of the *Unbearable Lightness of Being*. If our existence is a singular occurrence, then we have no frame of reference to compare our choices and actions. Without this frame of reference, we can never judge our choices as correct or gravely erroneous, which suggests we cannot take responsibility for them. This is what it means to live with lightness. The question posed by Kundera is which kind of life do we want: an ephemeral life that is light or a dense, weighty life that is burdensome?

When Avi first read *The Unbearable Lightness of Being,* he agreed with Kundera's ontological description of how we come unto existence. His recent actions, however, forced him to reevaluate the nature of being. As he stood out on the balcony, he felt his existence to be weighed down by the burden of choice. He questioned Kundera's connection between linear time and the lightness of our being. He felt heavy and burdened by an existence that felt immensely dense. The guilt was building inside him. The burden he would have to carry would eventually crack open his psyche. Avi stood on the balcony lost in thought, as though the heaviness of his choice – the unavoidable permanence – was just striking him now.

"You seem to be deep in thought," Alena said, walking behind him. Her heels clacked on the wooden balcony floor. "Is everything alright?"

"I'm going to miss you, Alena!" Avi embraced Alena for what seemed to be an eternity.

"I'm going to miss you too, Avi. You better call me every day."

"Of course I will. Will you come and visit me in Boston?"

"Avi, I thought you were coming down here on the weekends."

"Yes, I will. But you can come visit me on occasion, right?"

"Well, I can come with my uncle when he goes on his lecture tours. How is that?"

"I was hoping you would come alone."

"I don't think my mother would let me go off to Boston and spend the night."

"Yes, of course. Where's my head. I have an idea, Alena. I'm going to Israel in the summer and I remember you telling me that you will visit Egypt. Why don't we meet in Cairo? I always wanted to see Egypt."

"Are you sure you want to meet me in Cairo?' Alena was confused. She knew that Avi wanted to leave New York in order to leave her. She knew this shortly after meeting his mother. She had too much respect for Avi to embarrass him. She simply went along with the charade. She also had pride and was not about to beg him to stay. She couldn't understand why Avi would want to meet her in Cairo.

"I would love to meet you in Cairo," Avi continued. "Do you still have plans to go?" Avi was not entirely sure why he asked her to meet him in Egypt. Part of him wanted to believe that it was not over between them. His guilt was a crisis of conscience. He was in love with Alena, but felt there was no other way out. As he stood there on the balcony desperately trying to find a way to reverse what he had already set in motion, he realized it was too late. He could see the disappointment in her eyes. His fate was on an unalterable course. Alena smiled calmly, as she had for months.

"Of course, we're going to Cairo. Where in Cairo do you want to meet?"

"How about the Nile Hilton? When will you go?"

"Why don't we make a promise now to meet at the Nile Hilton on June 24th at noon? What do you think? Will you be there waiting for me?"

"Yes, of course, I will. The question is: will you be there, Avi?"

"I promise you I will be there."

"Wait, but you're Israeli. How are you going to go to Egypt?"

"We have a peace treaty with the Egyptians, remember?" Avi smiled and for a moment believed his own words. He wanted to meet Alena in Cairo. He thought, perhaps naively, his mother would change her mind.

"Well, I'll be there standing in the lobby of the Nile Hilton. Have you noticed, Avi, that you haven't even said you love me all day long?"

"Of course, I love you, Alena."

"Are you sure? You seem distant."

"It's just that I'm going to miss you."

"I will always be here, Avi."

"Thank you for everything, Alena." As soon as Avi uttered these words, he knew they were inauthentic. He thought of Sartre's notion of bad faith. Sartre argued that when we are under social pressure, we tend to project false values that betray our authentic selves. Avi was in the midst of his betrayal and it was eating away at him.

"Avi, we better get back to the others."

"Yes, I suppose." They returned to the living room where several people were waiting to say goodbye. Avi turned and saw David, who always seemed to be present for important moments.

"There you are, Avi," David said. "We were looking for you."

"Professor Said wanted a word."

"Hi Alena," David said, turning to her. "Your uncle has an amazing apartment. It's not what I expected at all."

"What did you expect?"

"I don't know, maybe more down-to-earth, but with a big library. I love the grand piano though. Does your uncle play?"

"Of course, he plays," Avi said. "What did you think, this is an ornamental piece?"

"Okay, okay. Sorry. I didn't know. What's the matter with you tonight?"

"Would you like to hear him play, David?" Alena asked.

"Hell, yeah. Thanks, Alena."

"Avi, why don't you come with me so we can persuade my uncle to play for us?" Alena could see his rising guilt. She was hurt, but she remained deeply in love with him. She hated to watch him suffer like this.

"Okay, Avi. What's wrong?" she asked after pulling him toward the kitchen. "You haven't been yourself all day. Look, I know that you're torn by this move, but we discussed this, remember? We are going to call each other and write often. We are also going to meet in Cairo, right? What's troubling you?"

"What is it that you want to hear, Alena? I don't want to go, damn it."

"Avi, you don't have to raise your voice. I'm trying to help you. No one is forcing you to go. You were the one who applied to transfer. No one is asking you to leave. You have friends here who care about you. My uncle thinks very highly of you and has already taken you under his wing. What are you running away from?"

"I'm not running away from anything. I just want to have an opportunity to attend Harvard."

"Fine, then you should go to Harvard without all this stress and tension. There are people here who want to say goodbye and wish you well."

Suddenly, the strident call of Orff's *Carmina Burana* poured through the apartment. Someone had put on the record. Alena once again witnessed Avi's reaction. He clenched his hands and tilted his head sideways. He gave Alena a frightening look, but she was not affected. Alena wanted to avoid a scene. She had to react quickly.

"Avi, look at me," she said, grabbing his shoulders. "Hold my hands. Everything's going to be alright. You are going to be fine."

Avi squeezed Alena's hands with such force that he almost sprained her wrist. As *O Fortuna* crescendoed and crashed to earth, , Avi saw Alena's face twist into a knot

"I'm so sorry, Alena. Did I hurt you?"

"I'll be fine. I wonder who played it. My God, they could have at least asked. It's as if this music triggers the demons within you."

"I better go, Alena. It was not a good idea to come today."

"Please don't go, Avi. At least let the others say goodbye." Avi noticed the tenderness in Alena's eyes. He wanted to hold her. He wanted to kiss her. He wanted to be with her. But it was too late.

"I'm sorry, Alena. I haven't been myself lately. Perhaps I can stay a while longer."

"I need a favor. Do you remember the first time I went to your apartment? You promised to play Moonlight Sonata for me. I want… no, I need you to play it for me now."

"Why now? I mean, I want to play it for you when we are alone."

"Avi, please play it for me." Alena's eyes teared up and Avi walked over to the piano. As he started playing, everyone gravitated towards the piano, mesmerized by Avi's virtuosity. Edward and Mariam Said stood next to Alena who was by now in tears.

"This is a special young man. He's tormented by something. I can hear it in his music." Said looked to his wife.

"Edward, he is in love with the one person he can't have. His mother would never approve of Alena."

"How do you know all this?"

"She told me as much. When his mother came for your debate with Eban, she rejected her outright." Mariam put her arms around Alena to comfort her. Avi played Moonlight with such dark melancholy that everyone viscerally felt his departure as something providential. Avi stayed to say his goodbyes. He thanked Edward Said and Mariam for their kindness. He greeted many of the Arab students who were there to wish him well at Harvard. His last words to Alena were filled with a certain density of despair and the kind of cowardice that would torment his soul for decades to come.

"I'll see you soon," he said to Alena.

It would be another sixteen years before Avi set eyes on Alena again. He saw her briefly at Edward Said's funeral. It was Mariam Said who contacted Avi to ask him to give one of the eulogies. Avi corresponded with Said over the years and developed a close relationship with his mentor. It was Edward Said, a few weeks before he succumbed to leukemia, who asked his wife to have Avi attend his funeral services. Avi, who was a professor of philosophy at Harvard, immediately flew to New York.

The death of Edward Said in 2003 hit him hard. As he spoke at the service, he was unable to control his emotions. The memories of his time at Columbia gushed forth. These haunting memories were so overpowering that he was unable to complete his eulogy. As Avi offered his condolences to Mariam Said and others, he noticed Alena from a distance. Their eyes locked for what seemed like an eternity. Tears trickled down his cheeks, but they were not exclusively for Edward Said. The tears were filled with the anguish of what he did so many years ago. The guilt and anguish that haunted him was simply too much for his psyche to contain. He wanted to walk over to her, but didn't know what he would say. He wanted to offer his condolences, but that seemed inauthentic. He found himself frozen in place, unable to move.

As he gazed into Alena's eyes, he was again struck by her beauty. The ravages of time completely ignored her. It was as if time itself bowed before her transcendent beauty. Several people interrupted Alena as she approached him. That physical space that separated them appeared to him as an oceanic gap that he simply could not bridge. Avi left without speaking to her. He simply lacked the words. The demons that haunted him for so many years prevented him from uttering a word. It would be another five years before Avi made contact with her.

XIX

Avi quickly learned that Harvard was very different from Columbia. He rented a small apartment in Cambridge and kept to himself. His phone calls to Alena became less frequent, and he shut himself off from the world. He immersed himself in academic studies and did his best to forget about New York. He tackled the Sisyphean task of taking 28 units, which would be considered academic suicide anywhere, but was especially so at Harvard. His daily routine was to attend classes until six in the afternoon and study until two in the morning. By the end of the term, Avi returned to Israel to spend the summer.

Although he was happy to be home, his family told him he seemed distant. Without the distraction of school, he constantly thought back to Alena and the magical time he spent in New York. Avi eventually began to remember his time at Columbia with a dream-like reality. New York seemed to be a series of moments, fleeting and yet concentrated in their capacity to induce a dislocated sense of temporal awareness. He knew that June 24th was fast approaching and he contemplated going to Cairo. He thought of telling his mother the truth. He paced back and forth in his room as he practiced how to confront his mother. It was Saturday, June 20th and he was running out of time. He went to the kitchen where his mother prepared dinner.

"Mother, I need to talk to you for a minute."

"Of course, Avi. What is it? Oh, did I tell you that President Herzog invited us to Beit HaNassi this Wednesday. He is so proud of you, Avi. Your uncle will be coming with us. I think he has some business to discuss with the President."

Chaim Herzog was the brother-in-law of Abba Eban. Beit HaNassi, which means *president's house* in Hebrew, is the president's residence in the Talbiya neighborhood of Jerusalem. Avi felt an immense weight crashing down on him.

"Do we have to go this Wednesday? I mean, perhaps we can go another time."

"Avi, what's gotten into you? Chaim is not just family. He's the president of Israel. You know what I see in your future, Avi? I see you marrying Hadasah and becoming prime minister one day." His mother stood over the kitchen sink rinsing some greens. She turned around smiling with maternal certitude.

"Oh mother, here you go again. I'm not even done with college yet and you already have my future planned out."

"It's *bashert,* Avi. You can't go against fate. You are destined for great things. Uncle Solomon agrees with me." *Bashert* is Yiddish for destiny.

"Mother, Uncle and I do not believe in fate. Human beings choose their own path. I don't have any desire to enter politics at all. I can see myself perhaps teaching somewhere."

"Well, I may not be an intellectual like you and your uncle, but I do believe you will have an impact on the world."

"I don't know about that."

"Avi why don't you go see Hadasah? She's been asking about since you got here. Go on, dinner won't be ready for a while."

"Mother, why did you reject Alena without even getting to know her?"

"I thought you told me you stopped all contact with her."

"I did, but I'm curious as to why you treated her with such contempt."

"I'm sure she is a lovely girl. But she is not the one for you."

"What does that mean, mother? She was the kindest person I've ever met. Did you know she drove me everywhere after my motorcycle accident? She was the most beautiful girl I've ever met."

"I know she is beautiful, Avi. I was rather surprised by her beauty, but she is not one of us."

"What does that even mean, mother? Are we Jews so exclusive that every *goyim* is a threat?" Goyim is the Hebrew term used to describe someone who is not Jewish.

"What's gotten into you, Avi? Tell me. How do you think things would have worked out between you two? She is Palestinian and you are Israeli. Your backgrounds are an ocean apart. You are too idealistic. The love you have for her is romantic; something out of a novel, but it is not practical."

"And I suppose Hadasah is more practical?"

"Of course, she's more practical. You grew up together. She's had her eye on you for many years. Haven't you noticed the way she looks at you? Her eyes just light up whenever you are around."

"The fact I'm not in love with her is of no consequence to you, is it?"

"What does love have to do with it? She will make you an excellent wife."

He turned to walk away and the phone rang. His mother answered it and smiled.

"Oh hello, Hadasah."

Avi waved frantically at his mother, motioning for her to tell Hadasah he was not home. She ignored him, smiling as before.

"He is actually standing in front of me." His mother handed him the phone. Avi gave his mother a look of frustration.

"Hi, Hadas." She told him she would be there shortly, and that his mother had invited her over. Avi looked at his mother resentfully. He knew that his life was demonstrably different now that he was home, and that his hard-won independence had been stripped from him. But this was worse than anything he imagined. He had to get out of the house.

In fact, there was nothing wrong with Hadasah. She was always a nice girl and had been very patient with him in social groups, when he was painfully awkward. She simply wasn't Alena. She was pretty in a provincial sort of way, but she was not an intellectual. His mother wasn't wrong about her making a good wife. He simply had known her too long to be attracted to her. But he wasn't against spending time with her.

He spent that afternoon with Hadasah and saw her again each of the next three days. They went shopping, walked through the park and she told him about her life away at college. He could admit it was refreshing to hear about life that wasn't crowded by intellectual pursuit. Hadasah had a way of putting him at ease, but he never went long without wondering about Alena.

More than anything, he felt trapped by the lofty expectations imposed by his family. The label of *Chosen One* that was attached to him since childhood became a haunting reminder of his existential confinement. This was especially true at home, where his mother was a constant reminder of the weighty expectations everyone had for him. The one expectation he resented, and couldn't comply with, was the arranged marriage his mother planned for him. He felt that fate would not win this battle. He told his mother he would not think of marriage until he completed his studies.

On the morning of Wednesday, June 24th, he was on his way to Jerusalem to have dinner with President Herzog instead of travelling to Cairo. Though he wasn't sure if Alena remembered to meet him at the Nile Hilton, he felt an enormous sense of guilt about not keeping his promise. He was growing resentful of a world that was conspiring against him, and he saw his mother as culpable. He returned to Harvard without offering Hadasah any promises of marriage or a hint of returning for her.

§§§

Avi completed his bachelor's degree in January of 1988. It took him a little over two years to complete his undergraduate studies in philosophy and comparative literature. He graduated *summa cum laude* and was accepted into the doctoral program at Harvard. He settled into a comfortable routine and tried to ignore the haunting memory of Alena. He attended classes during the day and studied at home in the evening. One day in February, Avi was studying at Café Pamplona near Harvard Square. As he sat outside reading Nietzsche, he noticed an attractive redhead sitting three tables away. He tried to ignore her and continued reading. He periodically glanced toward the young woman without realizing it. About an hour passed before the redhead got up to leave. Before walking away, she stopped by Avi's table.

"Excuse me, but I noticed you staring at me. Have we met before?"

"I'm terribly sorry. It was very rude of me. It's just that you remind me of someone I knew."

"Are you a student here?"

"Yes, I'm a graduate student in the philosophy department."

"I'm Catherine, by the way. I'm doing grad work in history."

"I'm Avi. I'm truly sorry for staring at you like this."

"She must have been someone special to you."

"Yes, she was indeed special. In fact, I have a picture of her in my wallet. You see, she had red hair." Avi searched his wallet for Alena's picture, but it was not there. He started to panic. It was the only picture he had of her.

"I don't understand. I always carried it with me in my wallet."

"Maybe you just misplaced it."

Avi searched frantically for the picture. He turned his wallet inside out, but could not find her portrait. It was the only visual link he had of her. He thought perhaps that his mother had taken it out. He looked up and the woman had vanished. He quickly packed up his books and rushed home to call his mother. As he was about to dial, he realized his mother would deny it, but he was convinced she took it. The loss of this one photograph was the single worst moment of his life. It precipitated a total psychological breakdown. The density of his despair was simply too much for his psyche to process. Consciously, he knew he could not let Alena fade from his memory. His guilt tore away at the thin layers of his rational protection. He desperately wanted to turn back the clock, to undo the damage he created.

To preserve the memory of Alena, he methodically and pathologically recreated each day that he spent with her. He recreated the first time he encountered her stunning beauty. He recreated the emergency room when he felt that an angel descended upon him. He recreated the otherworldly experience of making love to her for the first time. He recreated their daily drives together, when Alena picked him up in the morning and returned him home late at night. He spent countless days recreating every detail in order to remember. Though he was not an artist, he drew her face from memory, down to the number of freckles on her cheeks. His only obsession was to prevent Alena from becoming a fractured and disjointed memory .

Within a few months, Avi's construction of Alena started to take on a life of its own. On one seemingly uneventful day in April of 1988, Avi was studying at Café Pamplona. He was sitting outside working on a paper on Heidegger when Alena's voice seemed as real as someone sitting next to him. It was here that his psychosis started to take hold.

"Hello Avi," he heard from somewhere.

"I miss you."

Avi was unable to distinguish the voice in his head from other ambient voices surrounding him. The voice seemed real enough to him that he felt compelled to respond. It happened in a moment, and then he couldn't stop, though he knew it wasn't right.

"Alena, is that you? Oh God, I missed you Alena."

"I missed you too, Avi. I love you. Why did you leave me?"

"I don't know what was in my head? I'm filled with so much shame that I can't even ask for forgiveness."

"It okay, Avi. I'm here now. We are together again."

And this was the moment he saw her, clear as day. She wore jeans and a scarf around a blue blouse, and her red hair cascaded over her shoulder, just as it always had. She smiled and he saw the twin dimples bracketing her mouth.

"I'm in love with you, Alena. I just don't know how to live without you."

"I'm here now and everything will be alright again."

As Avi sat in the café having a conversation with an imaginary Alena, he blocked the outside world and dove into his own private escape. She seemed real to him. The lines between reality and fantasy grew blurry and he was unable to control a construction that he created. As Avi interacted with an imaginary interlocutor, he had no idea that Professor Scanlon, one of his Philosophy professors, was sitting behind him four tables away. His professor carefully approached him.

"Hello, Avi."

Avi froze and said nothing.

"Avi, are you alright?"

"Professor Scanlon. Hello, I'm sorry I didn't see you." Avi sat up stiffly. His mouth was arid and he felt light-headed.

Professor Thomas Scanlon, Jr. taught philosophy and religion at Harvard. Though he recently got to know Avi from the seminar he was teaching on foundational questions in moral theory, he felt that Avi's intellectual reach was beyond anything he ever encountered. It was very difficult for him to see one of his most brilliant students talking to himself.

"May I join you?" Scanlon asked sympathetically.

"Of course, Professor."

"I noticed you were having an interesting conversation just now. May I ask to whom you were talking to?"

"I was talking to Alena." Avi seemed confused and proceeded to introduce a phantom Alena to his professor.

"Alena, this is Professor Scanlon. He–"

Professor Scanlon stopped him before he could finish.

"Avi, there is no one here but us. Listen to me, I don't know what's going on in your head, but you need to get some help. I have a friend who is a psychiatrist at the medical school. I want you to call her tomorrow. You are one of the most promising students I've ever had and I don't want you to throw it all way. Do you understand what I'm telling you?"

"Yes, Professor. Thank you for your help."

Avi had no intention of seeking help. As soon as Professor Scanlon left, Avi resumed his conversation with Alena. He didn't care what others thought. Alena was as real to him as anyone else. Avi's condition quickly deteriorated over the next few weeks. He lost interest in his studies and couldn't sleep. He walked through Cambridge in the middle of the night, careful to avoid dark alleys and vacant side streets. Occasionally, he wandered into an all-night copy store or even through the freshman dorms on campus. But he never spoke to anyone and was in search of nothing in particular. His condition grew worse each day. He stopped grooming himself altogether. People who witnessed him talking to empty tables assumed he was a vagabond. The situation got so bad that several of his professors called him to a meeting. It was not only to encourage him to seek help, but also to save his academic career. Avi was doing poorly and no longer cared about his grades. In fact, he no longer cared about anything other than living in his imaginary world.

He believed he could control his impulse to talk to Alena all the time. He felt the world was conspiring against him. Avi eventually went to seek help in order to satisfy his professors. Professor Scanlon introduced him to Dr. Carola Eisenberg, who was the Dean of Student Affairs at Harvard Medical School. Carola Eisenberg, who was born in Argentina, helped establish Physicians for Human Rights, which went on to win the Nobel Peace Prize for its international campaign to ban landmines. As Avi walked into her office, he was surprised by its Spartan appearance. There was a small, unattractive desk with books and papers strewn haphazardly. There were bookshelves that towered up to the ceiling and more books piled on the floor.

"So, you are Avi Eban. Please have a seat."

"Thank you." Avi was pale and disheveled. His hair was unkempt and his eyes darted from Dr. Eisenberg, around the room and back.

"I've heard a great deal about you, young man. So you are from Israel, yes?"

"Yes I am."

"And your great-uncle is Abba Eban, correct?"

"Yes he is." Avi was reticent to speak, and Dr. Eisenberg's probing demeanor didn't assuage his concerns.

"You know, I truly admire Abba Eban's rhetorical skills. He is a powerful speaker. Professor Scanlon tells me you are one of his top students. Your other professors say you are exceptionally brilliant. I was told you finished your undergraduate work in two and a half years, *summa cum laude*. That's quite impressive. So tell me, why do you think you are here?'

"Forgive me, Dr. Eisenberg. But I don't want to be here."

"Well, there is the door. Please close it on your way out. I'm certainly not going to force you to stay."

"I'm very sorry, Dr. Eisenberg. I didn't mean to upset you."

"You didn't upset me. I simply want your perspective as to why you are here. I've heard about some of your odd behavior from Professor Scanlon, but now I want to hear from you."

"I don't understand why any behavior that deviates from the norm must be looked upon as something that disturbs our collective sensibility and, therefore, must be managed."

"How far are you willing to take this argument? Tell me, have you read Thomas Szasz?' Szasz was Professor of Psychiatry at the State University of New York. He was a critic of the moral foundation of psychiatry and the controlling aspect of medicine in modern society. His views were always controversial and considered to be outside the mainstream of modern psychiatric thought.

"Yes, I read the *Myth of Mental Illness.*"

"Do you agree with him? Is mental illness a myth?" Though Eisenberg was impressed with Avi, she knew he was using his intellect as a cover.

"I think to a large extent, it is. I love this quote from the *Myth of Mental Illness*. 'If you talk to God, you are praying; if God talks to you, you have schizophrenia.' If I exhibit eccentric behavior, it does not mean I have a disease."

"Perfect. Can you tell me about your eccentric behavior? Let's also remove the stigma of mental illness from our conversation, okay? Let's simply talk about the phenomena in question without attaching any labels to it, alright? Can we agree on that?"

"So you agree with Szasz, Dr. Eisenberg?"

"Not entirely, but I do agree that labels often get in the way of getting at the source of certain behaviors. Now, can you describe some of your eccentric behaviors for me?"

Avi grew tense and looked away. It was over now; the fear, any hope of seeing Alena, all of it. He didn't care, and felt compelled to answer her.

"I enjoy having conversations with someone who exists in my mind."

"So you have conversations where a person you know is trapped in your mind. Is this person manufactured by you or is this person real but no longer with you?"

Avi paused. He hadn't been asked this question before. He wasn't ready to give a genuine answer, and thought quietly for a few seconds. He responded only when the silence overwhelmed him, forcing him to stare at the giant bookcase.

"This person is real, but she is no longer with me."

"Interesting. I take it this person had an impact on your life, yes?"

"I was deeply in love with her, but I'm not comfortable talking about it."

"That's perfectly alright. Can we talk a bit about the voices in your mind?"

"Yes, of course."

Avi was surprised after his first visit ended. He felt as though his thoughts had been decompressed, and even looked forward to seeing her again. He found his talks with Dr. Eisenberg to be most helpful. Though he would be reluctant to reveal the details of his imagined reality, he was gradually finding it possible to cope with the loss of Alena. After several months of therapy, he was ready to reveal the identity of the voice that haunted him.

XX

It was November, 1988 and Avi was sitting at Café Pamplona, waiting for Dr. Eisenberg. Their sessions proved to be more beneficial when held in a less formal environment. With Thanksgiving fast approaching, Avi felt unsettled, given the potency of his memories during this time of year. Dr. Eisenberg arrived a few minutes late and sat down across from him. She wore thick glasses and a tweed jacket. She was bundled from the cold weather outside and took a few moments to unravel herself before smiling at Avi.

"Hello, Avi. I hope I didn't keep you waiting long."

"It's perfectly alright. I've been busy writing a paper."

"What is your topic?"

"It's on Nietzsche's 'God is dead' declaration. Where are my manners? Let me get you your coffee."

"Thank you, Avi, but I'm fine. I have to say, I've always found Nietzsche to be brilliant as a thinker, but flawed as a man. So tell me what do you have to say about his declaration?"

"I'm not sure it will interest you."

"I would have you know that I wrote a major paper on Nietzsche. So tell me, what is your position on his declaration?"

"I'm sorry, I didn't mean to imply–"

"Avi, it's alright? We don't have to talk about Nietzsche if you don't want to."

"No, it's perfectly alright. You see, I'm not entirely sure that Nietzsche was correct in announcing the death of God. His declaration seemed to be a bit premature."

"I'm not following you."

"When Nietzsche declared God dead, he was making an observation on the nature of faith in the modern world. He did not feel that faith was compatible in the age of progress. The reason I say he was premature in declaring faith in the divine to be dead is that faith, in the 19th century sense of the word, was weakening. He should have declared God to be ill. That would have been a more apt metaphor. I think it is we, the moderns of the late-20th century, who have killed God. We seem to have more faith in science and technology than we do in God. I suspect that our faith today is in the materiality of this world. Science has become the functional replacement for God."

"That's a remarkable statement, Avi. I doubt science has any ambition of replacing God. Science is a systematic methodology for investigating the natural world. It liberates us from the so-called authoritative texts and revealed knowledge."

"Perhaps the methodology is liberating, but I'm more interested in how the dissemination of scientific knowledge impacts us. Bertrand Russell, in his famous book *Why I'm Not a Christian,* says that he doesn't trust religion in that it limits his freedom. He doesn't care for any institution that uses normative language. You know, language that tells us how we ought to behave."

"Yes, yes, I know what normative language is, but what does all this have to do with Russell?"

"Well, science has become the dominant intellectual authority of our time. There is an army of experts and specialists instructing us on everything from what toothpaste to buy to how to vote. We are constantly told that we should not smoke, to watch our cholesterol, to exercise, and so on. To me that's normative language."

"Yes, but science tells us such things for our own benefit. Such pronouncements are not opinions, but the outcome of scientific studies. I'm sure you are not comparing scientific outcomes with religious pronouncements."

"Well, that is beyond the scope of my paper, but I think perhaps certain parallels can be drawn. When we listen to these scientific pronouncements, they are not offered to us using the language of science. That's what I find so curious. Science uses moral language to instruct us. 'Thou shalt not smoke,' or 'thou shalt exercise.' When did science derive such an authority to tell us what to do? That's a question I'm interested in."

"I don't understand your point. Do you expect science to speak to the rest of society in an esoteric language? That would not be very practical."

"You know what this reminds me of? It reminds me of the church during the Middle Ages making pronouncements and justifying such binding moral claims by telling people that theology is far too complex to explain. So it seems to me that both science and religion are saying- trust us, we know what we are doing."

"Here is the critical difference you are overlooking. Science is verifiable and reproducible. Religion is based on textual interpretation."

"I'm not sure if that difference matters."

"Well, tell me how have you been since I last saw you. It's been three weeks."

"I've been busy with school."

"How are the voices coming along?"

"I'm ready to tell you who the person is."

"What made you change your mind?"

"I feel perfectly comfortable talking to you. You've been wonderfully kind to me these past few months. I could not have adjusted without you."

"Who is she, Avi?"

"Her name is Alena Said and she is Palestinian. I met her while studying at Columbia."

"How did you meet?"

"I was walking on campus one day when I noticed her from a distance. I was immediately drawn to her. I didn't even know she was Arab. She certainly didn't look like any Arab I knew."

"What do you mean?"

"She had red hair and freckles. You know what's funny. She was standing behind a table handing out flyers for the Arab organization she was involved with. I didn't even notice the banner placed in front of the table. I was simply mesmerized by her beauty. I walked up to her to say hello. She handed me a flyer and wrote her phone number on the back."

"Did she write her phone number for everyone who took a flyer?"

"I don't think so." Avi told her the story of their first couple of weeks together at Columbia, beginning with his motorcycle accident. Dr. Eisenberg stopped him just as he was in the middle of explaining that he had no money to call a cab and was forced to call her in the middle of the night from the emergency room.

"Let me tell you what I think. I think that at a subconscious level, you didn't want to call a cab. You wanted to call Alena. It was the perfect excuse to call her."

"You don't understand, I didn't have any money on me."

"Let me ask you a question. Did you have money at home?"

"Yes, but..."

"You see, you could have called a cab and paid once you got home, but you chose to call Alena instead. You were smitten by her beauty and desperately wanted to see her again. When you were in the Emergency Room, you were frightened, weren't you?"

"I don't know what you mean." Avi was growing agitated.

"I think you do. Here you were, alone in a big city. Your family was thousands of miles away and you were freightened. You see, the motorcycle accident was not only a physical trauma, but an emotional trauma as well. It was your first time away from home and you didn't have your mother to tell you everything will be alright."

"I don't know what you are talking about. I was in the Israeli army. I wasn't frightened of anything." Avi cracked his jaw and tilted his head sharply. He knew Dr. Eisenberg was getting too close. He didn't want anyone to see him in a vulnerable state.

"Why did you just do that?"

"Do what?"

"Crack your jaw and tilt your head."

"I don't know. It helps me release some tension."

"I think it's more than that. I've touched a chord, haven't I? I think I know what happened to you, but I need to hear more before I can help you understand it. What happened after the Emergency Room?"

"She took me home and actually called me that night to check on me. She would pick me up every day to take me to school. She often treated me to lunch or took me to her home for dinner. We fell in love and it was the most magical time of my life. On one occasion she invited me to Said's home where I met Chomsky."

"This is extraordinary, Avi. Here you are, an Israeli, suddenly thrust into a Palestinian world, talking to Chomsky and Said. How did that make you feel? I'm sure you were aware that Chomsky, whom I met on several occasions by the way, is the greatest critic Israel has ever seen."

"I wasn't bothered by all that. In fact I reveled in it. I engaged them quite effectively. I also took a couple of courses taught by Said."

"What did you think of him?"

"I thought he was brilliant and very eloquent."

"So you and Alena were in love despite your very different views on the conflict. Tell me, did you ever get into arguments with her about politics?"

"We had a few arguments, but they actually improved our relationship. I mean I couldn't bear it to upset her."

"Did you change your views on the conflict?"

"Yes, of course I did. I got to see a different perspective. I mean I've always believed in a two-state solution, but now I feel that more needs to be done. We

Israelis need to acknowledge our role in Palestinian dispossession. I know it sounds crazy, but I don't think peace could come about without a radical shift in thinking from both sides."

"Why did you leave this paradise? From what you are telling me, you seemed very happy."

"Happy? I was in heaven and I left it all behind."

"Do you want to talk about it?"

"It's fine. We staged a debate between Eban and Said. It was an incredible moment in our history. My mother came to see the debate. When I introduced her to Alena, she rejected her outright. It was devastating for me. She didn't even give her–"

"Hold on a minute. What were you thinking when you decided to introduce Alena to your mother? Did you actually expect your Israeli mother to embrace a Palestinian girl, regardless of her beauty, as a potential daughter-in-law?"

"I don't know what I was thinking. I was living in this idealistic world where an Israeli was embraced by a Palestinian family. Her family did not mind if we got married, so I thought why would my mother mind?"

"So you left because your mother didn't approve, right?"

"It's not that simple. It was not the fact I left. It was how I went about doing it. I behaved in a…I was–" Avi broke down in tears.

"It's alright, Avi. Take your time. I know this is very difficult on you." Dr. Eisenberg held his hand and tried to comfort him. He stared into the table and tried to maintain his composure. He didn't want her to see him vulnerable in this way, though he recognized it was probably too late for decorum.

"Thank you. I…I was…I was a coward. I acted in a cowardly way. I knew my mother would not accept her so I started looking for a way to leave New York altogether."

"Why didn't you simply tell Alena the truth, that your mother did not approve and nothing would come of the relationship?"

"I couldn't do that. How could I face her that way? I was deeply in love with her. She was the kindest person I've ever met. She helped me in so many ways that I cannot possibly begin to explain. It was not simply the fact she drove me everywhere or always paid for lunch. She made me feel special. She always encouraged me. She helped me become a man. And what did I do to repay her? I betrayed her in every way imaginable. I engineered my exit by transferring to Harvard. I suspect she knew what I was doing, but she never said anything to me. I was supposed to meet her in Cairo, but I was a coward.

"Let's change course. It sounds like when you talk to Alena, you are aware that you are talking to someone trapped in your mind. Do you feel that way, or do you feel she is real?"

"She is as real to me as you are now."

"Does she talk to you?"

"Yes, of course she does."

"What does she say?"

"She always says good morning to me. She tells me she is proud of me and that she loves me."

"I see. Well, would you like to know what I think?"

"I'm not sure that I want to know."

"Let me start with Szasz. You told me you read his work, so you must be aware that he discussed the power of labels. As a child you were labeled as brilliant or perhaps a freak of nature. You were also labeled as obedient. The massive weight of these labels influenced the direction of your life. You internalized these constructs and, in fact, made them come true. You were a precocious young man who possessed extraordinary cognitive insights. You told me you speak six languages, doubled majored in comparative literature and philosophy, and graduated Suma Cum Laude. You earned your bachelor's degree in two and half years and you are now doing graduate work at Harvard. These same labels that helped you achieve extraordinary things are responsible for your psychotic break.

I'm sure you know what a psychotic break is, but do you recognize that you are experiencing it? Your break occurred when you realized that you lost Alena's picture. It must have felt to you that you lost her forever. As you said you recreated her in your mind, but what you may not be aware of is that you idealized her. She became an archetypal image of beauty and virtue. It was your guilt that drove you to do that; to elevate her to something beyond reason itself. Something else happened in the emergency room that shaped your perception of her. One day you may have an emotional memory of that moment. When that happens, you will know why you were instantly drawn to her. What you are experiencing now is massive guilt. In literature, we describe this guilt as self-inflicted demons. The psychotic break occurred when you were no longer able to distinguish between Alena's voice as something you created and reality itself. That's when your auditory and visual hallucinations began.

I suppose medication such as Haldol or Thorazine would be appropriate in this situation, but I don't think that will help you. You see, Avi, the solution to your problem is quite simple. You need to contact Alena and apologize. You need to explain to her what you did and why you did it. It's the only way for you to find peace."

"I can't do that. I just can't do it. I can't face her."

"Avi, if you don't do it, you may have to go on one of these medications to control your symptoms. The guilt you are feeling will not go away.

"What if I can control it? I have been able to control it for a couple of months now."

"I have no doubt you can control it, but it will never entirely go away until you address the root cause. Well, I have to go, but promise you will come and see me next week. I heard from your professors that your grades are improving. Please think about what I told you."

"I will. Thank you Dr. Eisenberg. I will see you next week."

Part V

Absolution

XXI

The Nobel Committee quickly postponed the award ceremony once news of the assassination attempt spread. Both the Israeli and Palestinian governments agreed to share information regarding the shooting. Alena was waiting in her hotel room for news on Avi when the phone suddenly rang. It was David Barkovic, returning her call.

"Thank you for calling me back, David. Please tell me how is he?"

"Foreign Minister Said, I'm sorry I couldn't get back to you earlier. He is out of surgery, but he is in a coma. The doctors are monitoring him, but there isn't much they can do now."

"David, you must let me see him. Please."

"I'm afraid that would be impossible, Foreign Minister."

"David, stop being so damn formal." She began sobbing and wiped away her tears. "Please…I'm begging you to let me see him. I just need five minutes."

"Hold one minute, please." David retreated into an alcove in the hallway outside Avi's room where he could talk.

"Alena, I can't just let you come and see him. Security is everywhere. How are we going to explain it?"

"David, please. There are words I need to say to him."

"Alena, believe me. I know, but it's too risky. Are you aware of the media circus both inside and outside the hospital? How am I going to get you in and out without the whole world knowing about it?"

"If you know what I want to say to him, then you know that I'm in love with him. Please, David, I'm begging you to let me see him."

"What would President Ashrawi say? I know she is on her way back to Palestine. Does she know about any of this?"

"She had the same suspicion as you, but I know she would not mind."

"Alena, listen to me. I will give you five minutes. That's all I can do. You know I can lose my job over this, but I know that Avi would never forgive me if I didn't let you see him. There is a Mossad agent that I trust. I will send him to pick you up. You're at the hotel, right?"

"Yes, I can wait in the lobby for him."

"No. Don't wait in the lobby. He will dress as a waiter who will come up and deliver food to your room. Your security people will have to let him take you through a back door of the hotel and he will bring you to a side door of the hospital where I will meet you. Can you get your security people to clear him?"

"Yes, don't worry about that. Thank you, David. I will never forget this." Alena immediately called President Ashrawi. While the phone rang, she wondered what the president would say, but decided it didn't matter. She had to see Avi regardless of the consequences. Rashad Al Amri answered. He was President Ashrawi's personal advisor.

"Hello, Rashad. I need to talk to Hanan."

"She is on the phone with President Clinton. Do you have information on the Prime Minister?"

"Yes, I do. Please put her on, it's imperative that I talk with her."

"Hold on, Alena." She could hear President Ashrawi on the other line, saying she had to take another call.

"Yes, Alena. Do you have any news?"

"Hanan, can you talk?"

"Yes, don't worry." President Ashrawi, who was in route to Palestine, waved her people away to give her some privacy.

"I just talked to David. He told me he would give me five minutes with Avi. He wants a Mossad agent to pick me up. The agent will take me to a side door of the hospital where David will meet me."

"Dammit, Alena. You are putting me in a very difficult situation. Why haven't you told me you were in love with him? Edward told me about you and Avi back at Columbia, but I thought that it was buried in the past. So the rumors are all true."

"I didn't want you to think any less of me. You know how our culture is."

"Alena, I'm not culture. I'm your friend." In fact, Hanan was more than a friend. She was Alena's longtime mentor and the reason for her professional success during the past twenty years.

"I'm so sorry. Please forgive me. I just want to see him."

"Does your husband know?"

"He suspected something in 2010, but I denied it. That's why I terminated everything with Avi."

There was a long pause, and Alena could sense that Hanan was considering her request. At the same time, Alena knew it didn't matter what Hanan said. She was going either way, and would force her security team to help her. She would see Avi at all costs.

"Alena, I'm sorry. This is too risky. No single person is bigger than the peace we've created with Israel. Our situation is too tenuous to take needless risks. I'm sorry–" Hannan heard a click at that moment. She stared at the phone and shook her head, certain of what would happen next.

§§§

Avi's mind continued to wander through time. He had no awareness that he was in grave danger. Instead he felt a sense of meta-consciousness, a kind of acute awareness that he was alive and experiencing certain memories. Though he couldn't control the direction, he started to recognize the existential meaning behind these seemingly random images. It seemed to him now, lying comatose and hooked up to machines, completely inert but with swirling activity surrounding him, that much of his life had been in search of absolution. It was a sense of absolution that he only felt now, surrounded by people but completely alone for the first time in his life. His mind wandered to 2007, twenty years after he left Columbia.

He was teaching an ethics seminar at Harvard where he taught since 1990. His first book, *The Second Death of God,* catapulted him to academic stardom. His fourth book, *Cultural Illusions,* became an international best-seller. Avi found himself in demand for lectures at universities around the world. *Cultural Illusions* was a response to, and an extension of, *Orientalism*. Edward Said wrote the foreword and praised the book as an intellectual *tour de force*. The *New York Times* hailed the book as "stunningly brilliant", and ranked Avi as one of the top five Jewish intellectuals of the 20th century. *Cultural Illusions* would cement Avi's reputation as a brilliant scholar and a writer of uncompromised integrity.

It was during the ethics seminar that one of his graduate students introduced the concept of atonement.

Although the discussion was an esoteric analysis of Kant's *moral influence theory of atonement*, Avi couldn't help but think of Alena. His thoughts of Alena had never stopped. Though Avi experienced spectacular achievements as a professor and a writer, his private inner world was always punctuated by periods of psychosis. He continued to have conversations with Alena. Twenty years removed from the trauma of his own cowardly actions, Avi was never able to overcome his demons.

As a middle-aged man, Avi found his life to be completely unassuming. He established a comfortable routine, despite the excessive demands on his time. His routine was defined by his academic duties, his writing, and life as a bachelor. The fact he never married was a great source of pain for his family, particularly his mother. He refused one potential mate after another, always insisting that he will get married when the right woman comes along. Hadasah, the one girl his mother picked out for him, was long married and had three children. For now, Avi was fully immersed in academic life.

Though his book tours and lectures kept him busy, he never stopped thinking of Alena. It was during his travels that he occasionally saw her from a distance. He had no idea if it was her or an illusion created by hope. Over time, his sightings of her gradually dwindled, despite the fact he never stopped following her decorated career. He knew that Alena went on to earn her doctorate in linguistics from Columbia and went on to teach there. He heard from Chomsky and Said that Alena married a Palestinian colleague at Columbia.

He read several of her books, one of which stayed on the *New York Times* best-seller list for several months. It was called *The Language of the Other* and it expanded on Said's and Spivak's notion of how subaltern groups are represented in literature. It was during his ethics seminar that Avi started to give serious consideration to contacting Alena. He never stopped wanting to call her to apologize.

Avi searched everywhere for absolution, and it was only after twenty years of searching that he realized only she could provide it for him. He remembered what Dr. Eisenberg told him; that Alena was the only one that can offer him peace. For all of his sophisticated intellect, he found it impossible to find the language that would allow him to apologize. He didn't know how to begin to ask for something as simple as forgiveness. He played and replayed possible scenarios in his mind. If he said to Alena that he was sorry for suddenly leaving, then, at least in his mind, it sounded presumptuous and arrogant. If he contacted her to simply say hello it would sound inauthentic and callous. Avi felt trapped by his own language games. His guilt ran so deep that twenty years was not enough time to put his life in perspective. He lived haunted by a secret past that he was unable to forget. His self-inflicted demons imprisoned and tortured his soul, and there was no escape in sight.

It was Sunday, September 9th, 2007, and Avi was in New Haven, Connecticut. He was preparing to give a lecture at Yale that evening. It was on this date 22 years ago that he first met Alena. He spent the whole day thinking of her. He decided to take a drive in his rental car and picked up his cell phone to call her. He knew the phone number of her office at Columbia. Over the years, he would call her office late at night simply to hear her recorded voice. It was Sunday so he felt comfortable enough to call. He knew her phone would ring four times before the answering machine picked up. The phone rang three times, and just as it was about to ring the fourth time, he heard a voice

"Hello." It was Alena. Avi panicked and didn't know what to say. He was paralyzed.

"Hello? asked Alena. "Is someone there?"

"Is this Alena? I mean, is this Professor Said?"

"Yes. Who is this?"

"This is–"

"Oh…my God! Avi? Is this Avi Eban?"

"Yes, it is. I just called to… I mean I just wanted to–"

"I cannot believe this. My God! My God! My God! How are you?"

"I'm fine. I'm so sorry to bother you. I just wanted to say hello."

"I cannot believe this. My God, how long has it been? At least twenty years. So how have you been?"

"I'm fine. Everything is fine. I'm actually giving a lecture at Yale tonight." Avi stammered. He felt his stomach flipping and beads of sweat forming on his brow. He breathed deeply and listened to her speak.

"I'm not surprised. You're a big shot now. My students bring you up all the time in lecture. How did you know I would be in my office today?"

"I didn't. I just thought I would call." It was Sunday, and Avi didn't know how to explain away this stubborn fact. He was hoping Alena wouldn't ask, and had no answer to this question.

"Well, I'm glad I was here to take the call. I can't believe I'm talking to you. The last time I saw you was at my uncle's funeral. Why didn't you say hello?"

"I truly wanted to, but you were surrounded by people and I didn't want to interrupt."

"Well, I remember you gave a very nice eulogy."

"Thank you. He was an extraordinary man and I owe so much to him."

"Thank you, Avi. You know Columbia has been trying to get you to give a lecture here, but you seem to be always busy."

"I promise to do it soon."

"You know that your book is assigned reading by many professors here."

"I did not know that. I assign your book to my philosophy students."

"Wow, I did not know that. I'm flattered."

Avi couldn't think of anything else to say. There was nowhere for the conversation to go. The silence choked him and he felt a prickly sensation in his throat.

"Well, I have to go," he said. "But it was so good to hear your voice."

"Likewise. Please don't be a stranger and call again."

"I will. Take care."

"Bye, Avi."

His body began to shake as soon as he said goodbye. He pulled the car over and tried to collect himself. It was hard to accept that he just talked to Alena. It felt surreal. She seemed pleasant as always, but he didn't want to call again anytime soon. He feared that Alena would think that all it took was a simple phone call and all would be forgiven. Six months passed before he called again. He asked her if it would be alright to send her an email, which she said was fine. Avi spent several weeks and wrote a dozen drafts before he finally, regrettably, exhaled and sent his email.

Dear Alena,

This letter is twenty years overdue. There comes a time in a man's life when the truth must be confronted without mediation and without reservation. I am writing this confessional to you in order to offer my deepest apology for my cowardly behavior all those years ago. Any explanation now would be too little, too late. I simply want you to know that I behaved badly, very badly indeed, and I'm deeply sorry for my actions. Please forgive me for the way I treated you. I know I don't deserve your forgiveness, but I feel that I must ask. What I did was unconscionable and unforgivable and I throw myself at your feet. I am reminded of William Butler Yeats's great line, 'I have spread my dreams under your feet; Tread softly because you tread on my dreams.'

I seem to have destroyed both our dreams. Please forgive me for not treading softly upon your dreams. I offer my apology to you without excuse or reservation. I also want to thank you for everything you've done for me. Thank you for picking me up from the emergency room. Thank you for driving me everywhere. Thank you for feeding me. Thank you for always encouraging me. Thank you for always believing in me. Thank you for your kindness. Thank you for helping me without ever expecting anything in return. Thank you for being the most authentic person I've ever met.

With Humility,

Avi

Avi hoped for a quick response. He checked his email every hour but nothing came. He assumed the worst – that

Alena would not forgive him. Several days passed before Alena finally replied. He was in his office at Harvard when he noticed the email. He had a lecture in five minutes, but forgot about it completely. He sat at his desk staring at the email before opening it. He clicked to open it and noticed it was short, perhaps four or five lines long.

Dear Avi,

My God, I never expected such a confessional from you. You are talking about things that happened a long time ago. I forgive you, Avi. If it is forgiveness you are looking for, then I absolutely forgive you. You should come down to Columbia when you have a chance. We can have coffee and talk about the good old days. Take care of yourself and I look forward to hearing from you again.

Warmly,

Alena

Avi read in tears. He reread her email several times. He cancelled his lecture and decided to walk to Café Pamplona. It was far more than he expected. He was looking for absolution and he felt he found it, but something was missing. He still felt unsettled. He wanted to call her, but didn't want to risk saying the wrong words. Deep down, he felt that he didn't deserve forgiveness, and this is perhaps why he didn't want to call. The gravity of his guilt weighed him down as if it was an immovable object. It was unyielding and singular in its positional authority. Though Avi was not consciously aware of the impeccable hold that guilt had on his existential identity, he was acutely aware of the need to find absolution.

Avi would call her every few months, hoping to find the right moment to ask to see her. Their conversations were brief and formal. He didn't know how to break through the thick fog of formality and simply ask her to lunch. He was gripped by fear and became overly cautious.

Alena sensed that he wanted to see her, but she was not about to propose lunch herself. It had to come from him. Avi could not have known that Alena wanted to see him. His heartfelt apology affected her, and she wanted to see him. Of course, she followed his meteoric rise to literary stardom, and now she was beyond intrigued.

The next time Avi called her was January, 2009. He was in his car, driving home from work. He had agonized about calling her all day and had gotten little work done.

"Hello?" Alena answered. The sound of her voice never stopped paralyzing him momentarily. He was prepared for it, but it didn't matter.

"Hi, Alena."

"Hi, Avi! It is so good to hear from you again. You seem to call every six months or so. I hope you had a wonderful New Year."

"I want you to know that I just accepted an invitation to speak at Columbia."

"What? Really? How come I haven't heard anything? Wow, that is so good to hear. I was beginning to think we were not good enough to have Professor Eban speak."

"I was wondering if you would like to have lunch."

"Of course I would. I truly want to see you, Avi. When is your lecture?"

"It's on February 12th. I thought perhaps we can have lunch before the lecture."

"That would be wonderful. What day will the 12th be?"

"Thursday. Will that be alright?"

"Some things never change, Avi. I miss the way you used to say 'alright.' Let's see, I have lectures until 1 pm. How about 1:30? Where do you want to have lunch?"

"May I get back to you on that?"

"Sure. So what is the topic of your lecture?"

"It's on Zionism."

"Hmm, can you be more specific?"

"It's a critique of Zionism. It's actually about the need for Israelis to acknowledge responsibility for contributing to Palestinian suffering."

"You're kidding, right? Wow, I can't wait to listen to your lecture."

"Well, I've kept you long enough. I will get back to you regarding where to meet for lunch. It was so good to talk to you, Alena."

"I enjoyed talking to you, too, Avi. I look forward to seeing you. Wait, let me give you my cell phone number."

This was the second time Alena offered Avi her phone number. He couldn't help but perseverate over this fact. Avi was instantly thrilled and terrified. He wanted to plan the perfect lunch. All he could think of was properly thanking Alena for everything she had done for him. After careful research, he decided to take her to Le Bernardin on 51st.

It was early Thursday morning when Avi decided to fly down to New York. He rented a car and drove down to 5th Avenue to buy a new Armani suit. He would spare no expense for what he considered to be a once-in-a-lifetime opportunity. For many years, Avi had saved a substantial sum from sales of his books. He opened a separate bank account just in case he reconnected with Alena. He made bimonthly deposits into his account. His last deposit showed his account to contain $184,742, from which he withdrew $2000 for this lunch.

He arrived at Le Bernardin fifteen minutes early and slowly grew nervous. He was alarmed when he realized it was 1:40 pm and Alena had not shown up yet. He paced back and forth outside the restaurant. Though he saw her a little over five years ago at Edward Said's funeral, he couldn't help but wonder if she changed. He imagined what her hair would look like and how she would dress. He played multiple scenarios regarding how to greet her, and tried to imagine his own behavior. As he paced back and forth several feet away from the entrance to the restaurant, he noticed a red-haired woman standing by the door and stopped, suddenly unable to move.

XXII

Alena approached *Le Bernardin* and immediately noticed Avi standing at a distance staring at her. Avi was incapable of apprehending the reality before him. The only woman he ever truly loved stood a few feet away, and he didn't know how to react. She grew impatient and threw her arms in the air in frustration. As Avi walked toward her, he realized that this reunion was going to be a disaster before it started. He walked slowly and deliberately, uncertain as to how to greet her. These initial few seconds moved in slow motion, and Avi found himself to be a spectator rather than a participant. He was awestruck by her beauty. He couldn't understand how time ignored her. Her alabaster skin hadn't aged a day. Her figure was as perfect as his fading angelic image of her. Alena gave him a quick hug.

"Why were you standing there?" Alena asked. "I thought you might have changed your mind about meeting me."

"I'm…I mean I was–"

"Relax, Avi. I know you're nervous and so am I, but we'll get through this. Why did you choose this fancy restaurant? My God, it's gorgeous."

They were seated immediately. Avi made sure of it by handing the *maître d* a $100 bill before she arrived.

"Wow, this is so luxurious. We have a lot of catching up to do. You have become everything I imagined and more. You teach at Harvard and you are a bestselling author. I heard or read somewhere that you never married, which is surprising to me." Before Alena could finish her thought, she regretted telling Avi that she knew he never married. She knew he was uncomfortable and exacerbated the mood by making him feel more unsettled. She could not have possibly known that she was the reason or that she haunted Avi's thoughts for the past twenty two years.

"I… I'm not sure what to say."

"I'm sorry, Avi, I didn't mean to put you on the spot like that. I'm nervous as well."

"It's perfectly fine. I take it you are married?" Avi knew she was married from Edward Said. "I'm sure you have children."

"Yes, a boy and a girl. Their names are Edward and Violet. Here are their pictures." She handed over her phone with pictures of the children.

"They are very beautiful. They both have red hair."

"You sound surprised."

"No, I'm pleased. I see you kept Edward's name alive. I love the name Violet."

"Thank you. I was actually going to name her Majeda, but settled on Violet."

"What a beautiful name, Majeda."

The waiter arrived, breaking the tension sharply. Avi ordered a 1990 *Chteau Latour Pauillac.* The waiter left the table with a smile. Alena stared at Avi, who looked at her with confusion.

"What?"

"You don't have to order such an expensive wine. Besides, I'm not sure if I'll like it."

"No, you'll love this wine. It's amazing."

Alena opened her menu and gawked at it. Avi saw her eyes hovering over the spine of the menu. He knew what she was thinking before she said anything. Maybe it was too much all at once, but he wanted so desperately to impress her.

"Avi, this place is so expensive. You didn't have to bring me here."

"It's the least I can do. I just want you to enjoy yourself. Please don't look at the prices."

"Okay."

They stared quietly. Avi already knew what he was ordering. He went online and studied Le Bernardin's menu repeatedly over the previous days, and quietly hoped Alena would ask him to order for her. Suddenly, he looked up and saw that Alena was looking at him.

"So, have I changed?" Alena asked with a smile.

"No, you have not aged a day. I can't believe it. But I've changed." Avi was not being fully honest. He actually believed that he looked the same as he did in college. This was not idle vanity, but the projection of trauma on his aesthetic self-image. It was during his psychotic breaks that Avi began to perceive his own reflection as an immutable image from a distant past.

"Let's just say you look more distinguished. Your hair is thinner and you put on a few pounds, but I like the change."

"You are very kind. I can't get over how you managed to look the same. It's as if the passage of time completely ignored you."

"Thank you, Avi, but I assure you that I have aged."

"Well, if you have it is imperceptible to me." The waiter returned with the bottle of wine and a linen draped over his forearm. He opened the bottle slowly and revealed the cork to Avi, who smiled and put it down. The waiter poured two fingers in the goblet in front of Avi, who sniffed it and smiled approvingly.

"Are you ready to order?" the waiter asked.

Avi ordered without thinking. He chose the prix fixe menu, with lobster as their entrée. The waiter skulked away and Alena began to feel comfortable at that moment. She felt like the center of attention in a way she hadn't in years. Though she was a well-respected professor at Columbia and a best-selling author, her life had been filled with the kind of boring routine that one simply becomes accustomed to, like comfortable old slippers. She married someone who was considerably older than her and she never felt the kind of passion she had with Avi back at Columbia.

Avi stared at her and she saw the same expression from college, the same way he held her with his eyes in his apartment so many years ago. Then she realized he was about to unburden himself.

"Avi, you don't have to do this"

"No, Alena. Please. This has haunted me for over twenty years. I want you to know that I'm deeply grateful for your forgiveness. I need to tell you what happened at Columbia. I did something that I lived to–" Avi's eyes were tearing up. He felt his cheeks burning and his eyes growing puffy. He paused and stared into the blank space on his table. "I did something that I lived to regret for over twenty years. I was a coward and I am truly–"

The tears trickled down his face. Alena touched his hand to comfort him.

"I am truly sorry for how I behaved. There is no excuse for it, but I want you to know the truth of what happened. As you know, my mother did not approve and I was not strong enough to confront her. I engineered my exit to Harvard in order to escape the situation. This one act of cowardice has haunted me ever since. I have regretted my choices and actions." Avi sniffled and Alena looked around the dining room. She held his hand and shushed him, but he couldn't stop. "I have regretted what I did ever since. The guilt was eating me alive and I..."

The waiter delivered the first course to the table.

"It looks wonderful, thank you." Alena told the waiter. She didn't want anyone to see Avi this way.

"Alena, I want to thank you for everything you've done for me. I've never met anyone as kind as you. Thank you for picking me up from the Emergency Room. Thank you for driving me everywhere. Thank you for all the times you've treated me to lunch. You would never let me pay and I've never forgotten your generosity. Thank you for always encouraging me." Avi had to stop again. His emotions surged, but he wanted to continue. Alena seemed to understand and gave him time. "Thank you for introducing me to your uncle. We formed a decade-long friendship and it was entirely because of your kindness. Thank you for being patient with me. Thank you for understanding. I became a better man as a result of meeting you. I never truly knew love until I met you."

"Avi, look at me," Alena said while holding his hands. Avi wiped away the tears and stared into his plate. "Please look at me. I have forgiven you. I am deeply touched by all this, but you need to forgive yourself. Now you need to eat something. You brought me to this five-star restaurant and you haven't even touched your food.

They ate their salad course quietly and Avi regained his composure. He smiled at Alena when a piece of lettuce fell clumsily from her mouth. They laughed together and Alena looked up at him.

"Tell me, Avi. How is your mother?"

"She is not doing too well. She is diabetic and has congestive heart failure."

"I'm sorry to hear that. I'm also sorry to hear about Abba Eban's passing. He died a year before my uncle. Did you attend his funeral?"

"Yes, I flew to Israel. It was a lovely service. How are your parents?"

"My father passed away twelve years ago."

"I'm so sorry, Alena. I only met him a few times, but he was one of the nicest people I ever met. He always made me smile. I remember him having huge hands. How is your mother?"

"Mom is doing fine. Would you like to see her?"

"Oh, God yes. Thank you. I loved Palestinian food because of her. How is Mariam? I haven't talked to her since Said's funeral."

"She's doing fine. She actually mentioned you a few weeks ago. She was thinking of that dinner we had at my uncle's home. Was it 1985 or 1986? It doesn't matter. She was just reminiscing about the good old days."

"Alena, please forgive me, but there are a few more things I have to say to you."

"Of course, Avi. What is it?"

"I want you to know that my views on the conflict have changed and I owe it all to you. I've learned to love the Palestinian people as a result of knowing you. I not only believe in establishing a Palestinian state, I am participating in making it happen."

"I know you are, Avi, and I'm so proud of you. I've read several of the articles you've published. I loved the one, what was it called? Oh yes, *Why Israel Failed the Palestinians*. I thought it was honest and powerful. Uncle Edward would have been very proud."

"Thank you, Alena. There are many people in Israel who are asking me to run for office. The Meretz party has asked me to run, but I'm actually quite happy teaching."

"I have the same problem. Hanan Ashrawi, you've heard of her, has asked me to run for a seat on the Palestinian National Council."

"Are you considering it? I think the Palestinian people could benefit from someone of your background and pedigree."

"My pedigree? What about your pedigree, Avi? Didn't you once tell me that you are related to Chaim Herzog?"

"Yes. I'm just not ready to enter political life. Do you enjoy teaching?"

"Actually, I do. I can't imagine ever leaving it. You know your friend, David, taught in the political science department for many years before moving to Israel."

"Yes, I know. I stayed in touch with him over the years. He's teaching at Tel Aviv University now.

"So you stayed in touch with him, but not me. Hmm."

"I'm deeply sorry about that, Alena. I simply didn't know how to face you." Avi stared into the table.

"I'm kidding, Avi. Let's talk about something else, okay?" Avi and Alena finished their lunch and left. They stood on the sidewalk and waited for the valet to bring their cars.

"Avi, I can't thank you enough for today. It was truly magical."

"Will you attend my lecture this evening?"

"Of course, I will. I wouldn't miss it for the world." As their cars arrived, Alena gave Avi a hug and whispered in his ear.

"Would you like to see me again?" she asked. He backed away and held her eyes with his. She smiled a knowing smile, like someone in on a secret. Avi was shocked, but she seemed more certain than he could imagine.

XXIII

Avi felt light-headed as he drove down Broadway toward Columbia. Given his tendency for psychosis, he wasn't entirely certain that what just happened was real. He was still in a fog minutes later when his cell phone rang.

"Hello?"

"Hi, Avi." He was in disbelief as he held his phone.

"I'm so glad you called." Avi said. He was breathless and stopped just in time as he drove up to a red light.

"Why is that?"

"I miss your voice already."

"Avi, I just left a few minutes ago."

"I know, but I miss your voice. I've been deprived of your voice for so long."

"That's very sweet. I just want you to know that I truly had a wonderful time. What you said in the restaurant had a deep impact on me."

"Oh God. You don't know, do you?"

"Know what?"

"You're the love of my life."

"Avi, I'm absolutely flattered. Can I see you after your lecture?"

"Yes, of course. I'll cancel this lecture right now."

"Haha. Oh, Avi."

Avi raced through his lecture that night. He stared at Alena, sitting in the second row, while he delivered his lecture. He had given this speech several times, but never with less interest in engaging the audience. He stared at Alena as he gave his closing thoughts. He cancelled the Q&A by telling the audience he had an emergency to tend to.

They talked for a few minutes before Alena had to leave. Avi promised her he would return to New York in a couple of weeks. Alena kissed him as they said goodbye. It was perhaps the most erotic kiss Avi has ever experienced. The kiss was on his lower cheek, just a few millimeters away from his lips. It was tantalizingly inviting, yet held a certain mystery. Her lips were as soft as he remembered them.

Avi returned to New York two weeks later, as promised. Though Avi wanted to have lunch at another fancy restaurant, Alena only wanted to go to Amir's. It was at Amir's that Avi began to realize that the love Alena had for him all those years ago was gradually returning. They discussed the events that defined them during the twenty-year gap. He noticed Alena did not talk much about her husband, which made him curious. He privately hoped she was divorced, but knew it wasn't his place to ask.

As Alena talked across the table, Avi couldn't grasp that the love of his life was sitting before him and smiling. He felt like he was back in college. When lunch ended, Avi told her he would be gone for a couple of weeks lecturing in Europe. Alena's demeanor immediately changed. The energy was wiped from her expression. He knew it wouldn't be long before she confessed her feelings.

Alena's emotions were powerful enough to undermine her moral compass. She was falling in love with Avi all over again. She embraced the sense of liberation from the dullness that defined her domestic life. She realized that her attraction to Avi was a betrayal to her husband. This was made worse by the fact she was falling in love all over again with an Israeli. There was nothing she could think of to rationalize her behavior.

Avi felt none of the morality that would later haunt Alena. He was unable to comprehend how an affair would destroy not only Alena's reputation, but tear apart her family. In his mind, it was fate bringing them together. His singular obsession was to be with Alena.

As he said goodbye to Alena, she gave him a hug that lingered for a few seconds. She whispered to him to call her once he arrived in London. Avi returned to Boston for a couple of days before departing. He called her from the airport before he left.

"Hello?"

"Hi, Alena. I'm at the airport."

"Oh, hello Majeda. How have you been?"

"Majeda? Alena, what's going on?" Avi completely forgot that Alena was home and couldn't talk. He immediately cursed himself for being so thoughtless. Alena had to quickly think of something so as to avoid any suspicion. Her husband, Faisal, sat next to Alena.

"Hold on a moment," Alena said. Avi heard her talking away from the phone. A long minute passed.

"Alena, what happened?"

"I'm sorry, Avi, but I couldn't talk. When does your plane depart?"

"In about an hour."

"I'm not doing too well, Avi. I miss you so much and it hurts. I never thought I would have these feelings again, but I'm in a great deal of pain. I'm falling in love with you all over again. What have you done to me?"

"Dear God, Alena. I've always been in love with you and I always will be."

"I will miss you terribly. Please call me when you get there. Wait, will your cell phone work in London?"

"Yes, I asked and was told it would work. I will also text you. Would that be alright?"

"Yes, of course. I'll miss you so much."

"Alena, I want to ask you a question."

"Of course, Avi. What is it?"

"Do you trust me?"

"Absolutely and without reservation. Why?"

"I just want to spoil you and I want to make it a surprise. If I give you instructions from Europe, would you follow them to the letter?"

"Avi, you are being cryptic, but yes I will follow them."

"Well, I know you are home and I don't want to create problems for you. I will text you when I get to London. If you can talk, then call me back. I love you, Alena."

"Have a safe flight, Avi. I love you. *Ba moot feek.*"

Ba moot feek is an Arabic expression of love.

§§§

Avi spent his time in Europe searching for ways to spoil Alena for a day. Though he was behind the learning curve when it came to technology, he went on the internet to research five-star hotels in New York, luxury car rentals, flower shops, yacht rentals, and first-class airline tickets. He thought of flying her to Paris, but realized that Alena was married and couldn't possibly fly across the Atlantic on a short notice. He decided to cut his trip short a few days to surprise her. His texts were cryptic.

Avi: *Set to return to Boston on Sunday, March 15th. Can you clear up some time on Tuesday the 10th?*

Alena: *How much time do you need?*

Alena: *I don't understand. If you are returning on Sunday, why do you want me to clear time on Tuesday?"*

Avi: *I thought you said you trust me.*

Alena: *Of course. I can be free from two till midnight. That work?*

Avi: *That's perfect. Can you stand in front of Tom's Restaurant at exactly 2:30?*

Alena: *You're being very mysterious. What are you planning?*

Avi: *Just want to treat you like the queen you are. Promise to be standing in front of Tom's on Tuesday?*

Alena: *I promise.*

Avi stayed busy planning every detail. He was driven by powerful emotions twenty-two years in the making. He wanted to show his appreciation for everything Alena had done for him. He started by renting a Rolls Royce Phantom with a driver. The plan was to meet the driver a half hour prior to Alena's arrival in order to give him special instructions. He reserved the Empire Suite at the Carlyle. The Empire Suite boasted 2,600 square feet on the 28th and 29th floors with sweeping views of Central Park.

He called the concierge to have 22 roses brought up to the suite, a bottle of Chateau Petrus, and a dozen chocolate-covered strawberries. He made dinner reservations at the Carlyle Restaurant. He arrived in New York at noon and hailed a cab to the nearest music store. He wanted to buy a

Kool and the Gang CD that he planned to have playing when Alena entered the suite. He went to the Carlyle to make sure everything was perfect. He gave a $100 tip each to three bellboys to open the car door when Alena arrived and escort her to the room. He then went to Sherry-Lehmann on Park Avenue to purchase a bottle of Dom Perignon. Finally, there was just enough time to go to Tom's and wait for the Phantom. The driver pulled up to the curb at 2:05 and Avi climbed inside.

"Thank you for doing this."

"My pleasure, sir."

"Here, this is for you." Avi handed the driver $500.

"Thank you very much, sir."

"I need a favor."

"You name it, sir. Whatever you need."

"I need you to do exactly as I tell you. When you pull up to pick up my companion, I want you to get out of the car and open the door for her. I also want you to pour her a glass of this Dom Perignon and give her the rest of the bottle to take with her. I want you to treat her with courtesy and respect. Her name is Dr. Said, so you will address her as such. You will take her to the Carlyle and under no circumstance will you tell her where she's going. If she asks, just tell her you are not at liberty to say. As soon as you are on your way, I want you to call me. She thinks I'm in Paris, so I don't want you to give anything away that I'm here."

."I understand completely, sir. Would there be anything else?"

"I will give you further instructions once you call me." Avi left the driver and hurried back to the Carlyle to check into the suite. Once there, he placed the CD on track eight for the song *Cherish*. He clutched the CD remote to press play when Alena arrived. The suite was preposterously gaudy. Avi never splurged like this in his life. It wasn't in his personality, but that didn't matter now. He waited a half hour before his phone finally rang. It was the driver.

"Hello?"

"Yes, sir. Dr. Said is in the car and we are on our way."

"Excellent, put her on."

"Hi, Avi. What have you done? Oh my God, this is too much."

"Nothing is ever too much for you, Alena. Listen, I'm still in Paris, but I want you to enjoy your surprise."

"Where are you kidnapping me to?"

"How is the Dom Perignon?"

"It is the best champagne I've ever had."

"I'm glad you like it. I will call you this evening to see how everything went. Have a wonderful time. Can I speak to the driver?" Alena handed over the phone.

"Yes, sir?" asked the driver.

"Call me once you drop her off."

"Of course, sir." Avi paced back and forth until he was struck by the spectacular view of the skyline. He stared out to it, picking out buildings he recognized. He arranged the flowers on a table so Alena would notice them as soon as she walked in. He planned on hiding in one of the bathrooms. After what felt like an eternity, Avi heard the door open. He ran to the bathroom and pushed play. *Cherish* was playing as Alena walked into the suite. She lost control as soon as she saw the flowers and began to cry. Avi came out of the bathroom and embraced her to help calm her down.

"But I thought…I thought you were in Paris."

"I arrived this morning. I couldn't wait to see you again."

"You did all this for me? Why? How? No one has done anything like this for me." Alena's tears were gushing forth.

"I will tell you everything, but first I want you to come here and read the card that came with the flowers." Avi gave Alena the card to read. She decided to read it aloud.

"In all my life, I've never met anyone more beautiful. Love never dies." Alena felt light-headed and was grateful Avi was holding her up.

"It's alright, Alena. Come sit down."

"I don't know what to say, Avi. I'm speechless."

"Tell me, how was the Phantom?"

"It was unlike anything I've ever experienced. The driver was very nice and polite. I kept asking him where he was taking me, but all he could say was that he was not at liberty to tell me. I knew you told him not to tell me. At first I thought he was taking me to the airport so we could pick you up. Why did you do all this? My God, it's so extravagant. It must have cost you a fortune."

"Alena, money is no object when it comes to you." Avi turned her to face him and kissed her. They embraced quietly and Avi wiped the tears away from her eyes. He pressed the small of her back into him. He never felt closer to anyone in his life than he did to her at that moment. He pulled away from her slightly and looked at her.

"Avi, what is it?"

"It's just that you have no idea how long I've waited to kiss you again. Part of me can't believe you are here with me now."

"What about me? I can't believe this is happening either. It feels like I'm in a fairytale."

"Let me give you a tour." Avi gave her a tour of the massive suite and she kissed him in one of the bedrooms. It had giant marble columns and a luxurious canopy bed. Avi led her to the bed and started to unbuttoned the top of her blouse. She pulled away from him and held both hands up.

"I'm so sorry, Alena. I'm rushing you."

"It's just that I'm–"

"No need to explain. I understand. Do you know we have a reservation for dinner at the Carlyle Restaurant downstairs?" He walked over to the table where the champagne was and picked up the chocolate-covered strawberries.

"Oh, I love chocolate covered strawberries." Alena smiled and took one. Avi could admit that she never looked more beautiful. She wore a black skirt and white blouse which fell lavishly over one shoulder, just as it did when they were undergrads together. They sipped wine and laughed at their good fortune before descending the stairs slowly and finding their seats in the august dining room. They were led to a private table in the corner and sat across from each other, Avi staring at Alena as he had dreamed of doing so many times over the last twenty two years.

"Wow, Avi, this restaurant is stunning."

"Yes it is. Let's try the Beluga Caviar."

"Avi, are you insane? It's $285 dollars per ounce."

"Alena, please don't look at the prices."

"Avi, how are you doing this? You seem to have thought of everything."

"Will you please let me spoil you for a day?"

"Avi this is the most magical day of my life. I just don't want it to end."

"Well, what if the magic doesn't have to end? How difficult would it be for you to meet me in Europe?"

"Are you kidding? Wow, I would love that. I suppose I can tell my husband that I've been invited to give some lectures in Europe. Would one week be enough?"

"Yes, it will have to do."

"Spring break is coming up in about a week. Why not? Let's do it."

"Great, I will take care of everything. I have a huge favor to ask you. Would you meet me in Cairo this summer? I want to meet you at the Nile Hilton."

"Avi, you don't need to do this."

"Alena, I'm begging you. This is profoundly important to me. I never made the promise I made to you and would like to find some redemption. By the way, did you…?" Alena knew what he was about to ask.

"The truth, Avi, is that I waited for you at the Hilton for several hours. Though I knew you weren't going to show up, I waited for you in the hope of a miracle."

"I'm deeply sorry about…"

"Shh, not another word."

XXIV

Avi and Alena were in Europe within a week. It happened so fast. They spent two days in London, and another three days in Paris. Avi showered Alena with the finest restaurants and the most opulent hotels. Alena was having the time of her life, and the experience left her with a dizzying sense of disbelief. Their final stop was Norway, where Avi had a commitment to give a lecture at the University of Oslo. He reserved the Nobel Suite at the Grand Hotel. As usual, he had chocolate-covered strawberries and wine brought up to the suite. Avi and Alena knew that numerous Nobel Prize winners had occupied this suite. As they walked through the marble entryway to their room, Alena challenged fate by telling Avi she thought he would one day win the Nobel Prize.

Alena knew as they travelled across Europe that this was the best time of her life. The world Avi offered her seemed magical. It felt as if time stopped, and her dreams had overwhelmed reality. She had trouble grasping what was happening. No one had ever paid such careful attention to her before. It was as though his life depended on her happiness. He was unrelenting in his attention to her, and she privately wished it would never end.

At the same time, Alena struggled with the moral implications of her actions. Being a good person was central to her self-identity, and she knew her life with Avi made her a bad wife and mother. She could only avoid these thoughts for so long before they suffocated her. She knew this fairytale wasn't going to last – none of it was. She only feared that Avi didn't know it, and she would have to tell him.

For the moment, Alena focused on her blissful happiness. Her first act in the Nobel Suite was to take a quiet bubble bath. Avi walked in after a few minutes to hand her two chocolate-covered strawberries and a glass of wine. It was at that moment that Avi witnessed her transcendent beauty in all of its naked splendor.

" Let me get you a pillow so you can rest your head."

"What are you doing to me, Avi? If you keep spoiling me like this, I may never want to leave."

"Well then, I need to spoil you some more. Here let me put this pillow so you can rest your head. Why don't you have another strawberry, don't you like them?"

"Avi, why are you doing all of this? Is it because the guilt you've been feeling all these years? If it is guilt, you know that I've forgiven you. You don't have to do things for me out of guilt."

"You don't know the half of it, do you? There is so much that I need to tell you. I was so deeply in love with you in college. Do you remember that picture you gave me? You gave it to me for my birthday."

"Go on."

"I need to tell you what happened next. Shortly after I lost your picture, I had a complete nervous breakdown. I was frantic and didn't know what to do. All I knew was that

I couldn't allow myself to forget what you looked like. I started to reconstruct every single day I spent with you. You see, I constructed you in my mind and then something disturbing happened. I started to talk to you in public. I experienced what is generally referred to as a psychotic break. I suffered from auditory and visual delusions where I actually believed I was talking to you." Alena sat up from her bubble bath and stared at him in shock.

"What?"

"It's true. I was so consumed by you that it undermined my mental health completely."

"Avi, how did this happen? Why didn't you tell me?"

"I couldn't. I couldn't face you. I was haunted by demons. The guilt was eating me alive. I didn't know what else to do. I couldn't just let you slip away from my memory."

"But why didn't you call me? You didn't have to suffer alone. I was hurt, but I would have talked to you."

"I simply couldn't. I betrayed you and acted in a cowardly way. I didn't think I would ever speak to you again. It took me over twenty years to gain enough courage to call you."

"What happened when you started to speak to yourself in public? I mean, I'm sure people noticed."

"Yes, I eventually worked with a psychologist for a

while. She was quite helpful and over time I was able to control it. Alena, I've thought about you every single day for over twenty years. You're a constant force in my life, and I've never been able to figure it out."

"Avi, don't bother trying. Fate brought us together once again. I fell in love with you all over again. It's out of my hand. I can't explain it, but when I'm with you, I feel more alive than at any other time in my life. I can't explain why I feel this way anymore than you can."

"I feel all of that. But there is something else. I think it may have something to do with the emergency room. I don't know why, but my thoughts keep going to the emergency room."

"Do you think it's because I came to pick you up?"

"I'm not sure. Maybe. It's not just the emergency room. I mean, I've always found it historically romantic that an Israeli and a Palestinian can fall in love. There is something special about that."

"I feel the same way, Avi. I've always felt there is something special about us."

She looked away from him and down to the marble floor. The guilt and shame of having an affair was gradually growing unbearable and she wasn't sure how to resolve her feelings. She thought occasionally about her husband, who did nothing to deserve this, and she knew the time would come soon when she wouldn't be able to avoid it.

§§§

By July, 2009, Avi fulfilled his redemptive dream by meeting Alena at the Nile Hilton in Cairo. He had endured months of tedious lectures and toured several campuses, all of it cheerlessly save for the thought of seeing her in Cairo. The moment he saw her in the hotel lobby provided the puzzle piece that made him complete for the first time since he left New York all those years ago. They spent three days constantly together and had lunch at the Felfela Restaurant near the Pyramids of Giza on their final afternoon in Egypt. Avi savored every moment, uncertain of when he would see her next. He avoided the subject, preferring to talk about anything but their future.

"You know, the falafel here is not bad," he said. "But I prefer Amir's." He smiled at her across the table.

"Avi, we're in the heart of the Middle East and you prefer the falafel in New York?"

"I know it seems odd, but I will never forget the first time you took me to Amir's."

He paused and stared at her across the table. She looked back at him quizzically. She knew that look on his face, the wide-eyed one that meant he had something important to say to her.

"What?" she asked.

"I have to ask you something. Were you attracted to me when you took me to Amir's?"

"I think I was attracted to you when I took you home after your motorcycle accident. Do you remember when I asked you for your phone number after I dropped you off?"

"Of course, I remember. How can I forget that? I spent hours pacing back and forth in my room, hoping you would call. Do you know that when you called, I ran toward the phone and hit my leg on the coffee table?"

"Really? Did I tell you that when I made that call, I picked up the phone at least a dozen times before I actually made the call? I was so nervous. I didn't know what was happening to me. I never felt this way about anyone."

"I'm so glad you came to Egypt with me. I really like the Egyptian people. I didn't know how funny they are. Wasn't it funny what the waiter said about us when he found out you are Palestinian and I'm Israeli? How did he say it? Oh yes, he said, 'you solve problem now.' Do you think fate is speaking through him?"

"I thought you didn't believe in fate."

"Alena, thanks to you I will believe in flying elephants."

"Why did you tell him I was your wife?"

"I can always dream, right? Are you upset?"

"Heavens no. I would be honored to be your wife."

Alena held Avi's hands and smiled. Her smile slowly evaporated and she pursed her lips. Avi had to admit that she was beautiful when she was frustrated. He didn't understand how this could be true, but he believed it for more than twenty years now.

"What is it?"

"It's just that I feel like I'm living in a dream and at some point I will have to wake up. I'm not in love with my husband, but I still feel guilty about what I'm doing. I don't have to explain to you what having an affair means in Arab culture. I sometimes feel that discovery of what we are doing is inevitable."

"Alena, we discussed this before. I asked you if you felt guilty and you've always said no."

"I didn't want to upset you. I was also having the time of my life and didn't want to spoil things. Maybe I was selfish because I didn't want the dream to end, but at some point we have to wake up from this dream."

"What are you saying? I thought you were having a wonderful time. Did I do something wrong?"

"Avi, I'm not like you. I can't just rationalize this affair by ignoring my responsibilities."

"You keep saying affair. I never thought of us as having an affair. You are the love of my life and now I'm finally able to be with you. Do you know why I never married? I couldn't move past you. I was so deeply in love with you that no one stood a chance."

"I know you love me, Avi. And I love you too. Maybe I'm just exhausted from this trip. I miss my children and I'm ready to go home. So tell me, once we return home, when will I see you again?"

"I can come down in two or three weeks. Would that be alright?"

"Yes, of course. I'm going to miss you."

"I want you to know that I'm willing to drop everything to be with you." Avi stared into her eyes as he always had. She stared back at him, and the entire world stopped. "I can move back to New York so I can see you every day. I can try to get a teaching position at Columbia."

"Avi, what are you saying? That is preposterous."

"Why is it crazy? When do I begin to live for me? All I want now is to be with the one person I love more than anything else in this miserable existence. All my life I denied my own happiness for others. It's enough. I've done enough, Alena. Why can't I be happy too?"

"Because it's not that simple. I want to be with you more than anything, but we can't be selfish like this.

"What are you saying, Alena? Don't you want to see me again?"

"Of course, I want to see you. If fate wants us to be together, it will happen. But now is not the time."

They returned home the next day. They continued to see each other every few weeks as professional colleagues. They talked about collaborating on a book, and Alena explained to her friends and family that they were discussing their roles in the conflict, and their prospects for peace. It was important work, and her family understood the value of giving them space. During this time, Avi grew improbably closer to her family. He met her husband and found him to be friendly. Alena's children developed an attachment to Avi, and he adored them. He spoiled them with extravagant gifts at Christmas, too many gifts, in fact, for a new family friend. There was a part of Avi that simply wanted to repay Alena's kindness. At the same time, he was deeply in love, and wanted to spoil Alena and her children. He grew adept at masking his true feelings with distant affection. Alena never told her husband that she was romantically involved with Avi back in college.

By August, 2010, Alena was unable to continue the charade. She feared their relationship was coming to a head. She spent a weekend alone while her husband and children visited his parents. It was the beginning of September, and the new semester had just begun. She had papers to grade and lectures to refine, but all she could think about was Avi's reaction.

For his part, Avi was excited about calling her from Boston. He was coming to New York to see her. It was the 25th anniversary of their first encounter, and he had to see her on the 9th, the day they first met. He realized something was wrong as soon as she picked up the phone. He heard the apprehension in her voice.

"Hello, Avi. How have you been?"

"I miss you, Alena. Wait, what's wrong."

"Nothing. It's nothing."

"I'm making plans for us on September 9th. Do you know what this date means?"

"I'm not sure if I can, Avi."

"Why? It was on this date 25 years ago that I encountered your transcendent beauty. Don't you remember?"

"Yes, of course. But it's not that big of a deal."

"What do you mean? Of course it's a big deal. Are you alright?"

"I'm fine, Avi."

"No, you're not. What is it?"

"I just don't see why we have to be intimate. Maybe we can just be friends for a while." Before Alena finished speaking, Avi felt his world collapsing.

"What are you saying? I can't believe this is happening. Don't you want to see me again?"

"Avi, I didn't say that. I just want us to be friends for a little while. I need…I need a break from this. From us. The pressure is just too much sometimes."

"Did I do something wrong?"

"You did nothing wrong. I just don't know what to tell you right now."

"Please tell me what I did wrong so I can apologize."

"I just don't know what to say. I have to go." Alena was on the verge of tears. Avi was persuasive. She was afraid if she told Avi the truth he would work to change her mind. She knew their affair would end disastrously for her. She simply let him believe that she was no longer in love with him. She hung up before he could protest and that was it.

Avi called her frantically the next day. She didn't pick up and he kept calling until she finally did at her office.

"What…what is it, Avi?" He could tell she sounded frustrated.

"Why are you talking to me this way? What did I do to deserve this?" Avi was in tears as he spoke to her. He didn't know what to say or do to change her mind.

"I told you, you did nothing wrong. I just don't think it is a good idea for us to continue seeing each other."

"Is it my appearance?"

"Why do you put yourself down like this? I just don't want to do this anymore. I can't."

"Did you fall out of love with me? Is that it?"

"I don't know what to tell you."

"What does that mean? Why are you doing this? Can you just tell me something I can understand?"

"Avi I have to go."

Avi was frantic. He couldn't fully comprehend what was happening. He was losing the love of his life all over again, like a stab wound into scar tissue. He wrote Alena countless emails. The emails revealed his emotional turmoil, from sadness and hurt to drunken fits of despair. Alena responded with short bursts that solved nothing. Avi was deeply hurt, angry, and confused. He did not want to give up. He didn't understand how Alena could be so brutally cold to him. He couldn't understand what he had done to deserve this. He continued to call and write emails, but she seemed to be beyond his reach.

Avi began drinking to drown his sorrow, and it showed in his work. He arrived to lectures ill-prepared and neglected his office hours. He was prickly toward the university administrators and avoided people altogether. Eventually, Harvard asked him to take a semester off. It was a rare move by a university for a tenured professor. By December of 2010, Avi was drinking heavily and experiencing severe bouts of psychosis. He was trapped in the past, and only found comfort in the image of Alena he created in his mind all those years ago. Many of his colleagues grew worried and tried to intervene. They encouraged him to seek help. They saw his life unraveling up close. Harvard decided to put him on sabbatical for the entire year when the semester ended. Avi found himself without a job, and lost in the dark shadows of despair.

§§§

On January 14th, 2011 Avi read about the revolution sweeping Tunisia. It was on this date that President Zine El Abidine Ben Ali was removed from power. Avi did not realize at the time that this was the beginning of a fundamental change in the Arab world. The change that was about to happen was sweeping and unprecedented. The Egyptian revolution was underway within a few short weeks, with millions of people occupying Tahrir Square in Cairo. Avi sat in disbelief on his couch, watching the events unfold on television. This was a revolution organized by young, dissatisfied Arabs who used the latest technology to force the old order to change. By February 6th, 2011 President Hosni Mubarak – who was in power for nearly thirty years – was forced out. There were similar demonstrations throughout the Middle East and Gulf States. The political landscape of the entire Arab world was changing, with profound implications for Israel.

Avi knew immediately that he had to return to Israel. He understood the immense gravity of historical moments such as these. He called his friend, David, who was by now teaching at Tel Aviv University, and asked him if there would be a teaching position available for him. David laughed and told Avi that Tel Aviv would be honored to have him. Avi moved to Israel in the hope of putting Alena out of his mind. He started teaching and writing again. He joined the Meretz party and became actively engaged in Israeli political life. In March, 2012 Avi was appointed Minister without Portfolio and was quickly considered a rising star in Israeli politics.

Avi had no idea that Alena followed a similar path and also returned to the West Bank to enter Palestinian politics. Hanan Ashrawi, who became the first woman elected to the Palestinian National Council, called Alena in March, 2012, to ask her if she would be willing to move to the West Bank and assist her with upcoming negotiations with the Israelis. Alena also witnessed the Arab revolution with astonishment and quickly accepted Ashrawi's offer. She moved her family to Ramallah, which was the center of Palestinian politics. Ashrawi, who was a protégé and close friend of Edward Said, looked upon Alena as someone who could help the Palestinians realize their own state.

By 2015, the Meretz party scored a stunning victory by winning 39 seats in the Knesset. The 120 seats of this unicameral legislative body were designed in such a way that no single party would ever gain a majority on its own. Following an election, the President would nominate a member of the Knesset to become prime minister. Avi was nominated to become the 20th Prime Minister of Israel and immediately formed a coalition government. His message to the Knesset and the Israeli people was clear – peace with the Palestinians through the establishment of a Palestinian state. Avi used his persuasive power and the prestige of his family to gradually change public opinion. In his numerous speeches, he referred to the profound democratic changes that swept through the Arab world and argued that Israel must also change to reflect the new reality of the Middle East.

Within months of taking office, Avi opened negotiations with the Palestinian Authority. Alena was asked to head a delegation to negotiate the final solution, which would result in a Palestinian state. It was during negotiations that Avi tried to understand why she rejected him so flatly. Alena simply told him that whatever assumptions he made about her were false. Despite his inability to win back the love of his life, Avi offered unprecedented concessions during negotiations. He agreed to accept the pre-1967 borders that would form the boundary of the Palestinian state. He compromised on the right of return by negotiating a maximum number of Palestinians that would be allowed to return to Palestine. Those who were unable to return would be compensated for their loss. He agreed to have East Jerusalem as the capital of Palestine. These concessions were costly for Avi as the Knesset threatened a vote of no confidence on several occasions.

The bilateral negotiations were mediated by the United States, Russia, and China. Palestine was officially recognized as the 194th country by the United Nations. A signing ceremony was held at the White House on November 2nd, 2017 to mark the 100th anniversary of the Balfour Declaration. Following the establishment of Palestine, Avi continued his efforts to make peace with Syria, Libya, Iraq, Kuwait, Yemen, Sudan, and several other Arab states. He opened negotiations with Iran and strengthened the peace between Egypt and Israel. He became a hero to many Arabs and Israelis for his honest acknowledgement of Israeli wrong doing.

The Arab world followed his courageous lead by acknowledging their mistakes and contributions to the century-long conflict. The Middle East was entering a new era of peace and cooperation. Israel was no longer the hated outsider and the Arabs were no longer viewed as terrorists bent on its destruction. Avi was a lock for the Nobel Peace Prize. He was hoping Alena would receive the prize as well, but it went to President Hanan Ashrawi. Avi never stopped thinking of Alena during negotiations. It was the love he had for her that shaped the outcome.

When Avi was shot, Alena lost all sight of her moral compass. She was compelled to tell him her true feelings at all costs. She couldn't have peace until it happened. She didn't care about a scandal or what her family would say. Her political and professional life was instantly meaningless. To the outside world, Avi was a champion of peace. But to Alena, he was the only man she ever loved. Nothing else mattered; she had to tell Avi how she felt.

XXV

As Alena paced back and forth in her room waiting for the Mossad agent to pick her up, she decided to call David once again. David knew it was her when the phone rang. But he was surrounded by people and couldn't answer. Instead he sent her a standard message telling her he would call back in a few minutes. Her phone rang minutes later.

"David, where is the agent who was supposed to pick me up?"

"I'm sorry, Alena, but I had to get clearance from President Ashrawi and there were some details I had to take care of to prepare for your arrival. You should know that President Ashrawi is very upset, and I'm pretty sure she was unhappy with me. But the agent is on his way now. He should be there in a few minutes."

"Oh dear God! Thank you, David. Thank you so much." Several minutes later, there was a knock on Alena's hotel room. Alena opened the door.

"Foreign Minister Said, I'm agent Yoni. Would you please come with me?" Alena went with the agent, who took her down the stairs and out through a side door of the hotel. A car waited with the rear passenger door opened. They barreled into the car and drove away quickly.

"Thank you for doing this." Alena flattened her skirt and exhaled.

"My pleasure, Foreign Minister."

"Any word on the Prime Minister?"

"Mr. Barkovic will fill you in once we arrive."

"Can you drive any faster?" she asked the driver as soon as they pulled away from the curb.

"I don't think it would be wise to draw attention.."

"Yes, of course. I understand." The car pulled up to the front entrance of the hospital minutes later, where a throng of media members were clustered. There had to have been hundreds of reporters there and dozens of media trucks, with satellite booms hovering overhead.

"How are we going to get past this circus?"

"Leave it to me, Foreign Minister." The driver drove around to the back of the hospital and parked near a side door.

"Please wait until I open the door for you," Agent Yoni said. He got out and walked around the car, opening the door for Alena. He covered her with an overcoat as he escorted her to the door. David awaited them inside and ushered her quickly down the hall as they approached.

"Where is he, David? Please take me to him."

"Foreign Minister Said, please follow me." David led Alena to an empty room in the hospital. He closed the door behind them and his voice ricocheted in the sterile room.

"David, what are we doing here? Please let me see him."

"This is highly irregular, and I can't be held responsible for what's going to happen."

"David, just take me to him.

"You're going to be sanctioned by the Palestinian government, and possibly relieved of your duties. You have to exculpate me and my staff from any participation–"

"Dammit, David. I don't care about any of this. Don't you see? There's nothing else that matters. Nothing!" She was screaming and pointing at David. He saw the taut muscles of her neck and relented.

"You have five minutes and then we have to get you out. Do you understand?"

"Yes, now please take me to him."

"You need to put this on." He handed her a ball of pale green scrubs. She hadn't noticed he was carrying them.

"Why?"

"Alena, no one here can recognize you. Now please put them on and wear this cap. I will be outside. Please hurry." Alena emerged after a moment, and David discreetly led her to Avi's room. Alena noticed several security guards and Mossad agents eyeing her tensely.

"Remember, you have five minutes. That's it."

"I understand."

"If anyone can reach him, it's you," David said, opening the door for her. "Good luck."

Alena walked in and saw Avi lying in bed dressed only in a hospital gown. She was instantly overwhelmed by shock and disbelief. The man she knew was gone. He was always so full of life, his brilliant eyes absorbing the world before everyone else. Now he lay lifelessly connected to machines. He was reduced to so little. A maelstrom of emotions swirled as she approached him. There were tubes connected to his mouth and nose, two sets of intravenous lines, and several machines next to him. She burst into tears. She held his hand and bent down to kiss his mouth. As she sat down next to him, she tried to come up with words to speak.

"Avi, I know you can hear me. There are words to say. Do you remember? You used to say that to me. You always told me that I'm the love of your life, remember? I never used these exact words to describe my feelings to you. I'm so deeply sorry, Avi, for not saying this earlier. You are the love of my life." Tears streamed down her cheeks. "Do you hear me, Avi?"

The EKG monitor beeped angrily at her.

"You are the love of my life. I don't care who knows it. I don't care anymore. I've spent years worrying about a scandal. I stopped seeing you because I, too, was a coward.

Are you listening to me, Avi? I shouldn't have done it. I wish I can take it all back. I wasted years of happiness by avoiding the only man I ever loved. I was scared, Avi. That's the truth. You know how we Arabs look upon affairs, especially for women. I was scared. I love you! I know you can hear me, Avi. You are the love of my life! I can't…I…I can't live without you. You know that. It's not too late for us. We can finally be together. My children are grown now. We don't have to be tied down to obligations anymore. Why should we live a lie? Why? Why?" David suddenly opened the door and she swiveled her head to him.

"Alena, you need to wrap it up."

"Please, David. Give me a couple more minutes. I'm begging you." The strain on her face was clear.

"Dammit. Alright, two minutes." David quietly closed the door behind him.

"Avi, I don't have much time. I need you to wake up for me. Please follow my voice." Do you feel me holding your hand? Do you feel me kissing your lips?" Alena kissed him again. "Please don't leave me, Avi. I can't continue on without you. I want to tell you something I've never told you before. I always believed that we would be together again. You've done so much for everyone else. You denied your own happiness to satisfy your mother. You've embraced the Palestinian people as no Israeli has ever done. It's time for us to realize our own happiness. Do you hear me, Avi? What am I to do without you? You've taught me so much. Please don't leave me. I'm begging you not to leave me."

"Alena, I'm sorry," David said, opening the door. "But there is simply no more time."

Alena stood up and kissed Avi one last time.

"Find your way back to me," she whispered to Avi. She turned and walked into David's arms. David reflexively embraced her and she wiped the tears away from her eyes. Agent Yoni was behind David, waiting to escort Alena back to the hotel

"I need to talk to you privately for a minute," she said to David.

"I simply don't have time, Alena."

"Then make time, dammit." Alena stood back from David and glared at him. He glanced back to Agent Yoni, who shrugged.

"Give us a moment," he said to his Secret Service agent. Then, turning back to Alena, he said, "Come with me." He led her back to the same private room and asked agent Yoni to wait outside.

" What is it?"

"Do you know who the shooter is?"

"Not yet, but I promise you once we know we will share that with your government."

"David, you know this cowardly act was designed to undermine the peace between us. The shooter could be Arab,

Palestinian, or Israeli."

"I know that and that's why we have every available Mossad agent working on it."

"Not good enough, dammit. We have an agreement in place to not only share intelligence in matters that affect both our nations, but also cooperation."

"Alena, this is different. It is an internal matter and we are working on it."

"I realize it is an internal matter, but if we don't have a joint investigation, the rumors will spread like wildfire. By allowing our agents to work with your people, we would be telling the world that we stand together; that terrorists, wherever they come from, will not derail this peace."

"Can I tell you something?" David interrupted.

"Yes."

"I didn't suspect anything between you and Avi until yesterday. I must have been blind or something, but I simply couldn't believe it. When I confronted Avi yesterday about it, he categorically denied it. Then just last night, he told me everything."

"I asked him not to say anything. What did he tell you?"

"First of all, he realized from the conversation you had with him last night that you will no longer reciprocate his love. He was exhausted from constantly thinking of you. I think he felt a sense of relief by telling me."

"What did he tell you?"

"He told me about the time you picked him up in the emergency room; that you are the love of his life. He told me about 2009 and the romance that was reignited. He told me that you were both here in Oslo almost ten years ago. He also mentioned the trip you both took to Cairo. It's as if he knew something was going to happen. I don't know how to explain it."

"I see."

"Alena, I will contact Prime Minister Rabin-Pelossof to persuade her to accept a joint investigation." Dalia Rabin-Pelossof was now the acting prime minister.

"I appreciate that, David. I will contact President Ashrawi to inform her of where we are. You promise me you will contact me when he wakes up."

"I promise you, Alena. You will be the first to know."

"Thank you, David. I will never forget your kindness." Alena gave David a hug and walked out of the room. Agent Yoni escorted her back to the hotel where she waited for absolution.

Epilogue

The following day, the shooter was caught. It was largely assumed the shooter was either Arab or Israeli, but it turned out the shooter was someone who had little to do with the Middle East. He was neither Arab nor Israeli. The shooter was someone who wanted to ensure his immortality by shooting a historical figure.

It was absolution that defined the tragic nature of their lives. They searched for something that transcended their separate yet intersecting paths. Avi, who always felt as an outsider as a result of his exaggerated intellect, fell in love with the enemy, but it was the enemy who saved him. It was the enemy who humanized him. In time, Avi came to realize that the enemy was not the convenient representations of a dehumanized other. The enemy was within. The enemy was fear. For Alena, the search for redemptive possibilities required a fundamental change in the prism by which she perceived the conflict.

Her identity was tied to a two-sided framework that defined the suffering of her people against an enemy determined to reduce them to a historical footnote. Alena had to navigate herself out of this black-and-white mode of understanding. She had to come to terms with the fact that her enemy was a victim of historical madness. She had to leave behind the wilderness of hate and embrace the humanity of her enemy. The love between Avi and Alena became epic not simply as a result of the oceanic divide that kept them separate and removed from each other, but also as a symbol of the human spirit to break down walls that are artificially designed to keep people apart.

The fact that an Israeli and a Palestinian fell in love was, in and of itself, not historically dramatic. But when this love rises to the level of shaping history itself, it becomes a testament to the indomitable human will to conquer our deepest fears.

As Avi learned to love the Palestinian people through Alena's eyes, so, too, did Alena learn to love the Jewish people through his eyes. If Avi's journey through life was a search for absolution, both personal as well as collective; Alena's journey was also about absolution. Understanding Jewish suffering was not enough. She had to embrace Jewish suffering as her own. As she stood there in front of Avi, she recalled the numerous times he discussed Gramsci's observation that history deposits an infinity of traces upon our consciousness. These historical traces; the traces of Jewish suffering, were filtered through a biographical and ideological prism that prevented Alena from truly appreciating the concentrated moral degradation that Jews had to endure for centuries.

It was Avi who fundamentally changed her. She recalled watching *Schindler's List* with Avi and the impact it had on her. She cried for the Jews. She remembered the famous Talmudic saying: *To save one life is to save the world entire,* and it changed her forever. By embracing Avi she embraced the Jewish people and by embracing the Jewish people she loved Avi passionately. She began to see the necessity of Israel through Jewish eyes. Palestine and Israel represented a land that stirred the imagination of two people who bitterly fought for the right to claim it as their own.

In the end both people realized something so utterly simple and yet horrifyingly distant- by removing the 'otherness' from their respective identification, they can embrace a land that animates their historical sense of purpose and direction. They can embrace fate by embracing each other as joint caretakers of a historical location that witnessed rivers of blood and the silent weeping of those who dream of a New Jerusalem. This was Alena's journey. This was her absolution- to find redemption for herself and all Palestinians who were incapable of allowing Jewish suffering to reach them. Their inability was not the result of ethical distance. Rather, they were busy reacting as victims of those who were themselves victimized a thousand fold.

Seconds after Alena left Avi opened his eyes and in so doing kept the eyes of millions opened to new possibilities.